DANCE

OF THE

ASSASSINS

DANCE
OF THE
ASSASSINS

HERVÉ JUBERT
Translated from the original French by
Anthea Bell

An Imprint of HarperCollins*Publishers*

Dance of the Assassins
Copyright © 2002 by Éditions Albin Michel S.A.
English language translation copyright © 2004 by Anthea Bell
All rights reserved. No part of this book may be used or reproduced in any manner
whatsoever without written permission except in the case of brief quotations
embodied in critical articles and reviews. Printed in the United States of America.
For information address HarperCollins Children's Books, a division of
HarperCollins Publishers, 1350 Avenue of the Americas, New York, NY 10019.
www.harpereos.com

Library of Congress Cataloging-in-Publication Data
Jubert, Hervé.
    [Quadrille des assassins]
    Dance of the assassins / Hervé Jubert ; translated from the original French by
Anthea Bell.— 1st American ed.
        p.   cm. —(The devil's dances trilogy ; bk. 1)
    Summary: A sorceress and a police detective track a reborn Jack the Ripper
through historically re-created cities, from Victorian London to Montezuma's
Mexico City.
    ISBN-10: 0-06-077717-6 — ISBN-10: 0-06-077718-4 (lib. bdg.)
    ISBN-13: 978-0-06-077717-3 — ISBN-13: 978-0-06-077718-0 (lib. bdg.)
    [1. Fantasy.] I. Bell, Anthea. II. Title.
PZ7.J8578Qu 2005   2004028084
[Fic]—dc22   CIP
                                                                AC

Typography by Christopher Stengel
1 2 3 4 5 6 7 8 9 10
❖
First American Edition
First published in France under the title *Le Quadrille des Assassins*
by Éditions Albin Michel S.A. in 2002
First English language edition published in 2004 by Hodder Children's Books

DANCE
OF THE
ASSASSINS

LONDON

*Historic City
with Changes of Set*

POPULATION: tenants 7000,
tourists 2000.

CHRONOLOGICAL PERIOD:
nineteenth century.

PLACES TO VISIT: the British
Museum, the Crystal Palace, the
Tower of London, Buckingham
Palace, etc.

ACCOMMODATION: all categories.

SETS CHANGE: every other day.

DOCKLANDS DAY

Mary stopped in the middle of Westminster Bridge. The cold froze her breath in the air before her face, and she thrust her gloved hands into the folds of her skirt. People were walking past her in both directions, their backs bent. All sounds were muffled by the fog above the city.

She tried to make out Westminster Abbey, but its Gothic façade was hidden by the fog. Mary turned her collar up and buried her frost-reddened nose in it. She went on, treading firmly as she crossed the bridge.

As she came closer to the docks, the outlines she saw were fewer and more blurred. The street lights came on when she reached the other bank. A horse whinnied somewhere nearby, on her right. Mary looked for the cab, and a rectangular shadow made off into the dark. A whip cracked, and then silence engulfed the young woman like a cloak of icy terror.

She realized that she was alone under a streetlamp,

standing in the trembling circle of light cast by the gas jet as it struggled with the darkness. Slowly, Mary raised her eyes to this conflict overhead.

"Light against darkness," she murmured.

A shiver ran down her back.

"You're out of your mind, my girl!" she told herself in firmer tones.

A moth was fluttering round the street lamp. A speck of soot stuck to Mary's cheek. Abstractedly, she brushed it away, leaving a black smut on her face. She was still fascinated by the silence and the trembling light. A shadow emerged from the fog, startling her as it stopped in front of her. A London bobby. He touched two fingers to his forelock.

"You want to get home, miss. Going to be a real pea-souper tonight. And I reckon," he added, looking her up and down in an ungentlemanly manner, "I reckon you're walking the wrong way."

Mary thrust out her chest and favoured the policeman with the sulky pout she did so well.

"I'll go where I think fit, Officer. I'm sure there are damsels in worse distress than me for you to rescue on the other bank."

The bobby grunted and shrugged his shoulders, and was about to move off when a cannon shot rang out in the distance. He went over to the parapet and leaned out over empty space. Mary cautiously did the same. You couldn't see a thing. Down below, the River Thames flowed along, with a sound like a heavy bolt of cloth unrolling for all eternity. The fog broke into drifting swathes of mist below the bridge. Darkness reigned all around. A second cannon shot echoed through the air.

"What's going on?" asked Mary.

"The Woolwich cannon. That'll be for some convict that's escaped. Making for Lambeth, most likely."

He touched his forelock to her again and set off in the direction of Westminster. The fog instantly swallowed him up. Mary sighed. She told herself she was a fool. The Doctor was waiting for her, and she didn't want to miss that appointment. She made for the festoons of lights indicating the Longshore warehouses. She must pass them before reaching the Black Dog, which was among the most disreputable public houses in one of the seediest parts of this low-life area. The guidebooks said that to appreciate it fully you should go there on your own. The gloved cutthroats of Whitechapel . . . Mary Graham was determined to dance with Evil tonight.

The Black Dog lived up to its description in the guidebooks. Raucous laughter and the sound of bows scraping over fiddle strings filled the low-ceilinged little saloon bar. Four blind fiddlers, their feet tapping, were playing beside the dance floor where couples circled round and round. Mary was dancing energetically, her skirt flying around her legs, her hair coming down. She had been screaming with laughter since the beginning of this jig, which seemed to have gone on forever. She abandoned herself to the circling movement as she was tossed from arm to arm.

A sudden dizzy fit made her stop short. She stood there swaying and getting her breath back. The floor tilted slightly, then settled in its proper place. The couples went on dancing. Cheerful merrymakers, gathered around the dance floor, beat time, clapping their hands in unison. Mary wasn't drunk, far from it. She had ordered nothing stronger than half a pint of ginger ale, which was rather too bitter for her liking, but either the spicy ginger or the suspense of waiting was beginning to affect her.

She could have stayed in her room at the Charing Cross Hotel, she could have dined with some self-styled Scots laird, or played whist, or studied the catalogue of manufactured goods on display in the Great Exhibition, which was soon to open. She could have gone drinking with one of those dandies who haunted the lobbies of the grand hotels in the hope of adventure.

She could have done any of those things.

Arms outstretched, she made her way over to a table and sank heavily onto a rickety chair. A couple beside her were embracing. Mary sighed as she watched them.

"Were you expecting me, miss?"

Mary's heart jumped. Slowly, she turned her head to see an elegant figure standing beside her table. He was not very tall, and his figure was partly hidden by the cape thrown over his shoulders, but his stocky silhouette contrasted with his delicate, almost feminine features. Mary wondered if the Doctor plucked his eyebrows. At first she felt disappointed. She had been expecting someone more virile, but the charisma emanating from the man dispelled that first impression. And then there was his hoarse voice, deep but sometimes rising higher . . .

"I believe we have an appointment," the Doctor continued.

Mary's nerves were jangling. But for the crowd in the Black Dog, including several people who must have come from the better parts of town for reasons much like her own, she would have offered herself to the stranger here and now. Come on, quick! her blood sang in her ears as she tried to compose herself.

The Doctor seemed to understand, for he came round the table and offered her his arm. Mary rose. She was a little shorter than he was. She gazed into his eyes and saw that their whites were fascinatingly pure, without a single vein or thread of blood showing.

"Shall we go?" said the Doctor.

"Yes, let's."

Gathering up the folds of her skirt in one hand, Mary let him lead her to the door of the public house. No one noticed them leaving as they stepped out of the stuffy atmosphere of the Black Dog into the chilly London night. The alleyway curved ahead of them, lit here and there by gas lamps. Leaning on the Doctor, Mary felt the strength in him. She also noticed the serpentine pattern of the waist-coat he was wearing. It had a curiously solid look, almost like a suit of armour.

"I know a furnished room not far away," the Doctor began.

But they could wait no longer. There was a deserted park on their right where a wall would hide them from view. She pulled the Doctor into the dark, leaned back against the wall and held his arms firmly. She was in deep shadow, for only their heads rose above the wall, making them look like dark rag dolls. Mary tilted her head back, offering him her neck.

The Doctor began to unbutton her bodice, never taking his eyes off her. He felt her bra strap.

"I thought a corset might be right for the period, but not very practical . . ."

Mary's heart began thudding. The hand went down. She abandoned herself to the moves the man was making.

She was ready. Now the Doctor was holding both her arms above her head with one hand. Mary tried to free herself. He tightened his grip. She looked straight at him. And her blood froze.

The man's eyes were empty, expressing nothing at all. Mary thought of the darkness below Westminster Bridge, of fog and death. She tried to scream. Letting go of her, he hit her hard on the chin. Her head struck the wall. Dazed, she let herself slip to the damp ground.

"You bastard!" she muttered. "Who d'you think you are?"

She tried to get up. Blood was running down her chin. The Doctor had taken a step back and was watching her with the same lack of interest as before. He was undoing the cords laced through the eyelets on both sides of his waistcoat. One side opened out to reveal a collection of shiny knives held in place by leather straps. The man chose one, taking his time. Mary, watching this scene, couldn't believe it.

"I'm dreaming," she said, huddling where she was.

She looked at the way back to the street. Three paces and she could get there. The man was wiping his blade on the waistcoat. She made for the street. He caught her as she fled and hauled her back into the shadows. Mary began to scream. Placing one hand over her mouth, he raised her with the other. He leaned back against the wall.

"You're ill, Annie Chapman. We're going to make you better."

"Mary—Graham," she gasped, her throat constricted by horror. "My—my name's Mary Graham."

She was paralysed, on the point of fainting away. The man's eyes stared at her. Their whites had now been invaded by two bloodshot patches spreading towards the pupils.

A cannon shot rang out in the distance, very far away. Mary thought of the London bobby and felt tears running down her cheeks.

"The terror of it!" whispered her murderer, leaning his weight gently on the blade. "Ah, the terror of it!"

Roberta Wakes Up

Roberta Morgenstern was sipping a cup of vanilla tea infused with cardamom, telling herself that no day begun in the company of Percy Faith and his Orchestra could be entirely wasted. Swallows were swooping above the rooftops, and the sun climbed slowly in the morning sky. Roberta counted to ten. At ten and a half a ray of golden sunlight fell on her face. She let the warmth envelop her, savouring it like warm tangerine sauce. Percy Faith's violins died away on a note of happy nostalgia.

"And we now continue our musical matinée with 'My Bloody Valentine,' played on the accordion by Miguel Puerto Rico."

The melancholy notes of the accordion filled the little apartment. Roberta went into the kitchen and rinsed her cup, humming the tune on the radio. Well now, she wondered, what shall I do today? Take it easy until noon, lunch in the park, siesta, take it easy until evening. Do some knitting, do some reading, go to bed.

She left her tiny kitchen and went into her sitting room, which was crammed from floor to ceiling. On top of a bow-fronted chest of drawers stood a large collection of miniatures, portraits from the past. A brightly coloured bunch of dried flowers was reflected in a mirror surmounted by two chipped cherubs. There was a large black cat asleep on a sofa covered by a tartan rug. His stomach rose and fell at irregular intervals, and he was making little grunting sounds. Roberta leaned over him.

"Still fighting, Beelzebub?"

The cat's whiskers rose vertically into the air, stayed there for a moment, and then drooped again.

Tightening the belt of her dressing-gown, Roberta made slowly for the bathroom. In the normal way two mirrors would have reflected this windowless white-tiled room to infinity, but the mistress of the house had cast a classic spell to stop them showing anything at all. Pure vanity on her part. The sorceress stood in front of the opaque glass and broke the spell again:

"Reflect, let images appear, but do not show the next world here."

You can never be too careful.

The mirror trembled and then showed Roberta her reflection. She examined it critically. She was somewhere between forty-five and fifty-five, with a good life behind her, a life full of excellent meals, delicious liqueurs, and marshmallows. Not enough exercise. Well, none at all, to be honest, except what came naturally. Roberta's love of comfort and a certain preference for making as little effort as possible had done nothing for her figure. Still, she'd come to terms with it. She had always been a dumpy little thing, even before discovering the joys that came with adolescence.

Her nose was podgy and her cheeks chubby, but never mind that. Roberta might be short and plump, but she had two features about which she was rather vain: her hair, which was curly and shone with natural red-brown highlights, striking evidence of her vitality (no stupid ad agency would convince her otherwise), and her eyes.

Roberta had inherited those magnificent green eyes from her maternal grandmother. They had always been her principal instrument of seduction, and still were. When her eyes had captivated the person on whom they were resting, they could make him forget everything. They were a constant source of surprise and satisfaction in her life. It was to her green eyes that Roberta owed her optimism and her tendency to look on the bright side.

Roberta sighed. So did the mirror.

"*Ex ungue leonem*," she said in learned tones.

The habit of reciting Latin tags was recommended by the College of Sorcery, where she had studied diligently up to Grade Three level. A little quotation in a dead language on waking up was rather like rinsing your mouth out. Intellectually speaking, of course.

Beelzebub chose this moment to come into the bathroom and jump up on the washbasin. He had miscalculated his leap. He missed the side of the basin, slipped, and landed in the waste bin. As it happened, Roberta had just lifted the lid, so all that could be heard of the cat once it had closed over him was a plaintive mew.

14

"The lion may be known by his claws," Roberta translated. "And you," she added, turning to the mirror, "go blank again, that's an order, and stay blank until I give the word."

The mirror obediently turned opaque, as if invisible fog had drifted over it.

Roberta went into her bedroom, took off her dressing-gown, and put on a BodyPerfect girdle and a dress with a pattern of periwinkles and forget-me-nots. The colours had washed out long ago, but she'd never been able to bring herself to part with it. Anyway, she could hardly change her wardrobe every week, not on her salary as an investigator with the Criminal Investigation Department.

Better water my black-eyed Susan for a start, she told herself.

She was just opening the sitting room windows when the phone began to ring.

"Not at home!" she snapped.

The flowers looked rather pale. The mains water in Basle definitely had too much lime for a black-eyed Susan. The phone went on ringing. Roberta reached out to her right and took the mynah bird off the perch where it was sleeping. The bird looked at the witch with an expression of genuine panic.

"Go on, birdie, do your job or I shall have what little meat you've got under those feathers for Sunday lunch."

The mynah bird flapped its wings twice and made for the phone, took the receiver off the hook and put it down on the table. Someone was shouting at the other end of the line. The mynah bird ignored the caller, and began talking

15

in a heavy German accent:

"Miss Roberta Morgenschtern is out gone, but I can ze message take . . ."

"However often you hang up I shall call back, you stupid fowl! Come on, Roberta! I want to talk to you!"

Major Gruber, head of the CID, was a man of bulldog tenacity. Roberta picked up the phone, and the mynah bird returned to its perch, where it fell asleep again almost at once. Gruber was shouting, swearing, and uttering threats. It was some moments before the sorceress got the chance to ask, "You think my black-eyed Susan can wait?"

"It can wait. I want you here at the office. On a matter of the utmost urgency. Now."

Gruber hung up. Roberta looked at the receiver, at the mynah bird sleeping on its perch, and at Beelzebub as he emerged from the bathroom with several used cotton-wool balls clinging to his tail. She'd been a witch for thirty years, for over twenty of those years she'd been giving the CID the benefit of her experience as a clairvoyant, and she still hadn't found any spell strong enough to enable her to say no to Major Gruber.

Picking up her canvas bag, she looked back at the room before opening the door. Beelzebub had curled up on the floor between the bathroom and the sofa and was dreaming again already. Roberta slammed her front door without a thought for the neighbours.

The offices of the Criminal Investigation Department were on the sixty-ninth floor of the impressive Community Building, an enormous concrete hexahedron situated between Police Headquarters and the militia barracks. This being Sunday morning, the administrative quarter of the city was lifeless. The tram, running its reduced Sunday timetable, had dropped Roberta off at least two hundred metres from the building. As she walked towards it, it grew slowly larger. Too slowly for her liking. This was a good chance to air her large stock of rude remarks about Major Gruber and his terrible timing.

A high-powered sports car shot out of a side street with a noise of tormented metal. It turned and made for Roberta, who jumped aside at the last moment, and saw a blurred, roaring shape pass by. One of those mechanical monsters that only a few privileged barbarians could afford these days. The State encouraged motor manufacturers. There was even talk of progress in the industry. Roberta knew perfectly well that this kind of economic recovery, which respected the lives of neither hedgehogs nor human beings, could only mean the end of civilization as she knew it.

She continued on her way, keeping an eye on the car, which squealed to a halt at the foot of the huge flight of steps leading up to the Community Building. A leather-clad young man jumped out and ran up the steps four at a time. He banged on the door, got no reply, came back down to his car, looked for something in the glove compartment, took out a piece of paper, read it, went up the steps again—more slowly this time—knocked on the huge bronze door of the building once more, came back down the steps . . .

"What's all this racket in aid of?" asked Roberta,

addressing the silent and empty air.

She was now at the foot of the building, and cast an interested eye at the vehicle as she passed it. Its bodywork was still warm. You had to admit that there was something about these sports cars, all the same, she told herself.

"Hey, you!" said the young man, addressing her.

He was twenty-five, if that. A pretty face, almost untouched by life. Not a mark on it, and no doubt he'd have skin like a peach under those expensive, showy leathers. Roberta stopped and watched him approach her without saying a word. The fool was waving his piece of paper about. The witch noticed the Ministry of Security stamp on it.

"I was told to come to the Community Building," he began, "but no one's answering the door."

"Well, it's Sunday. The place is empty."

She was lying through her teeth, but she saw no reason to help this moron. Turning her back on him, she made straight for the real door, a discreet wooden affair tucked away under the great flight of steps. She knocked twice. The spyhole slid silently aside, the caretaker recognized the sorceress and opened the door. It closed behind her.

"Oh, this is the end!" said the young man furiously. He too marched up to the door, knocked twice as he had seen Roberta do, and the caretaker's eye appeared at the spyhole.

"Yes, what is it?"

The young man held his piece of paper up to the glass of the spyhole, so that the caretaker could read it.

"Clément Martineau. The CID sent for me. On business of the utmost urgency. National security depends upon it."

The caretaker sighed and closed the spyhole. Roberta, standing in the shadows, said nothing.

"He's got an invitation card, miss. Can't really leave him outside, can I?"

The witch thought about it. Martineau. The name rang a bell. And Gruber had sent for him? At the same time as he'd sent for her, and in much the same terms?

"I'll get a start on him." She tapped the caretaker's shoulder. "How's your back doing, by the way?"

"Oh, much better since you gave me that ointment!" He waved her away. "You start on up. I'll keep him kicking his heels for a while."

The lift waiting for Roberta took her up to the sixty-ninth floor. She hesitated before getting out. Wasn't what she was about to do rather childish and stupid, not exactly the accepted idea of good manners? Well, that stupid twit and his noisy toy had almost squashed her flat. She immobilized the lift by pushing the Stop button and then set off, a spring in her step, for the frosted glass door bearing the words: CID. ENTER. DO NOT KNOCK.

"Morgenstern! And about time too!"

Major Gruber was seated behind his ebony desk, immaculately dressed in his usual anthracite-grey suit, his throat imprisoned by his collar. Roberta couldn't remember ever seeing him except behind that desk, dressed in that suit, barking out orders.

She sat down, folded her canvas bag, put it on her knees, and waited. Five minutes passed in total silence. Then she heard panting breath and a loud knock on the door. A malicious smile lit up the Major's face.

"Ah, here's our young adventurer. Come in!"

Clément Martineau came into the office. He was pale, sweating, and trembling at the knees. He stood to attention in front of Major Gruber as best he could.

"Clément Martineau, sergeant, assistant editor with the Cont— Contracts Section, Ministry of Security, reporting for duty, sir."

"Contracts Section!" said Roberta. "With the Bumf Department, are you? Nobody would think it, not the way you drive."

Martineau hadn't seen her. He took a couple of steps backwards on identifying the person who had so graciously slammed the door of the Community Building in his face.

"You!" he said in surprise.

"Me!" said the happy Roberta.

"Now, now," said Gruber with remarkable amiability, pouring oil on troubled waters. "We're not at the theatre, you know. Sit down, Martineau."

Martineau sat down, and the Major pushed a black file over the desk to them. Roberta knew Gruber's colour-coding: black stood for Sensitive, Death(s) Involved. Had they gone back to the days of organized crime on a grand scale? Her heart began to thud.

The Major slowly opened the file and took out a set of photographs. He looked at them for a moment in silence.

"I hope you've had your breakfast," he said, addressing neither of them in particular.

Then he slid the photographs over to Martineau and Morgenstern. CID shots with the typical CID reference marks on them. At first Roberta couldn't make out what the subject of the photos was. A vague shape, part of a wall . . . Then she turned a picture round and finally saw what it showed.

A woman, young and quite pretty, was seated on the ground, leaning against a wall. Her stomach had been carefully gutted and its contents placed between her legs.

"St. Christopher help us!" breathed Martineau.

The other shots showed the same body either in close-up or from a distance. Roberta hadn't seen such a sick murder for years. It was astonishing that there'd been no reports in the press. Most of the time the media got its tips from the militia.

"Name of Mary Graham," Gruber told them. "Aged thirty-two. Found in this unfortunate condition yesterday morning. Fould handed the case over to me scarcely two hours ago."

"Yesterday morning!" Roberta exclaimed.

The invention of tracers had improved Security so much that people were beginning to wonder whether there was any need at all for the CID these days. Four times out of five, murderers were arrested immediately by militia linked to the tracers and to Central Filing. The CID should have been informed at once. A tracer ought to have picked up the murderer by now. And what about the evidence? What state would the crime scene be in by this time?

"This woman was murdered in one of the Historic Cities," explained Gruber, adding for the benefit of the young man, who might not be as well up as Roberta on recent legislation. "The Historic Cities are outside our jurisdiction. In fact this crime might have passed unnoticed if one of the local tenants hadn't got wind of it and told the Ministry."

"Who exactly told you?" asked Martineau.

"A flower-girl. She can be ruled out."

Roberta inspected the photos.

"This was in London?" she surmised.

"On Docklands Day, in the late nineteenth century," Gruber confirmed. He took back the photos, put them in the folder, closed it and gave it to Roberta.

"I want you two to find me the butcher who did this, using our good old traditional methods of investigation to track him down. Morgenstern, you're in charge. Martineau, Roberta Morgenstern here will show you the ropes. She's your immediate superior, understand?"

"Yes, sir."

"You'll be at the landing stage on the North Quay in an hour's time," Gruber told the young man. "Morgenstern will be waiting for you there. Right, you can go."

The young man got to his feet, saluted the Major, sketched a hesitant wave to Roberta and then left the office. Silence fell between Gruber and the witch again. Roberta was gently stroking the black leather folder.

"Why lumber me with that brat?" she inquired.

"A little company will do you no harm, Roberta. Or you could get set in your ways and repetitive, like that mynah bird of yours."

"Don't make me laugh! Sonny Boy there comes from the Contracts Section, and you're putting him on a homicide case in a Historic City outside our jurisdiction!"

"Sonny Boy came top for theory in the police exams."

"Oh, great, so he knows his police manual off by heart. He'll be able to tell the murderer his rights while he's being made into mincemeat."

"I've no choice, Morgenstern. He wanted to go out on a case, and this is the only case we have."

Roberta heaved a long and weary sigh.

"Yes, all right," admitted Gruber. "So he has an influential family. In fact, but for his family, I doubt whether the CID would still be in existence."

Roberta could see from Gruber's face how much it cost him to confess this.

"Martineau . . . I've heard that name somewhere before."

"Martineau Cement Industries."

"Martineau Cement, of course!" exclaimed Roberta. "Didn't they put up the Building?"

"I want you to find me that murderer!" the Major said, suddenly peremptory. "He's a sick man. He won't stop at Mary Graham."

"I thought there was no such thing as a serial killer these days," said Roberta, adding casually, "er—I suppose our young novice doesn't know anything about my modest talents?"

"Nothing at all. You can tell him if you like. But let me remind you that the Ministry of Security isn't supposed to pay clairvoyants, wizards, or witches."

"You don't pay them very well."

"Look, you're not even supposed to exist, Roberta. Except in children's books. So think yourself lucky to draw a salary at all."

The witch rose to her feet. She didn't need the Major to

tell her when an interview was drawing to its close.

"And Morgenstern!" The Major called her back as she was about to go through the doorway of his office. "I'd advise the circumspect, velvet-glove approach."

"To Sonny Boy?"

"To Palladio. The Historic Cities are his crowning achievement. You're about to go digging for dirt on his territory, and although he has no choice in the matter, I suspect he won't look very kindly on your arrival in London."

"*Oculos habent et non videbunt*: they have eyes and will not see," Roberta snapped back before closing the door of the CID offices.

DEATH THROUGH
MARY GRAHAM'S EYES

The Pelican class hydroplane was making its way through the water with a gentle, swaying movement. Morgenstern and Martineau were sitting on the upper level above the nose of the craft, where they could admire the vast expanses of the lagoon stretching all the way to the curved horizon.

The young man had been silent since they left. The witch put it down to shyness. However, the fidgety way he had been behaving for the last ten minutes showed that he wanted to start a conversation. He took the plunge.

"Er—how long have you been working for the CID, Mrs. Morgenstern?"

"First, it's Miss. Second, no need to remind me, but about twenty years."

Martineau sorted out these items of information and whistled when he realized the significance of the last one.

"Then you were here before the militia and the tracers!"

"You could call me a veteran, yes. I'm of the old school. You like them, do you?"

"Sorry?"

"The tracers, the militia, those nano-whatsits that go everywhere, gather information, put it on file, predict what's about to happen and alert Security. You like them?"

Martineau took a few minutes to think about it.

"I like to see Good winning out over Evil. Tracers and militia are only tools."

Well, the young man had been born not long before the introduction of those microscopic auxiliaries which aided police procedure to an extent previously unknown, so why would he *not* like them? To see crime go unpunished again? The Historic Cities were the last enclaves where the tracers had no power. And the result was nothing to write home about: a woman murdered and her killer still at large.

Martineau took a copy of *Historic Cities News* out of a side pocket on his left in the cabin. It contained a series of articles on cities in the Network and their main attractions, features of interest and festivities. For London there was quite a long piece on the famous Tower where the crown jewels were kept.

Another article, headlined "Not For Those of a Nervous Disposition," was about two of Count Palladio's other creations. The cities of Lisbon and San Francisco were designed to be destroyed once a week and then rebuilt within two days. Lisbon staged the reconstruction of a devastating fire, guaranteed to be extinguished every time, while San Francisco had earthquakes running to a fixed schedule. You had to have a medical examination to visit those cities. People with heart conditions, children, and senior citizens were not admitted.

Not in my line, thought the young man.

An envelope slipped out of the magazine and fell at his feet. Martineau picked it up and turned it over. It was blank. Unsealing it, he took out two sheets of paper and a mauve card. He read the contents of the first sheet of paper and put it aside. The second bore the enigmatic words: "I killed Colonel Gardiner."

The mauve card was a voucher for a free visit to the Tower of London. Martineau pocketed it, realizing that Morgenstern was returning to the fray.

"Do you know why people like the Historic Cities?" she inquired. "Why they're always fully booked?"

"It's the anonymity," he replied at once. "Because tracers aren't allowed there."

Roberta nodded triumphantly.

"Yes, OK," said Martineau. "I can tell you don't like tracers, but I can't go along with you there. Anything can happen in the Historic Cities—and go undetected. This murder could easily have escaped the attention of the CID, right?" The young man was getting quite excited. "Central Filing *is* Security!" he announced, very sure of himself.

"The Historic Cities aren't bound to Central Filing, but they keep records of everyone who goes in and comes out," said Roberta. "That's how the whole world used to work before the tracers came along."

Martineau knew about access to the records of the Historic Cities Network, and he also knew that they would be no use at all in helping them to find the murderer.

27

"Exactly," he said. "You sign your name, you wave your papers in front of someone's eyes for a split second, and they let you in regardless!"

Roberta said nothing, preferring to end this conversation. However, Martineau was in full flow.

"The problem of Evil!" he exclaimed. "That's what we're after, with or without tracers!"

Roberta massaged her temples, wondering how to deal with the problem of Martineau.

"Evil . . . er, do you think the Devil himself eviscerated that young woman?"

"No, of course not. There's no such thing as the Devil," he replied with a childlike smile.

As a matter of fact, the Prince of Darkness had not manifested himself for so long that the College of Sorcery had recently opened an inquiry into his existence. God was dead, as everyone knew, but what about the Devil?

"You could be right," Roberta conceded, mollified.

The engines of the Pelican suddenly roared as it rose from the lagoon. A dam stretching far into the distance passed below the fuselage of the enormous hydroplane, which came down on the surface again to complete its voyage, weightily skimming the water. A voice addressed the passengers:

"Welcome to Historic Cities territory. The temperature in London at present is twelve degrees. The weather is overcast, with clear periods. Palladio Sealines would like to thank you for travelling with us. We hope to see you again soon."

"God save the Queen," muttered Roberta, examining

the huge stage set of the city standing out against the horizon.

The sorceress had expected Count Palladio to meet them in person when the Pelican landed. An official cable from the Ministry of Security had informed him of their arrival. Three people were waiting on the landing stage: two police officers and a man of desiccated appearance in a black suit like an undertaker's. The undertaker look-alike approached Roberta and Martineau with a forced smile.

"The Count presents his apologies," he said, getting in first, "but tomorrow is Crystal Palace Day, and he's needed while they put the Palace up."

Roberta looked round. She had never been to one of the Historic Cities, but seen from this vantage point there was nothing special about London. You might have thought yourself in any mainland port.

"Is the Count aware that a crime's been committed on his territory?" she inquired without animosity.

"He'll see you tomorrow at the opening ceremony. My name's Simmons. Walter Nathan Simmons. Everything's been done to ensure that you can make your inquiries as smoothly as possible. We'll look after your luggage. Follow me, please."

Simmons escorted them to a quay where a remarkable vessel was moored. Its deck was about thirty metres long and bristling with a forest of masts. Propellers rotated at the far end, keeping the hull above the water and whirring with a muffled sound. Both ends of the hull were as sharp as a war galley's. Two propellers turned slowly on horizontal axes at the prow and stern of the craft.

They went on board, the gangplank was drawn up, the propellers whirred, and the ship rose lazily into the sky above London.

"Welcome aboard the *Albatross!*" said Simmons. "This is a promotional ship publicizing Verne City, the great project at present occupying Count Palladio's mind night and day."

"The *Albatross?*" repeated Martineau. "You mean Robur's *Albatross?*"

"That's right, the airship out of Jules Verne's *Robur the Conqueror*," replied their guide enthusiastically. "Made of similar materials. Powered by electricity—nothing but the form of energy has been updated. Jules Verne was vague about that anyway. You're in luck!" He had to shout to make himself heard above the noise of the propellers going full speed. "The sky over London is almost empty today!"

Martineau leaned on the handrail protecting them from the void below. Roberta, on the other side of the deck, was looking at the fantastic scene unfurling before their eyes. The craft rose high enough to give them a view of the whole of London. Then it turned slowly on its own axis and began flying over the Historic City built by the Count from scratch in the middle of the lagoon.

Roberta knew the basic principle of the Cities: the end product of theatrical tradition, the failure of early electronic experiments with virtual reality, and a number of brilliant ideas from past ages. Such places had been dreamed up in the old days by visionaries: architects, novelists, illustrators. It was the Count who had brought them to life. Profitable life.

This crowd of women in crinolines and men in top hats, these carriages, street sweepers, newspaper vendors, old ladies, families out walking together, all these people in the streets on the eve of Crystal Palace Day were not actors or bit-part players. They genuinely lived in London, worked here, and paid rent which went towards maintaining the vast amount of machinery concealed within the entrails of the city.

But most of the money came from tourism. The Pelican, which had been crammed full, must already have disembarked its cargo of fresh currency. At this time of day the passengers would be in the wardrobe departments trying on skirts, corsets, and outfits for navvies or house painters.

The *Albatross* was following the curve of a deserted Regent Street. Hydraulic jacks shaped like flying buttresses held the façades of the street close together, almost touching. They flew over this empty stage set at a height of a hundred metres, emerging from it right above a very busy main artery. An incredible number of pedestrians, horses, cabs, and omnibuses were competing for space in the road. A steam engine was crossing a metal railway bridge that soared above all the hurry and bustle. Seen from the *Albatross*, the engine looked like a toy.

"How can anyone *want* to live in such conditions?" marvelled Martineau.

"Fleet Street's always crowded at this time of day," explained Simmons. "And modern cities have disadvantages of their own, wouldn't you agree?"

The vast traffic jam disappeared from sight, giving way to a view of a huge expanse of grey rooftops.

"The British Museum," their guide proudly announced. "Where the masterpieces of the past are kept."

The witch, who had joined the other two, looked down at the huge glass roofs.

"*Replicas* of the masterpieces of the past," she pointed out. Tearing herself away from the view of the Historic City, she spoke to Simmons in a tone that forced Martineau to turn and look at them. "We're here to catch a murderer, not play at tourism. I suppose London does have some kind of police force?"

Simmons looked upset at having this subject brought up so soon.

"London is a very law-abiding city despite its bustling appearance and the—and recent events. We have about fifty security officers in the city, yes, but most of the time they have nothing to do but settle quarrels between neighbours and break up minor pub brawls."

"About fifty. Who's in charge of them?"

"Er—I am," admitted Simmons.

King Solomon protect us, thought Morgenstern. "And have you got far with your inquiries, Mr. Simmons?"

"Well, er—not really. We thought we'd better wait for you to arrive. This situation is rather new to us, you see, and—"

"Yes, yes, we see," Roberta agreed.

"Let a few tracers and militia loose in there," said Martineau in offhand tones, pointing at the replica of Trafalgar Square over which they were flying, "and you'll find the murderer before this ship even casts anchor. If it's got an anchor."

The young detective looked pleased with himself. He didn't immediately notice that Roberta was casting him a furious glance, and the forced smile on Simmons's face had given way to a much less agreeable expression.

"What on earth are you thinking of?" asked Simmons.

Martineau went red in the face. Had he dropped a brick? Roberta came to the rescue.

"Count Palladio drew up a charter which was countersigned by all our governments," she explained. "It clearly stipulates that no tracers may be introduced to the territory of a Historic City. Obviously we intend to use other methods of investigation to find the murderer." Here Simmons looked curiously from Roberta to Martineau and from Martineau to Roberta. "We wouldn't want to have to leave London before even beginning our inquiries, would we, Martineau?" she finished.

Martineau was struck speechless for several moments. Of course he knew that tracers and militia were not allowed in the Historic Cities, but he hadn't realized just how sensitive a subject it was—or how far Palladio's power extended where their presence in London was concerned.

"No. No, we wouldn't," he agreed sheepishly.

Simmons looked reassured. The incident was closed.

The ship narrowly missed the dome of St. Paul's. The cathedral, constructed on the edge of the lagoon, was still unfinished; the scaffolding outside ran all round the choir and had its feet in the grey water. They left this scene behind them and flew down a street full of shops towards a kind of fortress built on the banks of the Thames. Further on, a large bridge had raised its central section to allow a

33

clipper with shining brasswork to pass through. The *Albatross* sounded its horn. Down below the clipper replied.

"The Tower of London and Tower Bridge," announced Simmons proudly.

"The Tower of London," repeated Martineau, gazing intently at its walls as if hoping to discover their secret.

The airship's propellers were turning more slowly as they approached the space now left free between the towers of the bridge.

"Here we are," announced Mr. Simmons. "Just coming in to Security Centre."

Two of the crew members were letting out landing platforms fitted to the back and front of the *Albatross*. The vessel gradually moved towards the axis of the river and ended up gliding towards the bridge sideways on. Roberta's heart missed a beat at the sight of the huge structures towards which they were racing.

"We'll be crushed!" she gasped, her throat constricting.

"Don't worry," Simmons reassured her. "The crew can perform this manoeuvre with their eyes shut."

"I'd rather they kept them open," said the witch.

They were now almost between the two towers. The Thames seemed a long way below them, and they had a view of the façades of buildings plunging down towards the river.

"Cast 'em out!" shouted a man on one side of the ship.

There was a loud report. Two ropes shot out from one of the towers towards the *Albatross*, snaking almost of their own accord around the capstans clustering on the platform. The same manoeuvre was performed on the other side of the vessel, which swayed slightly and then stabilized, creaking. The propellers slowed down even more, returning to the purring sound they had made while the vessel was stationary as the passengers came on board.

The ropes, wound in from inside one of the towers, were bringing the ship closer. A covered gangway dropped from a window flanked by gargoyles and came to rest on the deck, where part of the handrail had swung back. Sketching a bow, Simmons indicated the gangplank.

"We've got a little surprise for you. You'll like this."

Morgenstern never liked surprises. She looked at the grey waters of the Thames flowing below them, at the imitation city that showed none of its real nature, at the bridge slowly dropping back into place in the clipper's wake.

Carriages were driving by on both banks. Children were bowling hoops. A woman in a crinoline pointed them out to a man in a bowler hat.

Followed by Martineau and Simmons, Roberta set foot on the gangplank. A cormorant uttered a nasty squawk behind her just as she entered the bridge tower.

Simmons took them down staircases and through a long tunnel to his headquarters in the Tower of London. They went to the wardrobe department first. It was compulsory to wear period costume when you walked the streets of a Historic City. Martineau emerged from the men's wardrobe in a tweed suit, its check trousers tucked into woolly socks, and with a shabby cap perched on his forehead, making him look thoroughly disreputable. Roberta took longer to emerge from the ladies' wardrobe.

She finally made her entrance in a magnificent mourning outfit, carrying a black silk umbrella. She had been afraid the skirt would get in the way as she walked, but it turned out to be quite useful for keeping people at a distance, which she liked. As for sitting down, she'd tackle that problem later. Simmons complimented Roberta on her elegance and Martineau on his very convincing pickpocket look.

"No need for you to sign the register," he told them. "Government representatives are exempt from that formality."

Morgenstern and Martineau exchanged swift glances. Simmons led them to the heart of the Tower of London, where the Security Centre, as he called it, was based.

It turned out to be an ordinary police station full of screens, consoles, and busy staff. About a hundred cameras covered the city, Simmons explained, most of them trained on buildings and watching for any sign of subsidence. No accidents had yet happened in any of the Historic Cities, and there must be no danger at all of one of the fake façades falling and crushing a passer-by. The men who worked here—architects, hydraulics experts, and engineers—were hand-picked for the job, and they never made mistakes.

Burying her hands in her black fur muff, Roberta immediately saw that Simmons and his men were not going to be the faintest use to them in solving this case.

"There's no crime in the Historic Cities, you see," he pleaded, correctly interpreting the expression on the witch's face. "We have no regular police force or filing system. The bobbies on the beat are tenants like the rest. They know their roles by heart. And when they do chase crooks, the crooks are actors specially hired to lend the reconstruction more authenticity."

"It looks as if one of them at least is a master of the art of authenticity," Roberta pointed out. "Unless Mary Graham was an actress too? What talent!"

"Mary Graham had been a tenant for four months. She was staying at Charing Cross, in a room in the Charing Cross Hotel opposite the station, while she waited for an apartment to fall vacant. Her reasons for going to the East End on a foggy night on Docklands Day were no one's business but her own. The Black Dog is popular with both tenants and tourists—they go slumming it there when they want a real thrill. What you get at the Black Dog is bogus low life. Cardboard crime."

"The blade of the knife that killed that unfortunate young woman wasn't made of cardboard," murmured Roberta. "Can you take us to the public house?"

Simmons bit his lower lip, looking awkward. "I'm afraid the Black Dog is out of bounds just now. The foundations have been folded away to let the scene-shifters put the Exhibition up."

"Folded away?"

Simmons tried to explain. "Hyde Park with its elm trees and the Serpentine take up a lot of space. Anyway, the crime was committed outside the Black Dog, not in it. Come with me and I'll show you the surprise I mentioned."

Roberta and Martineau followed Simmons down a

37

spiral staircase which plunged deep into the Tower of London itself. The temperature suddenly dropped. They must be below the level of the Thames.

They found themselves in a round room illuminated on all sides by projectors. Large air-conditioners were fitted here, keeping the temperature at around zero. Part of a wall and a patch of waste ground had been placed in the middle of this installation. Mary Graham sat at the foot of the wall, her skin shining slightly under a thin layer of ice, just as it did in the photos Gruber had shown them.

"We removed the whole crime scene, brought her here and kept her at a temperature that would preserve her and allow a post mortem to be carried out *in situ*," explained Simmons.

"Good idea," agreed Roberta.

It was the first time she'd seen anything like this. She moved deliberately towards the fragment of stage set. The ice on the ground cracked underfoot. Roberta crouched down in front of Mary.

The young woman's legs were folded under her, her head was turned up as if to the sky, her eyes were wide open.

"Good," murmured Roberta.

Removing her hands from her muff, the sorceress took one glove off and reached out to touch the body. Idiot, she reminded herself, you won't feel anything at this temperature.

"Martineau!" she called over her shoulder.

No answer. Turning, she saw the young detective deep in conversation with Simmons.

"I'll bet my bottom dollar you've studied Goddefroy," the young man was saying.

"*An Elementary Handbook of Police Technique*," agreed Simmons. "I swear by it."

He seemed highly excited. Leading Martineau over to the corpse, he pointed out various parts of the scene that had been frozen just as they were. Although Morgenstern was directly in front of them, they ignored her.

"Two factors allow us to define our knowledge of the killer and his methods more closely," began Simmons, in the tones of a schoolmaster testing a pupil. "Can you spot them?"

Intrigued by the challenge, Martineau knelt down in front of the section of wall, sniffed around the corpse like a spaniel, then rose and paced up and down in front of the scene for several minutes, sometimes muttering to himself, sometimes grunting with satisfaction. Roberta had moved aside to watch him. The heir to Martineau Cement Industries finally brought his little performance to an end and turned to Simmons.

"No trace of anything on the body itself apart from the marks left by the killer. However, two clues should repay further investigation."

He put his hand behind Mary Graham's head, moving it away from the wall at the risk of breaking it. Roberta expected the frozen neck to snap right off and send the head rolling at her feet, but no such thing happened.

"The killer left some very clear prints here. It would be a good idea to lift them."

Simmons showed him an enlarged photograph of the

prints concerned, with a scale to show the size beside them. "And the clues don't stop there, Mr. Martineau."

The investigator crouched down, snapping off several bits of frozen earth. He pointed to a place on the ground just in front of him: a footprint this time.

"Our man has small feet. He takes size six and a half in shoes. So we're after someone measuring between one metre sixty-seven and one metre seventy-two."

"You base your calculations on Barbillon's table of averages?" inquired Simmons.

"And wait a moment," added Martineau, still concentrating. "There's a third clue too. Did you spot it, Mr. Simmons?"

Only too obviously Mr. Simmons had not spotted it. Slightly annoyed, but nonetheless interested, the self-styled detective and head of Security went over to the section of wall that his brother in criminology was inspecting.

"Here." Martineau pointed to the wall just above Mary Graham's head. "See those threads from the fabric of the victim's clothing?"

Simmons took out a monocle to examine the clue. If he could have climbed up on the unfortunate Miss Graham's body to get a better view, no doubt he would have done so. "How on earth did I miss that?" he wondered.

"The direction of the threads shows that they were pulled out in an upward movement. So we can reconstruct the killer's methods." Martineau demonstrated on the rest of the wall, placing one hand on the stones and holding an imaginary object in the other. "He leans on the wall and raises her—like this—before killing her." He rubbed his hands and stepped back. "Which suggests uncommon muscular strength," he concluded, very pleased with himself. "He wears size six and a half shoes and he's strong. That's a good start."

"And we have his prints," added Simmons.

"We have his prints, but *you* don't have any filing system," Martineau pointed out.

"True. But we'll find some way to catch him, never fear."

Roberta, who had taken off her other glove, applauded ironically.

"Fascinating, gentlemen. Fascinating."

She went back to the body, from which Simmons too had moved away, and laid her hand over Mary Graham's eyes as if to close them. The frozen eyelids were stuck to the eyes themselves and did not move when she touched them. Roberta returned to the two men, one hand held over the other like a lid.

"You may know your theory, but don't forget you're about to plumb the nastiest depths of our delightful human species," she informed Martineau caustically. "Violence, murder, sadism, madness. Your systems and tables of averages aren't going to cast much light on the shadows where our murderer lurks, or help us understand how he operates."

"We don't have to understand, we just have to show how he does it," replied the young man.

"Very true," agreed Simmons.

Roberta sighed. Well, never mind, Sonny Boy had made it easy for her. Let him indulge his enthusiasm—he might even find something out.

"You're free to take samples and do any cross-checking you like, Martineau. Carry on, gentlemen. I have to go and check up on a few things myself before meeting Count Palladio."

"We've reserved you a suite at the Savoy," Simmons made haste to tell her. "I can escort you there at once."

"Don't bother, my dear Watson. I'll find my own way. But I'd be glad if you'd send everything you have on this murder to me at the hotel."

"I'll send it right along, Miss Morgenstern." Roberta imagined a courier already racing towards her suite with a black folder under his arm. "But do let me show you out."

Roberta left Martineau at the scene of the crime. The young man was examining a frozen leaf and talking to himself.

Simmons escorted the sorceress out of the building. She thanked him and assured him yet again that she really did want to go to the Savoy under her own steam, seeing London like any anonymous tourist armed with a Palladian Guide.

Alone at last, she was free to open her hand and inspect the broken eyelashes lying on her palm. In other circumstances she'd have taken Mary Graham's eyes too without a second thought. But with Martineau and Simmons behind her, even holding forth at length on the merits of their respective methods of detection, she had thought it better not to tempt Providence.

And now, Miss Graham, said Roberta to her hand before closing it again, now we shall see whatever it was you saw.

★ ★ ★

42

The lobby of the Savoy was as big as a billiards room. The Prince Edward Suite, occupying a whole corner of the grand hotel on the Thames and the Victoria Embankment, had been reserved in the name of Morgenstern. A page-boy took the sorceress to her door and left her without even waiting for a tip.

Roberta found that she had two magnificently decorated reception rooms, a truly luxurious bathroom, and a bedroom with a wrought iron bedstead which had delicate wildlife ornamentation and seemed as if it might lend itself to all sorts of extravagant purposes. A wide balcony looked out over the Thames. Despite the overcast London weather, the heavy barges ploughing their way along the river, and the industrial vapours casting their gloom over the East End, the view was unique. A fake, but a unique fake, thought Roberta.

The walk from the Tower to the Savoy had tired her. Palladio's London was truer to life than the real thing, and its streets wore you out. As she wove her way through a tumultuous, noisy, colourful crowd, the witch had found she had to concentrate hard to avoid the carriages bearing down on passers-by without warning. By the time she reached the Savoy she was cursing the Victorian age, with all its drawbacks.

Sorceress she might be, but Roberta was a pragmatist too. Palladio's achievement, she realized, lived up to his claims: for a whole hour she had completely forgotten the existence of the mainland and her own hometown of Basle.

The hoops of her crinoline made a sound like grinding

scrap iron when she tried sitting on the bed. She took the crinoline off and lay down for a rest. The ceiling bore a painted relief showing cherubs at play with flying fish.

Getting up to go and splash her face with water in the bathroom, Roberta saw an enormous cabin trunk beside the dressing-table. Her little flower-printed fabric travelling bag, placed on top of it, looked no bigger than a bowl of potpourri. She opened the trunk to find that it was a hanging wardrobe containing a dozen dresses and as many hats, along with assorted footwear, shawls, and handkerchiefs embroidered with her initials.

A card had been left on the dressing-table. It read: "Welcome to London, Miss Morgenstern. I look forward to meeting you at noon tomorrow for lunch in the air at the Crystal Palace." The message was signed *Palladio*. Roberta put the card down again.

A surprising gesture on the Count's part. He had a reputation for being a dried-up, unfeeling, reclusive billionaire. But perhaps that reputation was an invention of the tabloids on which Palladio had several times declared war. A man so loathed by the gutter press couldn't be all bad, thought the witch.

And what did he mean by lunch in the air?

Roberta went over to a desk with feet carved like little dragons. A folder stamped with the Historic Cities logo was waiting for her there.

"Thanks, Mr. Simmons," she said, picking it up. Searching her bag, Roberta found the file that Gruber had given her. She put both files on the bed and opened them to compare their contents.

44

The material provided by Simmons told her that Mary had only recently become a tenant of London and liked the dissipated life. She had inherited a considerable fortune made on the mainland, and lived on the interest. You could count the witnesses who had been questioned on the fingers of one hand. A bobby had passed Graham on Westminster Bridge as night was falling. Most of the customers in the Black Dog remembered a young woman who was obviously drunk and seemed to be waiting for someone. But she had not been seen leaving the pub, and no one had noticed her murderer.

Roberta sighed. Simmons's file told her as little as Gruber's. However, she had something else to go on. Something more revealing than the prints found by Simmons that couldn't be checked against anything, or Martineau's fanciful calculations.

The sorceress opened the little make-up box in which she had deposited Mary Graham's eyelashes. Looking in her bag, she took out a tobacco pouch, cigarette papers and a cigarette holder. She recited a spell over the eyelashes, which crumbled to black dust. Then she rolled a cigarette, tipping the contents of the make-up box into the brown tobacco, licked the paper, and smoothed the white tube with an expert hand. She put it in the cigarette holder and made for the balcony, taking a shawl out of the trunk as she passed. Throwing the silky folds of the shawl round her shoulders, she sat in a rattan chair and raised Mary Graham's visual memory to her lips. Courage, my dear, Roberta told herself. Then she said out loud, looking towards the Thames:

45

"Ye hours pursuing your eternal round, cease moving now, to stillness you are bound."

A seagull skimming the surface of the river was suspended in mid-flight. The fog assumed an icy, opaque look. Roberta looked fixedly at the end of the cigarette, which lit up, throwing out sparks. The witch puffed at it, and Mary Graham's life up to the moment of death unfurled before her eyes. She saw a child's nanny. A red scooter. A green field with white sheets blowing in the wind. Women, more women. No men. City scenes. Roberta recognized a theatre. A meeting with a famous actor one night. Paris. Venice. Graham began paying regular visits to the Historic Cities. London . . .

Here we are, thought Roberta. The images were clearer now, and the fragments of memory more eloquent. An evening at the theatre, a boat trip, men this time, a great many men, Westminster Bridge looking hazy in the fog.

A bobby passed before her eyes and disappeared again. Walls, musicians, dancers whirling round on the floor. Roberta's view blurred, stabilized, and focused.

There was a black shape sitting opposite Roberta, floating like a mirage. Impossible to identify it. The witch felt perspiration running down her back. "Oh, concentrate, Mary, can't you?" she breathed. The street. A series of street lamps. A stretch of waste ground. A section of wall. At last, a clear image: an image of the man's eyes. They were black and expressionless, the whites perfectly pure. Mary Graham's vision blurred again and contracted, perhaps under the influence of pleasure. Or terror.

Details came into view. A waistcoat with a complex pattern. Those eyes again. A fine, elegant hand. The line of Mary's vision suddenly swung left and then back again. It was now terrifyingly precise. She was looking at her executioner's torso. His waistcoat opened to reveal a collection of blades of different lengths, curved, straight, slender, pointed.

Mary's vision focused on the man's mouth. Cruel lips, curling back to show the enamel of white, well-tended teeth.

"Say something!" the witch ordered.

The man's lips began to move in slow motion. Roberta followed every syllable. Suddenly the line of sight moved up again to the now bloodshot eyes, and then contracted for the last time, like a fading TV picture. The End. En route for the next world, Miss Graham.

Roberta crushed the cigarette out with her heel. The seagull had not moved a metre since she cast the spell, but meanwhile the witch had seen a whole life pass before her eyes. She was exhausted. She felt like throwing up, or weeping for Mary. She began trembling like a leaf, and the shawl did not warm her.

She gave a brief order, and time began moving again. The gull flew low over the water, the fog was freed from its icy straitjacket. Roberta thought about what the murderer had said. She had read his lips as she had been taught to do at the College of Sorcery.

Why Annie Chapman, she wondered. Why did that bastard call her Annie Chapman?

She rose and quickly noted down the few visual facts she had gleaned from her experiment, not that they gave her much to go on. The waistcoat, the colour of the man's eyes, the appearance of his hands and lips. Picking up the phone, she asked the Savoy switchboard to get her a number. CID Central Filing replied after two rings.

"Morgenstern here, code number 6372. Can you tell me what you've got on an Annie Chapman? From any period."

"Hold the line, please," replied the automatic answering service.

Roberta waited a few moments. Then the voice spoke again, telling her what Central Filing had on Chapman.

Night was falling over London when the sorceress put the phone back on its rest. She had covered several pages of her notebook with hasty scribbling. Feeling pleased with herself, she looked in the dressing-table mirror.

"*Dimidium facti, qui coepit habet,*" she told her reflection, which replied, with a wolfish smile: "Well begun is half done."

You'll never get anything done if you don't make a start, young Martineau told himself severely, caught in the trap of his own speculations. He was pacing round the scene of the crime like a palaeontologist with a fossil, waiting for inspiration to strike as he sought an answer. The air conditioning had been turned off to let the body reach a temperature where it could be laid flat without breaking. It was time to return Mary Graham to solid ground.

She had already lost her shining carapace, and tears of icy water were running down her cheeks. Her lips sketched a melancholy smile, and her eyelids, with their broken lashes, closed slowly on eyes now veiled by death.

48

"The man was strong and he took size six and a half shoes," repeated Martineau.

The fingerprints were useless in the absence of any records against which to check them, as Simmons had been forced to admit once his first enthusiasm wore off. According to the Historic Cities charter, no one—whether a tourist, an actor or a tenant—could be made to provide personal details for the files, even though it was common practice in the rest of the League. It didn't seem likely that the murderer would have given his prints voluntarily, unless he had decided to take the ultimate responsibility for his bloodthirsty habits.

Simmons, called away on some kind of urgent business, had made his apologies and left Martineau alone with the corpse. A curious, increasingly peaty smell rose as the ground thawed out. A rivulet of rust-coloured water trickled between Martineau's feet. Mary Graham's body slumped. But for her gaping stomach you might have thought she was asleep.

The young investigator was determined to get results. He saw it as his duty. He didn't want to end up in either Martineau Cement Industries or the Contracts Section of the CID, and if he was going to avoid that fate he must come up with the goods, fast.

More modern methods are called for, he told himself. Was this place being watched? He didn't know, but anyway, an observer would see nothing but a few fireworks.

The young man took a round tin and a marten-hair brush out of his inside jacket pocket. Going over to the wall where the murderer had left fingerprints, he opened the tin. The motes of dust inside it were dancing a magnetic ballet. Triangles turned to stars before exploding and re-forming to create even more complicated shapes, which destroyed each other in their own turn.

"Dear little tracers," Martineau whispered, "I've got work for you."

He brought the brush close to the moving surface. A light flurry of air rose, covering the hairs of the brush as some electrostatic miracle caused a swirling effect. Martineau took the brush away from the box, which he closed with a snap. He brushed the fingerprints very carefully, starting again twice. Then he stood up, shook the dust off his brush and put it away. The tracers, airborne and now enriched with the murderer's DNA from the prints, rose on a slight draught and were carried to the ventilators leading to the outside air.

"Good luck, my little detectives," said the investigator.

He had turned his vibration recorder on. It was true that London, like the other Historic Cities, did not allow tracers to be linked to Central Filing, which would have meant installing relay stations of the kind you saw on the mainland. But there was nothing to prevent tracers working on closed circuit. If a single one of those motes of dust found the man who had left the fingerprint, Martineau's vibration recorder, acting as a relay station, would tell him at once. And then it would be child's play to locate the murderer.

The young detective was very pleased with himself. He leaned on the wall to step over Mary Graham's left arm, but stopped when he realized he was about to tread on her.

"Sorry, Miss Graham," he apologized.

Standing on one foot and trying to keep his balance, he was just about to jump over her intestines when they began to move. Martineau's throat constricted as he watched them curl. They moved again and rose slightly. He crouched down to observe the phenomenon more closely. Picking up a stick, he plunged it into them. Mary Graham's head suddenly dropped on her chest. Martineau looked aside to watch the movement.

"Oh, my God," he murmured, his mouth dry.

Something about the size of a small cat jumped at him, taking off from his shoulder and bouncing back from the other side of the room. Martineau just had time to see the creature scurry into a hole in the floorboards and disappear from sight.

A rat! It was only a rat!

"That's about enough for today," he said out loud, his voice shaking.

He started out along the corridor leading back to ground level, whistling one of the latest hits and trying to relax. But more than once he looked behind him to make sure he was not being followed, and the beating of his heart roared like thunder in his ears.

CRYSTAL PALACE DAY

✦

"We can do eggs any way you like. Scrambled, boiled, poached, fried, omelette?"

"Boiled, please," said Roberta.

"Boiled for madam," said the waiter, with a cheery smile. "How about you, sir?"

"Scrambled."

The waiter nodded and moved away from their table. As the witch admired the Savoy restaurant she heaved a deep sigh. Sunlight came flooding into the great hall with its panelled walls and ceiling. Red sandstone urns emerged from beneath fountains of brilliant green foliage. There was a luminous radiance about the light, a primeval purity no longer to be found in mainland cities like Basle. Morgenstern was looking particularly chirpy this morning, but Martineau had dark rings round his eyes.

"Didn't you sleep well, dear boy?" asked the witch.

Dear boy, indeed! He was still searching for a suitable retort when the waiter brought them two plates loaded with smoking bacon and sausages grilled to perfection. Roberta poured more tea into her cup and raised it to her lips, little finger elegantly crooked.

"Incredible. Absolutely incredible," she murmured.

Martineau helped himself to a cup of black coffee, almost drained it in a single gulp, and immediately poured himself another.

"What's so incredible?" he inquired.

"This tea. A pure Darjeeling, not one of those blends the industrialists try to palm off on us. Mmmm! Delicious! Divine! I shall have to drug the hotel manager and get my hands on several packets of this miraculous substance."

Martineau told himself the woman was perfectly capable of doing just that. Then, before they had even started in on the sausages and bacon, their eggs arrived.

"Did you get Palladio's invitation?" Morgenstern asked.

Martineau nodded. "We meet at the Crystal Palace at twelve noon," he said. "So the Count's finally going to see us. Do you know what he looks like?"

"No idea. He's always steered clear of the media."

Martineau held his rasher of bacon aloft on his fork, wondering at which end he was supposed to start eating it.

"Did you have time to check up on whatever it was yesterday afternoon?" he asked, a serious expression on his face.

"Uh-uh," replied the sorceress.

"So you found something out?"

"I think I ought to be asking you that, dear boy. It was your job to examine the scene of the crime. What do we know about the murderer apart from his shoe size and his figure? Can I have your cheese?"

The young man passed his plate over to his colleague, who devoured the piece of Cheddar almost in a single bite. How on earth did she do it? All he could manage at this time of day was coffee. And then more coffee.

"You don't look in very good shape, Martineau. Bad dreams?"

It had been the middle of the night when he returned to the Savoy, and he had found it very difficult indeed to get to sleep. He did recollect dreams, or rather nightmares, which suggested that sleep had finally claimed him only to turn his mind inside out, before throwing it up again, a total wreck, on the shores of early dawn.

"Bad dreams, yes," he agreed, adopting the evasive tone that Morgenstern herself seemed to favour when she wasn't holding forth at length. He wiped his lips on his napkin and asked, "You won't be needing me before midday, will you?"

Roberta shrugged her shoulders. "No, no. I thought I'd take a little stroll, but I don't want to dragoon you into window-shopping with me. I'm not as cruel as all that."

"Right." Martineau rose. "Then if you'll excuse me, I have something important to do. See you at the Crystal Palace."

The young man left the restaurant at remarkable speed. Morgenstern, spoon in hand as she prepared to dig into the marmalade jar, watched him go.

"So the heir to the Martineau company has secrets of his own, does he?" she asked herself out loud.

A dignified elderly gentleman breakfasting at a neighbouring table looked the sorceress up and down with a strange expression on his face. She dug her spoon into the jar and spread a generous layer of marmalade on her slice of white toast while going over the day's priorities in her mind. Second, catch the murderer. First, do justice to the breakfast on this table.

The cab had just dropped Clément Martineau off outside the entrance to the Tower of London. A tourist party was making its way along the path that would take them to admire the Crown Jewels. Or their replicas, as Morgenstern would have pointed out. The inquiry agent opened the envelope he had found on the Pelican hydroplane, took out the card, and once again read the enigmatic sentence: "I killed Colonel Gardiner."

The sombre old medieval prison consisted of four towers linked by high battlements. Visitors were channelled towards a nearby building with two Yeomen of the Guard in Elizabethan costume outside it, carrying halberds. Martineau went up to them and showed his ticket. One of the Beefeaters took it and put it in his pocket.

"Green door on the left," he said, pointing to a door concealed behind a projection in the wall. "You have ten minutes to find out who killed Colonel Gardiner."

And taking no further interest in Martineau, the guard turned his attention to another group coming down the path. Feeling like a burglar, the young man made his way over to the green door and pushed it open. A stuffy odour rose to his nostrils. He slipped through the doorway and closed the door behind him.

Dim light filtered through a series of sombre stained

glass windows into the room he had just entered. Martineau waited for his eyes to get used to the darkness. Gradually he saw a silent, motionless army taking shape before him.

Infantry and cavalry were ranged side by side. No fewer than thirty horses stood there, neither moving nor whinnying. The young inquiry agent approached the first horse a little apprehensively. The man seated on the animal was wearing a heavily reinforced suit of armour bristling with spikes and spurs, and a helmet shaped like an artillery shell. A crest of ostrich feathers tumbled to his iron-clad shoulders.

Martineau patted the horse's collar, which made a hollow sound. A set of floodlights on the ceiling suddenly illuminated the room.

"You have eight minutes left to find the killer of Colonel Gardiner," announced an expressionless voice.

"Yes, right," replied the young man stupidly, dazzled and suspecting that he was speaking to a pre-recorded voice.

He began going down the line, reading the information printed on cards at the foot of the dummies. Who was this Gardiner, and who had killed him? He suspected that it might not have been a real murder, but the rules of the game as laid down by Palladio Sealines did stipulate that players must not be deliberately led astray. So now what?

The armed figures turned out to represent former kings of England in ceremonial armour or robes of state. Henry VI, Edward IV, Henry VII, James I, Henry Prince of Wales—the resonant names echoed like the words of some ancient tragedy written in blood and gunpowder. The suits of armour were engraved with battle scenes, showing monarchs got up to look like Hercules and cavalry furiously charging the enemy guns.

The royal figures were brandishing what must have been their favourite weapons, identified by the cards: steel mace, Toledo blade, Maltese sword. The last figure, of a child of twelve imprisoned in his metal carapace, was particularly moving; the young Prince of Wales held a weapon the right size for him, a short sword adapted to his boyish arm.

"You have three minutes left," said the voice.

He'd lingered too long. Gardiner—who *was* this Gardiner? Martineau hadn't seen the name anywhere. Anyway, surely a mere colonel wouldn't be here on horseback among the kings. After the line of horsemen an exhibition of weapons began, laid out in glass cases, displayed like trophies or hanging on the walls.

"Two minutes," said the voice inexorably.

I killed Colonel Gardiner, said Martineau to himself, trying to concentrate.

Swords, maces, pikes, lances, halberds, daggers—grooves in some of the weapons were still black with enemy blood.

"Rifle and shield of the Count of Mar," read Martineau. "Sword worn by the Pretender on his proclamation as king in Scotland."

"Thirty seconds."

The young man had looked in all the glass cases. This was impossible. How could he have missed the killer? He turned and saw an axe fixed to the wall.

There was just time to read: "This Scottish mountaineer's axe killed Colonel Gardiner at the Battle of Prestonpans."

On impulse, Martineau took hold of the handle and pulled it towards him. The axe fell from the wall, but stopped short just above his head. A door concealed behind a tapestry opened in front of him, and a female voice begged artlessly: "Oh, do hurry up! I must tell you my secret!"

"Coming!" replied Martineau.

He went through the doorway, and the door closed behind him.

He was in total darkness. Not a breath of air, not a sound. Something behind him gently pushed him down, making him sit on what proved to be a padded seat. He felt a movement below him, and a bar swung into place over his chest to prevent him from falling.

He was on a scenic railway, in a little car which as far as he could tell was moving quite slowly. Martineau felt himself turning right. The car passed over a set of points that made it rattle and turned it towards the first spectacle: a scene of medieval torture.

It showed a man fixed to a table by his wrists and ankles. The torturer was leaning over the victim's legs, racking them with a vice. The victim let out frightful screams, and his bones gave a series of sinister cracks as the car turned left and approached another scene.

This one showed two children in a four-poster bed clinging to each other, gazing at a light that filtered under the door of their room. Only dummies, Martineau told himself, but he wasn't quite sure about that when he saw the door open and heard the children moan in terror. The executioner appeared in the doorway. Although Edward IV's sons, the terrified little princes, struggled to escape, they were in chains. Martineau tried getting out of the car, but the safety bar held him prisoner, and refused to move an inch.

The car turned again, slowing down this time. The next scene showed two figures in a dungeon cell, its floor covered with straw. A young woman, her face invisible, had placed her head on a block of wood and was waiting for the blow as the executioner raised his axe, preparing to bring it down on the condemned woman's neck.

The young man felt he had to get out of this nightmare as quickly as possible. He slipped under the bar, hauled himself out of his seat and landed on the cell floor. The woman was sobbing, but the man did not move. Martineau hesitated for only a split second. Then he made for the executioner, flinging himself and the other man against the wall of the cell. The huge figure put up no resistance, letting Martineau bring him down like a big rag doll. Nor did he move when the young man rose to his feet again, slightly stunned by his own courage.

The young woman had not stirred since he intervened. Martineau knelt down beside her and put out a hand to turn her head.

"The first letter of the mystery word is M," announced the head, before falling to the floor at the young investigator's feet. The dummy was not very well made. Its face had obviously been patched and stitched up, it had grotesque eyes and a mere sketch of a mouth.

Martineau rose again with a gulp of surprise. His one idea now was to get out of here, leave this mockery of a dungeon and return to the open air and the real world.

A door opened in one of the cell walls, letting him out into the open. Ten seconds later, the inquiry agent was walking down the path to the rest of the Tower of London, telling himself he was an idiot and trying to calm his heart, which was pounding hard again.

It was a perfect day for a visit to the Great Exhibition. Couples were strolling down the shady avenues of Hyde Park, and starlings twittered in the branches of the elm trees planted by landscape gardeners. The sun, with only a few cotton-wool clouds in it, shed gentle, radiant warmth on the park. London was enjoying wonderful late summer weather.

Roberta was on her way towards the immense edifice of the Crystal Palace, which looked like a giant hothouse or a transparent railway station. She had put on the lightest outfit she could find in her wardrobe, but she still looked like a meringue.

But the witch was more worried about Martineau than her dress. He seemed so inexperienced! Enthusiastic, too, not that that was necessarily a bad thing in Criminal Investigation. A little innocence and an injection of fresh blood would do Major Gruber's branch of the force no harm.

"Miss Morgenstern!"

The young investigator was hurrying uphill. He still wore his pickpocket's costume, which he seemed to like. He stopped in front of Morgenstern, gesturing to show that he was too breathless to speak. Roberta waited, hands folded on the knob of her parasol, its tip planted in the turf of the park. It was a very elegant pose.

"Have—have you just arrived?" he asked when he had finally got his breath back.

"No, I'm just leaving." Martineau looked foolish. "Yes, of course I've just arrived, dear boy. Why on earth are you in such a state? Even the Liberty sales wouldn't have that effect on me."

"I—I went to see the Tower of London."

"An instructive visit, I hope?" Morgenstern walked on. "Come on, we mustn't be late. It seems that Palladio is a busy man. It's a great honour for him to agree to see us at all."

The young man was hurrying along beside the sorceress, who glanced at him, a mocking smile on her lips. "Aren't you afraid of getting arrested in that pickpocket outfit?"

"It's just the thing for catching our murderer, Miss Morgenstern," replied the young man, his voice steadier now. "I can melt into the crowd, keep my eyes skinned and wait."

"Chapter Five of your Goddefroy, I suppose. 'Shadowing and Tailing.'" Martineau slowed down, slightly annoyed by his superior's tone. "Sorry, but it's a long time since I worked with a partner who could recite the police code off by heart. Your demonstration in the Tower was impressive. No, I mean it. Congratulations."

Martineau looked at the sorceress, trying to make out if she was still laughing at him. But Morgenstern was in a good mood, and she had nothing against this lad who dreamed of glory and adventure. Nothing except their first meeting and the racket of that sports car.

"So what conclusions did you reach after studying the scene of the crime?" she asked, opening her parasol to keep off the deceptively strong heat of the sun, which had just come out from behind a cloud. "You didn't want to tell me this morning."

Martineau patted the vibration recorder hidden inside his waistcoat. "Too soon to draw any conclusions yet," he said. "But we ought to know who committed that dreadful crime soon."

"Oh, look!" cried Roberta, asking no more questions. "Here comes Mr. Simmons. A charming man. Such an elegant way of carrying himself, too!"

Simmons, clad from head to foot in green, could almost have merged with the grass of Hyde Park. Bowing slightly to Roberta, he said, "Welcome to the Exhibition!" Then he escorted them to the turnstile admitting visitors to the Crystal Palace.

The perception of space can play tricks on you. Roberta sometimes amused herself by going into one of the many old churches in her native Basle and observing the sombre weight of the building, while the apartment blocks outside were all transparency and lightness. Entering the Crystal Palace was the opposite experience: the space inside was hugely extended, spreading in all four directions along the gigantic arms of the transept as they ran off into the distance. Light made its leisurely way through the vaults of glass, here falling brightly on a machine at rest, there diffused in milky radiance around a crystal fountain. Motes of gold swirled in the air above the pale wooden floor, like insects celebrating the coming of twilight.

"Fantastic," commented Roberta. "Simply fantastic."

"The Count is expecting you," said Simmons. "He loves the Exhibition, never misses a chance to visit it when he comes to London."

Simmons set off at a rapid pace, but Roberta hesitated to follow him. She wanted to stroll round like the other visitors clutching their Exhibition guidebooks, stopping to examine the machines with close interest. Meanwhile, Martineau went in pursuit of Simmons without bothering about Morgenstern. She let him move away and then set off in a different direction, taking her own curiosity as a guide.

A raucous sound attracted her to part of the American section, where a small crowd had gathered behind a barrier. A peculiar musical instrument was being demonstrated on the other side of the barrier: a huge case with a keyboard and four violins, fixed to the ends of poles, being played by mechanical bows. A young man was striking the keys energetically. The bows tormented the strings of the four crucified violins, producing a tune very distantly reminiscent, as far as Roberta could make out, of Haydn's Austrian national anthem. Rubbing her poor ears, she moved away from this discordant sound.

Further on, she passed a revolving plinth that visitors could swivel. On top of the plinth was a delicate marble statue of a naked girl taken by surprise as she stepped out of her bath. A great many elderly gentlemen were clustering around the girl, each providing his own commentary. What a delightful period this is, thought Roberta.

A muffled thumping brought her out of her thoughts. She followed the sound across the transept, and found herself at the foot of a mechanical monster three metres high by six or seven long. This machine bristled with any number of levers, cogwheels, handles, and moving sheets of metal which were shifting back and forth, grunting and spitting out jets of vapour with a deafening noise. Children hid among their mothers' skirts as they watched the invention at work.

"What on earth is it?" Roberta wondered.

Guide in hand, a bystander told her. "An envelope-sealing machine made by the firm of Stephenson. It can seal two thousand envelopes an hour."

"Goodness me."

Roberta left the envelope-sealing machine and moved on. A little farther off the Germans were exhibiting their marvels. One stand was attracting a lot of visitors. Elbowing her way through the crowd, Roberta saw a number of scenes created by a Stuttgart taxidermist: a family of foxes outside their earth; a wild boar brought to bay by the pack; a majestic stag with two huge hounds suspended in midair, jaws gaping, as they flung themselves at its flanks. It reminded her of the scene that Simmons had reconstructed in the cellars of the Tower of London.

The displays of taxidermy were flanked by little charades showing small animals in human dress: weasels dressed as students were chasing a duck; a couple of frogs sheltered under an umbrella; a class of rats and mice were listening attentively to their teacher, a cat.

"Miss Morgenstern!" someone called.

That was Martineau's voice. Roberta looked round, but try as she might she couldn't see the young man anywhere. The transept was some way off. A group of elm trees marked its centre.

"Miss Morgenstern!" called Martineau again, closer this time.

"Yes, what?" said Roberta, turning round, still unable to see him.

A shadow fell on her, too heavy a shadow to be a cloud, unless the cloud was made of iron. Looking up, the witch saw a curved hull hovering some ten metres above the Exhibition.

"Ah, the *Albatross*," she murmured.

The propellers of the ship were at rest, but two cables attached to her bows and stern linked her to tracks hidden in the roof of the Crystal Palace. Her engine must be moving her along them at snail's pace.

A set of metal steps was lowered from the ship's rail to the floor of the building. The bottom step came down gently right in front of Roberta, and Martineau signed to her to climb up. Picking up her skirt in both hands, she went up the steps. As she set foot on the bridge of the *Albatross* a man came to meet her, saying in a deep voice, "Welcome aboard, Miss Morgenstern. Antonio Palladio at your service."

Roberta should have fallen for the Count's charm. Instead, she instantly distrusted it. She'd seen him somewhere before, she was sure she had. But when and where? Morgenstern didn't believe in coincidences, and Palladio was not the man to leave anything to chance.

Martineau, on the other hand, like Simmons and the ten or so other people on deck, was bowled over by their host's charisma.

Roberta moved away from the Count, pretending to lean on the handrail to admire the scene below. The green of the elm trees moved slowly away under the hull. Several pigeons flew up from the trees and settled at Palladio's feet. They began waddling round him, cooing plaintively. Even the animals fall for him, thought Roberta, more suspicious than ever.

"So now that we're all here, let's have lunch," their host invited the party.

A table had been set up between two deckhouses. Roberta followed Palladio, and so did the other guests, all of them as docile as the rats who followed the Pied Piper.

Towards the end of the main course Roberta Morgenstern realized who Palladio reminded her of: her old Professor of the History of Sorcery, Monsieur Rosemonde. As a girl she had been madly in love with him. But Palladio was even better-looking than Rosemonde. He was just the way Roberta imagined her ideal man.

The doubles of Queen Victoria, Joseph Paxton, and Isambard Kingdom Brunel, who shared this distinguished table, seemed very pale creatures by comparison with their host. Martineau, seated between the Queen and Morgenstern, was entirely won over.

Conversation was in full flow, although most of the subjects so far broached were rather dull. Queen Victoria described the theatrical performance by Sarah Bernhardt she had seen a few days ago. Brunel and Paxton were discussing technical matters in a knowing way. Martineau was all ears, while Morgenstern kept remarkably silent. The Count had only to say a word or make a gesture to attract everyone's attention.

"I hear the Criminal Investigation Department has been having rather a slow time of it recently?" he suddenly inquired point blank, as a waiter refilled Roberta's glass.

If he wanted to get her talking, he was welcome, thought the witch. "Well, we seem to have a case on hand again, thanks to this city of yours," she replied in the same affable tone.

Palladio nodded, and turning to his other guests said gravely, "I must tell you that an atrocious crime was committed in London three days ago. Miss Morgenstern and Mr. Martineau are here to clear the mystery up."

"A crime!" exclaimed Victoria. "In London? How dreadful!" But the pseudo-Queen looked delighted.

"Dreadful but interesting," agreed Paxton, swirling the wine in his glass. "What exactly happened?"

Roberta could see a morbid glint, like a flock of bats taking flight, come into the eyes of the tenants. She sedately ate a mouthful of roast lamb with mint sauce before replying.

"One of your neighbours was found disembowelled in a little yard in the East End. A sadistic murder committed by a deranged criminal. He may be visiting the Exhibition at this very moment. Unless of course he's sitting here among us at this very table, in the classic tradition of the English detective story."

Roberta turned her most dazzling smile on the company, noticing with satisfaction that Victoria had turned pale and gulped down half the contents of her glass at once. The wine was really excellent.

"And how far have you got with your investigations, Mrs. Morgenstern?" asked Paxton.

"Miss Morgenstern." Roberta turned to Count Palladio. "Tell us about your Historic Cities, would you, Count? Just why did you build them?"

Their host's mind seemed to be elsewhere, for he turned a vague gaze on Roberta—and the sorceress saw his yellow, bloodshot eyes turn as clear as they had been a moment ago. She thought she must have been dreaming. No one had reacted to this sudden change.

"Oh, it was a desire to restore cities like London to their former glory, a taste for history, and a love of the theatre. You see, I was born in Venice, a city that has turned the masquerade into an art."

I bet it has, thought Roberta. Her mind was working furiously. There was nothing natural about the Count's charm. Certain spells allowed you to disguise your real self under a new, fictional but fascinating appearance. Roberta knew a very simple way to find out whether the Count was using this trick to mask himself.

"Each city is modelled on the Venetian lagoon," Palladio went on, leaning towards Victoria. "London, perhaps, was the most difficult. The skill here lies in the machinery that makes parts of the city change over as time passes and the sets need shifting."

Roberta was staring intently at the Count's profile.

"Your ancestors were stage designers, sir, weren't they?" asked Paxton.

"Designers and architects. The Palladian villas . . ." mused their host.

Roberta bit her tongue hard. For a brief moment, no longer than an electric shock, she saw Palladio's face in a distorted projection. It then settled back once more into a perfect likeness of Monsieur Rosemonde, hardly aged at all by the passage of the years.

"Are you all right, my dear?" he said, turning to Roberta in concern.

"Fine," she replied, a napkin to her mouth. "I bit my tongue, that's all."

She rose and walked up and down on deck as if to take her mind off the pain. Martineau hesitated for a moment or so, and then joined her.

"Amazing, isn't he?" he said enthusiastically.

Industrial products were still passing beneath the hull of the *Albatross*, prototypes of machines that looked like metal fossils on the bed of a crystal sea.

"And his inventions are truly Titanic," the young man continued.

"Who does he remind you of, Martineau?"

The young man hesitated, rather thrown off balance by the question. "Well, as it happens, I was wondering the same thing just now. I think he reminds me of Goddefroy."

"The man who wrote the *Handbook of Police Theory*?"

"Technique. Police technique."

"Describe him. Physically."

Martineau seemed surprised by Morgenstern's abrupt

manner. "Well, rather stout. Brown eyes. Bald. But his charm lies in his fine mind, his capacity for analysis, his powerful deduction . . ."

"Charm, eh?" muttered Morgenstern.

Yes, Palladio conveyed a different image of himself to everyone, an ideal image. A magic spell masked his true face, Roberta thought, but she still had to confirm her theory. The Count, like everyone else in the city, was one of their suspects. She went back to her place, followed by her colleague.

Brunel was talking to the Count, whom he revered, about a project for a Leviathan class liner linking all the Historic Cities: London, Paris, San Francisco, Venice. What a cruise that would be! But currents, contrary winds and the low draught of water in the lagoons would make the task difficult.

Roberta stared at the glass walls of the Crystal Palace rising on both sides of the ship and commanded, with all the strength she could muster up: "Reflect, let images appear, but do not show the next world here." The spell worked on her bathroom mirror—no reason why it shouldn't work on the walls of the Crystal Palace too.

Sure enough, the glass sparkled, a wave of light passed through the reflected image of the ship, and at last the sorceress was able to see Count Palladio in his true shape.

The creature sitting at this table had certainly been a man once, centuries ago . . . The Count's body was covered with oozing, stained, mottled skin. His head drooped on his chest, twitching now and then. Two vicious little yellow eyes darted from guest to guest. His ears were ragged round the edges, and his face was a single liver spot erupting with boils.

The witch was looking at a nightmare vision, a human being forgotten by Death but plagued by Time for an eternity. She felt a hand placed on hers, and slowly looked away again. No one had noticed anything. Not that there was anything for *them* to notice.

"Are you back with us, my dear?" inquired the perfect likeness of Monsieur Rosemonde.

Roberta took her time replying. She looked at that smooth hand with its flawless nails, and then raised her eyes to the Count's.

"It's this building—it makes one melancholy," she said distractedly. "I do apologize. A slight absence of mind, that's all."

"Don't apologize," exclaimed Paxton, whose brainchild, after all, this place was. "It's a disturbing factor that we couldn't have foreseen—and the Palace is dedicated to light, too!—but a remarkable number of women do feel faint under my crystal vault. Who'd have thought so much glass could induce dreams?"

"Nightmares, too," added the sorceress.

"Paxton, you are a poet," said Victoria. "I did quite right to support your project."

The guests exchanged mutual congratulations and drank to each other. Roberta dared not look at their reflections in the crystal walls. Her eyes moved over the grey-brown fleck that was the Count without lingering on it. Only a fourth-level charm could conceal his true appearance. But there was no spell, to her knowledge, that could keep the Count alive. A man several centuries old had invited them to lunch. And as far as the witch knew immortals were no part of this world.

"Miss Morgenstern may be thinking of her inquiries," suggested Palladio. "We're so excited! Can you tell us how far you have got with your investigations?"

Martineau said nothing. He was watching Roberta.

"I know who killed Mary Graham," she responded quietly, watching the Count's reaction in the huge mirror of the walls.

The mummy-like head was suddenly raised. The eyes, precise as pins, turned to Roberta.

"You know who killed Mary Graham?" repeated the smooth, perfect likeness of Monsieur Rosemonde. "What amazing news! Tell us more!"

Simmons and Martineau exchanged startled glances.

"The murderer goes by several names: Montague John Druitt, Severin Klozovski, Dr. Roslyn D'Onston Stephenson, and—oh, I forget all the others."

Simmons, white as a sheet, whispered, "Almighty God, how the . . ."

Roberta took pity on him and did not hesitate to reveal what else she knew. "I made a little inquiry on the side. The killer knew his victim not as Mary Graham, but as Annie Chapman. I rang the CID archives. The woman Annie Chapman really existed, just like Victoria, Paxton, and Brunel." The sorceress glanced at their three reincarnations before turning to the Count. "If our man likes a historical reconstruction as much as you seem to, I have every reason to think that three more innocent female tenants risk losing their guts to the Ripper over the coming nights."

A silence of several seconds followed this comment.

"The Ripper, of course," murmured Martineau. "Jack. Or someone who thinks he's Jack the Ripper."

"What evidence can you offer?" asked Palladio after several moments' thought.

Roberta threw her napkin down on the table violently, making the other guests jump, Martineau included.

"You think Mary Graham slipped and gutted herself on a stone? There's a killer at large in your Historic City, a tenant who takes his new part very seriously indeed. And he's not working alone."

"What do you mean?" asked Martineau.

Roberta gave Palladio a look that spoke volumes. She had trapped him. The Count told Victoria, Brunel, and Paxton to go over to the other side of the ship for liqueurs, and his guests complied without even appearing offended. Palladio's charm seemed to work as well on his old cronies as in seducing new ones.

"What exactly do you know?" he asked, once no indiscreet ears could hear.

"The killer wears a waistcoat with a very unusual serpentine pattern. I sent its description off to the various city wardrobe departments. About a dozen tenants are wearing a similar costume, but in spite of my repeated requests no one would tell me who they are."

"And for a very good reason, Miss Morgenstern. The success of my Historic Cities lies in anonymity. You can't—"

Roberta brought her fist down on the table. "I don't

73

care if your little reconstructions are a kind of Lunapark for perverse, depraved billionaires. But Historic City or not, you're under the jurisdiction of the Ministry I work for. Refuse to cooperate and I'll have London closed down for serious infringements of state security."

"You wouldn't dare," said the Count.

"We'll see about that," Roberta snapped back. "And don't trying turning your charm on me. I see through you, Palladio. I see you as you really are."

With considerable pleasure, Roberta studied the image of the wizened old man, who started with surprise at this announcement. Simmons provided a diversion.

"As for me," he said, pursing his lips, "I should be interested to know how Miss Morgenstern has discovered so much about the murderer."

Roberta looked at him like a cat watching a mouse. "Why not ask her straight out?" she replied. "Perhaps she'll tell you."

Palladio raised a placating hand. "White magic," replied the Count. "Or black magic, never mind which. I didn't know Mr. Fould employed people like you in the Ministry."

Roberta was on dangerous ground here: Martineau wasn't supposed to find out that she was a witch. Not like this, anyway. It wouldn't be the end of the world, but it could give Gruber ulcers. Everything depended on the Count and the tone he chose to take. Palladio held her gaze, not daring to go any further. Finally he gave in.

"Simmons," he ordered, "tell Security. I want the tenants concerned brought in and kept in isolation."

"But sir, there's no precedent!"

"There's a first time for everything."

Simmons raised one hand to his ear and issued a series of brief orders. Martineau had risen to his feet. "What did you mean about Miss Morgenstern?" he asked the Count. "When you said 'people like you.' What does that mean?"

Palladio did not reply. It was up to Morgenstern to wriggle out of this on her own. Roberta decided on the unvarnished truth and, as usual in a crisis, charged straight in.

"I'm what's commonly called a witch, dear boy. I make potions. I cast spells. And I can see a murderer through the eyes of the murder victim."

"A witch?" repeated Martineau. Roberta saw surprise struggling with disbelief in the young man's face. Finally he burst out laughing. "A witch! Oh, that's a good one!"

Simmons was already coming back towards them.

"Nine tenants have been tracked down," he said. "The bobbies are on their way."

"What about the tenth?" asked Roberta.

"They're still looking."

Simmons moved off again to follow the investigations from a distance. Morgenstern looked the Count up and down. He returned a mocking smile.

"Where did you learn that little conjuring trick?" she asked, indicating the glass walls of the Crystal Palace.

"Oh, I've had time to learn from the very greatest," replied Palladio enigmatically. "Are you aware of the risks you run, Miss Morgenstern?"

"Threats, eh? You flatter me, Palladio. I've only just

arrived," she replied, with a beaming smile. "It's you who should take care."

"Take care of what, dear lady?"

"Of fourth-level charms. They're useless against certain third-level commands."

And Roberta launched into an incantation aimed at the Count who, judging by his expression, had only just understood the danger. His disguise melted away like the mortal remains of a man defeated. The old man materialized, slumped in his wheelchair, features distorted by rage, shouting and swearing at once. Stunned, Martineau gazed at this apparition. Simmons, who had not yet seen his master's changed shape, hurried over.

"The bobbies have just tracked the tenth man down," he said. "In Park Lane, making for St. Paul's. There's a woman with him."

"Curse you!" Palladio managed to spit at Morgenstern. He was drooling greenish bile.

Now Simmons saw Palladio. He turned pale as a sheet. On the other side of the ship, Victoria, Brunel, and Paxton were transfixed. Roberta took Martineau's arm and pulled the lever that worked the stairway. The steps down to the floor of the Crystal Palace unfolded, and they raced down them, ignoring the imprecations hurled at them by Palladio from the deck of his ship.

"Are—are you really a witch?" asked Martineau, once they had left the *Albatross* far behind.

"I'm a witch," Morgenstern confirmed. "And you know what, Martineau?"

"What?" he repeated, looking as if he were both dazed and hallucinating.

Well, too bad about Major Gruber's ulcers, she thought.

"Everything they ever told you when you were little, the stories they told to send you to sleep, all those tales of fairies, dragons, monsters, pots of gold at the end of the rainbow . . ."

"Yes?"

"They were true."

THE TENTH MAN

They were almost running as they left the Crystal Palace, with Martineau asking a question at every stride. Morgenstern had great difficulty in answering him while saving enough breath to keep up.

"How did Palladio change his shape?"

"A charm."

"How did you find out?"

"Instinct."

"Will you . . . will you show me what Mary Graham saw before she died?"

"I'll show you what the next victims will see if we don't get a move on."

The young inquiry agent had taken the fact that Roberta was slightly different from most people remarkably well. Indeed, perhaps rather too well. When he asked how you became a witch, or the male equivalent, she planted herself in front of him.

"You don't *become* a witch or a sorcerer, Martineau,

you're born that way. I can teach you a few tricks if you like, but we have a Ripper to catch first. So if you could think up some means of getting us to St. Paul's as quickly as possible—and don't ask me to fly us there," she warned him.

"OK, OK!" he agreed. "The idea never so much as crossed my mind," he added, lying through his teeth.

Several carriages were driving through Hyde Park beside the Serpentine. Martineau marched up to a phaeton and snatched the reins from the driver's hands without a word of warning. His arguments must have been very persuasive, for the man hurried meekly off. Martineau took his place, cracked the whip twice, and drove the phaeton over to Roberta, who had not moved.

"Jump in, my lady," he invited, drawing up beside her.

The sorceress climbed into the carriage and seated herself beside Martineau, looking at him suspiciously. "What did you do to that unfortunate driver?"

"Oh, nothing. Just a game I used to play as a boy."

"Come on, Martineau, don't make me ask you everything twice."

He turned away, so that Roberta could see only his back and the movement of his shoulders, and then he turned to face her again. The sorceress screeched. His eyes were rolling, his mouth distorted, and he was slobbering and breathing heavily.

"Huuung—huungry!" he articulated convincingly.

Roberta started roaring with laughter. "Let me guess," she said. "Frankenstein's major-domo?"

Martineau passed a hand over his face, and the fright

mask disappeared as if by magic. "The man who escaped from Bentham, beheaded people out walking, and kept their heads hanging from his belt."

"You have hidden talents, Monsieur Martineau."

Clément shrugged. "To be honest, I always did worry my parents a bit."

With great enthusiasm, he cracked the whip above the heads of the two horses. They galloped towards the houses bordering the park faster than was really wise.

Martineau drove the phaeton the way he drove his car, like a suicidal madman without a thought for anyone else's life. The tenants of the Historic City jumped aside, shouting angrily, as they approached.

"Look!" exclaimed Roberta, pointing to the sky.

The *Albatross* was passing directly above them as they drove over the reconstruction of Piccadilly Circus.

"Do you think he's making for St. Paul's?" asked Martineau.

"Yes. Palladio wants to pip us to the post. We must get there first!"

Martineau started down a crowded street lined with large shops. The dome of St. Paul's was visible at the far end. Ignoring the bobbies blowing whistles, he urged the horses to press on through the crowd. He felt as if they were labouring upstream along a river of top hats, caps, and parasols, but at least they were making some progress.

Then the investigator suddenly felt his vibration recorder spring into action. It was telling him that a tracer had just picked up the murderer. Taking the little tin box out of his waistcoat pocket, he opened it and studied the interior with a mocking smile.

"I'm a sorcerer too, you see, Miss Morgenstern. I predict that we're going the right way. Gee up there!"

The tin box contained a holograph of the city, and a red light was blinking on the spot that marked St. Paul's straight ahead of them.

"Tracers? Are you telling me you've let tracers loose in London?" said Roberta indignantly. "So what about Simmons and his warnings?"

"Oh, I listened to them with interest," said Martineau, choosing his words carefully.

They made their way out of the busy street and reached the forecourt of the cathedral. The wide esplanade was curiously empty. Dark clouds had piled up, veiling the sky above the dome. The sun disappeared just as Martineau and the phaeton drew up at the foot of the steps outside the building.

"Our man's chosen his setting well," said the investigator, shivering. He jumped out of the carriage and helped the witch down. "No sign of the *Albatross*," he added, examining the sky.

His little tin box began vibrating again. When he opened it he uttered an exclamation. The first red dot had not moved, but a second was now approaching the cathedral, making its way along a nearby alley.

"Two? But that's impossible! Yet the tracers can't be wrong."

Roberta studied the holograph over his shoulder.

"We'll think about that later. You see to the second, I'll look after the first."

"I don't know whether—"

"And no argument, or I'll turn you into a toad!"

Roberta climbed the steps of St. Paul's, making straight for a side entrance. She opened the door and slipped noiselessly into the monumental building.

The nave was plunged in an unreal twilight. The rows of chairs looked like a congregation at prayer, and the side aisles were two dark avenues that Roberta's eyes could not penetrate. She held her breath and listened, all her senses on the alert.

St. Paul's was singing. Stone cracked under the pressure of its great mass. Wind blew round the columns, sighing softly, and the pulpit and choir stalls responded by creaking.

A laugh made Roberta jump. It came from the choir. The sorceress went up to the transept crossing and studied her surroundings, taking cover behind the statue of an Evangelist over five metres tall. A young woman, still laughing, was making her way up a spiral staircase built into one of the huge pillars supporting the dome. A dark, cloaked form followed her, and disappeared in its own turn.

Roberta counted to ten and then passed through the pool of pale light in which the crossing was bathed. She stood close to the pillar with the staircase and listened. There was a faint panting sound, and then the laugh again. It stopped short.

Time for action, my girl, she told herself.

Rehearsing the spell she planned to use on the murderer, she began to climb the stairs.

Martineau was walking down an alley next to St. Paul's, holding his tin box open in front of him like a compass. He was doggedly following his red dot. Another few metres and he'd see the killer. Or one of the killers, anyway. This was extremely odd: a tracer could pick up only one person at a time, since every individual's genetic sequence is unique.

On sudden impulse, he hid in a doorway as someone turned out of a road just ahead of him.

Martineau sighed. It was only a bobby, identifiable by his black gabardine and helmet.

"Excuse me, officer!" he called, emerging from his hiding place. The bobby stopped but did not turn round. "Excuse me." Martineau approached at a trot. "I'm a CID man. My colleague and I are after a murderer. She—my colleague—is in the cathedral, and—"

Martineau fell silent. His box was beginning to vibrate again. He opened it. As well as the dot inside St. Paul's and the one immediately facing him, two new dots had just appeared, one beside the cathedral, the other right opposite the investigator himself.

Raising his head, he heard a sound like the hum of a million insects. The *Albatross* was passing above him, with no lights showing.

"I—" was all he managed to say before a blow to the jaw sent him crashing to the ground, unconscious.

Roberta was climbing the stairs with the utmost circumspection. Loopholes in the pillar showed her the paving of the choir farther and farther below as she climbed each spiral of the staircase. It suddenly came out on a sort of landing. There was the man, with his back to Roberta. He

83

was leaning over something, muttering, and the girl was nowhere to be seen.

I'm too late, thought the sorceress. She concentrated on the walls around the landing and murmured, under her breath, the spell she had composed in advance:

"Iron rings and chains appear, seize and hold him captive here."

Four rings appeared, set into the stone walls. Four coiled chains began to unfurl. The man stopped muttering. He turned, saw the iron chains snaking out towards him, and tried to run for it. The chains uncoiled around his wrists and ankles, flinging him roughly back against the wall.

Roberta climbed the last few steps and approached the Ripper. The stout, paunchy man was spluttering with mingled fury and helplessness.

"Who—who the devil are you?"

"You first," Roberta ordered.

The man was prey to nameless terror. This woman must be an apparition sent by his late wife! He tried to fall on his knees, but the chains prevented him.

"My name's Van Holst. Wilhelm. Holst of Van Holst Steelworks. Please!" The steel magnate began whimpering like a child. "Please don't hurt me!"

Van Holst Steelworks? Well, it made as much sense as the heir to Martineau Cement Industries working in the CID.

The landing looked out over the drum of the dome. Roberta heard the woman calling her lover. The sorceress took a few steps forward and saw the paving of the choir about fifty metres below. A gallery protected by a slender balustrade followed the curve of the drum to where the stairs continued up inside the dome to the lantern. The woman was on the far side of this gallery. She hadn't seen Morgenstern.

"Wilhelm, darling, what are you doing?" she cried impatiently.

Roberta was wondering what line to take when a nasal, distorted voice was heard. It came from the stairs that the woman was about to climb.

"Here I am, darling."

By some strange effect of the cathedral acoustics here in the Whispering Gallery, Roberta heard the murderer panting as clearly as if she were in the young woman's place.

"Are you there?" The bird-brained creature was already making for the shadows.

"Don't!" shouted Roberta. "Keep away!"

The other woman turned her head just as two arms took hold of her, pulling her violently back against the wall of the dome. There was the muffled sound of a struggle, and then silence.

Roberta took a deep breath and looked at the empty space below. "One, two, three," she counted, before setting off to walk round the gallery, her own back pressed to the stone wall.

Two figures were coming up the nave of St. Paul's, a man and a woman. Their heads were turned up to the dome and the dark form of Roberta, who was now halfway round the gallery.

"What do we do if the sorceress manages to intervene?" asked the woman.

"I've told the Count," replied the man evasively.

He was wearing a bobby's uniform, and was not very tall. His face was sunburnt, his eyes flashing with rage. The woman was wrapped in a cloak that came down to her ankles. Her androgynous face, neither masculine nor very feminine, shone as if she were constantly perspiring.

"Reviving the midwife was not a very good idea," said the man. "She's too unstable."

"If Jack's arrested we shall have to wait."

"Yet more waiting!" muttered the man.

Roberta reached the foot of the stairs at the far side of the drum, heart pounding. The steps, as steep as those in a Mexican temple, rose up to the lantern between the double wall of the dome. She began to climb them, breathing hard.

It was exhausting, and the going was tough. She stopped at least three times to calm the beating of her heart. Why hadn't she left the cathedral to young Martineau? What a fool she was! She'd been imagining herself back in her early days with the CID, when she could leap easily from rooftop to rooftop in pursuit of criminals.

Well, no. To be honest, she had never in her life leapt easily from rooftop to rooftop.

She reached the lantern. The little rotunda was empty. Footsteps visible in the dust stopped in the middle of the floor.

"They can't have vanished into thin air!" swore Roberta between her teeth. "Miss? Miss, can you hear me?"

The sorceress sensed the vast void of the dome beneath her feet. Suppose a floorboard gave way . . . A *plink* broke the silence. Roberta let the sound guide her. A dark stain on the ceiling above was growing. *Plonk.* She could see a closed trapdoor. *Plunk.* Roberta raised an arm, trying to reach the trapdoor, and flinched back, uttering a small cry. A drop of warm, sticky liquid had hit her in the left eye.

"By Satan's horns!"

There was a sound of running footsteps above her head, and the crash of broken glass. Roberta ran to one of the windows and opened it wide, leaning out. It had a view of the lagoon. On the outside, where the machinery of the stage sets showed, the city was a tangle of beams, struts, and joists supporting vast theatrical façades. The base of the sets was plunged in darkness. But Roberta saw the murderer leaping nimbly from one landing to another.

"Jack!" she shouted.

The murderer stopped and looked at her. He was too far off for her to make out his features, but Roberta clearly saw the scarlet smear on his chin. Jack raised his top hat, waved, and jumped down on a landing that finally hid him from the witch's eyes.

The sound of a roaring engine suddenly shook the lantern. The *Albatross* was flying round St. Paul's like an enormous bird of prey. The Count, in his own shape, was seated in the prow. He saw Roberta and gave the crew an order, which they carried out. The *Albatross* stopped orbiting the dome and made off towards the lagoon, where it soon vanished from sight in the thunderclouds piling up over the city.

Roberta was enjoying a plate of cream of asparagus soup while Martineau sipped a twelve-year-old whisky to restore his strength. The lobby of the Savoy was deserted. Most of the guests were in bed at this late hour, but a cheerful fire roared in the Tudor-style hearth.

The witch had cabled the latest news to Major Gruber. The corpse retrieved from the belvedere above the lantern of St. Paul's was a tenant of the Historic City by the name of Mary Ann Bigelow. Like Mary Graham, she had been disembowelled.

Mr. Van Holst, a tourist, had been discreetly taken back to his hotel, Claridge's, and then, along with the other pseudo-Rippers, put on board a special Pelican class hydroplane going back to the mainland. These men would be questioned by the Ministry of Security, but Roberta knew they would soon be eliminated as suspects. The killer was still in London, and could strike again whenever he thought fit.

"Will Gruber declare a state of emergency in the Historic City?" asked Martineau, making a face. He had been suffering from a terrible headache ever since the supposed bobby had knocked him out without warning.

"I shouldn't think so. A state of emergency wouldn't help us solve this case, nor would cordoning off the city."

"Solve this case—you sound like my Goddefroy handbook. We've got two corpses on our hands," said the investigator, rising to his feet, picking up a poker and waving it at the mauve-flowered wallpaper, "not to mention a killer who scurries about the city like a rat inside the walls of this hotel."

Martineau was playing with the poker as if it were a

sword. Roberta kept a close eye on him as she finished her asparagus soup. You never knew what the effect of a knock on the head might be.

"Do you think the Major will send in militia?" he asked.

"I've no idea. I'm not Major Gruber."

"Well, a few militia wouldn't come amiss. It looks like the killer isn't working alone."

"Good heavens!" Roberta widened her eyes in mock surprise. "You mean you didn't knock yourself out on your own? Sure you didn't stumble and throw yourself at a wall head first?"

"Ha, ha, ha," said Martineau, finishing his whisky. "It wasn't just that bobby either—there were the other two people the tracers picked up, *and* the real killer. Making four in all."

Roberta, whose taste for laborious argument was strictly limited, made no comment.

"Did you know the Count has left the city?" asked the young man, when his partner preserved her silence. "Simmons left me a message before setting off with his master."

"Well, Palladio's got a right to leave. So long as he doesn't impede the course of justice and we know where to find him."

"He's gone to Venice. He never leaves his Historic Cities anyway."

"I'm not surprised, in his condition."

"His condition, yes," murmured Martineau, remembering the sight of the deformed old man. "What age can he be?"

"He's no age anymore, Martineau. He should have been dead long ago."

The young investigator poured himself another whisky. Morgenstern watched him with interest. She was curious to see the effect of alcohol on her young colleague.

Martineau began again, in a slightly thicker voice. "This city is a rat-hole." He gestured at the luxurious room. "Rats everywhere. Watching us."

"If you were right about that, Martineau, we'd have left by now. But I haven't seen a single rat since we arrived."

The young investigator stationed himself in front of Morgenstern, swaying slightly.

"Oh yes? Well—what would you do if there *were* rats?"

Roberta sat back in her chair. The boy wasn't putting on an act anymore. She replied impatiently, "What do you mean, if there were rats, Martineau? What are you getting at?"

Morgenstern's abrupt tone sobered him down briefly, enough for his mind to advise him not to play games.

"I did see a rat. Under Mary Graham's corpse. It scared me out of my wits."

Roberta jumped up, caught hold of the lapels of Martineau's jacket and shook him till his teeth rattled, although he was a head taller than she was.

"And *now* you tell me?" She let go of him and marched out of the lobby, saying, without turning round, "One death could have been avoided, Martineau. You'd better get moving if you don't want another on your conscience!"

Taken aback, the young man looked at the bottom of his

glass, wondering what this was all about. What had come over the witch? He threw the end of his whisky into the fireplace and hurried after her. As the alcohol caught fire, a purple flame rose above the logs. It was shaped like a grimacing mask, and it had two horns.

"Can you tell me what we're doing on the River Thames at two in the morning?" asked Martineau in a muffled voice, hands dug into his pockets, coat collar turned up to his ears, knees firmly pressed together.

They were sitting in the back of a small steam launch going upstream. The wooden bow made its way through lowering fog that kept visibility down to five metres. There was no sound but the chugging of the launch, the boatman whistling, and Martineau's complaints. A gap in the fog showed them the sombre mass of Tower Bridge passing overhead. The two towers were like gigantic sentries.

"Quite sure you want to go there, ma'am?" the pilot asked again. "Could be risky these days, calling on the Romanies."

"The Romanies!" exclaimed Martineau.

The fog dispersed. All of a sudden the view cleared as they came out into a loop of the river. A rectangular shape was marked off by wooden posts planted in the water. Shellfish clung to the poles, feeding. There was a lopsided pontoon in the middle of the rectangle. Judging by the ten or so torches lighting it, and the presence of three huts, people lived there. Two more pontoons were linked to the first by roped footbridges. The pilot brought his boat in to a partly submerged landing stage.

"I'll drop you off, but I'm not waiting. You'll have to ask *them* to take you back."

Roberta gave the pilot a pound note and climbed out on the quay, followed by Martineau. The launch immediately moved away into the fog. The witch clambered up some steps to the pontoon, where a wizened little old man with a face furrowed by wrinkles, waiting at the top of the steps, welcomed her with a big hug.

"*Bienvenudo Chovexani Day*," he said. "Welcome, Witch Mother."

"*Nais Tuke*," replied Morgenstern. "Thank you."

The Romany jerked his head in Martineau's direction.

"It's all right, the *gorgio* means well," she said, patting the young man's shoulder.

"A good boy, is he?" grumbled Martineau, moving sulkily away from Roberta.

"You've come because of the *ruv*?" asked the Romany.

Roberta nodded. The man signed to her to follow him.

"What's a roove?" asked Martineau. "And what, for heaven's sake, are we doing here? Who are these people?"

"*Ruv* means wolf," said Roberta. "I'll leave you to guess who the wolf is."

They reached the middle of an empty space in between the three huts on the first pontoon. Embers were glowing there in a metal brazier, and several people lay asleep, wrapped in blankets. The Romany sat down beside the brazier. Morgenstern and Martineau copied him.

"So what can we do to help you rid us of that demon?" asked the Romany.

"Demon?" said Roberta, taking her hands out of her

92

muff and holding them above the glowing embers. "I thought we were dealing with a human being?"

The man let his eyes wander for a few moments. "You're on the trail of a *chakano*," he said, "a Son of the Stars. If he were a human being we'd have dealt with him ourselves by now." And he repeated his question. "What can we do to help you?"

Roberta leaned over the brazier. Watching her, Martineau thought that her face with its high cheekbones, lit from below, really did look rather like the face of a sorceress at a witches' Sabbath.

"I need a Gustavson," she said.

The man smiled, rose without a word, and disappeared into one of the huts.

"A Gustavson?" repeated Martineau. "What's a Gustavson? Some kind of magic weapon?"

"In a way."

The man came back with something in his hands. He held the object out to Roberta, who took it gently and began stroking it with her fingertips. Impelled by curiosity, Martineau rose, went over to the witch and bent over the thing on her lap. Without warning, she raised it and held it under his nose. He jumped back.

"A hedgehog!" he cried. "A disgusting hedgehog!"

Some of the sleepers grunted. Martineau lowered his voice.

"I hate hedgehogs. I've hated them ever since I was little. And they're full of fleas."

Roberta smiled. She seemed to be listening to some internal voice.

"He doesn't like you either. According to him, you smell of *boba*." The Romany roared with laughter. "It's true, you do smell of *boba*. Where on earth can you have picked up a smell like that?"

Martineau sniffed his jacket, watching the hedgehog as it settled a little more comfortably in the folds of the witch's dress. He preferred to ignore her remark and preserve a lofty, contemptuous silence.

Roberta stroked the hedgehog's prickles, singing him a strange song. After a few minutes the little animal stood up on all four paws, yawned, jumped down on the boards of the pontoon, trotted over to one of the huts and slipped away beyond it.

"Now all we have to do is wait," announced Roberta, making her muff into a pillow and lying down to spend the night where she was.

The Romany adopted the same course of action. Martineau wasn't going to copy them without understanding what was going on. "Wait for what?"

"Wait for the Gustavson to bring us news," said Roberta, her voice already drowsy. "He's a telepathic hedgehog, Martineau. He's going to talk to the rats he knows. If one of them has seen the murderer they'll all know where he's hiding, and Jack will be picked up tomorrow morning. Now, do go to sleep. We're going to need all our strength for the last round of this fight."

"A telepathic hedgehog?" Martineau had never read about such a thing in any police manual at all. "Telepathic hedgehog?" he repeated, staring up at the stars.

Then weariness overcame his amazement, and a few

minutes later he was making his own contribution to the ensemble of snores shaking the pontoon.

Martineau was fighting a bobby. As so often when he fought in dreams, his fists struck empty air. The bobby smiled, sure of himself. He opened his gabardine to reveal a waistcoat with a serpentine pattern. Martineau, paralysed and fascinated by the pattern, was caught like an insect in a spider's web. A change came over the bobby. Palladio's shrivelled face was smiling at him. His mouth yawned open to show a moist abyss into which the young man plunged.

"Eeech!"

He sat up in a hurry, to dispel the nightmare. The sky had taken on a milky hue in the east, but everyone else was still asleep. Martineau stretched and looked at the pontoons, now drowned in the morning mist.

The investigator moved away from the brazier and went round behind a hut. Only the lagoon and me, he observed with satisfaction. Standing on the very edge of the pontoon, he undid his flies and peed as far out as he could.

He was just doing his flies up again when a prickly ball trotted between his feet, squeaking. Martineau instinctively stepped back. He felt the void catch at the small of his back and send him falling. Flailing his arms like windmills, he lost his balance and plunged into a keep-net full of wriggling fish. The odour rising from the net was disgusting.

"About time we went home," he muttered, clambering up on the pontoon again with much acrobatic effort.

When he got back to the middle of the pontoon Roberta, now awake, was listening to the Gustavson.

"Oh, there you are, Martineau. Good heavens, what happened to you? And what's that smell? It's—"

"Horrible, yes, I know." He removed a silvery blue fish from one of his waistcoat pockets and threw it casually over his shoulder. "At least I don't smell of *boba* anymore. Did the hedgehog talk?" he asked, rather wishing it had been made to talk under torture.

Roberta nodded. "The rats have been watching Jack for some time. He's living in the Dead City, in the Red Foundlings' orphanage."

"Dead City?"

"I'll explain on the way. Can you take us there?" she asked the Romany, who had been following this exchange in silence.

"Of course. We couldn't refuse a *Chovexani* like you anything," he replied with a wink.

The motorboat moved away from the pontoon, going farther up the Thames than they had ever been before. They were now outside the inhabited area of the Historic City and making their way out into the lagoon. There was nothing in sight but the grey surface of the water.

A strong wind began to blow, and enormous ventilator fans appeared, planted in sets of five in the choppy waters. Some were switched on, others were out of action. Rust was eating away at their structure.

"This is where the fog comes from," the Romany explained. "Among other jobs we see to the fog and mist effects."

He steered past the blades of two of the inactive ventilators. The boat crossed another vast stretch of water. Then a statue standing in water up to its waist appeared on their left as if by magic. It wore a curious three-cornered hat.

"Admiral Nelson," the Romany introduced it. "His statue marks the place where the Dead City begins."

"Morning, Admiral!" Martineau greeted him, raising his cap.

Debris began appearing here and there. A broken column, a submerged building, a dome with water lapping round it. A ruined city was forming around them, the replica of a London which looked as if it had been swept away by some gigantic tidal wave. The Romany steered round the funnel of a locomotive resting on the bottom of the lagoon. With alarm, Martineau looked at the dark mass of the engine three metres below them in the water. It looked like a predatory beast waiting for some incautious swimmer.

The stage sets were now crammed close together, rising from the water. The Romany steered his boat towards a replica of Big Ben lying on its side, and tied up to the clock tower. Roberta jumped out of the boat and clambered up on the clock face, which was looking at the sky. Its hands pointed to twelve o'clock.

"The time of the crime," she commented.

Martineau joined her. The Romany stayed in his boat. "The Red Foundlings' orphanage is just behind the Lloyds building," he said. "I'll wait for you here."

"Aren't you coming with us?" asked the investigator rather anxiously. He had been involuntarily shivering ever since they passed the symbolic threshold of the Dead City.

"I'll wait for you here," the Romany merely repeated.

Taking Martineau's sleeve, Roberta drew him over towards Lloyds. "Romanies don't hunt the *chakano*," she explained.

"The Son of the Star, right?" grunted the young man. "So let's bump off this *chakano*. I need a shower, a cigar, and a good stiff drink."

They walked along the fallen clock and jumped down on to the steps of Lloyds, which was jammed up against Big Ben. The lobby of the building had not suffered too much from its abandonment. Martineau whistled, looking up at the height of the ceiling, the depictions of sibyls adorning the vault, the stained glass window imitating the sky, and the huge counter where the agents of the oldest insurance company in the world once stood.

"Evidently Palladio has ways of scrapping a thing that size," he pointed out. "But just how did it get here?"

"There must be a whole network of submerged railroads and tracks for changing the scenery. I thought I saw some railway trucks down under the lagoon. Got your little magic box there?"

"What? Oh—yes."

Martineau took out his tin box and opened it. The vibration recorder gradually produced a model of the shambles of buildings among which they stood. A red dot appeared on the extreme edge of the hologram.

"I can see him! The hedgehog was right!"

Roberta glanced at the winking evidence. "If you want to take out life insurance, now's the time," she said.

The inquiry agent took a six-shooter with a mother-of-pearl handle out of his trouser pocket. "This is my life insurance."

"*Si vis pacem para bellum*," agreed Roberta. "If you want peace, prepare for war."

They crossed the lobby of Lloyds. At the far side a swing door led into the ruined forecourt of the Red Foundlings' orphanage. The soot-blackened brickwork façade had once been part of the working-class sector of the reconstruction, now abandoned in favour of such features as the Savoy and the Crystal Palace. Martineau had his gun in one hand and the vibration recorder in the other. The orphanage was built on a starfish plan, like the prisons of the period, and the red dot was blinking faintly at the end of one arm of the starfish. Exchanging a brief glance, the investigators made their way into the building.

Paint was flaking off the walls from the floor to the stained ceiling, and water trickled down them. But the electricity was still working, and a festoon of bulbs lit the leprous corridor.

They made their way along cautiously, avoiding the debris lying in pools of stagnant water. Martineau's six-shooter felt slippery in his sweating hand. He decided to put it away again so that he could concentrate on the vibration recorder. They were near the end of the corridor now. Another equally dilapidated passage led to the wing that interested them.

"Wait a moment!" whispered the young man, on the alert.

His eyes were fixed on the box. Roberta joined him. "What is it, Martineau?"

She looked too. The first dot hadn't moved, but a second had just appeared on the far side of the building.

"Here we go again! Are you sure those wretched tracers of yours are working?" she asked crossly.

"Of course they're working! No two ways about it: either we have here two individuals with the same genetic code, or—"

"Or one man has divided himself into two and is waiting for us in two separate parts of the orphanage."

The investigator bit his lip. He was thinking hard. "All right, I'll go left and you go right," he suggested.

"No, we must stay together. I don't want to come back and find you're mincemeat. Let's take a look at the closest suspect."

She took the box from Martineau's hand and went ahead. They walked along fifty metres of corridor. The dilapidated ceiling sometimes gave them glimpses of the old dormitories on the upper floor, and once they even had to make their way round a heap of cast-iron beds forming a barricade. Finally they came close to the place where the tracers showed a presence.

Roberta took every possible precaution as she approached the doorway of the room. She had been mentally preparing her spells ever since they stepped inside the orphanage. Martineau had taken his six-shooter out again. The witch went in.

The room was small and circular, with beds arranged round a piece of apparatus that looked like a water fountain. A glass jar, now opaque with pigeon droppings, stood on top of a column of chrome-plated metal. Rubber tubes ran from this apparatus to the ceiling and then dropped towards the beds. Roberta went closer to inspect it.

Martineau, in the doorway, listened intently. The witch was in no danger: the room was empty, and concealed no psychopathic Ripper.

Then that noise again! He went back into the corridor. Stifled sobs, very close to him. He hesitated to alert Morgenstern. Leaning over the jar, she was trying to read something. He went to the doorway of the next room on tiptoe.

One of the beds had recently been in use. The witch looked at the end of the rubber tube resting on the sheet. It was red with blood. Blood that was still fresh. Disgusted, Roberta put it down and went back to the jar. Dipping her sleeve in a puddle of water, she rubbed the dirty glass vigorously.

The sobs were stifled now. Martineau glanced into the room. It had once been a bathroom, with a big bathtub and a broken porcelain basin. Moving forward, he jumped when something moved to his right, on the edge of his field of vision. He turned. A woman was crouched in a corner of the room, weeping.

My God, thought Martineau, feeling his stomach turn over. He put his gun away and leaned over her. "Ma'am?" he said. "It's all right. You have nothing to fear now."

Roberta stopped rubbing and looked into the jar through the clear window she had made. It contained half a litre of blood. It wasn't surprising that the tracers had marked two places for the Ripper's position. The witch opened the tin box. The red dot was throbbing at the centre of the hologram, right in front of her. She stared, wide-eyed, as she realized that the other dot was now in the next room.

101

"Martineau?" she whispered, thinking he was still just behind her.

"Ma'am?" the young investigator repeated, speaking to the crouching woman. He placed one hand on her shoulder, and at that she instantly rose to her feet, turning bloodshot eyes on him in the face of a Fury. Martineau, who had also been crouching down, was about to rise too. The woman kicked out at the young man's chest, sending him flying to the other side of the room. He hit the bathtub with a violent thud. He was winded, his back was on fire, and dazzling lights appeared in front of his eyes.

"Keep your hands off my baby!" screamed the woman, before running to the corridor.

Shakily, Martineau tried to follow her and fell into Morgenstern's arms.

"Where were you?"

"Jack—the Ripper's a woman!" he gasped. "That way!"

She had run left, towards a staircase. Steps could be heard racing up to the next floor. Without hesitating, Roberta climbed the stairs herself and found the dormitory where the Ripper was hiding. There was no other way out. The windows were walled up on one side of the dormitory and closed on the other. The end of the huge room was barred by a mountain of rubble. Cots stood on both sides of the dormitory like so many little cages. Roberta wondered if the Count had gone so far as to place real children in this picture of Victorian poverty.

"You can't get away!" she called. "Give yourself up!"

A shrill voice from somewhere Roberta couldn't locate

102

replied, "You just want to steal my baby! It's my baby! Mine, mine!"

Cautiously, Roberta moved along the central gangway. The farther she went, the darker the shadows grew around her. She wished Martineau was here. What on earth was he doing?

"I haven't come to steal your baby," she implored. "I've come to help you."

The woman did not reply. Roberta took a few more steps. She was in the middle of the dormitory now. The floorboards creaked beneath her feet. The sorceress feared they might give way. Everything was rotten here, with a smell of death and decay.

There was a furtive movement and a sound of breathing on her left. Then something scraped against the opposite wall. Roberta went that way.

"I've come to help you," she repeated, her voice less steady than before.

The reply came from just behind her. "I know you're lying!" said the Ripper.

Something whistled in the air. Roberta dived, and just managed to escape the scalpel blade. She tried running for the staircase, but the other woman blocked her way, looking at her with ferocious glee. She was clutching some kind of bloody object with one hand and brandishing the scalpel in the other. Roberta retreated towards the far end of the dormitory, trying to remember the spells she had prepared in advance, but her mind was paralysed by fear.

The Ripper raised her arm. Her eyes were the last thing that Mary Graham had seen. The blade came down through the air towards the witch's stomach.

A dull explosion sounded through the dormitory. The Ripper turned and let out a shriek as she made for the stairs. A second shot sent a flake of plaster flying, somewhere far behind Roberta. Martineau appeared silhouetted in the entrance to the dormitory, like a figure in a Chinese shadow play. He was holding his smoking six-shooter in both hands. The woman was still running towards him.

The young man fired again, twice. A piece of ceiling plaster shot into the air. The second bullet ricocheted off a cot and went through a window pane. Roberta concentrated hard as Martineau fired his last two shots. One bullet passed between the woman's legs, the last hit her shoulder but hardly slowed her down. She was only two metres away from the young man, who stood there motionless.

At last all Morgenstern's forces were back at her command. Two cast-iron cots rose vertically from the floor and fell on the Ripper, who stopped when she saw them sail through the air and plunge towards her. They closed over her like a cage. An unreal calm suddenly fell over the dormitory again.

Unsteadily, Roberta went over to Martineau.

"Well played, Morgenstern," he said in an expressionless voice. "None of my bullets would stop that wildcat."

The witch's back was bent, her eyes were hollow, her breath was coming fast. "Why don't you go and tell our Romany friend we've caught the wolf?" she suggested. "I'll stay here to make sure she doesn't slip through our fingers."

Martineau seemed to be suddenly waking up.

"It's over, then?" he asked.

"It's over," said Roberta.

At once the young man ran downstairs. Morgenstern leaned against the wall, looking at their captive.

The woman was pointing to a place on the floor, trying to say something. The witch came closer and knelt down to identify the bleeding object indicated by the Ripper, the thing she had held in her lap when Martineau was sniping at her in vain. She had dropped it before the cots closed over her.

"My baby," she murmured plaintively.

Roberta recognized human organs stitched together. She shuddered, picked up the nightmare doll and handed it back to the madwoman. The Ripper crouched in her cage, cradling her treasure, and stayed perfectly still.

By the time Martineau showed up again, Roberta had lost count of the number of times the Whitechapel Ripper had asked to be left alone. That was all she had asked of *him*, she said. She just wanted to be left alone.

PARIS

*Historic City
with Permanent Set*

POPULATION: tenants 2500, visitors 5000.

CHRONOLOGICAL PERIOD: seventeenth century.

PLACES TO VISIT: medieval quarter of the Île Saint-Louis, the Louvre, the Bastille, the Hôtel-Dieu, the cathedral of Nôtre-Dame, etc. This Historic City was consecrated by the Holy Father. Daily pilgrimages. Visits per week, per month, or per year.

ACCOMMODATION: all categories.

DO NOT MISS: Versailles (the château and the gardens).

PERMANENTLY ON THE PROGRAMME: The Pleasures of the Enchanted Isle.

A Cat and Two Salamanders

Isidore Goldfingers was pushing a small trolley of books along the Periwinkle floor of the Municipal Penitentiary. Isidore liked this job. He spent most of his time in the library, reading anything and everything to help him to forget the long years he must still spend paying his debt to society. Isidore wasn't a bad sort, and his crimes weren't serious, or not as he himself saw it. His judges had seen it differently.

Five years for robbing the pawnshop—what rotten luck! Isidore who, in his prime, had scurried swiftly over rich folk's rooftops, making their safes moan happily under the caress of his blowtorch, coaxing old locks open with his skilfully handled skeleton keys. Not for nothing had he been nicknamed Goldfingers, and he was trying to keep those fingers as nimble as they used to be. But it wasn't easy thinking up five-finger exercises between four grey walls which you shared with cockroaches and mice.

He sighed as he handed a library book to an old comrade

in crime who wasn't taking imprisonment too well. Isidore made him read travel books: Stevenson, Du Camp, Carter. Everyone had a right to a little escapism.

"Norbert!" he called. "Hey! Norbert Dipso!"

A grunt from the back of the dark cell was his reply.

"Found you a nice book here, mate. *Peter Pan*, it's called. Sounds like this guy Peter did a good flit."

Norbert the dipsomaniac didn't even get up to take his book, so Isidore slipped it between two bars to land on the floor of the cell. He went on his way, thinking of the good old days before the introduction of tracers and militia.

He clapped his hand to his neck as if a cockroach had landed on it. Thinking of those wretched robots—quiet as a tadpole's fart, they were—made him itch all over. Filthy informers going through the air in all directions, passing through your body, denouncing honest craftsmen like him to the cops. Oh yes, the pigs got all their work done for them these days. A crying shame, that's what it was.

Bloody tracers! Damn militia! They'd been the downfall of Isidore, Dipso, and hundreds of others. Crime wasn't what it used to be. These days you needed a university degree to rob a bank, you had to master electronic toys, crypto-camouflage, that sort of thing. Or else cover yourself with that disgusting plastic solution that kept the tracers from getting at your body, and if you didn't take it off pronto you'd die of suffocation after a few hours. Alternatively you could put yourself in the hands of some mad scientist to see if your genetic helix could be altered. Some said it was possible. Isidore wasn't too sure what he thought.

Anyway, he didn't want his genetic helix altered.

He stopped outside Cell 52. The woman in there was a real nutcase. Isidore couldn't make her out. Her eyes troubled him. On the Periwinkle floor, rumour said she was only in transit, she'd come from a Historic City and would soon be sent on to a high security jail.

"Well, well," he murmured, looking at the cover of the book she had asked for. *Atrocious Crimes and Famous Murderers from Ramses to the Present Day*, by Professor Ernest Pichenette.

How come the prison library had a book like that? He jumped, looking up. The madwoman was staring at him, hands clasping the bars.

"Was it—was it you wanted this book?" he asked, showing it to her.

"Hand it over."

Isidore held out the book cautiously. Terrible things came into his mind when he looked at this Fury. She glanced at the index of the Professor's encyclopaedia of bloodshed and paused, a triumphant smile on her lips.

"Good!" she said. "I'm in it!"

And she frantically leafed through the pages to find the chapter about her. Isidore was no fool. He knew the book had been written quite a long time ago. So how could this psychopath be in the learned Professor's freak show? She really was right round the twist.

The convict stayed where he was, watching the expressions that flitted across the Ripper's face as she read the chapter. Suddenly she laughed uproariously, surprising Isidore, who wasn't surprised by anything much in the usual way.

"That man Warren! What an idiot!" she exclaimed. "Fancy hiring a medium to find me! The poor sap!"

Isidore knew he had to continue on his rounds. But the woman was behaving oddly: she had retreated to the centre of her cell and was holding her head in her hands.

"No!" she cried. "No!"

A bluish aureole surrounded her, and golden sparks began dancing before her eyes. A sun had just emerged in the woman's belly. A sun that was growing and growing.

"Wow!" breathed Isidore, astonished. "Look at that!"

Gradually the Ripper's cell was engulfed by a kind of silent detonation. A great globe of light surrounded Isidore's library trolley and Isidore himself. He didn't even have time to register the fact that death was carrying him away in passing. A burning wind, hot as a furnace, raged like a hurricane through the corridors of the Municipal Penitentiary.

Eleazar Strudel's inn sign showed two salamanders biting their tails. The inn stood opposite a bronze statue of the Emperor in the middle of the historic centre of the Old Town. Its peeling façade was nothing to look at, and the opaque windows prevented you from seeing the interior at all.

The handle of the front door was shaped like a goat's head and looked less than inviting. Local children often dared each other to turn that handle. Those who ventured to do so found a strange mark left on the palms of their hands.

But it disappeared quite quickly. Eleazar was not a monster.

Once you were inside the door, the view was completely different. By friendly agreement between the dark and the light, the interior of the inn was brightly illuminated and decorated with attractive frescoes of aerial and aquatic scenes.

Eleazar Strudel sat in state behind his bar. He was a big man, round from head to foot, his bald head shone in the bright light, and his bottle-green eyes suggested an inborn talent for wielding the corkscrew behind him. He gazed with paternal affection at his regulars as they talked, ate and drank, laughed, and swapped good exorcisms in a cheerful, deafening roar.

Behind the landlord stood a black wooden sideboard laden with jars. Their labels were faded by time, but their contents were plainly visible: asps, birds' heads, infants dead before birth, strange plants, powders, and decoctions.

Strudel's inn was frequented by those magicians, witches and herbalists who lived on the fringes of society. It was a convivial place and served good fresh food. People returned to it with pleasure, but it didn't get a mention in any of the local guidebooks.

Plenty of lively discussion today, thought Strudel. In fact it was a positive seething whirlpool. The place was full, and it wasn't even lunchtime yet. Eleazar listened in on other people's conversations with an ear that he had fine-tuned over the years. Not a word escaped him.

Morgenstern pushed the door of the inn open. A few heads turned. Roberta had few contacts with the College of Sorcery these days, and not because she was known to be with the CID. Half the people in this room were civil servants; the other half told fortunes or wrote novels, and even included a weather forecaster whose predictions were no more accurate than anyone else's. It was just that Roberta had always been choosy about her friends.

She crossed the room and went round behind the bar to embrace Strudel.

"My bird of paradise!" said the landlord fondly. "I thought I'd never set eyes on you again!"

"And your grief took several kilos off you!" Roberta teased him.

Shrugging his shoulders, he took her into the souvenir-lined room behind the bar, which was reserved for the master of the house and his close friends. He had thoughtfully brought along two small glasses of Bohemian crystal and a bottle full of a liquid as sticky as sap. He filled the glasses with an expert hand, and they drank to each other. Strudel clicked his tongue with satisfaction, while Roberta's eyes wandered over the photographs of magicians covering the walls. They were all inscribed to Eleazar, who had a passion for conjuring tricks.

Morgenstern liked the Two Salamanders for several reasons. First and foremost for Eleazar, a happy man living on the outskirts of the closed world of sorcery, and generous with the fine wines he stocked in his bar. But she also came back to the Salamanders for its clients, who were given to gossip. More than once she had discovered matters of interest to the CID here. And the Two Salamanders let her assess the general temperature of the atmosphere, at present rising in line with the animation of the company.

"What's got them into such a state?" she asked Strudel.

The innkeeper uttered a small squeak. He couldn't conceal his own excitement. "Well, you for a start. Last time you were here you told me about your adventures in Palladio's Historic City and that female Ripper who was arrested, tried, and sent to jail. Something tells me there's another chapter to your story."

Roberta knew she would have to give him a little information for the sake of their friendship. She didn't grudge it, anyway.

"Yes, Gruber rang this morning. He wanted me to go to the Municipal Penitentiary where the madwoman was being held. The governor hurried out to meet me. He was very upset, poor man. In fact there was a lot of agitation in his little establishment."

"You mean the Ripper had escaped?"

"No, her cell had melted! So had everything else for ten metres around it. Five prisoners are reported dead, including the Ripper herself."

Roberta indicated that her glass was empty.

"Her cell melted? What on earth happened?" Strudel refilled Roberta's glass but forgot his own.

"The witnesses spoke of a blinding light, unbearable heat, and a silent explosion."

"A silent explosion . . . ah, Dr. Xanadu did that trick on stage in the twenties. I believe he used some kind of potassium."

"Dr. Xanadu had nothing to do with this, believe me. Or potassium either. The Ripper simply imploded. Cheers."

"People don't implode just like that," said Strudel.

"Oh, don't they? Remember your second-year lectures. It's the way some life forms disappear when their creator decides to return them to the void."

Strudel tried to read the witch's meaning in her magnificent green eyes. How often he had asked her to come and run the Two Salamanders with him! His head was in even more of a whirl than before.

"Well, yes, that's how an astral twin disappears," he said. Then, suddenly understanding the significance of what he was saying, he brought his powerful fist down on the table. "By the Great Houdini, you mean the Ripper was an astral twin?"

Roberta nodded. It was the only explanation for what had just happened at the prison. The Ripper must be an astral twin, a double of Jack who had died so long ago, and she had been skilfully brought back to life. By whom? Roberta could think of several possible candidates among the mad scientists of her acquaintance. She had one in particular in mind.

"Who'd want to bring the Whitechapel killer back to life?" asked Eleazar.

"Someone," suggested Morgenstern, "who would shrink from nothing to put the finishing touches to a reconstruction."

Palladio, of course. Roberta had told Strudel about the charm the Count had used to change his appearance. He had plenty of secrets to hide, so why not this one?

The innkeeper was drumming his fingers on the table in his effort to concentrate. "What are you going to do?" he asked the witch.

"Nothing. I'm going back to my flat, where I shall invoke the Great Moloch and ask him to make Gruber forget about me for a while. I wasn't at the jail. You and I haven't seen each other. I never existed. This business smells too strongly of sulphur for my liking. And I have a black-eyed Susan to keep alive too."

"Heaven help us!" exclaimed Strudel. "This doesn't sound like you!"

"I'm too old to go chasing about rooftops these days. Well, so what news of you?"

The innkeeper rubbed his jowls, leaving long marks on his face. "Everyone's talking about the next Sabbath. Carmilla Banshee is holding it in her Liedenbourg palace at the end of this week. They say the Devil's been invited."

"Nonsense. There'll be city police present to make sure no one tries conjuring up Satan."

"So you're not going," Eleazar concluded, disappointed.

The subject was closed.

"How's business?" Roberta asked.

"Business? Oh, much the same as usual. No, wait! You remember those boxes of powdered mole I had cluttering up my stock? They've been hanging about ever since the College banned the Black Mass. Well, they all went this week. To Paris."

"Paris?"

"The Historic City of Paris."

Now what, Roberta wondered, would anyone want powdered mole for? She cast her mind back to her old sorcery lectures. Powdered mole, diluted, was used to trace signs of divination during the Black Mass. In the past a notorious legal case had brought its use to light: one of the last witches burnt at the stake for Satanism had used powdered mole lavishly. Not so much a witch, more a monster who fully deserved to be in one of the horror stories published in the seventeenth century by the firm of Marteau. Who was it?

Roberta's heart began pounding. Her thoughts were coming thick and fast. London and Paris. Jack and—who was even worse than Jack? They'd been talking about astral twins only a moment ago.

On a sudden impulse the witch rose to her feet.

"Leaving already?"

"Where did you send your stock?" asked Roberta urgently.

"To Dame Guibaude, at the sign of the Eleven Thousand Devils in Fishing Cat Alley. But . . ."

Roberta gave her friend Strudel a quick hug and went out through the inn, weaving her way between the tables. The room was full of the deafening noise of conversation. She emerged into the open air and walked rapidly away to catch the first tram home.

The wind had risen, and was blowing clouds of dust round the statue of the Emperor. One of the dust clouds was a horned shape, spreading out its arms as if to embrace the world.

Roberta looked at her faded black-eyed Susan. She had been trying to reason with herself ever since she got in, not very successfully. Why see Evil everywhere? she asked herself. It was the Count's true appearance that had influenced her; ever since seeing it she had connected the worst of atrocities with his name and his treasured creations. This case was only a matter of a few boxes of powdered mole. Nothing to make a song and dance about.

All the same, she pored over her *Black and White Magic Cookbook*, open at the page headed "Assorted Powders." Her finger rested on the entry headed "Mole":

Powdered mole was used in the past to invoke Satan during the Black Mass. The officiating priest mixed it with sanguine and used it to draw cabalistic signs on the body of the victim or of the woman receiving the sacrificial blood. Such signs were believed to summon the Devil. The last recorded instance of the use of this powder dates from 1680. The archives of the Burning Chamber tell us that the famous poisoner La Voisin used powdered mole when invoking Adonaï during Black Masses held in the cellars of Paris.

Paris. La Voisin. The seventeenth century. The Historic City of Paris was set in the middle of the seventeenth century.

Roberta's imagination began working overtime. Suppose innocent children were being bled to death at this very moment in some obscure crypt? Her insides turned over as she pictured it. No. She was making things up. She needed a holiday. That astral twin business was getting her down.

The postman brought a welcome diversion. Roberta picked up a large envelope, opened it, and took out an expensively produced glossy magazine.

The Historic Cities again, she sighed.

They had been sending her *Historic Cities News* ever since her visit to London. Everyone who had been a passenger on a Palladio Sealines Pelican craft received it. Useless information, lists of dates, events, gossip, weather forecasts, the chit-chat of the day. Nothing very interesting. And not a word about the Ripper, of course. That had all been quietly dealt with and then hushed up.

Roberta's eyes fell on an article called "A New Bell Chimes." It described a mini-event in the reconstructed city of Paris:

> *An unexpected incident occurred on Monday morning in the parish of Saint-Jacques-de-la-Boucherie (1664). Everything seemed to promise a successful and festive occasion in the church. The precentors had brought out the vessels with the holy chrism. The censer was fragrant with incense, myrrh, and sweet-smelling pastilles, and the bell to be consecrated was hanging in the nave of the church. The officiating priest had sung the* Deus *misereatur* nostri et benedicat. *After the* Gloria Patri, *he traced the sign of the cross on the bell, and the tenth chapter of* Numbers *was sung. The rites were punctiliously observed: next the sub-deacon asked the godparents by what name they wished to baptize the bell. Imagine the amazement of the congregation when the name "Satan" echoed thunderously through the nave of the church. The deacon, in a convulsive fit, thrust the cross out in front of him, as if to attack those guilty of such sacrilege. The sub-deacon*

restrained him just in time. Confusion reigned in the church until the participants collected their wits. The bell was finally baptized by the name of St. Catherine. The godparents were unable to explain why they had acted as they did. Our correspondent Edmond des Amicis interviews them on pages 2 and 3.

Roberta didn't read the interview. She put the copy of the *News* down on a pedestal table covered by a lace cloth. Her cat Beelzebub reached out a paw, claws extended, and set about tearing the journal to shreds.

"Satan," she murmured to herself.

So he was back. People were calling on him. Now the witch was sure of it. If the Black Mass really was being celebrated in the Historic City of Paris, incidents of this kind would multiply and get worse. The more blunders were made, the more clearly they would herald the coming of the Goat and his demonic servants. Until *he* arrived. In person.

Roberta imagined herself calling Major Gruber:

"Hello, Major, Roberta Morgenstern here. Your favourite witch."

"And what can I do for you, my dear Roberta?"

"I'm just about certain that the Black Mass is being celebrated in Count Palladio's third Historic City. Admittedly I have no proof except for several boxes of powdered mole, a recent report in *Historic Cities News*, and my intuition. What do you think?"

"I think you ought to see a psychiatrist, my dear Roberta. Have a nice day."

And bingo! Gruber hangs up.

You're losing your grip, my poor dear Morgenstern. It's your age. It takes witches that way. A classic symptom. They see Evil everywhere.

"Hans-Friedrich? Where are you, poppet?"

The telepathic hedgehog had come home with the witch after her adventure in the Dead City, and was living in her flat. Roberta had christened him Hans-Friedrich, so now his full name was Hans-Friedrich Gustavson. The two of them got on very well, particularly since the hedgehog conveyed the thoughts of the mynah bird and the cat Beelzebub to their mistress's mind. Roberta finally knew what her pets thought of her, which was nothing to write home about. But the bird and the cat knew that she knew, and watched their step.

The hedgehog did not answer her call. Roberta began turning the flat upside down. She was always afraid Beelzebub might eat Hans-Friedrich, but the cat was enthroned on the pedestal table, where he had torn *Historic Cities News* to bits and was stretching voluptuously in the pile of shredded glossy paper.

"Oh, there you are!"

The hedgehog was hiding under three layers of cushions, all his prickles quivering. Roberta picked him up in one hand and stroked him affectionately. The little creature really did look terrified.

"What's the matter, little Hans?"

Closing her eyes, she got in touch with the hedgehog's mind. It was entirely possessed by a dark thought, evil enough to take your breath away. The thought was saying:

122

"My beloved Master will soon reply to the call. Then the weeping and wailing will begin, and trumpets will sound to usher in the riotous revelry. Miaow."

The thought was furry and yellow-eyed, and had claws.

"Beelzebub, you diabolical cat!" swore Morgenstern, turning towards him.

The cat, seated like an Egyptian statue with paws rigid and whiskers horizontal, watched her.

"So that's it! He's coming back, is he?"

Beelzebub licked one paw absently and ignored the question. Roberta made for her bedroom and set about packing a suitcase. She put in the hedgehog, who was soon buried under her BodyPerfect girdles, socks, and washed-out dresses. Thoughts were coming thick and fast in the witch's mind.

No use calling Gruber. He'd think she was crazy. She had enough money to go to Paris. She must find out what was up.

The case was packed in a couple of minutes. Roberta shot across her sitting room like a rocket and slammed the door behind her. Beelzebub uttered a sinister mew and jumped up on the windowsill to scrutinize the city built and inhabited by these wretched human beings. All the scorn in the world showed in the black, shadowy pupils of his eyes.

Gradually the faithful filled the single nave of the crypt which was standing in for a church. It could hold about fifty people at the most under its barrel vault, blackened by candle smoke. A plain stone cube of an altar marked the position of the apse. A chalice and a lectern with a closed book on it were the only visible liturgical items.

The company assembled in the crypt wore white veils and looked like mourners. They stood upright and motionless, but they were shedding no tears.

The priest celebrating Mass entered from a side aisle, approached the lectern, opened the book, appeared to be searching for a page for several minutes, and finally found it. Both hands placed on the lectern, the celebrant sized up the congregation with the cold self-confidence of one who has taken both God and the Devil into account.

Most of the congregation shuddered at the sight of the priest's androgynous face, with its smooth, curved forehead, narrow lips, and eyes hollow from some vigil or ecstatic trance. The priest's vestment was equally strange: black, with three crosses embroidered on it upside down.

The celebrant began the Mass in a husky voice, almost whispering:

"By the Omnipotent to whom we pray here, whom we adore for ever and ever."

The congregation murmured the words themselves. They sounded like an army of centipedes clicking their pincers on the paved crypt.

"By the power of the Key conveyed to us, O Vaycheon," and here the priest paused for the congregation to repeat the name, as with each name that followed, "Stimulamathon . . . Erohares . . . Retragsammathon . . . Clyoran . . . Icion . . . Esition . . . Existian . . . Eryona . . . Onera . . . Erasyn . . . Moyn . . . Mephias . . . Soter . . . Emmanuel . . . Sabaoth . . . Adonaï . . . I summon Thee. Amen."

A long silence followed this litany. The heads of the congregation remained bent. Some were shaking slightly. The priest, eyes closed, was the very image of concentration.

A gust of wind coming out of nowhere suddenly extinguished all the candles and plunged the crypt into darkness. A frightened "Oh!" rose from the congregation.

Fourteen red candles were lit at the same time. Standing in two chandeliers which had just appeared on the altar, they looked like fourteen outsize, skeletal fingers seen through a transparency. The flames sent contorted shadows dancing over the vault.

"We summon Thee, Adonaï," repeated the priest, speaking to the earth and the depths below. "We, Thy servants, Thy army of darkness. We make Thee this offering, the better to serve Thy cause."

One of the worshippers stepped out of the front row and approached the altar, dropping her cloak to her feet. Under it the young woman was naked. She lay on the stone slab, arms straight beside her body. Gobbets of candlewax fell, hissing, on the stone next to her. A smell of hot fat filled the polluted air of the crypt.

The priest picked up the chalice, which had a thick liquid at the bottom of it. Dipping two fingers in, the celebrant drew a triangle on the belly of the young woman, who did not move.

A worshipper came forward with a child, a little boy. He did not struggle, and must have been drugged. He let himself be led to the altar, eyes fixed on the candles. The scene was now a strange tableau: the celebrant in black, back turned to the nave, the motionless child, and the woman lying on the altar, motionless too.

Turning round, the priest took the child by the chin, and raised him at arm's length until their faces were level. The child did not flinch. He was breathing hardly any louder than before. The priest raised a knife and turned to the worshippers. All doubts of the nature of the androgynous face were swept aside.

After the sacrifice, the priestess La Voisin raised the chalice and cried triumphantly: "Come and drink."

The worshippers approached in serried ranks to take part in this bloody Eucharist. La Voisin allowed them just to moisten their trembling lips in the chalice that she held in both hands. Now and then she caressed a face, solicitous and kindly, like a mother caressing her children.

THE ELEVEN THOUSAND DEVILS

"Right, here we are. The Eleven Thousand Devils."

The façade of the inn was even less inviting than that of the Two Salamanders. Three potholed steps led up to a rickety door. The whole place was leaning forward, and the hovels on the other side of the road seemed to be flinching back to avoid a collision.

Roberta put her basket of oranges down on the first step leading up to this uninviting spot. Hans-Friedrich stuck his nose out of the basket as the witch tried opening the door. Locked. The place was closed. No sign of life inside.

Roberta must have walked a good half mile before reaching the medieval quarter of the Ile Saint-Louis. She felt that she had been crushed, jostled, and swept along by a crowd in perpetual movement, but this road seemed almost empty. Only a single citizen was coming down the street, whistling.

"Good day to you, friend," Roberta hailed him. "Pray where's the modish company?"

Almost in spite of herself, she spoke in an old-fashioned style. The Historic City was so convincing that no sooner had she left the wardrobe department, after choosing this orange-seller's costume, than she forgot her native city, the CID, and the League from which she came. However, this time she had observed the formality of signing her own name, Morgenstern, in the Historic Cities register.

"Forsooth, 'tis in the court there, good woman," replied the citizen.

"What court?"

"The tennis court." He pointed to the building beside the inn, which evidently belonged to it. It was just as dilapidated and bore no sign. "There."

Saluting her politely, the man pushed its door open. The sound of distant voices floated out into the street, and died away once the door had closed again. Picking up her basket, Roberta tapped the hedgehog on the head to make him get back into hiding, and entered the place herself.

The man she had spoken to was just turning the corner of a corridor lit by several small lamps. The witch was following when an arm emerged from the wall and grabbed her shoulder unceremoniously.

"There's dues to pay, orange-seller." A giant of a man was stationed in a booth to take the entrance money. "Two sous to watch the tennis. And an orange to quench my thirst."

He plunged his hand into the basket. Roberta looked for some small change in her pocket, and held out two coins at random. The porter took them and signed to her to go in. The farther down the corridor she went, the clearer were the voices.

"Fifteen!" she heard someone call.

She climbed a short flight of stairs and found herself in the tennis court. All the locals had gathered. It was a rectangular room, neither very large nor very high-ceilinged, with tiers of seats running round it. The witch was in the middle of one of the shorter sides of the room. The spectators, crowded together on the seats, were watching the white ball flying from one side of the court to the other. Roberta found a free seat and sat down to watch the game.

The players, a man and a woman, wore lightweight garments suitable for sport: short trousers, waistcoats leaving the arms bare, and wigs tied back with a plain bow. Each held a small racket. A net divided the court in two. The walls were covered with black drapes, which made it easier to follow the flight of the ball and lent the scene a funereal atmosphere.

The woman made a great effort to come up to the net, leaping forward and hitting the ball hard at her opponent. He missed, and the imperturbable umpire announced "Thirty!" as the spectators applauded and cheered loudly. The match must be approaching its climax.

The man won a point, bringing the score to deuce in the last game. Roberta put her hand in her basket of oranges in search of Hans-Friedrich, and laid it on his prickles, stroking him gently.

She had been planning to use the telepathic hedgehog long before the Pelican passed the dam marking off the territory of the Historic City. In his own way, Hans-Friedrich would act as a tracer—while Roberta would be like the militia, on the lookout for scenes of horror or Satanic rites. She was expecting the worst, and she had come here to tackle it.

Ever helpful, Hans-Friedrich listened to the crowd and transmitted its thoughts to the witch, whose eyes were half-closed as she watched the images passing through her mind.

Paris featured prominently, but hardly anyone was thinking of real, mainland Paris. Everyone here in the tennis court, whether tenants or visitors, had fallen for the illusion created by the Historic City. Festive scenes, visions of Versailles. Many of them had enjoyed the Pleasures of the Enchanted Isle. Roberta saw a naked woman, and switched the thought off once she had made sure that it was simply the memory of an amorous encounter.

A sudden lightning flash cut her vision in half. The sorceress opened her eyes. The woman player had just won a point, and the umpire was announcing that the next would be match point. Roberta concentrated, asking Hans-Friedrich to scan the tennis court slowly. More images flooded in. Roberta picked and chose among them, just as she had picked out oranges for the people who bought them from her in the street.

"Stop!" she suddenly ordered.

A blank had formed in her impressions of the excited crowd, a protected area against which all surrounding thoughts were brought up short. Roberta asked Hans-Friedrich to concentrate on this mental vacuum. She could feel the effort the hedgehog was making, but he could not penetrate the black hole of the void.

The woman player uttered a cry of fury when her ball

hit the net. Roberta saw the edges of the dark void in her mind quiver. Flames shot out, and its corona lit up like the corona of a sun during a lunar eclipse.

She asked her neighbour who the woman player was.

"Why, 'tis Dame Guibaude," he replied. "The best player in town. Mistress of the tennis courts, by my troth!"

The man rose to his feet along with all the other spectators. Dame Guibaude had just won the match. Her opponent was looking at the place where the ball had bounced as if he couldn't believe it.

"Dame Guibaude. Well, well," murmured Roberta, who had remained seated. "Seems as if powdered mole agrees with you."

The spectators were making their way down the side aisles to the exits. The witch concentrated on Hans-Friedrich's mind again. The image she had been receiving, steady and regular a few seconds earlier, was now like a universe expanding in all directions. The people leaving the tennis court where they had all been in communication were returning to their separate mental worlds. The shadowy void had shrunk.

Roberta was about to abandon her observations when someone's thoughts attracted her attention. She stepped back.

"What on earth is this?" she muttered.

She was seeing herself through that other person's eyes, wearing her Victorian outfit and standing on the deck of the *Albatross* moving slowly above the crowds in the Crystal Palace in London.

Roberta rose, looked for the source of this thought, and

spotted it at once. A man who was just leaving on the other side of the room.

No one knew she was in Paris. Had she been followed all the same? If so, it was as good as proof that something odd was going on in the Historic City. But if he was shadowing her, why did the unknown man leave without turning round? He ought to have waited for her to leave the tennis court and then followed. Dame Guibaude would have to wait.

"*Fiat lux!*" she breathed between her teeth. Let there be light! The witch put Hans-Friedrich in her pocket, left her basket of oranges where it was, and moved past the now almost empty tiers of seats to find out where the man shadowing her was going.

He led her over half the city. Fortunately seventeenth-century Paris was not too large, and moreover Count Palladio, for reasons either of space or of his budget, had left out whole quarters, so it wasn't as far as it might have been to the northern boundary of the city, for which the man seemed to be making with determination.

Roberta would have liked to read his mind, but Hans-Friedrich's tremendous efforts at the tennis match had exhausted him, and he was asleep in her pocket. The witch couldn't bring herself to wake him and make him tackle this new task.

They left the alleyways of the Ile Saint-Louis behind them and crossed the Seine. The man walked past the Louvre and went into the church of Saint-Germain-l'Auxerrois. Roberta followed him, hiding behind the pillars so as not to be seen.

But that proved useless; he had spotted her and seemed to be trying to shake her off. His tactics were simple, almost childish: I'll go into a church, take advantage of the dim light to get up to the apse and leave that way. And so on, until my pursuer tires of the chase.

Roberta wasn't in the habit of giving up so easily, so they visited, in succession, the churches of Saint-Eustache, Saint-Merri, Saint-Paul and Saint-Louis, Saint-Gervais and Saint-Protais. All those saints made the witch's head whirl.

This little expedition gave her some idea of the religious enthusiasm in the city. The churches were crammed with worshippers, their relics were all on show and the priests wore vestments of gold and silver.

Roberta guessed that the original city had never been quite so devout. However, the Historic City of Paris had become a place of pilgrimage after receiving the blessing of she forgot which pope, or maybe anti-pope, but never mind that. All she wanted was to keep her eyes on the man who still hadn't shown his face. He was now walking along a trodden earth path going up the hill of Montmartre.

This little game had gone on long enough. Roberta was on the point of speaking to the man when he got in first, turned round and came back downhill towards her with a resolute step. He had taken off his wig, and his face, heavily made up and now drenched with sweat, was running like a mask of white wax. Roberta watched him approach without saying a word. She had recognized him all right— but she could hardly believe it.

"Madam, you have been following me for nearly an

hour!" thundered the young man. "Kindly explain yourself!"

His voice was all the confirmation Roberta needed. Yes,
it was Clément and no mistake!

"By the Great Zoroaster, Martineau, what on earth are
you doing here?"

On hearing his name the young investigator widened
his eyes, and bent his head to look hard at the woman now
taking her cotton bonnet off.

"Morgenstern? Roberta Morgenstern?"

"None other! But by the Scarlet Goat, wouldn't you say
the presence of both of us here calls for a proper explanation?"

Butterflies were chasing one another above the vines
that clothed the hill. A trellis concealed a little restaurant
slightly higher up the hill. There must be a fine view of
Paris from there. The young man gave Roberta a broad
smile.

"I would indeed. Let me buy you a drink, my dear sorceress. I've got no end of things to tell you."

"Forsooth, then 'tis true—the Ripper was an astral twin?"
repeated Martineau. "Tell me, prithee, how can that be?"

"Martineau, this is just you and me. In private. So forget
the forsoothery and talk normally, if you don't mind."

"Yes, right, sorry. Well. So the Ripper has returned to
the void from which she came. And tracking her down
served no good purpose?"

"Well, it served *some* purpose. Otherwise we wouldn't
be sitting here over this jug of plonk discussing it."

"You're right. Cheers. To justice and fair dealing," said the investigator, raising his glass.

"And the crimes without which we couldn't make a living," added the witch.

They drained their glasses and shared some sliced sausage that the proprietor of the restaurant had just brought them.

"OK, so the Ripper was an astral twin," Martineau summed up again. "Goddefroy doesn't have any of those in his list of criminal categories. How do you make an astral twin?"

"You just need a *ka* tank, something to start fermentation and act like the primordial soup, and a relic or some item that belonged to the person you're twinning. And you have to know the right spells, of course."

"A *ka* tank?"

"For the *ka*—it's ancient Egyptian, meaning something like soul."

"Could you do that yourself?"

"Yes, but any twin I made wouldn't stay stable for as long as six hours."

"Why not?"

"Because I don't usually travel with my *ka* tank."

"I see," said the young man. Roberta wondered if he really did. "Right, so the female Ripper was the double of the original Jack. Which confirms what I've found out for myself."

Martineau ordered another jug of wine and fell into contemplation of the Historic City lying below them. The roofs of Paris mingled in a pattern of blue and grey.

135

Church towers rose to the sky like black arrows. The lagoon surrounding the city, which was built on a fragment of mainland, could hardly be seen beyond the quivering heat haze.

"What *did* you find out, Martineau?" asked Morgenstern impatiently.

"You remember those prints Simmons took at the scene of the crime in London?"

Roberta nodded, thinking again of poor Mary Graham and the other woman, Mary Ann Bigelow.

"Well, once the Ripper was safe behind bars I searched the Scotland Yard archives for the period when the real Ripper was active. They'd kept his prints."

"And they matched the prints of our female Ripper exactly?" Roberta guessed. "If you'd been to lectures at the College of Sorcery you'd have thought of astral twins straight away. Why didn't you tell me what you'd found?"

Martineau looked rather offended, but cheered when the jug of wine arrived. "And if you'd read Professor Pichenette's book you wouldn't be in the dark about the second murderer."

"Pichenette?" asked the witch.

"Professor Ernest Pichenette, author of *Atrocious Crimes and Famous Murderers from Ramses to the Present Day*. This was my line of reasoning," continued Martineau, enthusiastically explaining his discovery. "If a historic killer like Jack was at large in London, the same thing could have happened elsewhere. So I consulted my Pichenette on seventeenth-century France. I looked for cases of interesting murderers and made a note of those

136

that could be checked. And here I am."

"Why Paris? You could have picked Lisbon. Or Venice, or San Francisco."

"I don't know . . . I supposed I picked Paris at random." Martineau heaved a weary sigh, clearly indicating that he wasn't going to repeat himself. "OK. So I set off for Paris with the names of several historic killers and my information about them. And I found one who filled the bill just before you started trailing me."

"Where, at the tennis match?"

"Aha!" said Martineau, in the tone of one who didn't want to say any more.

It was Roberta's turn to sigh. "Don't make me use the third degree on you, dear boy. You wouldn't like it."

"Dame Guibaude," he said. "The woman player."

So they had been led by two separate trails to the same woman: Morgenstern by following up Strudel's information, Martineau by reading the works of Pichenette. Two distinct and definite trails. But no Dame Guibaude featured in the army of murderers sent out by the Devil to roam the highways and byways of history.

"What's so special about her? Did she kill her cat, or what?" asked Roberta, making a joke of it. For she was afraid to hear what she already knew.

"Dame Guibaude is La Voisin," Martineau revealed. "The famous poisoner sentenced by the Burning Chamber to die at the stake. She bought children for an écu apiece to be sacrificed to Satan. That's what my Pichenette says, anyway. This woman must be another astral twin."

Roberta wasn't listening to Martineau anymore, but

thinking of the monster now at large in Paris. The historic La Voisin had expressed no remorse when the fire consumed her. She went on cursing her executioners until the roar of the flames drowned out her obscenities.

"How can you be sure that Dame Guibaude is really La Voisin?"

"I found an engraving of her. Look at this."

The investigator unfolded a sheet of paper showing the head and shoulders of a woman. Her lips were full, her nose hooked, her forehead curved. There was no expression in her eyes with their drooping eyelids. Her moon-like face was the same as the tennis player's. It was androgynous, as the Sun King's contemporaries had noted in the past.

"We can't rely on mere physical resemblance," decided Morgenstern, after a silence which Martineau dared not break. "We must make absolutely sure of her identity first."

"But how do we approach her without arousing her suspicions?"

Roberta looked worried too. "Yes—particularly as there's absolutely no penetrating her mental field," she remarked.

"Her what?"

Something moved in Roberta's right pocket. She gently took out Hans-Friedrich, who was just waking up, and put him on the table. Martineau rose to his feet and hastily retreated.

"You didn't bring that monster, did you?"

"Monster, indeed! Hear that, Hans-Friedrich?" She tickled the telepathic hedgehog under the chin. "This monster has already helped us to arrest one astral twin. Why not two? If he could get close to the woman when she least expects it and read her thoughts . . ."

"I don't see how." Martineau sat down again at a prudent distance from the hedgehog. "I've been following her for three whole days. She appears in public only between ten and eleven in the morning and two to three in the afternoon, at the tennis court. Between midday and two she's in her private quarters at the Eleven Thousand Devils, and she spends the rest of her time at Versailles. In the evening, when she's finished playing tennis, she makes for the Pleasures of the Enchanted Isle. A vaporetto takes her to the château and brings her back next morning for another tennis match."

"Who plays against her?"

"Anyone who likes. The porter takes applications half an hour before each match."

"We ought to try getting at her while her mind's on a match," decided Roberta. She stroked the hedgehog pensively, exploring the young man's mind without his knowledge. "You never told me you played tennis."

Martineau blushed, and replied, wondering just how the witch had found that out, "I lost in the semi-finals of the Martineau Cement in-house tournament." He paused. "You're not thinking of making me challenge that woman, are you?"

"Why not? Your game is pretty good—you should be able to keep the rallies going long enough for little Hans to explore her mind." The witch hefted the hedgehog in her hand like a ball. "He'll be getting very close to her. That way he ought to be able to find the answers to our questions . . . see what I mean?"

The young man's face lit up when he got the idea. "Yes. Yes, I see exactly what you mean."

As for Hans-Friedrich, he wasn't sure he had read his mistress's mind correctly. Surely she'd never do a thing like that!

"You're going to be a hero, young hedgehog," Martineau told him, suddenly sounding very friendly.

The hedgehog looked at the witch, looked at the young investigator, looked to right and to left, and decided that his chances of flight were too slim for him to try it. He finally curled up in the palm of Roberta's hand, making himself even smaller than he was already. Morgenstern took this opportunity to close her hand round the little animal. One question had been bothering her ever since she and Martineau had met here.

"Are you in Paris on Major Gruber's orders?" she asked.

The young man looked embarrassed. "Well, not really," he admitted. "I came under my own steam. But I suppose you're here on official business?"

Roberta used the privilege of her age and her seniority in the CID to refrain from replying. Martineau looked at her sphinx-like face for a moment or so. Then, tiring of it, he turned to scrutinize the city of Paris as he sipped from his glass. Bells chimed twelve noon. Roberta tapped the table and rose, rousing the investigator abruptly from his dreams.

"This is no moment to drop off to sleep, dear boy. Your tennis racket awaits you. And this time you'd better reach the final!"

The tennis court was crammed. Martineau had just received a great ovation: he had been holding out for five sets against an opponent who normally eliminated challengers with a minimum of shots. Arms raised, he acknowledged the applause from the tiers of seats.

"Don't overdo it, Martineau," said the sorceress between her teeth.

She was sitting in the front row along the shorter wall of the court, just behind him. As the inquiry agent passed close to her, Roberta slipped him the ball she had been hiding in the folds of her skirt since the match began. The audience had relaxed its attention, and Dame Guibaude was discussing something with the umpire. No one noticed their little manoeuvre.

The umpire called for a change of ends. Martineau winked at Morgenstern and made for the other half of the court, nimbly jumping the net and gleaning a scattering of applause. Dame Guibaude, already in position, waited for him to finish showing off. It was his service.

Roberta put her face between her hands to help her concentrate. Martineau threw the ball up in the air and simultaneously raised his racket.

"Sorry, Hans-Friedrich," the witch apologized.

The investigator struck the ball hard. It shot like an arrow between the woman's legs. She sent it straight back through Martineau's. Roberta missed her first opportunity—it had all happened too fast. Or had the impact knocked the hedgehog out? No, she had made sure he was well padded inside the ball, protected by cotton wool so that he wouldn't feel anything. And he could breathe through the seams. He might be upset by his enforced inactivity, but still, a hedgehog like Hans-Friedrich must have seen a thing or two.

Hard as Roberta tried, she wasn't receiving any images at all. The ball had already been back and forth over the net three times. The hedgehog's mental transmissions were blurred, indeed practically non-existent.

But at last an image did appear—a very distinct one. It showed her a child held at arm's length, a knife at its throat.

Roberta exclaimed and flinched away. Her neighbours muttered crossly. Dame Guibaude, taken by surprise, missed her volley and the ball ended up in the net. She turned round, furious, to see who had disturbed her concentration, but Roberta, like everyone else, was applauding her heroic young opponent. She took care to avoid La Voisin's angry eyes.

So it *was* La Voisin, or anyway her astral twin. They had been right. First the Ripper, now the famous poisoner. Just what was going on in the microcosm of the Historic Cities? The sorceress would have to probe the monstrous mind of La Voisin if she was to have any hope of finding out.

It is easy to situate thoughts on a time scale: vague as they may be, they all represent precise moments. So you can tell if a thought is upstream or downstream of the present, if it is a wish for the future or a memory of the past. The image of the Black Mass that Roberta had just intercepted was upstream, and very close. It was a memory only a few days old, and its clarity was further proof of that.

The sorceress now had the choice of following La Voisin's thoughts that way and going back in time, or exploring her ideas about the future to find out what she was planning. Martineau still looked fresh. The ball was holding up well, and the hedgehog was dutifully reporting in. Another volley began. Roberta opted to go on backwards.

Rally succeeded rally. Martineau and La Voisin were neck and neck now. Fifteen love, fifteen all, thirty-fifteen to La Voisin. Meanwhile Roberta was picking up information and reading the Poisoner's second life as you might read a book.

It was quite a short story, but punctuated by at least three Black Masses and three child victims. The faces of the congregation remained blurred, and so did the scene where the ritual took place.

One scene in particular caught Roberta's attention. It was night, a boat was going up the river, passing the Historic City and approaching a pontoon like the one she had visited on the outskirts of London. Three people slipped into a Romany encampment, waking no one. La Voisin was in the middle of this trio. She stopped beside a child, picked it up and carried it away as if nothing at all had happened.

The match was about to end. Roberta went on moving back along the stream of time, travelling very fast now. La Voisin had spent six months in the Historic City of Paris. Before those six months her mind came up against a wall as black as death itself. That was when she had emerged from the void as an astral twin.

143

La Voisin's first memory was blurred and vague. A man in a wig was looking at her and smiling. Or no, it was a painting. There were gardens seen from a window, white statues, fireworks. Versailles. La Voisin had taken shape at Versailles.

Before that all was blank, a territory of frozen and silent solitude across which strange, gigantic flames sometimes flashed. La Voisin's first life gleamed very far away, on the other side of a void covering several centuries. But Roberta didn't have time to get back there now.

"Deuce!" called the umpire.

Martineau's arm was tiring slightly, and he was breathing hard. He threw the ball up at an angle, missed his serve and began again. The ball moved gently towards La Voisin, who recovered her form and sent it forcefully back. Martineau ran and struck it. But as he returned to his position the ball fell back in his court.

"Advantage Dame Guibaude, match point!"

The spectators began drumming their feet on the wooden tiers. The noise was indescribable. Martineau was trying to get his breath back as Morgenstern signalled to him.

What the hell does she want? he asked himself, swallowing with difficulty.

The idiot doesn't understand, thought the sorceress. She closed her eyes and called, "Hans-Friedrich!" No reply. "Hans, I know you're in there." The hedgehog's mind moved sluggishly, out of annoyance rather than exhaustion. "You saw what I saw," Roberta went on. "She's been stealing Romany children. You are the Romanies' totem animal.

I just need a few more minutes to sound out this demon's mind. Give Martineau some help or we'll never make it."

"Aren't you feeling well, madam?" a woman sitting on her left asked.

The sorceress realized that she had been talking out loud. She shrugged her shoulders and started applauding like mad.

"Quiet in the hall, or I shall have everyone turned out!" the umpire threatened.

Silence fell over the tennis court as if by magic. La Voisin had picked up the ball in which Hans-Friedrich was hidden. Martineau, standing in position, was dancing from foot to foot, twirling his racket.

The woman threw up the ball and moved as if to serve to the right, but then served to the left instead. Anticipating her move perfectly, Martineau sent the ball back between her feet. La Voisin jumped comically to avoid it.

"Deuce!" said the umpire.

The young man felt as if he could read his opponent's mind. La Voisin was upset by this sudden change in the situation.

"Well done, little Hans," Roberta congratulated the hedgehog.

La Voisin served again, without thinking this time. A rally conducted from the back of the court began. The witch was concentrating on the Poisoner's thoughts. She picked up the thread again and began following it forward into the future.

The creature's mind was like a blue-green marsh, its surface as smooth and infinite as the lagoon, showing no visible hint of anything. Desperately, Roberta realized she had no choice but to plunge into this mental mud to study the monster's feelings. She held her breath, went down, and repressed revulsion as La Voisin's thoughts closed around her.

Another Black Mass, on a larger and more savage scale than those she had seen before. It was being celebrated in a cathedral in front of thousands of worshippers.

As the celebrant stood before a bloodstained altar, she was thinking: the heavens will open when the Devil descends, comes to me, and grants me ultimate knowledge!

Head down, Roberta made her way through a stained glass window in the building, and found herself hovering above a strange scene. A pasteboard castle was transforming itself into a firework display. A horseback procession moved past a crowd in fancy dress. An improbable number of torches was reflected in the still water of the pools. The reconstruction of Versailles, decked out for the Pleasures of the Enchanted Isle, lay below her.

A huge ovation filled the tennis court, bringing Morgenstern back from her journey of exploration. Martineau was on his knees. La Voisin had just won. The Poisoner turned to look Roberta's way. The witch thought she heard her say, "Listening at keyholes?"

She felt caught in the act like a naughty little girl. She tried to shake her head in self-defence, but turned her eyes aside. La Voisin seized this moment to slip away from the tennis court despite the applause, which showed no sign of dying down.

THE PLEASURES OF THE ENCHANTED ISLE

"We'll meet at five this evening, at the landing stage for the Enchanted Isle."

"Aren't you afraid of venturing into the lion's den?" Martineau had asked.

"Yes. But I'll have thought of a way to handle it by then," Morgenstern had replied.

They were standing outside the Eleven Thousand Devils, and she had left him without saying anymore. Martineau just hoped Roberta knew what she was doing—all they were really sure of was Dame Guibaude's real identity, and the atrocities that were to take place that very evening—perhaps on the Enchanted Isle of Versailles itself.

Anyway, he had two hours to kill before meeting the witch again, and he planned to spend them on the second part of his personal quest.

Lady Jane Grey had told him the first letter of the mystery

word when he went to rescue her from the executioner's axe in her dungeon in the Tower of London. Now he had to solve the second riddle in the Palladio Sealines puzzle game. He had found it in the Pelican hydroplane taking him to Paris.

He took out the envelope, which was just like the first, containing a sheet of paper and a card. The sheet of paper was a replica of the reply slip he already had. The card was a voucher for a meal at the Good Companions, informing him that this inn stood on the Pont-Neuf.

The afternoon was wearing on, and Martineau had skipped lunch because of the tennis match. Moreover, the landing stage for the Enchanted Isle was right under the Pont-Neuf, so it would be silly of him to miss this opportunity.

A quarter of an hour later he was outside the Good Companions. Its inn sign was a clear illustration of the state you were likely to be in when you left the place. The figures of two merrymakers cut out of sheet metal stood outlined against the sky, propping each other up so as not to fall into the gutter. Martineau was not much of a gourmet, or much of a drinker either. He could have counted the times when he had visited a restaurant without his parents on the fingers of one hand. But this was a special case.

He opened the door and was immediately welcomed by a powerful, savoury smell, while a wave of warmth escaped into the outside air. The young man felt as if he were stepping into a vast casserole. He looked down at his feet to make sure he wasn't treading on some giant slice of bacon.

"Did you want lunch, sir?"

A winsome and attractively curvaceous waitress, with a

148

cloth tied round her waist instead of an apron, waited for his reply. Her cheeks were pink and her forehead shiny. She was delicious.

"Er, yes. If it's not too late?"

"That depends what you want to eat," said the girl, nodding.

Martineau hesitated, but in the end he took out the card and handed it to the waitress.

"Oh, well, that's different! Come along, I'll give you the best table by the fire."

She led him to the warmest corner of the restaurant, where a fire was roaring cheerfully on the hearth. A comfortable armchair stood at a little table laid for one. The linen cloth was immaculately clean.

"Sit here, please, and I'll be back in a moment."

Martineau sat down, wondering just what this test consisted of, and what tricks the inventors of the game had thought up to prevent players from winning. At least the atmosphere of the Good Companions was nothing like that horrific scenic railway in the Tower of London. Surely they weren't about to poison him? Or challenge him to eat a whole sucking-pig in under thirty seconds?

"You can stop daydreaming—you'll never do it."

Martineau had not previously spotted the portly man of about fifty wearing monastic robes: a frieze habit belted with a rough cord. He was sitting at a table just like Martineau's. His tablecloth too was immaculate, and he was waiting to be served.

"Never do what, sir?" asked the young man, instantly on the alert.

"You can call me Monsieur Gorenflot here. Outside, it's another story. You'll never remember the second letter in the mystery word. This is my third attempt."

How could the man have forgotten a single letter? This unexpected fellow guest might be part of the plan. Yes, surely he must be something to do with the trap. But since curiosity is stronger than prudence, Martineau asked, "Why did you fail before?" A silly question, in view of the fact that he still knew nothing about the nature of the test.

"You'll find out soon enough," replied the man evasively. "But I can assure you that the Tower of London was a piece of cake compared to this place. Here she comes. Be on your guard."

The waitress was approaching with a steaming plate in each hand. So it seemed they were about to suffer some form of physical torture. That contravened the Rights of Man as laid down in the statutes of the League! This might be a Historic City, but the Count would have to answer for himself before a higher authority than the Ministry of Security if he turned out to be practising coercion.

The waitress put the plates down in front of Martineau and Gorenflot, went away and came back again with two unlabelled bottles of red wine. Without a word, she filled their glasses and disappeared into the kitchen once more. Looking at the contents of his plate, Martineau found his mouth watering as the delicate aroma rose to his appreciative nostrils. The wine had a deep, powerful colour. The investigator unconsciously caressed his cutlery. Gorenflot was looking at his plate with the same dazed expression as before.

"They really know what they're doing," he said. "Last time it was duck legs with cherries for the main course. I didn't last five minutes."

He too was wielding his knife and fork like a drug addict longing for a fix and undergoing some unbearable, tempting test.

"So where's the trap?"

"On your plate, in your glass, under your nose. Start eating and you won't be able to stop."

"I'll risk it," the young man decided. After all, if Gorenflot was still here to tell his tale after two unsuccessful attempts, the cooking couldn't be poisoned. Martineau was beginning to have a faint idea of the nature of the test. It must be something to do with over-indulging and temptation. Well, he had always been a young man of very moderate habits. This was going to be a pushover.

He cut up a large piece of the ham with pistachio nuts on his plate and swallowed it without hesitation. He didn't know a lot about these things, but the glorious sensation exploding from his palate to the marrow of his bones told him that this was great cooking. Gorenflot had followed suit. "The cunning devils!" he sighed. "They've simmered it in sherry!"

Martineau was already wiping his plate clean with a piece of bread. He had drunk half his glass of wine; it was a strong, robust vintage with a faint aroma of the cask in which it had matured. He was drinking flavours of oak wood, the soil, the sun. Such a wine deserved to fill more than half a glass. He emptied his glass and refilled it, also offering the wine to his companion, who didn't refuse. The waitress came to clear their plates away and went back to the kitchen.

"Well, well!" exclaimed the investigator. "This is a nice change from scenes of executions and torture victims, don't you agree?"

The other man had taken out an enormous cigar and was about to light it. He changed his mind and offered another to Martineau, who refused. He would drink just a little, he decided, but not smoke.

"Yes, scenes of medieval torture," remarked his fellow guest. "The Little Princes in the Tower, the execution of Lady Jane Grey." He puffed out a cloud of blue cigar smoke that immediately floated up the chimney above the fire on the hearth. "Count Palladio has a sense of drama."

"You already know one of the letters of the mystery word, then," suggested Martineau.

"So do you, or you wouldn't be here."

The young man raised his glass with a knowing smile. They were still drinking a toast when the waitress came back with a single serving dish, which she placed on Martineau's table. At first, seeing what looked like a snake coiled up between four large onions, he made a gesture of revulsion. Gorenflot was looking at the dish too.

"Eel *à la minute*," he breathed. "The chef's speciality!"

"Since it's just the two of you, I thought I'd serve it on a single platter," the waitress said. She began preparing their plates, cutting the eel into thick slices and arranging them like the petals of a flower before coating them with a yellow sauce. As she worked, she explained, "The eel has been skinned, quickly browned, brushed with anchovy butter, rolled in fine breadcrumbs, and then put back under the grill for ten seconds. It is served with a sauce flavoured with pimento and garlic."

"The great Dumas himself couldn't have done better," sighed Gorenflot.

"Will you stay with the Burgundy?" asked the waitress, noticing that the two bottles were almost empty. "Or we have a Gaillac which would go very well with a dish of this kind."

"Let's try the Gaillac!" cried Martineau happily. He felt as if his whole body were in a state of the utmost ecstasy. He had quite forgotten why he had come; it was enough to be here at all. Glasses were regularly topped up and emptied. Plates were mopped clean with bread, the second consignment of bottles was drunk. Martineau and Gorenflot enthusiastically discussed fascinating subjects of which they would remember nothing later. No doubt they had come up with brilliant insights on the state of the world, but there was no one to record what they said. A cheese board came round, as if in a dream, and a third bottle was opened for the two of them. The companions began laughing uproariously when they saw that they had finished this one too.

A last prompting of his conscience rang alarm bells in Martineau's mind. He was supposed to be joining Morgenstern. Soon. Where? Somewhere quite close. On the bridge. No. Under the bridge. He couldn't meet her in this state.

"So what about the letter?" bellowed Gorenflot all of a sudden.

"What letter?"

"The mystery letter, the second letter in the name of the city reserved for the Club Fortynu—I mean the Club Fortuny. The waitress. She tells you when you reach the dessert course. We've reached the dessert course, right?"

Martineau looked at the crumbs of his cheese, trying hard to concentrate. Naturally, dessert would follow cheese as night follows day.

"Mmm," he agreed, wondering why his head felt so heavy.

Gorenflot turned towards the kitchens. "Dessert! Dessert!" he started shouting.

The waitress approached empty-handed. The young man thought she looked rather blurred at the edges, but she was smiling. It was the first time he'd seen her smile. She had a pretty smile.

"Would you like dessert or the mystery letter?" she asked them.

"Dessert! Dessert!" Martineau roared.

"Sssh!" said Gorenflot. He turned to the waitress and adopted the pose of a studious pupil. "We're list—listing—listening, miss!"

She leaned towards them. "The second letter . . ." she said. The two guests widened their eyes comically. "The second letter is E."

There were ten seconds of silence. Gorenflot and Martineau looked at each other and burst out laughing at the same time. They couldn't stop. The young man found it impossible to get his breath back. He laughed till he cried. Gorenflot was laughing so hard he had to clutch his stomach. So hard that he slipped out of his chair and ended up sitting on the floor. He pulled his tablecloth and everything on it off the table as he tried to rise to his feet.

Martineau, perhaps slightly less intoxicated than his companion, was already trying to remember the letter revealed by the waitress. Had it been M? No, that was in London. Might it be A? But his brain refused to work. So much for the prize offered to the winner. In that case he might as well bring this meal to a proper conclusion. He began banging on the table and shouting, "More wine! More wine! More wine!"

The clock of the Samaritaine church struck five. Morgenstern, leaning her elbows on the parapet of the Pont-Neuf, was waiting for Martineau. She stroked Hans-Friedrich, who was only just recovering from his stirring experiences. Five on the dot, and the young man still wasn't here!

Roberta heard a bawling somewhere on the other side of the bridge. Two drunks were coming out of an inn. They were the very image of the Good Companions on its sign, staggering all over the place. They embraced and set off in different directions. One of them began crossing the bridge, steering an unsteady course towards Morgenstern, who at first refused to believe her eyes.

It was Martineau, much the worse for wear. The bridge, he felt, was swaying beneath his feet like the deck of a ship in stormy seas, but he marched bravely on like a good little sailor. No waves would scare him! His sights were set on the witch; she was his beacon, his harbour. A barrier reef or an army of sharks wouldn't keep him from fulfilling his destiny.

The young man stopped in front of Morgenstern, who was wondering how on earth he could still stand upright. He began to say something, thought better of it, and finally kissed her on both cheeks, saying thickly, "So there you are!"

These four words had cost him such an effort of concentration that he nearly capsized for good. The sorceress only just caught him in time, and pinched his forearm, hard.

"Hey!" protested the drunk, scarcely able to open his eyes now. "That hurt."

"Martineau, you're drunk as a skunk."

"I don't—don't deny it," he replied with a foolish smile. "Not got a headache p-p-powder, have you? Shomething to shober me up? Ooh, I do feel ill!"

This, the witch decided, was a critical situation. A couple of slaps weren't going to do the trick, and she really needed Martineau to have his wits about him at this moment. She looked at the river flowing under the bridge, which luckily was almost deserted.

Of course there was that ancient spell the Vikings used on men too drunk to go into battle. It was efficient but dangerous, like all Scandinavian spells. Their side effects were especially uncontrollable. You could cast them easily enough, but you never quite knew when they would wear off. However, Roberta had no choice, and Martineau had got himself into this fix, so it was up to him, not her, to pay for it.

The witch steered the investigator over to the parapet,

held him steady to keep him from falling, and looking at the grey waters uttered the words:

"*Nudlok gotli tulsa, Gotli valhalla noisy noisy.*"

Martineau opened one bloodshot eye and asked, of no one in particular, "Wosshe—wosshe shaying?"

Two watery arms shot up from the surface of the river, turning as they rose to the parapet, seized the young investigator, plucked him from the bridge and flung him into the air. Morgenstern flinched back. She hadn't expected anything quite so violent, and leaned over to see what had become of the poor lad who had just plunged into the water. Where was he? Turbulent bubbling indicated the spot. For a good ten seconds the water wrung him out like a bundle of dirty washing.

Perhaps I went a little too far, thought Roberta.

She was opening her mouth to countermand the spell when Martineau was thrown out of the river and five metres up in the air. He looked perfectly wide awake now. The watery arms were holding him round the waist. Roberta reversed the spell, and the young investigator was deposited back on the bridge beside his colleague. The watery arms withdrew into the river, which returned to its former calm.

"How are you feeling?" the witch asked.

The young man looked round him, trying to make sense of what had just happened. Taking pity on him, Roberta ordered his clothes to dry on the spot. A cloud of vapour surrounded Clément and evaporated above his head. His garments were now dry and warm.

"How are you feeling?" Roberta repeated.

The letter is E, Martineau was thinking. The second letter is E. First letter M, second letter E. But for this ducking he'd never have remembered it.

"Er—rather shaken. I think I know what happened, but I hardly like to talk about it."

"Then don't. Right, let's get down there."

She pointed to the landing stage beneath the Pont-Neuf. You reached it down a flight of stone steps. A vaporetto was coming upstream and would be leaving again soon, carrying tenants of the city who wanted to enjoy the Pleasures of the Enchanted Isle.

"We have to go to Versailles. That's where La Voisin seems likely to celebrate her next Black Mass, remember?"

"Yes, all right, all right. Don't shout, please." The young man rubbed his forehead. "Yes, I remember. And I'm still not sure it's a good idea. Don't you think we could perhaps—oh, I don't know—ask Gruber to do something?"

"Oh yes?" said Morgenstern. "On the grounds that a witch burnt at the stake in 1680 has an astral twin who is preparing to hold a Black Mass with all due ceremony this very evening? Anyway, even if Gruber listened to me, the militia would never get here in time."

"What about the Romanies? You said it's their children who have been sacrificed, according to what you saw in that monster's mind."

"They may be able to help us, but it's no good expecting me to muster an army before seven this evening and then take the château by storm."

"Why not?"

"Because it can't be done! Versailles is over an hour away by vaporetto."

"I don't like this at all. Palladio concealing his real appearance, the disappearance of the Ripper, the sudden appearance of La Voisin . . ."

"You'll have to get used to it. We're chasing phantoms, and in my view they haven't finished leading us a dance yet. Particularly if the Count's the dancing master."

Martineau remembered his first impression of Palladio. All through that lunch in London, the young man had believed in God. Even better, he had passed God the salt.

"You really think he's behind all this?"

"I don't just *think* so. I'm sure of it."

"Suppose he's waiting for us in person at Versailles?"

Roberta sighed.

The vaporetto had arrived. It would leave again shortly, so they had no time to lose.

"I entirely agree with you, dear boy. Does this Enchanted Isle look like a trap? The answer is yes, it does. But that's not the question you ought to be asking."

"That's not the—well, what is the question, then?"

The sorceress met the young man's eyes. "The right question is, what part of yourself are you prepared to sacrifice to save the child who's due to die this evening?"

It did indeed take the vaporetto an hour to reach the Enchanted Isle. The gardens were a glittering sight on the waters of the lagoon, like a carnival held in the middle of nowhere. Morgenstern and Martineau had landed and climbed up to the two gigantic terracotta urns that marked the entrance to the park, admiring the sumptuous palace of Versailles where anything was allowed—indeed, encouraged.

The view extended far into the distance. Although night was falling, you could see as well as in broad daylight, thanks to the torches planted around the flowerbeds or reflected in basins of water. The windows of the château were plunged in darkness.

The Pleasures themselves took place out of doors. The park was dotted with large marquees, and actors were performing plays in the style of Italian comedy on several stages made of trestles. The wind had risen, snapping at the canvas of the tents. Clouds raced over the moon, making it look like a white flame whipped by a whirlwind.

The crowd had scattered. Judging by the sound of the games being played in the wooded groves, they were a lot less innocent than the viol recitals beside the artificial lakes. Couples and solitary figures strolled along the avenues in a festive atmosphere of extraordinary luxury. The guests had come here to enjoy themselves in every possible way, and Palladio was certainly giving them their money's worth.

Roberta looked round for the pasteboard castle she had seen through La Voisin's eyes. She found it, and pointed it out to Martineau. The young man produced the map they had been given in the vaporetto and located the building on it.

"The Palace of Alcina." He looked at his watch. "There's supposed to be a firework display there in just under an hour's time."

"We must find out where the Black Mass is to be held.

I'll look in the château, you search the gardens. We'll meet in an hour's time by the Orangery. Good luck, Martineau."

"Good luck, Morgenstern."

The investigator had been to a number of grand parties before, among others those given by Martineau Cement. And while the Club Fortuny to which his parents belonged might be a reprehensible institution, its members knew how to live well. No party that he could remember, however, had ever come up to this one.

The main marquee contained a magnificent buffet. The basin of the Fountain of Neptune had been turned into a swimming pool where people were splashing about with happy abandon. Martineau went up to it to make sure the party-goers weren't actually bathing in champagne. The tenants of the Historic City were being entertained by jugglers, actors, and fencing matches. The young man even passed three dwarves leading monkeys on leashes. And he hadn't drunk a drop.

But what Martineau wanted most was a closer view of Alcina's palace. He was making his way towards it with determination when a girl suddenly barred his way. She was pretty, she didn't look more than fifteen, and she was holding a magnificent Spanish horse by the bridle. The young man tried to walk round her, muttering some vague kind of apology. But she stepped in his way again.

"Let me introduce myself. I'm Madame Du Parc. I have to act the part of Spring in the fancy dress procession that starts in half an hour, but we've lost Autumn. I expect Monsieur de La Thomillière has gone astray in a maze somewhere."

By some strange magic, Madame Du Parc's youthful beauty made Clément Martineau forget everything that had been going through his mind a minute earlier.

"I'm so sorry," he said.

"Yes, it's devastating. But *you* would make a perfect Autumn, Monsieur . . . ?"

"Monsieur Quinze-Juin," he replied without thinking.

The girl pretended to faint, and fell into Martineau's arms. He caught her gently; she was light as a feather. She opened her eyes again, with a charming smile.

"I love you," she whispered.

Martineau blushed scarlet. She stood up, brushing her dress down, and took advantage of the catatonic state into which she had cast the young investigator to whisper in his ear, nibbling its lobe in passing, "I always dreamed of saying that to a stranger."

Taking his hand, she drew him towards a nearby coppice. Martineau was completely disorientated, and so hot that had he been a compass he would have been pointing due south. Panic fought with the promise of pleasures to come and made his heart pound. Madame Du Parc, luckily, knew all about this sort of thing, and there wasn't much the young investigator had to do. He abandoned himself to her, following her example.

"The Enchanted Isle!" he sighed, when it was all over.

They were getting dressed again when a loud crashing noise was heard behind them, accompanied by a trumpeting that echoed back from the façade of the château.

"Heavens, my husband!" cried the young woman. "He's

playing the part of Summer, and he decided to ride an elephant—fancy that! Come on, or we'll miss the procession."

They emerged from the coppice, leaves in their hair. The girl recovered her horse, whose reins she had attached to a branch. Martineau, seeing everything in rosy hues, let her lead him to an enclosure where a chariot stood, draped in gold and silver cloth. Madame Du Parc abandoned her lover to embrace her husband, who was indeed perched on an Indian elephant.

Twelve men and twelve women stood beside the chariot. An old man with a scythe sat in the coachman's seat, very upright and dignified, and another man was holding a bear on the end of a chain. Several figures stood in the chariot, three of them representing Gold, Silver, and Brass. The fourth, an alarming figure bristling with iron, was portrayed by a giant of a man who reminded Martineau of the executioner in the Tower of London. He could have spitted an entire ox on the blade of his sword.

A little man was fussing about, running from character to character and giving instructions in a strong Italian accent.

"Ze Hours and ze Zodiac, zey no move-a. Ze Age of Iron, can 'e smile a leetle?"

The iron colossus with the piratical sword smiled as best he could.

"*Molto buono.*" The Italian director counted the Seasons. They were all present and correct except one.

"*Primavera, estate, inverno.*" Here he rushed towards Martineau. "And you—you *autunno.* You ride-a zis!"

He indicated a camel being held by two pages. The

animal appeared to be asleep on its feet.

"You want me to get up on that camel?" repeated Martineau.

"Izza drrrromedarrrry," the Italian corrected him, rolling his 'r's to great effect. "Zere—ve start in *cinque minuti.*"

The young detective knew that the procession would pass right through the middle of the crowd—and on top of the camel he would get a good view. He climbed the little bamboo ladder and settled as best he could in the saddle. Now everyone was ready, and the Italian gave the signal to start. The procession moved off towards the avenue, which was already lined by spectators.

Madame Du Parc's deceived husband was on Martineau's right. He was not actually looking at the young man, but all the same Martineau felt uneasy.

"Is it the first time you have enjoyed these Pleasures?" Du Parc asked him.

Martineau assumed a mask of innocence. He was preparing to reply when his eyes fell on one point in the crowd, and one face in particular—La Voisin's.

She was looking at him, but then the elephant's massive body obstructed his view. Martineau slid off the dromedary, both legs together, causing some confusion in the procession. He slipped under the belly of the elephant ridden by Du Parc and plunged into the crowd, where he had seen the Poisoner a few moments earlier. She was now making for the Palace of Alcina.

"We've lost Autumn!" cried Madame Du Parc in mock dismay.

The others laughed. Martineau ran towards the painted palace and went round behind it, just where La Voisin had disappeared. But there was no trace of the Poisoner. Martineau stepped back a little way and inspected the flimsy construction.

It was a cubic structure about a dozen metres tall, with walls imitating a carved façade in the Baroque style, but the details became more primitive as you got close. It was entirely surrounded by fireworks stuck in the ground. A painted *trompe-l'oeil* staircase gave access to the palace. The Poisoner must be hiding somewhere in there. There was open space all round it, so that ruled out any alternative bolthole.

Martineau went over to the flight of steps and set foot on it in some alarm. The illusion was so good that he had the impression of venturing into a child's dream. But the steps were solid, and led him into the structure.

Inside, the Palace of Alcina was a single room. Torchlight shone through the painted canvas walls from outside, so that Martineau was walking over a floor splashed with coloured light. The figures painted on the canvas danced at his feet like imps.

"We know who you are!" he shouted at the top of his voice, turning round on the spot. "It won't do you any good to hide."

He felt something slip past him, and turned round. The wind was playing with the flaps of the tent, and with his nerves too. One corner of the palace remained obstinately dark. Martineau moved that way.

"La Voisin?" he called, less and less sure of himself.

A man stepped out of the shadows. Monsieur Du Parc advanced towards Martineau calmly, one hand behind his back. He was followed by his wife. Instinctively, the young man flinched.

"You never answered my question, Monsieur Quinze-Juin," said the deceived husband. "So I will ask it again, in slightly different terms: is this the first time my wife has offered you her charms?"

Madame Du Parc was devouring Martineau with her eyes, and seemed to be revelling in anticipation of the violence that must be about to follow. Martineau stopped retreating. He had to face the situation, but this whole thing was ridiculous.

"I—oh, listen, will you? A horrible crime is about to be committed!" he pleaded.

"A horrible crime *has* been committed!" interrupted Du Parc. The man took off his glove and struck Martineau in the face. Martineau did not flinch. "A crime that will be tried in due and equitable form. Does a duel suit you, sir?"

"Look, I've got no time to waste on this nonsense," snapped the investigator, striding towards the exit. "We'll deal with the other matter later, if you insist."

Du Parc caught up with him on the edge of the platform where the Palace of Alcina stood and placed an arm across his chest, pressing against his windpipe. "We'll deal with the matter now. And if it's not to be a duel, let us have an execution."

He kicked the investigator's legs out from under him. Martineau fell to his knees and tried to turn, but the other man was gripping him firmly by the shoulders. His arms were forced behind his back. "You leave me," Madame Du Parc whispered in his ear as expert hands bound his wrists, "you leave me with warm and truly delightful memories."

"Wait!" protested the young man. Then he fell silent, feeling the cold touch of a blade on the back of his neck. He tried turning his head slightly. On his left stood the iron-clad giant from the procession, sword raised in the air with its blade ready to come down on him.

"Wait!" repeated Martineau feebly.

The investigator never saw his death coming, for he did not believe in it for an instant, even when the sword whistled through the air. He felt a burning pain—and then nothing. His head rolled down the flight of steps to the ground, hitting it just as the fireworks began to go off.

Explosion after explosion of colour rose into the sky, neither seen nor heard by the young man. The wind blew his hair in all directions, but could do nothing to wipe the look of utter astonishment off his face.

Roberta had entered the château through an open door in the north wing. She went through the History of France gallery, crossed the anteroom to the chapel, and then climbed a flight of stairs to the first floor. Now, judging by the card identifying the place, she was in the Salon of Hercules, looking at a pendulum clock showing figures of Victory crowning Louis XIV.

The sorceress approached the bronze profile of the king, tracing the bridge of his nose with her forefinger. She had noticed some extremely anachronistic glasshouses built on the model of the Crystal Palace behind the château. As with

167

that mixed-singles tennis match, you could have anything you liked in the Historic Cities. Count Palladio wasn't interested in the detail, only the general atmosphere and the overall impression. But he did seem to go to some trouble with the features of famous people of a given period.

This statuette of Louis XIV had Monsieur Rosemonde's face. That was a fact. And if Martineau had been here looking at it, its face would have been Goddefroy's. So the Count's power affected the appearance of objects around him, which meant that his abilities were as uncommon as the megalomania they proved.

Roberta went through the Salon of Hercules and the Hall of the Crusaders without lingering in front of the battle paintings. She found what she was looking for in the next room.

Salon of Diana, said a little card on the door.

Here on the wall hung the portrait of Louis XIV that La Voisin had seen when she was being brought back to life. So the *ka* tank used to create the astral twin should be somewhere in this room. Crouching down, Roberta found four symmetrical marks on the floor: the four feet of a heavy tank that had dug into the precious wood.

The witch was preparing to set off along this new trail when a burst of violin music suddenly broke the silence. Percy Faith and his Orchestra. "Reza." Roberta could have listened to this piece played non-stop for hours. The music came from the Gallery of Mirrors, a little farther away. It was very inviting.

Roberta moved carefully along the magnificent gallery. After the Crystal Palace, the Gallery of Mirrors, she noted.

What other *trompe-l'oeil* décor had the Count thought up for his Historic Cities? An armchair stood beside an old crystal wireless set in the middle of the gallery.

Here we go, she thought. Bending down, she let Hans-Friedrich jump nimbly out of her pocket. "Don't miss anything," she told him. "And when it's over go and tell the others."

The hedgehog transmitted an image of docility to show Roberta that he understood.

Percy Faith went on luring the witch his way. Violin music positively oozed over the gilded wooden decoration. The whole room was vibrating in unison with it. Roberta felt her bones tremble. She'd have sold her soul for this feeling to last forever. Captivated, she went over to the armchair. Hans-Friedrich Gustavson stayed with her, following her but keeping close to the skirting board.

"And we now continue our musical matinée with "My Bloody Valentine," played on the accordion by Miguel Puerto Rico," said the radio announcer.

The harsh sound of the accordion filled the Gallery of Mirrors, and immediately stopped. Roberta was remembering. She saw herself back in her flat, before the phone rang and Gruber sent her to London.

Armchair and radio set disappeared as if by magic. Something hard prodded the witch's back. She turned round. The Count, looking as he really did and seated in a wheelchair, was jabbing her with the pointed end of his cane.

"Palladio," breathed the witch.

"Good girl," croaked the old man in a quavering

voice. "Good, good girl."

Roberta pushed the cane sharply away. The Count jammed it between his knock-knees and began fiddling with the base of his neck.

The sorceress watched this little manoeuvre, wondering how the man still found the strength to breathe. He was wearing a collar perforated with a great many holes. It had a knob fitted into it for adjusting his artificial voice. The old man turned it and spoke at the same time. His voice rose to a high register and then came back down to bass. Finding an acceptable compromise, he set his hands free again. They flapped in the air in an uncoordinated way.

"You're an enigma, Miss Morgenstern. I don't understand either your stupidity or your obstinacy."

The Count had nearly succeeded in stabilizing the movement of his head. This, and his now steady voice, made him almost menacing.

"What's all this in aid of, Palladio? Why bring first Jack and then La Voisin back to life? What's your sinister project?"

The old man let his head nod for a few moments. "Wasn't one of my killers enough for you? Do you want to deprive me of the others too?"

"Well, it looks as if the one we *did* track down has given us the slip."

"Ah, those twins, they're so unstable."

A bright light illuminated the Gallery of Mirrors. The fireworks were exploding over the Palace of Alcina, shooting jets of colour into the sky.

"Dear me, you've missed your rendezvous with young Martineau."

"That's enough babbling, Count. You're finished, you and your perverse amusements. Wait until the Minister reveals what you're up to and then you won't laugh so heartily."

"It's a long time since I laughed at all." The old man brought his wheelchair a few metres forward. Roberta took a step back. "But the Minister will never hear anything about it, my dear. You should know that—coming to challenge me on my own ground, you and that rookie cop, without even telling the good Major Gruber. You have no idea what or whom you're tackling, Morgenstern."

Roberta was not sure what line to take, but above all she must join Martineau.

She decided to make for the French windows, and started that way. Suddenly, however, she collided violently with an invisible barrier. The witch felt the apparently empty air. She was surrounded by something cylindrical which she could not pass. Looking down at her feet, she saw that the floorboards traced the shape of a pentagram, and she was in the middle of it. The old man was watching her, crowing with malicious glee.

"What a laugh *this* is, eh, my dear colleague? Can you get out of this trap? You can't? What a shame! Floorboards made of wood from the Temple, and a fifth-level invocation to hold you captive. You do appreciate the attention I'm devoting to you, I hope? After all, I have only to snap my fingers to make you surrender abjectly."

"Snap your fingers then, you old wreck! If you can, that is!"

She tried and failed to think of some way out. If the

Count had imprisoned her with a fifth-level invocation she had no chance of breaking the spell. She herself had never gone beyond the third level of magic.

Palladio darted reptilian glances at Morgenstern. The cataracts forming in his sunken eyes gave them the colour of curdled milk.

"You've given me an idea. It's true that I have no time to waste on you, but still . . ." he said, smiling. "Let me tell you about it: the total decline to which I have been prey for centuries has allowed me to make some interesting discoveries in the field of entropy. I have christened one of them the Crystal Sickness. It's affected me for at least two hundred years, and believe me, I protect myself as best I can. During my long, wakeful nights I've amused myself thinking up a spell to reproduce it in suitable persons—such as you."

Palladio traced a figure unknown to the sorceress in the air, looking in her direction. She immediately felt her bones freeze and her whole body become fragile. Some kind of transformation was going on in her. She sensed it, but there was nothing she could do about it. Her body was too heavy now, her joints were about to give way. She was collapsing from the inside.

"As you have probably realized, your bones have taken on the basic properties of crystal: purity and fragility. Now for a demonstration."

Palladio raised his arms and cast them violently to his left. The sorceress was lifted in the air and sent flying to the right. She shattered against the invisible wall like a china doll. The Count did not let go of her. He threw her from the other side of her cage and let her drop again. The sorceress crashed to the floor, groaning. Her body had become a bag of skin with vital organs and splinters of crystal spilling out of it on all sides. She tried to speak, but her jawbone broke and scattered in a shower of glass on the gallery floor. She managed to raise her eyes to the shape of the Count looming over her. She would die of pain if he didn't finish her off first.

Someone had joined them: La Voisin. She was holding something out to Palladio. A bag—he examined the contents with satisfaction. He wheeled his chair over to the witch and stopped with one of its wheels up against her skull. Roberta, fighting unconsciousness, was horrified to feel her cranium split.

The Count rolled the contents of the bag over the floor a few centimetres from her head. Martineau's complexion was greyish, his lips were black and his eyes started out of his head.

"So now, my dear colleague," said the Count," you're wise to the chances of success in your pitiful enterprise. You won't prevent me from reviving Jack again. You won't prevent my Killers' Quadrille from forming to dance the Dance of the Assassins."

Taking his cane, he jabbed the pointed end into the witch's skull, which exploded into thousands of pieces.

"Very well, there's no more for us to do here," he said. "Is the Eleven Thousand Devils ready for the ceremony? The child hasn't escaped?"

"Everything is ready," replied La Voisin.

"Then let's catch your vaporetto and enjoy ourselves," said the Count in jovial tones. "We shall soon be leaving Paris. The Ripper is almost reconstructed. Come along."

173

Hans-Friedrich knew what he needed to know, and he had seen quite enough. He had found a mousehole big enough for him to scurry into it and lose himself in the building. No one was paying him any attention. He raced away with all the strength in his little paws.

Sensing his presence, Palladio turned. He pointed his cane at Hans-Friedrich just as the little animal disappeared behind the skirting board.

"Stop that hedgehog!" he shouted.

La Voisin did not react, or reacted too late. Hans-Friedrich wasn't hanging about to find out which. He followed the route taken by his late mistress, but passing through the spaces between the walls and the floorboards. Neither man nor beast pursued him. He was soon back in the grounds of Versailles, crossed them unmolested, and finally reached the landing stage, where he stopped.

A vaporetto was taking La Voisin back to Paris. Hans-Friedrich let it move away. Then he went down through the tall grass to the water that the Romanies had taught him to distrust.

He had heard terrible things about the lagoon: stories of aquatic monsters, huge catfish who sometimes attacked whole ship's crews. Why not wait for the next boat?

But a Romany child was soon to die, and the witch with the magnificent green eyes would never forgive him for his weakness. No, he definitely couldn't wait for the vaporetto to come back. Grunting, the hedgehog plunged into the water and swam bravely out into the lagoon.

Saint Satan, Pray for Us

The wind tore the clouds above the city apart. The moon, drowning in the storm, cast a metallic light on the banks of the river. Two motionless shapes were waiting there, like souls that Charon had forgotten to take aboard.

A boat was coming upstream. There were five men in it, grunting with effort as they pulled on the oars. One last stroke, and the prow of the boat thrust into the muddy bank. The two shapes approached it. The men jumped ashore and joined them. Something was passed from hand to hand. The oarsmen left the boat upturned on the bank, and then they all moved away to the nearest houses.

The group went to the Louvre quarter, leaving the imposing castle keep on the left and making for the dark shape of Saint-Eustache among its maze of medieval alleys. There were no longer only seven of them; fifteen, thirty, then fifty people advanced soundlessly through the streets of Paris. New arrivals came to join them from porches or back yards.

The close-packed little troop entered a tavern, a shady dive in Withered Tree Road. The public room of the inn was soon full. The two shapes were bending over whatever it was that had been handed to them. The others waited without a word, standing round a long wooden table.

"Well?" asked Martineau.

He put his hood back and contorted himself to get a sight of Morgenstern's face, which was still hidden in the shadow of her monastic habit. The sorceress was holding the hedgehog and petting him affectionately. Hans-Friedrich Gustavson was busy reporting to her on the recent events.

"You still don't like hedgehogs," replied Morgenstern, after what seemed to everyone an eternity.

"And I never shall. What happened at Versailles?"

Shaking her head, the witch let her hood fall back on her shoulders and let go of the hedgehog, who went over to nibble some dried-up food from the table. All the Romanies were intent on her. They too were anxious to know all about it.

"It's just as well we didn't go to the Enchanted Isle in person," said Roberta.

"So what happened?" snapped Martineau impatiently. He hadn't agreed to take part in this twinning business to be fobbed off with a partial report or a half-truth.

"Hans-Friedrich says you got your head cut off. I didn't do much better myself. Palladio had something special saved up for me. Never mind all that—we know what to think of the Count now. There's no doubt that he's behind this extraordinary masquerade."

The Romanies murmured. One man detached himself from the group, a short, stocky man with an axe in his belt. He clenched his fists as he spoke, containing his anger with difficulty.

"So now you know who's guilty it's time to arrest them, right? Have you seen my daughter? Is she alive?"

"She's alive. The Gustavson probed the mind of Dame Guibaude—well, I mean La Voisin. The ceremony will take place tonight, at midnight, as the ritual requires."

"It's only just past eleven. We can still save her," Martineau assured the man.

The Romany chief ranged himself beside the child's father, who was torn between rage and despair, and asked the *Chovexani*, "But we still need to know where the ceremony is taking place. Does the Gustavson know that?"

"Yes—it seems the Black Mass will be held in the Eleven Thousand Devils," replied the sorceress, exactly as the hedgehog would have said if he'd been endowed with human language.

"At the tennis court?" said Martineau in surprise.

"That's right. Where you put up such a good show with your dexterity, dear boy. Gentlemen, let's set off. We have an innocent soul to save. And this time," she added, glancing at Martineau, "there'll be no excuse for being late."

The façade of the Eleven Thousand Devils tavern frequented by Dame Guibaude showed no sign of life. The men, taking cover under the projecting roof of a gallery opposite, were watching the small door of the tavern. Roberta had had the greatest difficulty in persuading the

Romanies not to charge headlong into the tennis court. The building was bound to be guarded, and she thought there had been enough traps for one evening.

Raising her arms, she ordered imperiously: *"Purtasuu-vrazvuus, charias ruipazvuus, gardaspustesanduriazvuus."*

The little door opened, squealing on its hinges. Nothing else happened.

"Is that all?" complained the disappointed Martineau.

"I don't trust La Voisin, or doors made of solid oak. They're harder to deal with. But if there *were* any defences they're down now."

They went into the inn, walked right down the corridor, and entered the tennis court itself without mishap. Moonbeams shone in through the skylights in the ceiling. The tiers of seats were empty. The voice of the Romany chief echoed in the unoccupied hall.

"Where are they?" He was armed with a musket, which he pointed in the witch's direction. "Could La Voisin have deceived your double?" he asked, controlling his anger with an effort.

Morgenstern was not sure what to tell him. Martineau had retreated to a corner of the court, and was playing with a racket and a ball that he had found on the umpire's chair.

"My astral twin was dead by the time they mentioned this place," said Morgenstern, "but why would they lie? Anyway, Hans-Friedrich saw La Voisin leave the Enchanted Isle."

She took the hedgehog out of her pocket. He was fast asleep. She tried to wake him by stroking him. No reaction. The witch shook him up and down. The hedgehog let out a shrill squeak and tried to bite whoever was maltreating him. Roberta tightened her grip, put him down on the floor, and held him in place. Kneeling beside him, she made him probe the floor of the building below the tennis court.

She could see the ceremony as clearly as if she were there. It must be because so many people had gathered for the Black Mass. She heard a chant. "Clyoran . . . Ixion . . . Esition . . . Existian." La Voisin, wearing a black chasuble, was reciting the demonic names. No sign of the Romany child. But if they had reached the stage of invoking the Devil under his different manifestations, the sacrifice must be coming soon.

Roberta rose to her feet in a hurry. "They're very close—down there underneath us," she said, pointing to the gravel covering the floor of the tennis court. "We must find the way down."

The Romanies sprang into action. While some of them explored the tiers of seats, others got down on all fours and swept the gravel aside. But they found nothing. With the Gustavson's aid, Roberta explored the minds invoking the Devil beneath their feet, but the worshippers were too rapt in the ceremony to transmit any mental image of the way they had gone down to the floor below.

Martineau seemed completely detached from the frantic activity around him. He made as if to serve, throwing the ball up in the air and aiming at a point below one of the shorter sides of the court. Watching him with curiosity, Roberta noted the trajectory the ball would have followed if he had really served it. A wooden statue was looking at them from a dark niche under the roof of the court.

It must be St. Barbara, the patron saint of palmers or pilgrims. From a distance you might have thought the statue a miniature version of La Voisin.

"Do you know how St. Barbara died?" inquired Morgenstern. Having taken a course in Christian legend at the College of Sorcery, she knew the answer.

"No," said Martineau, "but I have a feeling you're going to tell me."

"Beheaded by her father."

The young man threw up the ball, pretended to be about to hit it and then caught it.

"Can you do it?"

"With the aid of the infernal powers," grumbled the young man, "I suppose it's possible."

He threw the ball up higher this time. Arching backwards, he took aim and struck it hard towards the ceiling. The small white ball hit St. Barbara's head, which tipped back and then, thanks to an ingenious spring mechanism, returned to its place. A series of mechanical noises ran round the tennis court. The umpire's chair swivelled a quarter of the way round to reveal a spiral staircase running down to the lower floor of the inn.

"There it is!" said Roberta.

She ran for the staircase, followed by Martineau and the Romanies. Only four or five steps at a time could be seen. A heavy smell of incense rose from the depths below, along with the sound of muffled voices. The Romany chief was about to rush down. Roberta stopped him, laying a hand on his arm.

"Let me make something clear," she said, looking him

straight in the eye. "That invocation greatly increases the power of anyone reciting it. La Voisin is dangerous. And her spells are certainly stronger than mine."

"Go on, sorceress!" said the Romany impatiently. "What are you trying to tell me?"

"Do you dream of killing the wicked people down there? Fair enough, but they may have been possessed. They may be acting against their real will. I'm asking you to spare them as far as possible. The Minister of Security will bring them to justice."

"Yes, yes, we'll spare anyone possessed," replied the Romany, anxious to get moving.

"Good. Anyway, for a start, I'll deal with the priestess. Or try to. Please intervene only as a last resort."

"Let's go then, *Chovexani*."

Roberta began climbing down the steps, followed by Martineau. They went round the spiral twice. The murmured words were becoming audible.

"Bring in the lamb," they heard La Voisin order.

Morgenstern reached the foot of the staircase faster than she had thought she would. The crypt did not lie very deep. The worshippers had their backs to her, and were looking at La Voisin, who was standing by an altar with a naked woman lying on it. The Poisoner had her hand on the shoulder of a little girl who was looking at her, perfectly docile. La Voisin slipped her hand under the child's chin as if preparing to raise her from the floor.

The ranks of worshippers were so dense that any direct approach was impossible. But the Romany whose child was about to be sacrificed plunged into the crowd as soon as he saw the scene. The others followed him, creating wild turmoil around them, while Roberta and Martineau kept back, watching from the foot of the stairs.

The sorceress saw the black shadow that was La Voisin slipping behind a pillar.

Confusion reigned for several minutes. Then the ranks of the faithful gradually thinned out. Some were lying on the floor, unconscious. The others were roughly rounded up and placed under strong guard. The Romany chief who had led the operation pulled their hoods back. The numbers of men and women were about equal, and their faces wore ecstatic expressions. They looked as if they had been drugged.

All this time La Voisin was making her way along the wall to the apse, with the sorceress close behind her. An underground passage opened up on their right. Morgenstern entered it with caution, went several metres and rounded a bend. La Voisin was walking calmly along a little way ahead. She stopped and turned, sensing the presence of her colleague. The two sorceresses looked at each other without a word.

"What are you doing?" Martineau asked Morgenstern in a whisper. "Shouldn't we stop her escaping?"

Roberta, keeping perfectly still, replied very quietly, "The Devil almost appeared to her this evening. With the power that's in her at this moment, none of us could stop her. Look at her eyes, Martineau. But not for too long."

The young man obeyed. La Voisin's pupils were dilated, flashing at intervals as if a storm were raging in each eye. Martineau felt their hypnotic attraction, and turned his glance away just in time. But Roberta was watching him anyway.

The Romany chief stopped behind them, and saw La Voisin in his own turn. The demonic woman smiled at the sight of him.

"Ah," she said to the man, "are you the father of the piglet I bled with my own hands? I recognize his sweet little features. It was with this very hand that I opened him up."

One of the man's sons had gone missing a few days earlier. He had hoped, if he did not believe, that the child had simply run away.

The Poisoner showed her left hand. Arcs of electric energy flashed between her fingers.

The Romany uttered a roar and rushed at her. Roberta tried to hold him back, but the man was making for La Voisin like a wild animal. She waited.

Martineau's eyes were riveted to the scene, and yet all of what happened next, or almost all of it, escaped him. The underground passage became a bubbling fountain. Hands armed with claws dissected the Romany. La Voisin's face could be seen now and then, like a pale moon in a sky of blood.

The Poisoner disappeared. Martineau turned back to the crypt, hands to his mouth, his chest heaving spasmodically. A young Romany, evidently the leader now, approached Roberta, who had not moved. Impassively, he looked at the scene of the massacre.

"She's gone," said the witch.

The Romany looked down the passage, which led into the darkness. "We must destroy the demon!"

"Destroy her?" said the witch. "Yes . . . yes, perhaps we could if we set a trap for her."

"What kind of trap would that wild beast fall into?"

Roberta thought of the article she had read in *Historic Cities News*, the story of the bell baptized first as Satan, then as St. Catherine.

"The trap rather depends on the bait. I know one she won't be able to resist."

"What is it?"

"A bell."

"Bells usually put demons to flight."

"This is a rather unusual one. It ought to attract her."

The Romany thought about the witch's reply. He must have found it satisfactory, since he said, "Very well: if you have the bait, you'll catch your prey."

Martineau and all the others were waiting for the Poisoner to show herself. Morgenstern had taken them to the top of the tower in the church of Saint-Jacques-de-la-Boucherie, explaining that the bell had been consecrated to Satan before it was baptized correctly as St. Catherine. The sorceress believed its sound would attract the demonic being as surely as a corpse will attract a flock of vultures.

But they had been waiting for three hours now, and nothing had happened. Martineau was sitting on the tie beam just above the bell itself, with the witch beside him. She was petting Hans-Friedrich and listening to what went on around them. The Romanies were occupying every hiding-place the church tower could offer.

The wind played a lugubrious melody in the louvres of

the building, the only sound to be heard apart from the heavy note of the bell chiming every quarter of an hour. Its tocsin, carried on the stormy wind, rose above the roofs of Paris, calling to the monster by name.

Martineau thought of the strange ceremony which had allowed the sorceress to create their astral twins. He had seen Morgenstern in her darkest aspect then. The young man remembered the tales of witches' Sabbaths and enchanted forests that his mother had told him when he was a little boy. Bubbling cauldrons, hairy animals with sharp claws, paranormal phenomena. Good and Evil mingling, moulded into one figure by fear . . .

My mother would have made a good witch if she hadn't married into Martineau Cement Industries, the young man mused.

He retained a vague and uneasy impression of that recent experience. Look at it one way, and he couldn't help thinking that Morgenstern belonged to a different world. Look at it another, and that same world attracted him almost viscerally. He couldn't explain why. The moves his CID colleague made had seemed so familiar . . . strange images had entered his mind.

Images of the air and flying, most of them.

Roberta hadn't extracted the vital juices of a bat, or mixed ingredients with toad spittle, and she certainly hadn't waved some fetish object bristling with bloodstained needles around in order to create their astral twins. All she had to do was give an order to the mirror as they stood in front of it in her boarding-house. The glass had clouded over. Then their reflections had simply waved goodbye before disappearing behind the frame of the full-length looking-glass, leaving the room, and boarding the vaporetto to the Enchanted Isle.

Martineau and Morgenstern themselves were left there looking at the reflection of the empty room. They no longer appeared in it. The young man's first reaction had been to make sure his shadow was still following him. It was, but his reflection had simply disappeared. He had hurried into the bathroom, watched with amusement by Morgenstern. The mirror there also refused to reflect him the way mirrors usually did.

Once again he felt the vertigo that had come over him then. A sense that the ground was opening beneath your feet and reality was collapsing . . . even this bell might be an illusion. The sorceress had assured him that they would get their reflections back once the astral twins ceased to exist, but Martineau had been wondering about it all ever since.

How could Hans-Friedrich have followed the twins if he was part of the prime reality? What version of the city were they in now? Were they in the original church of Saint-Jacques-de-la-Boucherie or one of its reconstructions? Well, since this was a Historic City it had to be a reconstruction anyway.

The young man realized that the witch was looking intently at him, trying to tell him something. She showed him the pocket mirror she was holding, and then threw it his way without warning. He just managed to catch it, and then looked in it.

His reflection was back. It was smiling at him, and it was not decapitated. Reality was back in force again. The young man tossed the mirror back to Morgenstern, greatly relieved. He had a certain talent for playing tennis and driving noisy sports cars—but haunting the fringes of illusion and juggling with the uncanny certainly wasn't his style. No, he'd leave that to enchanters and sorcerers.

"Here she comes," said Morgenstern.

Hans-Friedrich rolled up in a ball, his spines bristling. The bell had last chimed ten minutes earlier. Martineau took out his six-shooter and cocked it. There were at least four or five Romanies hiding in the upper reaches of the belfry above him, and their weapons were all aimed at the same spot: the place where the staircase came up through the belfry floor. This time La Voisin couldn't escape them.

"She's come in—she's starting up the stairs," said Roberta.

Martineau began swallowing and found he couldn't stop. His heart was making more noise than that accursed bell. For heaven's sake, why couldn't he calm down? He glanced at Roberta, who was staring imperturbably at the steps. But anyway the shadows hid them, and if they kept still there was no reason why the demon should see them. Not before they opened fire, anyway.

"She's on her way up. Whatever you do, don't move," ordered the sorceress.

A step creaked. Martineau's blood ran cold. He would never manage to leave his perch. His courage had melted away.

La Voisin's androgynous face appeared, pale as the moon. She looked round the interior of the belfry, assessing its depths. She was breathing hard, and her pupils were dilated; evidently she was still in the trance-like state caused by her recent invocation.

She climbed the last few steps, approached the bell, and put out her hand to it. At least six people had her in their sights. The possessed creature stroked the bronze of the bell with a sensuous, reverent hand, as if caressing an idol.

A rafter just above Martineau creaked. La Voisin raised her head, her face distorted by hatred, and located the origin of the sound. A Romany opened fire. Next moment all the others were firing too. A hail of bullets rained down on the demon. The noise was deafening. Chips of wood flew in all directions, and the smoke filling the belfry soon prevented anyone from seeing anything at all. Above the din, Martineau heard Morgenstern's voice.

"Stop firing!"

The witch had to repeat her order three times before the firing died away. Martineau realized that his own weapon was cold. Transfixed by fear, he hadn't fired at all. The Romanies and Morgenstern leaped down from their perches. Splashes of blood showed that the demon had been hit, but there was no trace of her body. La Voisin had vanished into thin air.

"This is impossible!" swore one of the men.

"Nothing's impossible," said Roberta.

A burst of firing rang out on the staircase, followed by a howl. A shoot-out must be in progress lower down. The sorceress and the Romanies rushed to the stairwell and disappeared from Martineau's sight. From his own perch, he listened to the fighting, his stomach turning over with terror. He heard inarticulate cries, salvoes of rifle fire, and the witch's brief orders.

"She's on the run!" shouted one man.

"On the run!" repeated Martineau, his mouth dry, hardly daring to believe it.

Then came Roberta's voice from outside the church. "There! Look, she's climbing the outside of the tower!"

Instinctively, Martineau turned his head that way. He saw La Voisin pass by, clinging spider-like to the louvres on her way up to the top of the church tower. The young man jumped down to the belfry floor and risked a glance out. The Poisoner, propping herself on a gargoyle, disappeared on the far side of the balustrade that crowned the roof. Looking down to the ground, Martineau saw Morgenstern's face turned up to him. Footsteps were already pounding up the stairs. The Romanies were on their way back.

He didn't feel capable of scaling the façade of the tower himself, but the tangle of rafters where they had been lying in wait must lead somewhere. Martineau found that he could easily jump up on the first rafter, then haul himself up by the second, and that way he climbed to the ceiling, where he found a trapdoor going up to the roof. He opened its latch with one hand and pushed it gently open.

There was La Voisin, sitting motionless on the edge of the void. She had one hand on a gargoyle, which she was automatically caressing as she looked at the view of Paris. Martineau got the trapdoor wide open and hauled himself soundlessly up on to the roof. Just three metres separated him from the Poisoner. He aimed his gun at her back.

"Hey, you!" he called.

La Voisin tipped her head to one side and rubbed her ear against her shoulder. She rose, as if regretfully, and turned to face Martineau.

Now that he had his weapon trained on the Poisoner, he wished Roberta were there. La Voisin moved as if to approach him. Despite himself, Martineau retreated. The wind was strong, and was blowing fiercely at him. He was trembling, and not just with cold.

"Hey!" she imitated him. Her voice was like a cackle. "Hey, you!"

She stepped forward. The young man was standing on the very edge of the abyss. La Voisin came closer. She could have touched him now just by reaching out her arm. Martineau's own hands were paralysed. Something kept him from pulling the trigger.

The Poisoner struck the young man's wrist with her arm as if with a scythe. His six-shooter tumbled through the air. Martineau stepped back again, arms flung wide. He felt like a puppet with La Voisin pulling the strings.

"Do you think the two of us will have time for a little game before the Count comes to pick me up?" inquired the Devil's servant, rubbing her ear against her shoulder again. Catching Martineau by the lapels of his jacket, she drew him gently towards her. Their mouths touched. She opened her lips and placed them on the young man's. Horrified, he felt sharp fangs sink into his flesh.

Suddenly La Voisin withdrew to sniff the air. She looked at a place in the sky where the horizon was turning pale. A dark, oblong outline stood out against the first light of dawn, the shape of an airship making straight towards the tower from the horizon. The wind carried the sound of engines their way. It was the *Albatross*.

The Poisoner kissed Martineau, taking a small piece out of his cheek as she did so. "A little souvenir. See you some other time, sweetheart."

Letting go of him, she pushed him casually backwards. The investigator saw her take a run and jump up into the air as the *Albatross* banked, brushing past the belfry. At that moment the trapdoor opened, and Morgenstern's face appeared.

La Voisin made a soft landing on the deck of the ship. It let out a hoot that must have woken all Paris, and then the *Albatross* was on its way, going full speed ahead. It turned west, catching up with the night as dawn pursued it. Its outline blurred and then shrank like a flame being extinguished just before it goes out entirely.

Morgenstern, treading cautiously, approached Martineau and stared at him with her mouth wide open. Why was she looking like that? Was it his injured cheek? But La Voisin had barely grazed it.

All the same, he felt his face as he asked, "What's the matter?" She had stopped with her hand held out to him, not daring to go any further. "Are you afraid I'll fall, Roberta?"

Martineau saw that the witch was looking at his feet, and he looked down too. He was standing on empty air, fifty metres of it between himself and the ground, and the space of a long stride separated him from the belfry of Saint-Jacques.

He had no time to say anything. Fear overwhelmed him, and the force of gravity suddenly reasserted its rights.

VENICE

Original City

POPULATION: tenants 500, visitors 7000.

CHRONOLOGICAL PERIOD: depending on the season.

PLACES TO VISIT: San Marco, the Doge's palace, La Fenice, etc. Visits per week, rates according to point of embarkation (NB: Venice is the only mobile city in the Historic Cities network).

DO NOT MISS: the Feast of the Redeemer (second Saturday in July).

Monsieur Rosemonde

❦

The College of Sorcery stood in the intellectual heart of the city, on the Hill of Famous Men within the Great and Prestigious University.

Roberta had begun studying at the College when she was eighteen. The urgent necessity of earning a living had forced her to abandon her studies after three years, but she remembered those years as a very happy time. All the more so because she had opted to take the History of Sorcery with Monsieur Rosemonde.

Passing through the main gateway, she crossed the courtyard, which was full of students studying ordinary subjects. They were the visible part of the University, and none of them had the least idea that the venerable building concealed a second College too, like a desk with secret drawers, or one of those Russian dolls used by certain witches to give them a glimpse of the abyss.

Remembering the tricks she and her girl friends had played on the low-flyers, as they called the University students, Roberta felt quite emotional. They, of course, thought themselves high-flyers, queens of the air, wedded to the eternal powers, guardians of universal knowledge . . . ah, the folly of youth!

Roberta crossed the main courtyard, climbed Staircase F to the first floor, and made straight for the reception desk of the School of Practical Studies in the oldest part of the building. The corridors were lined with books behind doors with grilles in them, books kept under lock and key as if someone feared they might escape.

In this department you might meet scholars researching into some recently discovered piece of masonry casting new light on the location of a lost city of the ancient world. A small group might be discussing the meaning to be properly attributed to a certain word used in a Festival of the Nordic Bear. Or you might find another group claiming that Columbus was just a fraud, but that was nothing new.

Passing the open door of a lecture room, Roberta saw a professor writing out a fragment from the *Book of the Dead* on a huge blackboard with energetic strokes of his chalk. The students were copying the hieroglyphics down in sepulchral silence.

The sorceress pushed open the library door. At the back of the room a young man was hidden behind piles of books. The stock-keeper was vigorously stamping volumes. Roberta couldn't see the librarian. Too bad—but anyway, no one was taking any notice of her.

She put out her right hand, found the switch she wanted and flicked it down. Then she went to the far end of a corridor leading to a door said by the university authorities to be out of use. After making sure that no one had followed her, she pulled it towards her. An electric lock whirred, and the door opened.

Roberta had not been back to the College of Sorcery since the last reunion of her own class, two years ago, but nothing had changed. The same book-lined corridor, the same smell of polished wood . . . the special wood used for shelves to hold those library books you must get special permission to read.

Memories of evenings spent studying, of amazing discoveries, of waiting for results, of the way her heart fluttered when Rosemonde entered the College amphitheatre all came flooding back into Roberta's mind.

She followed the corridor, climbed a spiral staircase, walked along a landing, climbed down to a mezzanine floor and went along the Celestial Maps corridor. She stopped outside Albertus Magnus Hall, which was empty, like the rest of the college just now. Cauldrons, retorts, and jars stood waiting, neatly lined up on white ceramic lab benches.

At last Roberta reached the amphitheatre, a rotunda built on the model of an anatomy theatre. Three sets of tiered seats traced a spiral from ceiling to floor. Twenty metres above it, daylight fell in through the skylight in the dome, which was cracked and stained with damp. Legend said that the ruins of a classical temple of Bacchus lay beneath the spot where the lecturer stood.

Monsieur Rosemonde was sitting in the lecturer's chair, legs outstretched, hands in his pockets, gazing intently at the blackboard, although it bore no cabalistic signs. When he heard the sorceress come in he rose to his feet, exclaiming,

"Roberta Morgenstern! My dear!"

"Monsieur Rosemonde."

She couldn't help blushing. She'd known the Professor of the History of Sorcery for twenty years, but he never changed: he was tall, with clear eyes and a high forehead, hair greying at the temples, and always impeccably dressed . . . Rosemonde waved his left arm, and a chair floated across the amphitheatre to his hand. He put it down opposite him and invited Roberta to be seated.

"You never seem to change!" she ventured to comment.

"That's what you think! *Tempus edax, homo edacior.* Which I daresay the poets would translate as, 'Time is blind but man's a fool.' However, I don't suppose you asked me to meet you here to discuss entropy?" added Rosemonde, with a little smile.

"No, I didn't. I need your advice. It's a case I'm working on, and it's getting rather complex."

"Begin at the beginning, then."

Rosemonde stretched his legs again and took a pipe out of his waistcoat pocket. A cloud of blue smoke swiftly rose to the ceiling, while the aroma of Dutch tobacco filled the amphitheatre. Roberta collected her thoughts, took a deep breath, and led Rosemonde to London and the streets of the East End on the evening of Docklands Day.

"So there was Martineau," she finished her story, "falling through the air. I cast a classic spell to keep him from breaking any bones at the foot of the tower."

"The Song of Icarus?" inquired Rosemonde, with interest.

"No, I used Newton's Dream."

"Harder but more effective. Good work, Roberta."

She hadn't told Rosemonde that Martineau was literally hovering above the void just before she came to his rescue. Her story was complicated enough anyway.

"Gruber was informed at once. The CID alerted the Ministry of Security, and Fould had the devil-worshippers arrested. Paris was cordoned off, and the militia went through it with a fine-tooth comb."

"No trace of the killers or Count Palladio, I suppose?" said Rosemonde.

Roberta shook her head. "The *Albatross* had vanished into thin air. A summons has been issued against the Count. And that's the trouble. I'm pretty well certain I know where he is, but the Ministry of Security has its hands tied for reasons of international politics."

"You have Venice in mind? Or there's the city reserved for the Club Fortuny. Fould has no access there."

"But no one's ever proved that such a city really exists. I wouldn't be surprised if it's just a myth thought up by the members of the Club. Otherwise at least we'd know where it is and what model it was built on."

"I'm not so sure of that. The richer people are, the more they like secrecy."

"Well, be that as it may, I'd plump for Venice. Palladio mentioned his Venetian origins to us in the Crystal Palace. What's more, London, Paris, and the other Historic Cities are only concessions, licensed to occupy the international lagoon—but they're not outside the reach of the law. Whereas Venice is an original city, an autonomous sovereign state, protected under agreements signed during the Dominions period from any military invasion. So it's a problem for the Ministry of War, not for Security. God knows when the generals would decide to besiege Venice, or whether Fould would manage to persuade them it's a good idea."

"Not God. The Devil, maybe," murmured Rosemonde, rising to stretch his legs. He went over to the blackboard and traced a perfect circle on it freehand. Then he drew a pentagram inside the circle, and wiped it all off again with his sleeve. "So how can I help you, Roberta?"

"You're a sorcery expert, and we've been up to our ears in sorcery since the beginning of this business. What do you know about Palladio and the Killers' Quadrille? That's what he called it in the Gallery of Mirrors before finishing off my double. Who exactly *is* Antonio Palladio?"

Rosemonde did not reply.

"I know you never mentioned this Quadrille in any of your lectures, or not as far as I remember. Yet surely there's some—some historical explanation of all this?"

"There's an explanation of everything, Miss Morgenstern. Even the mystery of Palladio."

The professor rummaged in his brown leather briefcase and produced a file bearing the seal of the Records Office. Intrigued, the sorceress opened it. The file contained a number of sheets of paper covered with vigorous handwriting, and a bound leaflet which, judging by the marks of mildew, was older than the handwritten sheets. It was marked with a seal in the shape of a clenched fist.

"So the Records Office has been investigating the Count, has it?"

"And this was all they could find on him. I'll leave you to read it now—there's someone I have to see outside College—and I'll be back in half an hour."

When the Professor had left, Roberta wondered how this file could have come into his hands. The Records Office was even fussier about strict confidentiality than the Ministry of War. She studied the first part of the file. It was a letter bearing a clearly written, dashing signature, and it was dated 15 March 1810. Roberta plunged straight in.

My dearly beloved,

Allow me to tell you a ghost story—a tale that may seem to you grotesque coming from the pen of a man like me, but nonetheless it is a scrupulous record of the incident, exactly as it happened.

Venice had surrendered without resistance, and the Venetian aristocrats came to see me, one after another, as if to pay homage. Those interminable meetings were very tedious. Now and then I took refuge in some secluded building, on one occasion a Dalmatian church that contains some very fine paintings. Well then: I was holding audience in the Doge's palace when I first saw Antonio Palladio. This was on the 19th of January in the year 1798.

Palladio cut a good figure: a man of mature age, hard-featured, a soldier's face. He did not kneel, but stood upright before me, and whispered so quietly that none but I could catch his words: "Death makes a mockery of swords, conspiracies, and cannon. But I know a way to cheat Death itself. Are you interested?"

I was young, and must have been either mad or foolish. Be that as it may, I invited Palladio to dine with me that very evening. I had already had thousands of occasions to see Death at work. My mind sometimes dwelt on the matter, and now it obsesses me, as it does every man who has come close to Death too many times.

The breadth of Palladio's culture made our dinner fascinating. He spoke to me of the last three centuries as if he had lived through them himself. At last he confided his project to me. I listened attentively. The man was an alchemist, and was asking me for ingredients that I did not yet possess, but he was no fool and knew that they were within my grasp. We parted, having fixed upon a very strange rendezvous: we would meet again in the land of the Pharaohs once I was its master.

I do not know what part should be ascribed to this encounter in the victories that followed, but one thing is certain: history was on my side.

It took me less than a year to assemble the Eastern fleet and take first Malta, then Alexandria. It was in El-Ramanieh, a small town lashed by the burning desert wind, that Count Palladio presented himself to me for the second time. I was in my tent, conferring with Desaix, Reynier, and Vial on the best route to take to Cairo.

What magic did he use to get past the sentries? The troops were strictly accounted for, and no intrusion was possible. He told me of a man called Panhusen, a scholar from the Museum and secretary to Kléber. This man had vanished into thin air in Alexandria, whereupon Palladio offered Kléber his own services. He spoke perfect Arabic. Good interpreters were few and far between, and any speaker of the local language was welcome in our ranks, so Kléber had engaged him.

I dismissed my officers, and we continued our conversation where we had broken it off months before. We were so close to Cairo now! I burned to get there, and could not sleep that night.

I struck camp next day, much to my men's surprise. We knew nothing of the Mameluke forces awaiting us in Cairo, and Nelson was harassing our fleet. Yet I insisted on our making a forced march for ten days on end. We bivouacked in difficult conditions. My brave soldiers put up with the terrible aridity of the climate without a murmur.

My haste was not for military reasons, yet it gave us the advantage. When we reached Cairo the Mamelukes were still disorganized, although they had powerful artillery on the banks of the Nile. The pyramids were finally within reach of our cannon.

I attacked that very evening. It took only a night for Reynier and Desaix, backed up later by Bon and Vial leading the second charge, to crush the enemy. We captured four hundred camels and forty pieces of artillery. Cairo proclaimed its allegiance within the hour. It was a great, a fine victory.

I had a country to organize, propaganda to print, religious leaders to win over, a command post to set up. But above all, I had to witness the incredible occult event whose arcane secret Palladio told me he had mastered.

In accordance with my instructions, my faithful Cartenier was waiting at the western gate of the camp. He had ready for us two magnificent stallions, horses such as only the Arabs can breed. My eyes must have been blazing, and I daresay I looked very strange in the Venetian's company.

We galloped to the Gizeh plateau. The tombs of the Pharaohs were like fragments of the night buried deep in the ground. How could any ordinary men have been interred in such cenotaphs? Were the ancient Egyptians giants?

Palladio stopped at the foot of the tallest pyramid, which Denon calls the pyramid of Khufu, and climbed up on some large blocks of stone. An Arab was waiting for him a little higher up.

That vexed me. This man, whom I knew only from our first encounter, might be luring me into a trap. There were many who desired my death then, just as there are today. I joined him with one hand on the hilt of my sword.

The Arab lit two torches and gave them to us. We entered the pyramid along an underground passage dug, so Palladio told me, by tomb robbers. Negotiating it was no easy task, and I lost a button off my coat there. We emerged in a gallery made by the Pharaoh's workmen, which went down into the depths of the tomb. At the end of a downward climb which seemed to last a century, we came out in an empty room built to a square ground-plan. The walls were covered with mysterious hieroglyphics. A stone sarcophagus, eroded and empty as an old tooth, was sealed into the flagstones of the floor. Palladio produced a pot of ointment and took out a little of its contents on a spatula. Placing this small quantity of ointment at the bottom of the sarcophagus, he took a lock of hair from a small box and removed several strands, which he also laid in the sarcophagus, and then moved away. I did so too, retreating to a corner of the underground room.

The woman he intended to bring back to life had died in the sixteenth century, and he had known her personally.

Palladio raised his arms and murmured some strange words, looking in the direction of the sarcophagus. Suddenly the interior of the tank-like space was illuminated by a white, blinding, icy, glaring light, which made us resemble ghosts. The light disappeared as suddenly as it had come, and this is what I then saw by the pale flames of the torches which, very fortunately, had not been extinguished.

A hand emerged from the sarcophagus, fingers outstretched. A woman rose to her feet. She was naked, and might have been about thirty years old. Do not be jealous, my dear one. The woman who stood before me could no longer love or be loved. It crossed my mind that she might be a clever accomplice of Palladio who had slipped into the sarcophagus, under cover of the bold pyrotechnical effects, to play the part of a female Lazarus.

In a choking voice, she cried: *"Antonio tchecuo me, pardone."* For she spoke Italian with the accent that may still be heard in the more remote regions of the peninsula. *"Ichabella,"* replied the Count, in the same archaic accent. I no longer doubted that I was witnessing a personal reunion. The young woman, showing no shame, stepped out of the sarcophagus. She had not noticed my presence. She walked over the floor of the room, felt her arms, frowning in concern, passed a hand through her hair and let it fall to the nape of her neck, which she probed. Her index finger came to a halt at the top of her spinal column. Then she bent over, uttering a howl of pain that froze my blood. As for Palladio, he was petrified.

She flung the Venetian to the ground. He tried to escape her hands as they clawed at him, but in vain. The Fury was about to kill him.

Palladio had woken this woman from her eternal slumbers. By the same token, he had revived untold suffering in her. Man must remain no more than man. To wish to pass that limit—ah, what inconceivable folly! It was for me to restore the proper order of things. That, after all, was why I had been sent to Egypt.

I immediately drew my sword and struck the creature's head off. The body startled me by contorting violently and flinging itself against the opposite wall before it collapsed. Palladio, stupefied, was watching me.

A terrible odour of putrefaction spread through the vault. The corpse was decomposing and liquefying before our very eyes. Soon nothing was left of it but a few pools of a diabolical whitish substance. When it was all over I sheathed my sword, left the pyramid alone, returned to camp and fell into a leaden slumber.

A strange story, is it not? And none of it is invented. I never saw or heard of Palladio again. I sometimes regret that I did not kill him, demon that he was, so that the woman could finish in the next world what she had begun in ours.

Your devoted

Napoleon Bonaparte

Roberta gathered up the sheets of paper and put them away in the file. How would historians whose special field was the study of the Emperor Napoleon react to that letter? Ladies and gentlemen, the fantastic is at our gates! The witch imagined herself on a platform haranguing an audience of academics as tight-lipped as oysters. The fantastic lies in wait for us, whoever we are! And Death is not the least insoluble of its secrets.

Roberta sighed, and turned to the pamphlet with the fist-shaped seal. It was written in Italian, a language that any self-respecting witch ought to know. The thoughtful Monsieur Rosemonde had added a set of notes to the document to cast light on any obscure points. She could therefore plunge straight into the account, which seemed to be the minutes of a meeting, as if she had drawn it up herself.

Upon the twenty-third of July 1570, the Ten meet in the Black Chamber to try the case of Antonio Palladio, a spy in Government pay. Present: the defendant, the ten representatives of the noblest houses of Venice, and your humble servant acting as clerk. The indictment is read out by Innocente Contarini. The judge appointed to try this case, as appointed by the custom of the

Balotino, is Giuliano Morosini. The accused conducts his own defence.

INNOCENTE CONTARINI: We are here to try a rather unusual case, implicating one of the outstanding members of the White Hand, a body which, since its creation, has given us no cause for anything but self-congratulation. Antonio Palladio is accused of a double murder not sanctioned by the White Hand, and of contravening the first article of his guild. Let the guards bring in the witness.

(A hooded man is brought before the Ten. His hands are tied behind his back. He is in a state of agitation.)

MAN: I . . . who are you? Where am I?

IC: You have nothing to fear. (*To the guards.*) Untie him. This is not the man who is on trial. (*The guards unbind the man.*) Now, tell us about the night of twelfth July, just before the Feast of the Redeemer, when you were on your rounds in the Scalzi quarter.

MAN: Oh, so that's it, is it? I've already told that story a hundred—

IC: Then tell it again.

MAN: All right. Well, the company was a little edgy . . . do I have to keep this hood on?

GIULIANO MOROSINI: Kindly just tell us your story, my man.

MAN: Very well. The Feast of the Redeemer began next morning, and whoever you may be, I daresay you know what that's like. People take strong drink, tempers rise, there's scuffling. To cut a long story short, I was in the Scalzi quarter when I heard shouting from somewhere near the Grand Canal. And then silence.

IC: Were you on your own, soldier? Weren't you all supposed to stay in pairs?

MAN: Well, yes. But my colleague had gone off to close down a tavern still open after hours. He said he'd meet me a little farther on.

IC: And a little later, eh? Very well, continue.

MAN: The shouting came from the Palazzo Cambini. I went over to it and knocked on the door. I waited several minutes. Then I knocked again. Finally a young man opened to me. His clothes were covered with blood.

(Here the man falls silent. Palladio, who seems detached from the scene although he is the person most concerned in it, now raises his head.)

MAN: His expression was like the Madonna of the Church of the Salute—Santa Maria forgive me!—ecstatic and desperate at once.

GM: Never mind the stylistic literary effects, my man. What did you do next?

MAN: Er, well, I was taken by surprise. The man jostled me and ran off. I did run after him, but I was on my own, and there could have been people in the palazzo needing my help. So I double-locked the door behind me. The murderer would soon be picked up anyway.

IC: You double-locked it, did you?

MAN: Yes, that's right. I had only to follow the trail of blood upstairs to a room looking out over the canal. The scene was illuminated by a dozen lanterns. Do I have to describe it?

IC: We have brought you here for that very purpose.

MAN: Signor Cambini is . . . was a good, noble man. To see

the patriarch like that . . . he was lying across a bed, his eyes wide open. Well, one eye wide open anyway. A dagger was driven into the other. A very beautiful young woman lay at the end of the bed. She was dead too, but I couldn't find any wound on her. I left the palace and called the guard, who turned up promptly.

IC: And you arrested the murderer three days later?

MAN: Well, yes. He didn't even put up a fight. He seemed to be expecting us.

IC: We thank you, soldier. Your evidence is valuable.

(*Innocente Contarini rings an invisible bell. Two guards come for the soldier and lead him out of the Black Chamber. The prosecutor turns to the Ten and resumes his account.*)

IC: Antonio Palladio assassinated Arnolfo Cambini and his mistress for no apparent reason. We assume that it was a crime of passion but we can produce no proof. The defendant can explain it himself if he will be good enough to do so. But first I would like Marco Trevisan[1] to tell us something of the man who was once his pupil. Would you be so kind, Master?

MARCO TREVISAN: It is with great emotion that I speak to you, brothers, in this hour, a sad one for the White Hand. If I must speak of this man, then you may expect to

---

[1] Marco Trevisan was a member of the Great Council, his ancestors having acquired that privilege in perpetuity. A rich landowner with several hectares of vineyards on the mainland, and a brilliant merchant who could do business with Greeks and Turks alike, he also had a glass factory on the island of Murano. He was responsible for the Council of Ten's espionage system from 1535 to about 1565. It has been clearly established that the making of glass daggers was a speciality of his workshop.

hear a eulogy, an account of faultless conduct—up to that fateful night.

IC: Speak, Trevisan. You know the defendant better than anyone.

(Palladio now looks openly at Trevisan, and his figure straightens progressively as the master gives his account of his pupil.[2])

MT: Antonio was a street urchin when I first came upon him. He was thieving in the markets of Torcello and led a gang of boys. The police were keeping an eye on this gang. According to the late Sergeant Zanotti, who drew my attention to him, the lad seemed to be particularly clever. He had a great talent for disguise. At the age of twelve he could pass for an old woman, and he could steal anything at all with disconcerting ease. He was once caught by a police patrol from San Vitele. They imprisoned him with irons on his hands and feet; at dawn he was found to have disappeared as if by magic, as easily as a bird might have flown out of the window. This exploit won him the nickname of Martinetto, "The Swift." I believe that, like those birds, he lived under the rooftops, in some nest where he hid his poor treasures. I set a trap for the young prodigy. He walked straight into it, and I offered him the usual bargain: five years in my service learning to use a dagger, during which time he was not to leave Venice and would be under

---

[2] This remark (like the similar following and preceding passages) has been added to the minutes in the margin, in pencil. These notes are evidence of the original character of this document, which the clerk will have written out in a fair copy to be given to the lawyers working for the Ten. The fair copy of the minutes has not been found, since all the paperwork in the attorneys' offices was destroyed by fire at the end of the eighteenth century.

what I assured him would be very strict surveillance. Either that, or slavery in the galleys. Antonio chose the dagger. He soon exceeded all my expectations, and, as I would like to remind you, those of this Council. His induction into the White Hand as a member and the presentation to him of the dagger, events which took place here eight years ago, were unanimously approved.

GM: We doubt neither your worth nor that of the defendant, Maestro Trevisan. We are simply trying a crime which places the guild of spies in a very delicate situation so far as the great families of Venice are concerned. I am not saying that the . . . thoughtless action of Antonio Palladio casts suspicion on the White Hand itself. But it does make it far too visible. Spies, like monks, should work in silence. And noblemen do not care to be assassinated.

MT: I am aware of that. Antonio has worn my dagger with honour and courage all these years, and he has never tarnished its brightness. I—

(*Here the patriarch turns pale, and looks at Palladio, who at last takes up the story.*)

ANTONIO PALLADIO: It is time for me to answer for my crime. I killed Arnolfo Cambini and the woman who was with him, Isabella, in a moment of madness which in no way excuses my action. I deserve to die.

GIULIANO MOROSINI: That is for us to decide. If you wish to speak, do so. But be clear about it. Madness or not, tell us the how and why of this double murder. Explain yourself.

(*Palladio addresses no particular individual among them, but keeps his eyes on the panelling of the Black Chamber.*)

AP: I knew Isabella before I met Padre Trevisan. She was living on the Giudecca. Her father was a fisherman, but he died at sea, and she went to live with her mother's family in Verona, while Trevisan took me under his wing. Years passed by. I learned my trade, I made my first moves in the great game.[3] Isabella came back into my life when I was just twenty. It was as if we had parted only the day before. I lived with her in perfect happiness for four years.

IC: Cohabitation on the part of its spies has never been looked upon very kindly by the Council, although it is not actually forbidden. Were you able to hide the true nature of your activities all that time, never mentioning the names of those who were paying the rent of your little house in the San Stefano quarter? How did you manage it?

AP: I could teach a deaf mute how to hold his tongue. In any case, you would have killed her if she had suspected anything at all, or am I wrong?

IC: You have never been wrong, Antonio. Apart from that night, and we are anxious to hear about it from your own mouth.

AP: It all began last year. Isabella became mysterious and strange. We were trying to have a child, but without success. She was visiting witches, hoping to become pregnant, and I did not like that. I was following the Englishman, so I was

[3] The agents of the White Hand spy network used a special vocabulary based on an archaic Italian variant of the game of chess, the *scavione*, which has ten pieces for each player and four colours instead of two. The moves allowed are more complicated than in classic chess, and inspired those fascinating chess matches in which the possibilities of the game are limited only by the player's imagination.

away a good deal at that time.

GM: Christie, you mean? You did brilliantly in finding the evidence of his guilt.

AP: He's still in the Piombi prison, I suppose?

GM: If he's still alive. But we are here to talk about you, not him.

AP: Jealousy, suspicion, and black moods gnawed at me for months. I was desperate, and couldn't talk to Isabella anymore. Our arguments became violent. Once I beat her, and then went straight to confession. I was distraught.

GM: You were in love.

AP: I was mad. I followed her all over Venice, but she managed to elude me—me, Antonio Palladio! Ah, *she* would have made you a good recruit, had the master spies noticed her.

(*The Ten exchange glances of annoyance. The defendant does not seem to notice, for he continues, in a shaking voice.*)

AP: She was not at home that evening. I hadn't slept for several nights. The Festival of the Redeemer began next day, and I had drunk more than I should. Isabella was always repeating, "I'll explain soon, and then we'll be happy again, you'll see." But she never did explain. One of my informers came to tell me he had seen her enter the Palazzo Cambini. He found me drunk. You can easily guess the rest. I made a hasty, confused journey of which I now remember only fragments, hurrying from San Stefano to the Scalzi quarter. Getting into the palace was child's play. I went up to the bedroom, I found the two of them, and . . .

IC: And?

(*The silence which has fallen on the Chamber seems to last forever.*)

214

I take the opportunity to change my pen.)

IC: You killed, fair enough. But you killed with the dagger, the secret insignia of your confraternity![4]

(*The defendant shrugs his shoulders, looking as if he cares nothing for this world now.*)

AP: What am I expected to say to that?

IC: Maestro Trevisan has so perfected his teaching, then, that he has taught you to scorn death?

AP: Death?

(*Palladio begins to laugh. His laugh is truly satanic.*)

AP: What has death to do with me? I am immortal.

(*Innocente Contarini, no doubt detecting an insult here, prepares to reply, but the judge of the Ten puts an end to this exchange and has the guards called. They take the prisoner away.*)

IC: He went mad, and mad he remains.

GM: We are considering a crime of passion, and there is no avoiding the implications of such a case. We must now rule on it and bring in our verdict as quickly as possible. There has been too much delay. Trevisan, clerk, I will ask you to leave us now.

"Well?"

Roberta jumped, and almost dropped the historical document. Rosemonde had come back and was standing just behind her.

---

[4] The glass dagger is the subject of Article 1 in the rules of the confraternity of the White Hand. It states that: " The glass dagger is given to the new spy by his master. It is purely symbolic. Those who use it to kill or wound will be obliged to leave the White Hand for an indefinite period," which was a veiled way of saying that those who dishonoured the dagger would die.

"Goodness, you frightened me!"

"May I?"

Rosemonde bent to retrieve the papers from the witch's lap. He put the contents of the file together again and threw it carelessly down on the desk in the middle of the amphitheatre. Then he leaned against the blackboard.

"1570, 1798, and the present day," he said, enumerating the dates.

Roberta changed position and crossed her legs. Her mind was in turmoil, either because of what she had been reading, or for some other reason.

"I get the impression that the mystery around the Count is thickening." She was finding it difficult to concentrate. "Are you sure the two Palladios are one and the same? It could be a coincidence."

Rosemonde raised his eyebrows, drew his head down, and thrust out his chest. His former pupil had just asked a question for which he had prepared an answer some time ago.

"Well, if you look at it like that . . ."

Roberta wilted and sat back in her chair to listen.

"Now, we know nothing about the verdict of the Ten," Rosemonde began in a didactic tone. "The Guild of Spies was perhaps the most discreet and one of the most active confraternities in the Serenissima. However, we come upon Antonio Palladio again in 1574, at Sultan Selim's court in the heart of the Ottoman Empire. The Venetian had introduced himself to the Sultan as a man condemned to death *in absentia* at home. He offered his services and the plans for the Battle of Lepanto, which had been drawn up months

216

ago in the Doge's palace. Whether Palladio was working for himself or for the Ten is another matter—be that as it may, Selim suffered a crushing defeat at Lepanto. Logic suggests that at the very least he would have beheaded Palladio. But the Venetian stayed at the Topkapi palace in Constantinople for three more years, and not as a prisoner. Indeed, Selim thought very highly of him. The intellectual Sultan devoted three lines in his *Thoughts* to Palladio.

The Venetian constantly taught forbidden secrets. Greeks, Ethiopians, Mages, and mountebanks imparted their knowledge to him. Nor was Lazarus himself forgotten.

Theatrically, Rosemonde allowed the echo of his voice to die away in the vaulted ceiling of the amphitheatre. Roberta, entranced, did not move. She had travelled twenty years back in time, to the days when the Professor's lectures thrilled her every Sunday morning. Today it was even better: the enchantment was still there, and she had Monsieur Rosemonde all to herself.

"Those lines are the first evidence we have that Palladio was already doing research in the field of sorcery. The Mages exiled by Christianity took refuge with Selim, bringing with them arcane books, magic implements, and objects like the femur of St. Lazarus, which ended up in Topkapi."

"Lazarus certainly knew all about rising from the dead," Roberta commented.

"In 1574 Palladio's protector Selim died. He was now *persona non grata*, and he fled. Several months of silence follow. Then we discover the Franciscan friar José Luis

Salamanca finding him cast up by the sea on a beach in Maracaibo. The friar, who was keeping a journal of his life among the South American Indians, describes a black wooden box which the shipwrecked man, although unconscious, was clutching to his heart. It contained the handle of a dagger with a blade once made of glass, but now broken." Here Rosemonde took a deep breath. "But Palladio tired of the jungle, and left Brazil to return to the Old World, making for the Jesuit seminary at Rheims in France. This was in the year 1580. The Count was now calling himself Antoine Martinet and teaching dialectics, or if you prefer, the art of lying. He trained several spies sent by Rome to infiltrate the society of Elizabethan England."

Rosemonde picked up a stick of white chalk from the groove below the blackboard, and began drawing figures without heads or tails.

"Four years later Palladio reverted to his real name, and installed himself at the court of Ivan the Terrible. Our Venetian friend, a character somewhere between Rasputin and Machiavelli, already seems to have been well known in powerful circles. The boyars gave him the mission of toppling the tyrant from his throne. It took him only six months to do it. But Palladio was after something other than political intrigue. He left Moscow before the Tsar's head was even cold on top of its pike."

Rosemonde wiped away the figures on the blackboard and leaned against the desk, hands deep in his pockets.

"Now let's leap two centuries forward and move to the East. We are at Jaizalmer in Rajasthan in 1785. The Maharajah's scribes record the arrival of a Venetian with

218

three bags of gold, a merchant who organized one of the most prosperous spice caravans of the time, trading between Asia and the Mediterranean basin. Palladio bought a small palace and stayed there for ten years, during which time he was feeling his way, trying to put what he had learnt into practice. When he was discovered resurrecting a dead child his house was set on fire, his goods confiscated, and he only just managed to escape, leaving Jaizalmer poorer than when he had arrived there. But he had brought a dead child back to life. He had succeeded."

Rosemonde fell silent. Roberta took up the tale.

"Just in time to return to Europe and meet Bonaparte ..."

"Yes, a young man with bright prospects who would allow him to carry out his experiments. Palladio had become an extremely good sorcerer. Too good, perhaps. It was nearly his undoing. The great days of magic were over." Rosemonde sighed, as if he regretted it. "After the episode in the Great Pyramid, Palladio worked in secret and in isolation. Which was a good thing, or no doubt his achievements would never have come down to us."

Roberta rose and went towards the Professor.

"You knew I was going to ask you about the Count beforehand, didn't you?"

"Do you doubt my skill as a historian?" laughed Rosemonde. "Didn't I teach you clairvoyance when you were a young pupil of mine? I've had time to prepare for your arrival. And anyway, it's not so long since the College of Sorcery was taking a great interest in Palladio."

He seemed to be looking for a cigarette, found a packet, and then thought better of it.

"There are still many shadowy areas in his life. But certain clues allow me to say that the Count has come to some kind of agreement with a being often mentioned within these ancient walls."

La Voisin's ecstatic face came back into Roberta's mind. So did the Black Masses, to invoke . . .

"The Devil," she breathed. "Of course. Palladio must have made a pact with the Devil. That would explain his immortality." She returned to her point at once. "Why was the College interested in Palladio?"

"When we were considering the struggle against . . . er, Satanism, I was asked to draw up an inventory of those pacts with the Devil that are preserved in French and Italian libraries. All the librarians cooperated with me except one, in the Libreria Marciana, the Venetian library, which was already in the Count's hands. I could not get access to the documents through the official channels, although I was aware that the library contained such pacts. However, I did not know just how many, or what their value was. I therefore appealed to an Italian colleague who managed to get into the Libreria. Palladio did indeed have original pacts. Four of them, in fact. One signed by the Count himself."

The Professor allowed several seconds to pass before continuing.

"So Palladio was spying for the Council of Ten up to that terrible night before the Feast of the Redeemer in 1570, and the assassination at the Palazzo Cambini. He was arrested three days later. Meanwhile the festival was in full swing. In the grip of fever, the young man conjured up

Satan, who promised him immortality in return for whatever he usually asks, perhaps the mortal's soul. By the same token, Palladio escaped capital punishment and Time itself. He was immortal now, and travelled in many continents over the centuries."

"And I met him in London looking like a man several hundred years old. If he asked for immortality, you could say that the Devil did him down."

"That's very much in the Devil's line, don't you think?" said Rosemonde. "I'm sure it all turns on his deceit—the astral twins, the Historic Cities, everything. You were asking me what I knew about the Killers' Quadrille. My reply is that there are four pacts in the Libreria Marciana."

The Professor certainly had a gift for dotting his i's and crossing his t's. Roberta felt excited by the new turn events had taken.

"I suppose your colleague didn't manage to take copies of those pacts?" she asked, not very hopefully.

"His body, or what the catfish had left of it, was found floating in the lagoon. All I know about the pacts is the catalogue number of the portfolio containing them: MS Italian IV 66 5548."

"MS Italian IV 66 5548," repeated the sorceress, thoughtfully. It was her turn to sigh. "So the third movement of the Quadrille will be danced in Venice."

Roberta had been studying ways of getting into the Libreria Marciana for over a week. She had done some research in the Basle municipal library, tried the Historic Cities Network, and asked Strudel to find her a magician or sorceress familiar with the area.

Eleazar had come up with a retired sorcerer called Nicodemus who had a passion for automata and clockwork mechanisms. Nicodemus had tried to consult the archives of the Rainieri brothers, masters of Venetian clockwork toymaking, but he too was refused access to the Marciana. The library had been privately owned ever since Palladio bought the floating city. And its surroundings seemed to be particularly well guarded.

Roberta was going to have to organize an outright burglary. And to do that she needed plans of the layout of the Libreria—recent plans. She knew that large-scale renovations had been carried out in the building over the last few years. Without those plans the sorceress hadn't a hope of getting hold of the pacts.

Beelzebub jumped on his mistress's lap and settled down there, after lovingly digging his claws into her thighs. The cat didn't often show affection, so Roberta started stroking him while she let her thoughts wander.

She hadn't been able to get the Devil out of her mind since her conversation with Monsieur Rosemonde—the Devil and his old connections with the College of Sorcery in the days before he went underground.

She had been twenty when the College signed the White Magic Charter with the Mayor. Changes had been taking place for some time, but the tracers had, so to speak, brought matters to a head. If the College were to survive, it must come out into the open.

The Charter specified that all black magic was now proscribed, teaching in the College must be interdisciplinary, and research was to explore fields useful to non-sorcerers. Invoking the Devil was forbidden. In exchange, the existence and location of the College would remain secret from the public at large.

The witch certainly had nothing to complain about. The tracers had practically eliminated crime from the mainland and hadn't upset her private life in the slightest. Even better, they had indirectly allowed her to work for Major Gruber.

All the same, the ban on invoking the Devil for any reason at all meant ignoring the darker side of a witch's nature. Although Roberta had been revolted by La Voisin's methods, a small part of her couldn't help admiring the woman. Monster as she was, she had the audacity to offer herself to her Master even after experiencing the agony of the stake . . .

Roberta brusquely removed her hand from Beelzebub's silky fur, realizing that her mind was wandering. La Voisin, a good example? Definitely not. Banning invocations of the Devil had made the College respectable, and a sorceress must surely welcome that.

Beelzebub dug his claws into Roberta, who unceremoniously threw him off her lap. The cat cast her an outraged glance and stalked into the kitchen, tail erect, making his rear end look like an indignant exclamation mark.

Roberta's skirt was covered with black hairs. It must be covered with tracers too. She brushed it down energetically. A quantity of golden dust motes flew up before falling gently towards the floor again.

They told a story about the tracers in the corridors

of the College, a story which had always intrigued Morgenstern. The last real Sabbath had been held two years before she began her sorcery studies. The Devil had always attended those Sabbaths, and he was invoked in due form with the sacrifice of a goat this time too. Not only had he failed to turn up, he had been silent ever since. As it happened, the tracers had appeared just before he was invoked ... perhaps the Devil didn't want to feature in the Records Office's statistics?

Someone knocked at her door. Roberta went to open it in her slippers. Young Martineau was standing outside, looking contrite.

"Miss Morgenstern," was all he said when he saw her.

Ever since his acrobatics on top of the tower of Saint-Jacques, the young investigator had been a puzzle to the sorceress. Like the Devil's silence or Palladio's motivation.

"Clément Martineau! What brings you here? Nothing wrong, I hope?"

"May I come in?"

Roberta didn't have to glance behind her to know that her flat looked like a battlefield, but she wasn't about to leave Martineau on the landing while she bustled about doing housework. Anyway, she hated housework.

"Come in, and try to find a space on the sofa spared by the enemy," she invited him.

Martineau came in, moved a pile of magazines and sat down. He had a leather briefcase under his arm, and placed it flat on his knees. The scar left by La Voisin at the corner of his lips had changed his face, which looked harder around the jawline.

"Tea, coffee?" asked the sorceress.

"I'd love a coffee."

She went into the kitchen to brew it, and came back a minute later with two steaming cups. Not many people could stand the bitter flavour of the mocha she made. She had inherited the recipe from her grandmother in sorcery, a lady of pure Armenian descent.

"Sugar?"

He shook his head and unflinchingly sipped the liquid. The sorceress observed him with interest. So Martineau was one of those rare people who could swallow her coffee without groaning!

"Have you recovered from all the excitement?"

Martineau put his cup down gently and, after thinking the question over for several seconds, replied indirectly, "I wanted to thank you for saving my life on the tower."

So he hadn't realized that he was keeping himself aloft in the air of his own accord. He thought he'd simply slipped.

"Don't mention it, dear boy. Gruber told me you took a holiday after Paris?"

"I—I heard that the Count had disappeared," said Martineau.

Roberta leaned forward and spoke very softly. "We're not on his case anymore. It's up to the War Ministry to act now. You heard what Gruber said? You did your job and now it's over."

"No, it's not over. I apologize for disturbing you at home, but I've had enough trouble finding your address already."

"Yes, how did you do it?" asked Roberta in surprise. That detail had escaped her.

"The porter at the Community Building sent me to the Two Salamanders, and I went to see your friend Strudel."

"Eleazar talked to you?"

Eleazar never talked to non-initiates, except to utter terrible platitudes that would have sent an insomniac dachshund to sleep.

"I spent yesterday morning with him. Charming man. He gave me that spruce liqueur of his. In short, he told me all about his friendship with you." Martineau made a vague, airy gesture. "I asked how you were getting on with the inquiry, and he told me where to find Monsieur Rosemonde. I made an appointment with him at once."

"You made an appointment with Monsieur Rosemonde?"

Roberta could hardly believe her ears. Was the young detective taking a rise out of someone? Out of the whole College, maybe?

"I saw him yesterday afternoon. He told me what he knew about this business. Count Palladio's life story, the pacts in the Marciana. Well, all that." Martineau's tone of voice was playful.

"Wait a minute, Martineau. Where did you see Rosemonde?"

"At the College, of course! That's where he asked me to go."

Roberta was stunned. No outsider, no "low-flyer," had ever been admitted to the College. She was dreaming, that was it, she must be still asleep.

"Listen, I know you want to go to Venice to consult the

226

pacts in the Marciana," the young man went on. "And I know the Marciana is very well guarded."

"It is indeed," replied the witch, who had decided to act as if she were taking this improbable conversation seriously. "So I suppose you can get me in."

"Yes."

Roberta sighed. "Don't try to be funny, Martineau. We'd need plans to get into the Libreria. That library is better guarded than the City Hall itself."

"You're right, we do need plans." He opened his brief-case, took out a packet of folded papers and handed them to Roberta. "Here they are."

The sorceress decided that she wasn't dreaming after all. She unfolded a number of large-scale architectural plans. They revealed the mysteries of the Marciana, ground plans and elevations, floor after floor. They indicated the position of the technical galleries. And the plans were dated only last year.

"How on earth did you get these?"

"It was one of the best deals Martineau Cement Industries ever did. Palladio commissioned my father to take charge of the refloating of the city. Martineau Cement got the job of reinforcing all the buildings so that they could stand up to the wear and tear of the lagoon. And various modifications were made to the Marciana at the same time."

Roberta refolded the plans as carefully as if they were precious maps of treasure islands. Martineau waited in silence.

"What are you doing over the next few days?" she asked at last.

He shrugged. "I don't have anything much planned. My car's parked down in the street. A Palladio Sealines Pelican takes off from the South Quay landing stage in about an hour. If we want to catch it we'll have to hurry."

"Are you thinking of driving me there in that noisy vehicle of yours?"

"Yes, by St. Christopher!" said the young detective enthusiastically.

"Come on then, Clément!" exclaimed the sorceress.

A ray of sunlight penetrated the grey atmosphere of Roberta's flat and fell straight on Beelzebub, who was watching the two detectives, his whiskers quivering. The cat gave a mournful mew, and stepped aside to return to the shadows.

MS Italian IV 66 5548

"Ah, Venice!"

Roberta was holding on to the rail with both hands, taking deep breaths of sea air. The floating city occupied a large part of the horizon. There was a clear view of church domes, the upper storey of the Doge's palace, and the campanile. Martineau's nose was buried in his Palladian *Historic Cities Guide*. She snatched the book from his hands and hid it behind her back.

"Hey, what's the idea?" he exclaimed.

"Take a look around you, dear boy!" Roberta made a sweeping gesture at the lagoon. "You'll have plenty of time to swallow that indigestible guidebook once we've reached the jetty."

"Give it back!" he snapped, looking like a sulky little boy.

The witch gave it back, whereupon the young man put it away without making any attempt to open it again, and looked at Venice itself. They were entering the Grand

Canal, which was crowded with boats of every kind. A gull passed the bows of the craft, skimming the grey water until it reached the medieval façade of the Doge's Palace, and then soared above the building in fantastic flight.

"Have you ever been to Venice before?" he asked the witch.

"No, have you?"

"Several times."

"With your father?"

"Well, yes."

A boat with a load of vegetables passed level with the vaporetto. The man steering it waved to them. Roberta responded vigorously.

"When the Count bought Venice from the World Heritage Organization," said Martineau, "he refloated it, as he put it. The city was in a terrible state, half drowned. He turned it into a floating city to save it from the muddy inferno which was swallowing it up. My father explained the whole principle to me when he took me to see the building site."

The vaporetto moved smoothly along the jetty extending from the Piazza San Marco. It was early afternoon. Crowds of tourists were making their way along the esplanade. Since most of the people in Venice were visitors, it was rather different from the other Historic Cities in the Network. Most tourists didn't bother to go to the wardrobe department, and it wasn't obligatory to dress in Venetian costume here—except, of course, at carnival time.

Roberta and Martineau were the last to disembark. They both had small travelling bags slung over their shoulders.

"We can drink chocolate at Florian's!" exclaimed Roberta, with sudden enthusiasm. "Embrace the Tetrarchs! Lose ourselves in Veronese green!"

There was a loud splash. Martineau had just missed the gangway, and was dog-paddling in the water between the boat and the steps down to the lagoon. Several tourists were pointing at him, convulsed with laughter. He hauled himself up into the piazza looking resigned, his shoes full of water and squelching.

"What on earth do you think you're playing at?" asked the sorceress.

"I keep doing it since we got back from Paris. I fell into a fountain outside my own flat. Crazy, eh? I get quite scared these days crossing the least little stream. It's like a curse!"

"Er . . . did you have anything to drink on the Pelican?"

"Just the quarter litre of wine they served with the conger eel. I drank that, yes. What are you getting at?" He pointed an accusing finger at the sorceress. "Don't tell me it's because of what you did to me in Paris?"

"You were dead drunk in Paris. Not a pretty sight," she reminded him mercilessly.

The young man began turning round on the spot, breathing heavily. He could have strangled the witch! But he was afraid she might turn him into something nasty before he touched her.

"It was a Viking spell that sobered you up," she added. "Viking spells take quite a while to wear off. Keep away from the booze and you'll be all right. It'll pass off in time. And if it doesn't, then at least you'll be doing your liver a favour." Then, taking pity on him, Morgenstern dried him off as she had on the Pont-Neuf, with two quick gestures and in the twinkling of an eye.

Mollified, the young man asked tentatively, "Could you teach me that trick?"

"We'll see."

"Right. Well, I suppose there's nothing we can do before nightfall?"

"Not really," agreed the witch.

"Then I'll be off. There's something important I have to do. Let's meet here at the end of the afternoon."

Roberta planted herself in front of the detective, hands on her hips, and looked at him suspiciously.

"Playing the Lone Ranger again? What exactly are you cooking up?"

"It's a surprise," replied Martineau with a disarming smile. He strode off towards the basilica, calling back to Morgenstern above the crowd, "And don't worry. I haven't sold out to the enemy!"

But anyway it suited the sorceress for Martineau to do whatever it was he had in mind this afternoon. She too wanted a little walk on her own before tackling the Marciana.

Martineau crossed the esplanade and did not stop until he reached the statuary group of Tetrarchs built into the base of St. Mark's. He hid behind the marble brothers and took out the envelope he had found in the Pelican. It was the third envelope since he'd started visiting the Historic Cities.

He had found the letter M in London and the letter E

in Paris. One more letter and he could send in his answer to Palladio Sealines. Then he might be one of the lucky winners of the puzzle game, "Find Three Letters to Visit a City." First prize was a week for two at the private Historic City reserved for the Club Fortuny. Martineau was near his goal now. Just one more puzzle to solve, and the dream holiday would be his.

This time the envelope did not contain any Open Sesame to help him, only a plain sheet of paper with a message which was enigmatic, to say the least. He read it out loud, since there were no indiscreet ears around to overhear him.

"The lion's mouth will tell you where to go." He folded the paper and repeated the words, looking at the crowd. "The lion's mouth will tell you where to go. So in the city of lions . . . yes, right."

Luckily he had boned up on his Palladian Guide well enough to know where the organizers of the game were sending him.

Leaving the basilica behind him, he walked past the Doge's Palace until he reached the Porta della Carta. A group of tourists was waiting on the white marble paving of the courtyard.

"*Signore e signori*, the tour is about to begin!" announced a guide. "We will start by climbing the Scala dei Giganti, the Giants' Stairway, to enter what was once the private dwelling of the Lord of Venice."

Martineau attached himself inconspicuously to the rear of the group. The guide led them up the steps. Passing between the monumental figures of Mars and Neptune, the group hurried through the first-floor rooms with scarcely any time to admire the huge pictures hanging from the walls and on the ceilings.

"It was here," said the guide, "that the judicial organizations of Venice met. The *avogaria* tried legal cases, the *provveditori* supplied the galleys, and the *censori* exercised censorship. We will now go up to the next floor and the hall of the Great Council."

Another gigantic stairway was climbed, and they entered a rectangular hall of incredible dimensions.

"Over here you can admire Tintoretto's *Paradise*. This canvas has been restored thanks to Count Palladio, the man who saved Venice from sinking into the lagoon."

The tourists, Martineau included, craned their necks to admire the concentric areas of the artist's idyllic vision, adorned with gold and other embellishments. The guide led them out of the hall and through a suite of smaller rooms. The young man didn't remember their names; what interested him was still to come.

They climbed yet another staircase, crossed the Hall of the Council of Ten, passed through a kind of antechamber panelled in black wood, and finally reached the Hall of the Compass. The guide took up his position in front of an ancient strong-box built into the wall. Its small metal door was on the level of his belt.

"The Sala della Bussola," he began, "is famous for containing one of the last two denunciation boxes in which the Venetians, born conspirators and informers that they were, deposited the names of people they suspected of immorality, heresy, espionage, or worst of all fiscal fraud."

The guide opened the denunciation box. Martineau jostled several people to get a view of its contents, but to his great disappointment it was empty.

"Notes were placed in the box on the other side of the wall, where there is a gallery open to the public. The boxes were called lions' mouths because on the informer's side of the wall they were shaped like the heads of lions. We will now pass on to the Armoury . . ."

Martineau left the group to continue its tour, and checked that there was no one who might take him by surprise. The room they had crossed was empty now. He opened the strong-box, felt its base, and found a latch which he opened without a moment's hesitation.

A piece of paper had been left in the double bottom of the denunciation box. The investigator took it out, put it in his inside jacket pocket without stopping to read it, closed the box again and left the Sala della Bussola like a burglar, his treasure close to his heart. He was jubilant. Bull's eye!

The guide was just closing the Armoury when Martineau reached it. He made haste to attach himself to the group again. Like the rest, he went down a spiral staircase and found himself in the palazzo courtyard at the foot of the Giants' Stairway. He sat down at the first café table he found in the Piazza San Marco and unfolded the piece of paper, expecting to see the third and last letter printed there in black and white.

"You will find me on the Zanini stake," he read, his heart beating fast. "Oh no!" he exclaimed, bringing his fist down on the table.

Well, Palladio Sealines might be leading him on from

one riddle to the next, but the inquiry agent was one of those people who are spurred on by obstacles. He took out his Palladian Guide and turned its pages feverishly, trying to make sense of the strange message of which he was now the lucky recipient.

Roberta was thinking of Palladio and his life, or his successive lives: Martinetto the pickpocket; the spy in the pay of the Ten; the murderer blinded by jealousy; last of all the adventurer pursuing his own ends from century to century, secret, sombre, sinister.

The more the sorceress thought about his history, the clearer did the trail of the Prince of Darkness become. Palladio had sold himself to the Evil One here in Venice, some time between 12th July 1570, the night of the double murder, and 23rd July of that year, the day of the trial during which the defendant claimed to be immortal. The pacts would soon confirm it. But why was the Count so keen to resuscitate famous historical killers?

MS Italian IV 66 5548. The answer lay there. Or so at least Roberta hoped.

She came out into a small square much like all the *campi* to be found in Venice. Gaps opened up between the paving stones. The sorceress knew that in the past they had allowed water to drain away from the city during the high equinoctial tides.

A few intrepid pigeons landed at Roberta's feet. Some of them began showing off, stalking round the square like matadors. A *bel canto* tune emerged from a house with projecting stonework carved in diamond shapes.

Roberta wondered what the Palazzo Cambini looked like—the place where Palladio had murdered Isabella and the man he took for her lover. Did it resemble the large buildings surrounding this square? The sorceress examined the paving stones for bloodstains, but found none. Sighing, she retraced her steps to return to the noise and bustle of the Piazza San Marco.

The enigmatic smile of the statues watching her pass, the buildings that looked too heavy to float on the lagoon, this whole grotesque theatrical set was a good illustration of the atmosphere that Palladio had tried to re-create in his Historic Cities. Ever since they set out on the trail of the first murderer, she and Martineau had been walking through an endless gallery of mirrors.

And what, the witch suddenly asked herself, what, I wonder, is young Clément up to now?

She passed Florian's, forgetting the promise she had made herself to go in. The café windows caught her reflection for a moment. Several customers turned to watch her pass by.

Where was that woman with the enigmatic expression going? In what *trompe-l'oeil* effect of this operatic city would she lose herself? No one could tell. But one thing was sure: neither the Devil nor anyone else seemed likely to stop her.

The gondola went along the Grand Canal, bobbing like a cork. Martineau had never really found his sea legs. He much preferred driving his car on its rally tyres along a pot-holed road, with the hood down. Although this was really much the same kind of movement.

Especially with that Viking curse still sticking to him. Just let those ancestral Scandinavian spirits try grabbing him again! He'd take them to the Sorcerers' Tribunal—if such a thing existed.

Some of the palazzi were dilapidated, others had recently been restored. Venice had a timeless charm and nobility, something that must have been natural to Palladio too before he became a strange creature clinging desperately to life, thanks to some kind of black magic learnt between the Serenissima, Cairo, and Istanbul.

Traffic on the water was dense. The gondolier was trying to avoid the breaking waves in the narrow passage left for him by the big vaporetti. He was making straight for a row of stakes planted in the lagoon. Each post was painted a different colour: red and white, green and white, blue with a yellow top . . .

The gondolier pointed out one of the stakes to the young man and steered his craft towards it.

"Zanini!" he cried, nodding vigorously. He was pointing to the first stake, which was bi-coloured, red and white. The gondola bumped into the wooden post. Martineau rose to catch hold of it, while the gondolier energetically plied his oar to give the boat some kind of stability. A week for two in the Club Fortuny city, Martineau reminded himself. He'd have earned it too, after surviving the horrific scenic railway in London, that lunch with Gorenflot, and now this.

He let out a cry of triumph. A letter X was carved into the worm-eaten wood. The young man had found his third letter.

A wave larger than the others raised the gondola and sent it implacably back towards the Grand Canal. Martineau, hands clutching the gunwale, looked at the surface of the waves, trying to see if any embryonic arms were hoping to seize him. He shouted at the lagoon in a sudden frenzy, "Well, what are you waiting for? Do I have to be dead drunk before you lay hands on me?"

He was on a high. He could have climbed a mountain, fought a dragon, trampled on the murderers one by one.

And he wasn't watching the gondolier, who was obviously losing control of his boat and clinging desperately to his oar. A vaporetto passed a little too close, engine roaring, sending a surge of grey water towards them. The wave tossed them violently aloft. The gondolier was sent flying from his little platform and fell into the lagoon.

The man flailed frantically at the surface of the waves, swallowing great gulps of water. He obviously couldn't swim. Ridiculous as it might seem for a gondolier, he was drowning. The detective was going to have to dive in to save him from the lagoon.

Martineau thought he heard Morgenstern's voice pointing out, "Lesson number one: never challenge the primordial powers."

The façade of the small building was rather insignificant by comparison with the beautiful palaces that were the pride of Venice. The proportions of the Scuola di San Giorgio degli Schiavoni were austere and less than graceful. The plaster of the outside walls was flaking away here and there, and the statues had disappeared from their niches. Nonetheless, the sorceress opened the little door and went in.

The interior was a single low-ceilinged room of modest dimensions, with two sets of black wooden pews. A veiled woman was kneeling before the altar. The walls were covered with paintings and dark wooden panelling.

This chapel was nothing like the magnificent interiors intended to display power that could be found all over the city. Roberta had entered a place of prayer reserved by the Council of Ten for the Dalmatians of Venice. The hall of the Scuola was like a study intended for meditation.

But the sorceress had not come here to pray. She was here to see the paintings that had made this place famous. Each measured a little over two metres long by fifty centimetres high. The St. George cycle was on the left, the St. Jerome cycle on the right. The Venetian artist called Carpaccio—a man whom Palladio might have met in person—had painted them in the sixteenth century.

Roberta approached the canvas depicting the triumph of St. George. The warrior saint was holding the dragon on the end of a rope, while horses pranced in the middle ground of the picture behind him. A small crowd was admiring his brave deed. Fantastic architecture rose on the horizon. Carpaccio's paintings were both beautiful and sinister, like those alluring flowers whose stamens are full of poison. Look at me, they were saying, admire me. And if you weren't careful you would go in without thought, and find yourself admiring quite a different aspect of the world of the painting.

"I have a feeling that Carpaccio painted his pictures

from the inside, not the outside," Roberta's mother liked to say. "Otherwise there's no explaining the effect of transparency, the detail, the totality of his art."

A clock chimed. Roberta was due to meet young Martineau in the Piazza San Marco, and she must make haste if she wanted to abandon herself to the atmosphere of the paintings and plunge into that other world, just as she did when she was a little girl and ventured to peep behind a forbidden door.

She remembered that when her father had asked what she was looking for in his studio, she had said vaguely, "Something."

"But suppose it's a nightmare you find?" he had asked.

"I'll turn it into a dream," the little girl had replied with unshakeable confidence.

"And suppose you find a dream?"

Roberta still missed her parents.

The woman who had been praying had left, unnoticed by the sorceress, who was now alone with the painter. Roberta stationed herself in front of *St. George and the Dragon*.

The horse was a creature of monumental splendour. The warrior's lance traced a diagonal line through the picture straight to the mouth of the monster, whose paws were raised. Its tail was contorted to emphasize the pain it was suffering. Human remains lay beneath the dragon. A legless torso was propped against a low wall, like the fragment of a classical statue.

Magicians and witches had a gift that even the College could not explain: it was known as immersion. Roberta's mother had been able to move in person through the works of Brahms, the paintings of the Flemish primitives and many great works of literature. She often took her husband with her, when she went into the pictures of Van Eyck and Broederlam. They had spent their honeymoon in a pretty house lent to them by the Arnolfini.

Immersion was all a matter of taste. It was your personal inclinations that allowed you to immerse yourself physically in a particular work of music, literature, or art.

Roberta's own tastes had allowed her to visit nineteenth-century Paris courtesy of the pen of Emile Zola, to gallop full tilt over the frozen lakes orchestrated by Prokofiev, to marvel at the night sky over Baghdad thanks to Rimski-Korsakov's *Scheherazade*, and to join Perrault's Cinderella in a fairy-tale castle.

And Percy Faith wasn't by any means the end of her list.

Vittore Carpaccio, however, was the only artist for whom mother and daughter had shared a liking. His few extant pictures were their secret garden, although neither of them had ever had the chance to enter his most important cycles, the pictures preserved in Venice.

Roberta narrowed her eyes, concentrated on a detail of the painting, and let her senses carry her away. Her peripheral vision gradually blurred. The painted shapes began to move. There was a distant sound of clashing armour. The odour of rotting flesh rose to her nostrils. She heard the heavy breathing of a man making a violent physical effort, and the roaring of the dragon.

Now she was right inside the picture, behind the little wall against which the torso, head, and shoulders of the corpse were propped. Very quietly, Roberta rose to her feet.

She was astonished by the detail and violence of the scene. St. George was incredibly clear-cut. His armour cast dark reflections around him, and as for the dragon, it might have been carved from marble. The lance passed right through its muzzle and it fell, uttering a howl that seemed to shake the stones themselves. The saint retreated, drew his broken lance out of the creature's mouth, and struck the creature's flanks. It was still groaning faintly. Roberta almost felt sympathy for the monster and dislike for the saintly figure in armour, whose face, now that she saw it straight on, was distorted by hatred and ferocity.

How Roberta wished her mother were here with her! How often they had dreamed of entering the picture like this as they studied old reproductions of Carpaccio's works in the Scuola San Giorgio! At that time Venice had been derelict, a kind of no-man's-land abandoned to the pirates of the lagoon, and visiting it was impossible.

A woman began to shout. The Princess of Trebizond had seen Roberta. St. George turned angrily, and he too saw the witch. He said something incomprehensible, cast his lance aside, unsheathed his sword, and dug his heels into his horse's sides. Whinnying, it set off at the gallop.

The sorceress hastily retreated just as the charging steed was almost upon her.

Then she was outside the picture again, standing facing it. St. George's lance was a perfect diagonal between his arm and the dragon's jaws. The Princess of Trebizond was no longer shouting, but watching the scene from one side of the painting with a kind of fatalistic, unchanging detachment.

Yet the sorceress could still smell the odour of the

monster and hear the wet, leathery sound of its wings beating the air as its enemy the saint pierced its entrails.

"Homunculus alive!" she muttered, shaken by her experience.

The clock chimed five. It was high time to go and meet Martineau.

"And at the end of this corridor we ought to find a door coming out on the first-floor landing."

"Or alternatively we might find death," commented Morgenstern, gloomier than ever.

Martineau, who had the architect's plan spread out in front of him, cast a despairing glance at the witch. "What's bugging you? You've been looking like death since we met just now. Anything I can do to help?"

"I don't think so, Martineau."

Roberta's morale was at rock bottom, but she didn't know why. Depression had descended on her just after she left the Scuola. Martineau himself was in a very good mood, but seemed unable to communicate his delight. Anyway, Morgenstern herself didn't feel like communicating, except to moan a bit.

"Let's get moving," she said, and set an example by starting out along the gently sloping service corridor. Pipes of different colours ran along the ceiling five metres overhead.

"Ah, here's our door."

The metal panel had a pneumatic handle. Martineau operated it, and they came out on the first-floor landing of the Libreria. The door closed again behind them. On this side, its colours merged with those of a Renaissance tapestry that moved slightly and then fell still, making the door perfectly invisible. The detective leaned over the banisters of the staircase.

"The ground floor down there is stuffed with sensors, but as far as Martineau Cement knows there's no security system installed up on this floor. Which is just as well, because this is the one we want."

The Stations of the Cross were carved over the entrance to the reading room. One scene in particular caught the witch's attention: a picture of a small crowd climbing the hill of Golgotha, mocking the tortured Christ. The artist had even carved the tears running down his cheeks.

"Is there a problem?" asked the young man. "Will you need your special door-opening spell to tackle this one?"

"What?" said Roberta, emerging from her trance. "No, no. I was just admiring the carving. Lovely work, four-teenth century. Florentine."

She turned the handle, and the door opened without a sound.

"Just look at that!" she said, delighted.

The reading room of the Libreria extended ahead of them, running far into the building. Golden late afternoon light fell through the windows looking out on the Piazza San Marco. The noise of the bustling crowd in the Piazza was muted by the double glazing of the library windows.

The room itself had a series of shelving units on two levels all the way along. A spiral wrought iron staircase led to the upper gallery. Below it were cupboards, busts, and display cases containing the most valuable works in the library. Tables with feet carved like lion's paws stood here and there with huge geographical maps spread out on them, four tables in all, in different parts of the room.

"I'll just take a look at what's in those display cases," said Martineau, evidently about to go that way. But Roberta suddenly grabbed his collar and yanked him violently back before he could set foot on the floorboards. He turned towards her indignantly, clutching his throat.

"What's the idea?" he said crossly. "What's come over you?"

Roberta pointed to the floor just where he would have trodden, and at another place a couple of metres to the right. Two tiny, decomposed rodent corpses lay in the middle of the star-shaped pattern in the parquet. Their bones had crumbled to countless fragments. The star pattern was repeated all over the floor, from the doorway where they stood to as far as they could see.

"Pentagrams," explained the witch. "I was trapped by one of them at Versailles. An invention of the Count's. I wouldn't advise you to try it out."

"Great. What does it do?"

"It holds you captive and turns your bones to crystal. Then the slightest jolt is fatal."

"What now, then?"

Roberta studied the floor. There was no way of avoiding the trap. The stairs to the gallery were too far from the door. And they couldn't risk making a dash for it, even groping their way, for fear of getting partly or entirely caught in one of the shapes on the floor.

A grey shape began scurrying to the far side of the library, uttering little squeaks.

"What's that?" asked Martineau.

Squeaks from another source made the witch spin round. She saw a dormouse cross the landing. It scuttled past her feet and jumped down on the floor to join its companion at the other side of the room. The tiny rodent evidently knew the way by heart. It ran over two stars in a straight line, turned left, then right, then went straight ahead again. On a sudden impulse, Roberta followed it, telling Martineau, "Come on!"

The dormouse stopped on the edge of each star, sniffed, and then set off in a definite direction. Its twisting, turning route followed the harmless pentagrams among the patterns that the Count had set in the floor.

They were now in the middle of the reading room. Roberta had stopped counting the number of desiccated rodent corpses surrounding them, and was concentrating on the safe path chosen by the dormouse, which was now racing straight ahead like a rocket to join its friend. The two little animals disappeared behind the skirting board, squeaking.

"Morgenstern!" called Martineau.

His voice was too faint for him to be just behind her. The young man was only halfway over the floor, standing on one foot between a cupboard and the second table covered by maps. He obviously dared not put the other down.

"By Uranus, Martineau, what on earth are you doing?"

"I've lost the track," he whispered. "Where do I go next?"

The area of floor he had to cross was not very wide, but there were no dead dormice to tell him which way to go. Any of the eight pentagrams around him could be a trap.

And Roberta couldn't remember which way she had taken through that part of the labyrinth.

"What shall I do?" begged Martineau anxiously.

"Don't move."

One problem at a time. So long as he stayed where he was, he was in no danger.

The witch went over to a display case on the very edge of the booby-trapped area. It contained a number of works with invisible titles, their bindings ornamented with monsters or complex geometrical figures.

Roberta raised the glass top of the display case and picked up a book at random.

The *Liber de metallis transformandis et de natura eorundem.* She recognized this book on alchemy by the stamp identifying it: the "Book of the Transmutation of Metals and of Their Nature." She leafed through it rapidly. Roger Bacon and his inspired intuition . . . Putting it down, she picked up another: Giovanni Cinelli's *Treatise on Chemistry,* illustrated by the author. Next to it were the *Book of the Transmutation of Metal* by Hermes Trismegistus, followed by his *Study of True Science.*

"Morgenstern," groaned Martineau.

He was still a prisoner of the star patterns, poor boy. Roberta sighed and went through the works faster. She put aside the complete works of Christopher of Paris, the *Summa* of Albertus Magnus, Archelaus's treatise . . .

A black leather folder was jammed between the two volumes of Gratiani's *Liber de chemica.* It bore a faded label—MS Italian IV 66 5548. That was the catalogue number given her by Monsieur Rosemonde. Roberta picked up the folder and opened it.

Four parchment documents separated by loose sheets of India paper. Four different hands. Four languages. Four dates. Four signatures. But they were all marked with the same initial, a mark that the witch knew very well, for she had studied it at the College of Sorcery.

"Morgenstern!" cried Martineau.

Roberta put the folder under her arm and closed the display case before going back to the maze of star-shaped patterns.

"How long can you stay put?" she asked, her voice rather unsteady.

"You mean you can't get me out of here? For heaven's sake, Morgenstern, do something!"

Roberta looked at the corpses of the dormice who had fallen into a trap and were shattered to pieces, just as Palladio had shattered her astral twin in the Gallery of Mirrors. Martineau wouldn't be able to move without breaking his bones. If only she'd brought the Gustavson, he could have asked the dormice the way. But she had decided to leave him in Paris for a rest. What a fool she was!

"Suppose I just follow my nose?" suggested the detective desperately. "I could use my intuition."

"I wouldn't advise it."

But what other advice could she give? Wait until cramp disabled him? Morgenstern was feeling more helpless than ever. She was cursing Palladio and herself too for dragging the young investigator into this mad adventure.

"The one on my left . . . I'm sure that one's OK!" said the young man, trying to convince himself. He took a deep breath, closed his eyes, and stepped on the left-hand star. Morgenstern almost cried out, but she stopped herself. It was a miracle! The young man didn't seem to have fallen into a trap.

Martineau moved straight on over two more stars and then turned right, still with his eyes closed. He hesitated briefly, almost moved to the right, but finally went left. Straight on over two stars, then a left turn. Right and then left again. When he opened his eyes he was out of the trap. The sorceress hadn't moved. She was standing there like a statue, looking at him.

"How—how did you do that?" she asked.

He shrugged his shoulders. His hands were shaking slightly. "Maybe I was a dormouse in an earlier life?" he suggested. "I expect that's why I don't like hedgehogs. Too many nasty memories."

Roberta tapped the folder under her arm. "Well. I've found what we were looking for. Don't let's stay in this frightful place any . . ."

Her voice died away. She had just realized the full extent of her stupidity.

"What is it?" asked the young man.

Morgenstern went over to the wall at the far end of the room. It was a wooden partition with no door in it. The windows were out of reach. Martineau too realized what was wrong.

"Don't say we're stuck!"

"Well, well! Our two intrepid investigators!" exclaimed a voice at the other end of the room. "Anything we can do for you?"

Simmons was standing in the doorway of the reading room in his usual black suit, hands behind his back, a mocking expression on his face. Roberta tucked the folder into her waistband against the small of her back.

"Simmons!" cried Martineau, with obvious relief. "We're stuck! Go and get help!"

"Help?" said Palladio's henchman in surprise. "Why do you need help?"

He stepped on the first pentagram.

"Watch out!" yelled the young man.

Simmons went straight on to the second star, turned left and then right. He walked on without even looking at his feet. On reaching the first table he brought a rifle with a telescopic sight out from behind his back. Given the size of the gun, its bullets must be powerful enough to bring down a colossus from a considerable distance.

"Got the idea now, have you?" snapped Roberta, for Martineau's benefit. "Your friend isn't going to be much use to us."

Simmons was standing in the middle of the room. He stopped, raised his rifle, and aimed somewhere between the two investigators. They dropped as a deafening explosion shook the floor. A strip of wood shattered behind them. Simmons moved on again, rifle over his shoulder, ducking as if he were stalking game in some kind of safari.

"We have to get out of this fix," commented Morgenstern.

"Er . . . yes. But unless we change into dormice, I don't see how!"

Martineau thought that Roberta had taken him at his

word, because she went down on all fours. He copied her. She was evidently looking for the hole through which the dormice had escaped.

"A mousehole can be enlarged."

"Still there, are you?" called Simmons, who couldn't see them now they were at floor level. Judging by the sound of his voice he had moved yet closer. Crouching down by the hole, Morgenstern was murmuring something unintelligible while she scraped at the wood with a fingernail.

"What are you doing?" asked Martineau fretfully.

She suddenly rose to her feet and spoke straight to Simmons. "You can carry on, my friend. The witch-hunting season's open."

Simmons didn't wait to be asked twice. Martineau, who was raising his head to watch the outcome of Morgenstern's suicidal gesture, flung himself to the floor as a double detonation rang in his ears. Roberta hadn't moved an inch.

The young man heard the bullet whistle over his head. The part of the skirting board on which the sorceress had been working exploded. It was a good three metres from the place at which Simmons had been aiming, and was much too low for him to have hit it directly. A hole about fifty centimetres in diameter had just appeared in the partition wall. The sorceress knelt down beside Martineau.

"It's a question of the properties of matter," she explained. "Wood will attract metal when you give the right command."

"Wood will attract metal?"

"And we're attracting Simmons, so get through that

hole. Tell yourself you're a large and agile rodent being chased by a great big cat. A cat even more agile than you are."

Martineau scrambled through the hole and found himself in a windowless room, with pictures hanging on the walls. He raced for the door in one wall as Morgenstern joined him. The door was locked. Martineau slammed his shoulder against it, but only wore himself out.

"Yes, out of the frying-pan into the fire," agreed the sorceress.

The door was clearly protected by a magic spell, and refused to give way. Roberta ignored it and went over to one of the paintings, trying to make out its composition despite the dim light.

"Is this the time for cultural tourism?" said Martineau crossly.

She did not reply. If this canvas wasn't a forgery, or a copy made in the artist's studio, they might perhaps be saved.

"Ask Mr. Simmons to make our mousehole bigger so that I can get a better view," she said.

She seemed to mean it. Martineau complied, venturing close to the hole and sticking his foot out as bait. "Hey, Simmons! We're falling asleep here! What's keeping you?"

He withdrew his foot just before more of the wooden partition was shattered to pieces. The gap now came up to Martineau's waist. He could hear Simmons on the other side taking his time over reloading his gun.

"Coming!" Simmons sang out. "Just coming!"

"Right, we're safe," announced the witch. She took the young man by the sleeve and made him look at the picture,

253

which was now well enough lit for her. "What do you think?" she asked him.

"How do you mean, what do I think?"

"That picture. Do you like it?"

Martineau made himself read the caption underneath it. *The Dream of St. Ursula*, by Vittore Carpaccio. The painting showed a woman asleep in a huge bed while an angel approached her on tiptoe.

"Carpaccio. Yes, not bad."

"Do you or do you not like it?"

"I like it," said Martineau.

"Then look hard at some detail in it, never mind which, and relax."

"Relax? You must be joking!"

Simmons had finished reloading. He could be crouching down or already taking aim at them. Martineau turned to see what was going on. The witch took him by the nape of his neck and pressed a certain spot on it. Clément felt his body slackening, his mind taking flight, his eyes flickering.

"There. You're nicely relaxed now."

She took his hand in hers and led him towards the wall as if it didn't exist. Martineau felt his peripheral vision blur, and braced himself. The painted shapes organized themselves into a kind of anteroom. You could see part of a bed in the next room through an open door.

"Where are we?" asked the young man. His voice sounded strangely muffled in his own ears.

"In *St. Ursula*. We don't want to hang about here long. Follow me, and don't lose your way this time."

They slipped into the bedroom. Martineau recognized

the scene, although he was now viewing it from a different angle. The woman murmured in her sleep, uttering little groans. The angel was approaching the bed at snail's pace.

"We're inside the picture!" he suddenly realized.

He felt something catch hold of his trouser leg and tug furiously at it. A small dog with a yellow coat, paws planted firmly on the wooden floor, was trying to hold him back.

"Morgenstern," said Martineau, in a very small voice.

"Now what?" asked the sorceress. She didn't smile when she saw what was going on. "Don't move, Martineau, while I remember the spell that immobilizes such terrible monsters."

He tried to move his leg back, but the dog refused to let go. St. Ursula turned over in bed, muttering. Morgenstern, down on her knees, was talking softly to the animal.

"Good doggie. Let the nice gentleman go and you'll get a lovely lump of sugar."

The dog let go of Martineau's trouser leg and approached the witch, head lowered, tail frantically thumping the floor. Morgenstern gave it a sugar lump which she had indeed taken out of her pocket. The detective sighed.

"What do we do now?"

"We get out of this picture, we go through the St. Ursula cycle, we move on into the St. George cycle, and from there we get back to the real world."

"If I didn't know you, Morgenstern, I'd say you were totally nuts."

"Do call me Roberta, dear boy. And stop complaining. Lots of people would love to see this painting the way we're seeing it now."

The young man looked around him, but the sight of the

painted room left him cold. "How about Simmons? What do we do about him?"

"He's part of the other reality. It's as if we'd just left him by the roadside."

"But suppose he suddenly felt like firing point-blank at this picture?"

"Then the Ministry would report us missing."

The little dog suddenly turned towards the anteroom and rushed off that way, barking furiously. Ursula sat up in bed just as Simmons burst into the room. He raised his gun and aimed at the sorceress. The only thought that came into Roberta's mind was that Simmons must like Carpaccio's painting too. Well, at least that was a point in his favour.

The dog jumped up at him. Simmons struck it with the butt of his rifle, kicked it into one corner of the room, took aim and fired. The dog fell dead as thunder rolled through the painted room.

St. Ursula had fainted. The angel hadn't noticed anything. Simmons was aiming at the two fugitives again.

"Run for it!" cried the sorceress.

They rushed through the side door and found themselves on the banks of the Grand Canal. Night was falling as crowds hurried along beside the quays. A handsome bridge crossed this arm of the lagoon.

"What are we doing in the *Miracle of the Cross*?" wondered Morgenstern aloud. "It was never part of the St. Ursula cycle!"

"We're in Venice, aren't we?" Martineau pointed out.

"We are. So let's not wait for Simmons to catch up with us."

They made their way through a crowd of Venetian nobles, who stared as if they had no idea what Morgenstern and Martineau could be doing here. Two minutes later they were crossing the old Rialto bridge and plunged into the winding alleys of a Venice that was part real, part imaginary.

"This St. George cycle—how do we get to it?"

"By finding the St. Ursula cycle again and then reaching a particular scene in it," Roberta explained.

There was no sign of Simmons, but they still kept turning round to see if they were being followed.

"What scene?"

"*The Wedding*. It's set beside the sea, and certain stylistic details link the picture to the fight between St. George and the dragon. The feel of the landscape—the mast of a ship at a diagonal angle that's repeated in the line of the saint's lance."

"Was it art history or sorcery you studied?"

"A bit of both. Wait."

She had heard something. They were in the middle of a square that the painter had not finished painting. It contained a well standing against a background empty of detail, just a blank space. Roberta strained her ears, but the noise she had heard had died away. The young man pointed to the black folder still tucked into her waistband.

"Are those the pacts?"

"We'll have plenty of time to study them once we get out of here. There it is again!"

"What?"

The paving stones of the little square began shaking, and flakes of paint fell round them. A row of chimneys cracked and was carried away up to the golden yellow sky in a whirling cloud of dust. Two vast paving stones rose like the wings of a double door opening and pushed the unfinished well over. A horse reduced to a single continuous line rose to the surface of the paving and stopped in front of them. Simmons was perched on its back.

"How do you like this little sketch?" he inquired. "I found it under the top layer of paint."

The sketched horse conveyed a latent menace. Unfinished though it was, it was a perfect foil for the man sitting on it. If Simmons had thought, "Forward!" the horse would surely have moved forward. If he had thought, "Trample them!" it would have turned on the fugitives to trample them underfoot. The young man and the sorceress retreated to the other side of the square.

"Do you know how this pictorial world works? I mean, do you think imaginary things can turn real?" Martineau asked Morgenstern.

"Of course they can," she said, never taking her eyes off Simmons.

Martineau frowned, concentrating hard. Simmons reloaded his gun and pointed it at Morgenstern, whom he considered the more dangerous of the two.

"Palladio Sealines hopes you have enjoyed your trip," he said, forgetting to smile this time.

"Jump on!" cried the young man, suddenly hauling at the witch's arm.

He was sitting astride a motorbike that had appeared from nowhere. Morgenstern didn't try to make sense of it; she just jumped on behind Martineau. He started up, and the bike raced away, engine roaring. Simmons fired. The bullet hit the paving stones just where the motorbike had been a second earlier. As he prepared to fire again, his targets were making off at full speed through the winding alleyways of old Venice. The sound gradually grew quieter and then died away entirely.

Simmons lowered his weapon and patted his horse's non-existent collar. A clever lad, young Clément Martineau. With a vivid imagination too. But Simmons could be imaginative himself . . .

"Could you slow down a bit?" shouted Roberta over the detective's shoulder.

The young man had been riding at breakneck speed for a good five minutes, going as fast as he could through the tortuous succession of bridges, roofed passages, and winding alleys in Carpaccio's Venice, all of them faithful to the original. Martineau rode up a bridge, accelerating one last time. They rose in the air and came back down to earth several metres away in a shower of sparks.

They stopped in the middle of a huge square surrounded by buildings that looked like classical tombs. Painted figures were watching them from afar. If I decide to get off this infernal machine, thought Morgenstern, they'll run away howling. She got off the powerful motorbike, slightly dazed by the ride. Sure enough, the painted people did run away howling.

A radiant smile spread over Martineau's features. He looked elated, almost drugged, as if he were hallucinating. If the sorceress had told him to wear his tyres out riding round and round the huge square he'd have done it on the spot, laughing like a madman.

"Oh, marvellous!" she grumbled. She could feel a migraine coming on very fast. Oh for ordinary public transport! "Who taught you to ride like that?" she snapped. "Were you trying to kill us or what? Tired of life, are you, you stupid idiot?"

Martineau had been expecting to be congratulated on the skills he had just shown. "But I—we've shaken off Simmons!" he pleaded.

"Yes. See that round building over there?"

She pointed to the largest tomb. Its façades had evidently been designed by a master of perspective. The young man nodded.

"Then ride that wretched bike into it. Test the ability of Venetian painting to absorb shocks. Go on, and I'll take notes."

Martineau shrugged and turned off the motorbike engine, which was still idling.

"Very funny!" he said in some annoyance.

Three Venetian noblemen rather braver than their companions were approaching with a determined tread, their robes—yellow, red, and blue—bright against the immaculate ruled grid of the square in the background.

"Where are we?" asked Martineau.

"Back in the St. Ursula cycle. This is *The Wedding*."

The delegation in its colourful robes was now halfway to them. They could make out what the Venetians were waving above their heads: daggers and short swords.

"I suggest we skip the chapter on 'The Study of Weapons in Venetian Painting,'" said Roberta, getting back on the bike behind Martineau. "Quick, get us into the next scene."

The young man turned the ignition key and brought all his weight down on the kick-start. The engine coughed but failed to catch. He tried again, twice, three times, adjusting the throttle, but no luck. The three men were only fifty or so metres away now. And the rest of the wedding party, feeling bolder, was beginning to follow their example. A menacing circle had formed around the intruders and was closing steadily in on them.

"Like me to get off and push?" suggested Morgenstern.

The young man grunted. The bike began to move, but almost immediately stalled.

"Oh, hell!" he swore, bending over the engine. "Where the devil's the fuel inlet?"

Twenty more metres and the crowd would be on them. If they stoned this roaring demon to death they could chalk it up to the saint's credit. The witch knew spells to stop a certain number of angry attackers, but she couldn't hold a large mob at bay. They were going to be mincemeat!

A shadow came over the sky just as a foetid smell filled the air. Carpaccio's Venetians had stopped.

A dragon with a dog's head, a serpent's tail, and bat's wings was flying over them like a gigantic bird of prey. It darted a pointed tongue at part of the crowd and opened its jaws, hissing. A flame ten metres long shot down to the ground.

Everyone not transfixed by terror started running about in disorder. The dragon gave chase, amusing itself by raising barriers of flame here and there, turning the Venetian dignitaries into human torches, filling the square with a horrible smell of burnt flesh.

Martineau, still intent on starting the recalcitrant engine, hadn't seen, smelt, or heard anything. "This ought to do it," he said, jumping down on the kick-start again.

The motorbike finally started. Only then did the investigator realize that the crowd had disappeared. Scorch marks the size of houses blackened the esplanade. He was about to ask the sorceress what powerful magic she had used to disperse the crowd when she urged, her expression distraught, "Get going, Martineau!"

What could have got her into such a state? He'd had enough of all this secrecy. The young man thought it was about time she took him into her confidence . . .

Something very heavy dropped to the ground just behind the motorbike and Morgenstern's back. It was as big as an apartment block and had a green, shiny skin. The monster unfolded its wings, darkening the sky. Martineau recognized Simmons. In spite of the scales now covering him, his face hadn't changed.

"What . . . ?" he stammered in astonishment.

Morgenstern pushed in the clutch and reached for the handlebars. The motorbike started off with a roar. Clément took over at the controls again while Roberta wrapped her arms round his waist. The hot breath blowing down their necks told them that Simmons had only just missed his target. The sorceress saw the dragon take off behind them, gaining height.

"Which way?" he asked.

"Along the canal!"

Had she really said along the canal? Was she mad? There were any number of people walking beside the canal. Not to mention the ships by the quayside and the merchandise being unloaded from them!

"Turn left, Martineau!" shouted Roberta.

He throttled down just as a column of flame fell straight towards them from the sky. Martineau accelerated again and rode the bike through a tight set of S-bends to get back to the quays.

The dragon flew in front of them, roaring, barely two metres above ground level. Its head was following their course, while its heavy body tried to correct the momentum sending it the other way. Simmons spat another jet of flame, but it was lost far behind the motorbike.

Martineau was now making his way past the piles of barrels, the sailors, and the gangplanks of ships tied up to the quay.

"Make way! Make way there!" he yelled, hooting the horn frantically.

The space ahead of them was in a state of pandemonium. People were jumping into the canal or swerving aside at the last moment, and Martineau had great difficulty in manoeuvring the bike. There seemed to be an empty space far ahead, but he wasn't sure he could reach it.

Something exploded on their right. Simmons had just breathed fire on a caravel with a cargo of gunpowder, turning the whole canal into a sheet of flame. The dragon flew over the lagoon and swung round to return to the attack. They were stuck in the traffic jam caused by the panic. Simmons was coming back now with a great flurry of wings. Only ten metres to go and they would escape him.

"Out of the way!" shouted Martineau, as the motorcycle brushed past robes, fine fabrics, brocade.

The dragon had them in its sights, jaws open. Your turn now, my dear, Roberta told herself. She spread her arms, posing like a high priestess, and declaimed above the shouting of the crowd:

"O waves, be separated! O armies, be dispersed! May every obstacle be set aside, for me and for my people!"

A huge force sent people and barrels flying up in the air, leaving the way clear for them. Martineau stepped on the gas and made for the open space ahead. The dragon sent a hurricane of fire after them. They raced away from the inferno, the wedding, and the general chaos around them.

They were now riding along a deserted ramp, its details blurring as they went. The structure of the ramp came into view, only to be replaced by empty air.

They were flying towards a stony wasteland. The motorbike came slowly down and bounced off the surface of the painting. Morgenstern and Martineau were thrown in the air and dropped several metres away. The bike toppled over and came to rest against a low wall.

They were safe and uninjured.

The sorceress got to her feet, massaging her behind. She hated to think what colour it would be tomorrow. Probably as purple as an aubergine.

"Are we in *St. George*?" asked the young man, rubbing his forehead, amazed to find he was still alive.

Morgenstern nodded. This was certainly the same landscape she remembered visiting earlier, but minus the saint and the dragon. Martineau cast a critical eye on the human remains scattered around the place.

"I wouldn't mind getting back to our own world," he suggested.

"Motion unanimously carried. The way out is behind that wall."

The sorceress was preparing to go first when something hard prodded the small of her back. She turned, very slowly. The majestic figure of St. George was looking down at her from his steed. His face was full of scorn, his armour looked darker than ever.

The warrior raised his purplish-black lance. He slipped it into the leather holder slung over his horse's right flank and held it in place with one arm. The horse did not move.

"You," the saint asked the witch in a heavy accent, "you causa alla zis . . ." He gestured vaguely with his free hand, indicating the motorbike and the dead body parts. "You causa alla zis disorrrrder?"

He rolled his r's and spoke gutturally, deep in his throat. She didn't know what to say, but the saint did not seem to have taken particular offence.

"I alrrready see-a you. You disappearrrr! Pouf! *Come una nuvola.* You *strega*—witch!"

Roberta felt as if she were walking on eggshells. Vulture's eggshells. The warrior saint might be even more dangerous than the dragon they had just escaped.

"We kill-a *streghe* here," confirmed St. George, putting his hand to the hilt of his sheathed sword.

They would never have time to get round behind the wall, and she was terrified of the warrior. She had always imagined Death—her own death—looking like this: noble, implacable, half animal and half human.

The horse began pawing the ground. St. George looked suspiciously around. Then, without explanation, he moved away from their side of the painting. His horse furiously kicked the rock. Roberta saw the Princess of Trebizond, a silent, withdrawn figure, standing in her corner with the submissive, forlorn expression given her by the painter.

"Here! Martineau!"

The young man joined the witch, and they raced round behind the wall. St. George paid them no further attention whatsoever.

"He looked hopping mad," commented Martineau.

"You'd have come to my aid if things had turned out badly, I'm sure."

Martineau did not reply. There was a sudden gust of wind, and a flabby green dragon came down in the centre of the landscape, raising a cloud of dust.

"Martineau? Morgenstern?" called Simmons. "Where are you, my little dears?"

The young man would have liked to get straight out of the painting, but Morgenstern put a hand on his shoulder to make him stay put.

"Watch this!" she whispered in his ear.

"I can hear you!" hissed Simmons. He rose on his hind legs, head stretched towards the wall.

"Drago!" called St. George.

The monster turned to see who was summoning him just as the warrior galloped towards him, lance lowered. Its point plunged into Simmons's throat. He spread his wings in the sudden shock of pain. A rivulet of blood stained his throat and then his gigantic, dog-like, scaly chest.

"Wow!" murmured Martineau.

The two investigators stepped back and found themselves in the Scuola di San Giorgio degli Schiavone, which was dimly illuminated by moonlight, looking at the picture from the outside. St. George and the dragon were no longer moving. The roar of the scene had died away.

Morgenstern wondered if Simmons had died at the moment of being painted. She considered Carpaccio perfectly capable of immortalizing him at the height of his agony without going to the trouble of killing him first . . . but such idle speculation was for art historians, the sorceress reminded herself. The pacts were in their hands. That was all that mattered.

"Wow," repeated Martineau, who was having difficulty in coming down to earth.

ARCHIBALD FOULD'S OFFICE

The lift took Martineau up to a waiting room on the top floor of the Community Building. The young man got out and made for a double door covered with red velour. He knew that the tracers everywhere on this floor were keeping watch on him. Heart beating fast, he opened the door and entered the office of Archibald Fould, the powerful and much-feared Minister of Security.

A first glance showed him a view of the outside world seen through a wall of glass on one side of the room. The windows were lashed by the rain that had been falling non-stop in Basle for the last week. Another wall was lined with shelves. The Minister's desk stood in the middle of the room, massive and monolithic, like an altar. Blotters, a pencil box, paperweights, and files stood on it like so many cult objects.

Morgenstern was sitting in an armchair. Gruber, in his usual anthracite-grey suit, sat in another.

A young woman whom Martineau had never seen

before was with them, holding the black folder that Morgenstern and he had snatched from the Marciana. Smaller than the witch, she had tousled fair hair, a pale complexion and a retroussé nose. Her eyes were an even brighter green than Roberta's, and had a very peculiar effect on the young man.

Fould himself was nowhere to be seen.

Martineau moved towards Morgenstern, his one real ally here. The witch signed to him to look to his right, but he didn't understand. No one said a word. It wasn't normal.

"Well, here we all are, then. Find somewhere to sit down, Monsieur Martineau."

The voice that had finally spoken was both soft and steely. Turning, Martineau saw Archibald Fould with a lighted cigarette in the corner of his mouth.

The Minister of Security was very tall. His face expressed a mixture of lassitude, an aristocratic manner, and irony, the last no doubt because of his clear, keen gaze. The man was smiling, but his eyes hardly blinked. Martineau thought of a beast of prey bored to death.

"Let me introduce Suzy Boewens, seconded to us by the Ministry's Legal Department. Miss Boewens, this is Clément Martineau of the CID."

"Good to meet you," said the young woman in a low voice.

"Good to meet you too," said Clément, his own voice rising rather high.

Fould leaned on his desk to face his audience. With a watchmaker's precision, he removed a crumb of tobacco that had stuck to his lips before beginning.

"I have asked you to come here at the pressing request of Major Gruber. His last report on the case of the Killers' Quadrille, as it has been nicknamed"—here the minister looked hard at Morgenstern, who did not react—"his last report was rather disturbing. If I have followed the whole story correctly, it may be summed up as follows. Antonio Palladio, director of the Historic Cities, has brought at least two famous murderers back to life: a female version of Jack the Ripper and the damned soul of Catherine La Voisin. The former reduced part of our brand-new municipal penitentiary to rubble, the latter made her escape together with the Count. A couple of real Furies."

Gruber nodded.

"Morgenstern and Martineau of the CID then took it upon themselves to go to Venice and break into the Libreria Marciana to bring back—this."

Fould reached a bony hand out to Suzy Boewens, who gave him the folder. He opened it, consulted the pacts, picked out one and held it in front of his eyes, having first put on his glasses. Everyone knew what the pacts said. All the same, Fould went to the trouble of reading the parchment out loud:

"Between the Party of the first part and the Party of the second part, the signatories below, it has been agreed as follows. Clause One, subject of this contract: the Party of the first part requires the Party of the second part to carry out all infamous acts (perjuries, assassinations, desecrations, lies, etc.) which shall seem right to him, in his name. The Party of the first part shall thus maintain his power and see his name go down through history, century after century.

270

Clause Two, remuneration: the Party of the first part engages to grant all requests made by the Party of the second part. The Party of the second part shall be entitled to one wish. This wish, whatever it may be, shall be granted."

Fould sighed noisily. "This prose is more indigestible than a mayoral report."

Only Gruber laughed at this joke. The Minister, looking pleased with himself, continued reading aloud:

"Clause Three, termination of the said contract: should the Party of the first part fail to meet his obligations (see remuneration as laid down in Clause Two), the Party of the second part shall have the right to constrain the Party of the first part to answer for this pact under the following conditions: three similar pacts in addition to this pact and the signatories to each of them shall be brought together; the Party of the first part shall be invoked in the place and on the anniversary of the signing of the present pact. The Party of the first part shall then appear."

"The Party of the first part shall then appear," repeated Morgenstern.

"Clause Four, *Intuitus personae*. It is understood that the Parties shall sign this pact with their own true names. Should either of them contravene this overriding obligation (whether by ceding the present pact to a third party, by seizure etc.), Clause Five shall come into force." Fould smiled as he embarked on the next clause. "This is the bit I really like," he said. "Clause Five, sanctions. The Party of the first part is responsible for this section. Finally, Clause Six, duration of the pact. This pact is signed between the

271

Parties forever and a day."

Fould took the other pacts out of the folder and placed them on his desk. Turning his back on those present he looked down on the parchments, hands flat on the desk on both sides of them, pointing them out one by one from the right:

"Palladio, 1569, *giorno di Redentore*, that's the day of the Festival of the Redeemer *al ponte di Diavolo*, at the Devil's Bridge. The Count's pact."

Fould put his forefinger on the second and more recent parchment.

"1888, signed with a cross. You know whose this is, of course," said the Minister, turning to the investigators who had tracked down the Ripper.

The third pact was older, pitted with rusty marks. The edges were crumbling to dust. Its signature was complicated and full of flourishes, but the date and name could be deciphered when you knew what you were looking for.

"1665, La Voisin," said Fould.

There remained the fourth and last pact. It was written in archaic Spanish. The wording of the text was the same as that of the others, according to the Hispanic expert consulted by the Minister, but it was neither dated nor signed in the usual way.

A square symbol printed in red ink stood beside the Devil's signature. The symbol showed a small figure with a panther's head enclosed in a labyrinth. The moment she saw it Roberta had thought of an Aztec symbol, although she could not decipher its meaning.

Fould looked at the small clock on his desk, which said

twenty past ten. "Your specialist was supposed to be here at ten, wasn't he?" he asked the sorceress.

"Professor Jagrège will come," she confirmed. "But—well, he's a bit vague. He doesn't live on the same planet as the rest of us."

"I daresay not. Personally I live on a planet where meetings can't wait. I have to be at the War Ministry in half an hour. And in this weather," he added, glancing out at the torrent still bucketing down outside, "the ministerial cable car will be travelling at a snail's pace."

The Minister's cigarette had gone out. He threw the butt into an ashtray and took another out of an open box. He lit it, held it between two fingers, and went over to the wall of windows to look at the deluge.

"This case, I must say, is rather out of the common run." The office seemed brighter; were the clouds blowing away? The rain had been going on forever. A roll of thunder echoed through the wall of glass. "That's why I have asked Suzy Boewens for her advice, hoping to get a rather clearer view. Over to you, Suzy."

The lights flickered, making the darkness gather again. Picking up the pacts, Suzy began speaking, raising her voice to make herself heard above the sound of the downpour performing an apocalyptic finale outside.

"Miss Morgenstern, I certainly don't have to give you a lecture on Satanic Law," the young woman began.

"Go ahead, dear, you're welcome," said the sorceress rather condescendingly. "It's not on the College of Sorcery syllabus yet."

Gruber started nervously. He was always ill at ease when

people spoke of the College out loud. Particularly when Minister Fould was present, even though Fould was well briefed on the situation. Not that there was really anything to be ashamed of in working with magicians and sorceresses. As for Martineau, he had eyes only for Suzy Boewens.

"Pacts signed with the Devil generally follow a standard form," she continued, "and these are no exceptions to the rule. They contain X clauses concerning X points: subject of the contract, remuneration, sanctions, etc. What distinguishes them very clearly from anything ever seen before is part of Clause One. I quote." She picked up La Voisin's pact and read aloud. "Between the Party of the first part and the Party of the second part, the signatories below, it has been agreed as follows. Clause One, subject of this contract: the Party of the first part requires the Party of the second part to carry out all infamous acts (perjuries, assassinations, desecrations, lies, etc.) which shall seem right to him, in his name. The Party of the first part shall thus maintain his power and see his name go down through history, century after century." Boewens put the pact back on the Minister's desk. "To put it plainly, the Party of the first part is Lucifer and the Party of the second part, in this case, is La Voisin. The Devil wants to use La Voisin as his public relations officer. La Voisin didn't call the Devil up to request his services, it was he who wanted hers."

A flash of lightning shot through the grey twilight in which the office was bathed. A crash of thunder echoed very close, shaking the Community Building to its foundations.

"He likes to hear people speak of him," remarked Fould.

His phone began to ring. He picked it up, listened, and rang off again.

"Jagrège is on his way. He was held up by the flooding. Carry on," he told Boewens.

"Clearly the Devil recruited at least four killers of his own choice. Kill in my name and I will reward you, that was the gist of his message. Jack the Ripper, La Voisin, and Palladio signed. No doubt Professor Jagrège will be able to tell us the identity of the fourth. We don't know what Jack and La Voisin asked from the Devil in return before signing these agreements. Palladio, however, according to the Records Office report that Monsieur Rosemonde has shown me, must have asked for immortality. And in a way he got it, just growing older and older forever."

So Rosemonde has shown this girl the Records Office file too, Roberta couldn't help thinking, with a sudden pang of jealousy.

"The Prince of Lies has given yet another proof of his talents," Boewens went on. "La Voisin the poisoner died at the stake, for all we know Jack died peacefully of old age. The Count was cheated. No rewards, then, for those who killed in the Devil's name. Which brings us to the whole motivation of the Quadrille and the reasons why Palladio has decided to assemble the four killers."

The young woman picked up La Voisin's pact again.

"Clause Three, termination of the said contract: should the Party of the first part fail to meet his obligations (see remuneration as laid down in Clause Two), the Party of the second part shall have the right to constrain the Party of the first part to answer for this pact under the following

275

conditions: three similar pacts in addition to this pact and the signatories to each of them shall be brought together; the Party of the first part shall be invoked in the place and on the anniversary of the signing of the present pact. The Party of the first part shall then appear."

They were all expecting another flash of lightning to light up the office at this moment. Instead, however, the sun suddenly came out, making the wall of glass shine brightly and turning the raindrops clinging to it into crystal beads.

"Why did Palladio bring the killers back to life? To gather a sufficient number of plaintiffs to summon the Devil to account for himself. It's as simple as that."

"As simple as that," Fould repeated.

"Nothing new under the sun, Miss Boewens," said Morgenstern, suddenly going on the attack.

Everyone had turned to the sorceress. Martineau in particular was startled by the hostility in her tone. Fould came to the rescue of Boewens, who had gone red at this display of antagonism.

"Is there something you'd like to add, Miss Morgenstern?"

The sorceress turned to the Minister.

"Our problem now isn't to know *why* the Quadrille is to be assembled, but where and when. The Devil has to be conjured up on the anniversary of the signature of one of the pacts and at the place where it was signed."

"Morgenstern is right," agreed Gruber. "Now we know why Palladio created the Historic Cities. But in what part of the Network are these madmen going to hold their little ceremony?"

"Not London, Venice, or Paris," suggested Fould. "The Count must know that we'll be watching him."

"So the answer has to lie in the fourth pact."

"Obviously. And Jagrège had better hurry up," said the Minister again.

He stopped in front of Morgenstern, hands dug into his pockets. The cigarette smoke that accompanied Fould everywhere made him look like a giant with his head lost in the clouds.

"You're an experienced sorceress—I'd like to know what chance of success you give the Quadrille. The Devil hasn't shown himself for over thirty years. Why would he bother to respond to the murderers now?"

Morgenstern thought for a moment or so. "The sheer force of the invocation, supposing it really comes off, may make him break his silence."

"Anyway, his contractual responsibility leaves him no choice," said Boewens confidently.

"Contractual responsibility?" repeated Morgenstern. But in her heart she knew what the young lawyer was getting at.

"There's no one more litigious than the Devil," said Boewens. "He's based his power on pacts which amount to legal contracts. If he defaults on Palladio's injunction his silence could be regarded as evidence of guilt, and the Killers' Quadrille will set a legal precedent."

This was the first time Morgenstern had ever heard the Devil discussed in legal terms.

"The fact is," explained Fould, smiling broadly, "Suzy's our specialist in Satanic Law. It seems clear that the Devil is in a difficult situation over the Quadrille. Antonio Palladio may just succeed in making him account for himself—something never known before. And I don't like to think what Palladio will ask by way of compensation. So I've decided to throw my weight behind the Devil—and offer him the best lawyer available in the person of Miss Boewens."

"Mm," said the young woman, with a rather apologetic expression. "I'm to be the Devil's advocate—literally."

The office door opened, and a little man whose face was almost entirely covered by a pair of bifocal glasses came in. He wore a tweed waistcoat and plus-fours. He went straight over to the window, stopped halfway, and retraced his steps, saluted first the women and then the men, ending with the Minister, and introduced himself in a fluting voice:

"Jagrège. Practical Studies." Jagrège taught Aztec history at the School of Practical Studies, the antechamber to the College of Sorcery.

Without further delay, Fould gave him the pact marked with the symbol they had been unable to decipher. The specialist took it and spent an interminable few minutes going right through the parchment, murmuring as he read. "Hm . . . ah yes . . . really? Well, well!"

"Do you know what that mark means?" asked the Minister impatiently.

"*Motecuhzoma tchoitchi etzalqualiztli*," replied the scholar.

They all looked at him, baffled. He translated. "Motecuhzoma pledges his word on the fourth day of the feast of Tlaloc in his palace."

"Motecuhzoma?" said the Minister, still baffled. "Who would that be?"

"Motecuhzoma is better known by the name of Montezuma, the last emperor of the Aztec civilization when it was at its height," replied Jagrège. "Killed by Cortez, the Spanish conquistador who sacked his fabulous capital."

"Montezuma! Of course!" exclaimed Morgenstern. "Our fourth murderer!"

Jagrège turned on her furiously. "Murderer? Madam, I cannot let that pass. Montezuma was the greatest man of his glorious civilization: a warrior, a builder, a poet."

"Yes, to be sure," said Fould soothingly. "The fourth day of the feast of Tlaloc, Professor—when would that be in our own calendar?"

Jagrège's eyes were still flashing, but he managed to recover some semblance of calm. "Let's see." He took out a small diary and consulted it. "March. March the thirteenth."

Gruber buried his head in his hands. Roberta and Martineau sighed in unison. Suzy began pacing up and down. The imperturbable Fould repeated: "March the thirteenth. Are you sure?"

"In a week's time, if you prefer." Jagrège put his diary away, and added, "I don't know what's going on here, and I don't know how that document came into your hands. But I do know one thing: if anyone still celebrates Tlaloc it'll be between the tenth and the thirteenth of March this year. That's a fact."

And Fould had been hoping to mount a solid defence thanks to the talents of Suzy Boewens! He could wave goodbye to that idea.

Roberta took it upon herself to lift the last corner of the veil that had covered the mystery. "Professor, do you have any idea of the place where this pact . . . this document could have been signed?"

"That's obvious. In Tenochtitlán. Montezuma mentions his palace."

"Tenochtitlán?" repeated Fould. He had never heard of a city with any such name. Certainly none of the Count's creations had been founded under that title.

"Mexico. Mexico City, if you prefer."

Martineau swallowed the wrong way and had a terrible coughing fit before recovering some semblance of dignity. The Minister of Security was already escorting the eminent specialist to the door again.

"Thank you very much," Fould was saying. "You have been extremely helpful to our case."

Jagrège turned a stern glance on Fould, despite his ministerial status. "Whatever the nature of this *case* of yours," the scholar replied, "I trust you will not destroy that parchment for some obscure reason of state. This is a historic document, and material connected with Montezuma is too rare to be lost. Allow me to ask you a favour." Fould's nod encouraged him to go on. "Have a facsimile of the symbol made and send it to me." And having clicked his heels by way of saying goodbye to the company, Jagrège left.

The young investigator's mind was in a state of the utmost confusion. His mother had frequently told him that there was no such thing as coincidence, that nothing in the world happened by chance. He had followed the trail of the three mystery letters and triumphed. And now came Jagrège's identification of the fourth city . . .

Fould had returned to the middle of the room, and drew on his cigarette, but it had gone out long ago. He tossed it angrily into the ashtray.

"This business leaves me sitting on top of a volcano. I thought I only had to deal with the Ministry of War. Now I'm in a far more delicate position than before."

"I don't understand," interrupted Boewens. "Mexico no longer exists. It's not part of the Network."

Fould decided to enlighten her. "Have you ever heard of the Club Fortuny?" he asked the young woman.

"Of course. The billionaires who live in the Upper Town. A very select society indeed."

"Well, Palladio built a secret city for the exclusive use of the Club, a city which, as you rightly say, does not feature in the Historic Cities Network. I'm no billionaire, but all the same I know where and what that reconstruction is. I'll let you guess."

"Mexico," tried Boewens, whispering.

"That's where they're lurking. And they're going to invoke the Devil in a week's time," said Morgenstern reflectively.

Rising to his feet, Martineau said impetuously, "Then we must go there, just as we went to the other cities! Act as we did there! Merge with the crowd, follow the trail of the murderers, get them before they've gone too far."

Fould signed to him to sit down again. "Eight days, Monsieur Martineau. You'd have eight days to catch them. And the tracers would be no use to you this time."

"Why not?"

"Would they help you get into Montezuma's palace? They must have been banned from it! Don't forget, the fourth killer is lord of that city." Fould turned to Suzy Boewens. "I suppose the time available is too short for you to prepare a solid defence, but I'll ask you to do your best. Get to work at once. And let the Devil know that you're—offering him your services!"

"Do I send my offer through Box 666?" asked the young woman, suddenly hesitant in the face of the Minister's urgency.

"Do whatever seems best, but don't lose a second."

Suzy picked up the pacts and said goodbye all round before leaving the office. The Minister looked at the two investigators and the head of the CID. They had not moved a muscle.

"The Devil hasn't manifested himself for over thirty years," he said to the sorceress. "I suppose it's just about certain that he could assume any appearance he likes, am I right?"

"No doubt of it," replied Morgenstern, slightly taken aback by the Minister's question.

"Right. We'll never manage to get hold of the Quadrille in a week. So we'll send someone to Mexico—someone passing himself off as the Devil. It would be odd if Palladio didn't show up on learning that the big boss is in town."

Fould was right. Palladio would never let a chance like that slip through his fingers. It would even allow them to have someone on the spot at the moment of the invocation. But who would agree to take such a risk?

Morgenstern would certainly have offered, but Palladio knew her already. Although if the Devil could take on any appearance he liked . . .

Roberta felt Martineau's mind working furiously. He was pursuing the same train of thought.

Fould lit a final cigarette and took the time to inhale a few times in front of the wall of windows, which was now flooded with sunlight. The smoke made it look as if his outline were on fire. Morgenstern reflected that the Minister himself would have been perfect for the part he had just suggested.

"Morgenstern, Martineau," he began, without turning round. "I'm taking you off this case. The Killers' Quadrille is none of your business now. Go home and the Ministry will contact you in due course."

Martineau, scarlet in the face, rose to his feet. The sorceress did not move. Gruber's face was inscrutable.

"You heard," continued Fould. "Now I'd like to talk to the Major in private."

"Do you have to drive so fast?" asked Morgenstern.

She had made the mistake of accepting a lift in Martineau's car, and they were speeding through the city. The young man made straight for the vast puddles that covered the tarmac, raising great fountains of dirty water.

"Martineau!" begged Roberta.

He raised his foot and suddenly adopted a more civilized style of driving. He hadn't uttered a word since they left the Minister's office, but curiously enough, the fury that had made him fly off the handle had disappeared. The young man was now smiling as he drove with a light hand on the wheel. Some idea was brewing in his head, and Morgenstern would have liked to know what it was.

"I'm taking you to lunch at the Two Salamanders," he told the sorceress, without giving her any option.

A few moments later he was parking outside the inn. Roberta let the young man go first, and was interested to notice that he could turn the goat's head handle without being bitten or burnt. Eleazar Strudel even welcomed Martineau with positive delight.

"And our Morgan le Fay is with you too! What a happy day! I was about to shut up shop."

The place was empty. Roberta suspected that most of her colleagues were in Carmilla's Liedenbourg palace for the annual Sabbath. The high society of sorcery would have done better to pick Mexico as a site for invoking their old master.

"Coq au vin, apples with cinnamon, mystery dessert," suggested Eleazar. "Aperitifs on the house."

The investigators sat down at a table. Strudel had gone off to the kitchen humming a soldiers' song, and came back with two little Bohemian crystal glasses. The innkeeper shared their first spruce aperitif with them, poured the second, and went off again to see, as he said, to the stove.

"Well, Martineau? Just what are you thinking about?"

The young man, although convulsed with inner merriment, was making a great effort to conceal it.

"You believe Fould's going to send Gruber to Mexico to pretend to be the Devil?" he asked.

"It's nothing to do with us anymore. You heard the Minister, didn't you?"

"Do you think he'll sack us from the CID if we don't obey him?" asked the investigator, with a look of mock innocence.

As if addressing the feeble-minded, the sorceress explained. "We *can't* go to Mexico. Nobody except the Club Fortuny members knows where that Historic City is. And even if we did know, entry to it must be better guarded than the inmost sanctum of the Mayor himself."

"Look, when we went to Paris and Venice, Gruber didn't know what we were up to. It would be a shame to stop just when we're doing so well. Cheers!"

The sorceress was beginning to understand this young oddball. He must have some trump up his sleeve to be looking as confident as this. She tried several possible explanations and fixed on the least improbable. As she reminded herself, she was sitting opposite the heir to Martineau Cement Industries.

"You're a member of the Club Fortuny?"

"No, but my parents are. I've never set foot in Mexico, though. The Club wouldn't allow that."

Strudel came back with two portions of coq au vin and what, judging by its colour, was a decent table wine.

"I don't see what you're getting at," the sorceress admitted once Eleazar had gone away.

The young man slid a wallet bearing the Palladio Sealines logo over the table. Opening it, Morgenstern took out two tickets to Mexico. The lucky winner of the "Find Three Letters to Visit a City" game and the companion of his choice would be accommodated in the Tezcatlipoca Hotel in the House of Herons quarter of the city. A luxury Pelican craft would be waiting at the landing stage on the Western Quay. They could leave at once.

"I got it this morning, just before meeting you in Fould's office." Martineau refilled their wine glasses and handed Roberta hers. "So my little escapades have come in useful after all. Well, Miss Morgenstern, are you ready to finish the job we've begun?"

The sorceress slowly nodded her head. Her suspicions about Clément Martineau were rapidly being confirmed.

"It was only a game, you know," he said apologetically, seeing Morgenstern's expectant gaze. "There's no witch-craft about it."

"So you say," replied Roberta, looking at him very hard indeed. "So you say."

TENOCHTITLÁN

has many delights to offer. You can stroll by its canals, go bargain-hunting in its many markets, visit its temples, palaces, and museums, take part in the fantastic Tlaloc festivities, or simply enjoy the wonderful climate. You will be welcomed like a full member of the Club Fortuny. This dream week (6 days/ 7 nights) is your prize from Palladio Sealines, who are pleased to present you with this holiday.

The Devil Comes to Town

❦

After a single day in Mexico Morgenstern was sure of two things: first, it was going to be very difficult getting access to Montezuma's palace, and second, she adored the city.

When the Pelican hydroplane arrived, a water taxi in the shape of a native canoe hired by the Tezcatlipoca Hotel was waiting to take them to their hotel. They saw little of the city that first evening, apart from the immense buildings raised above the water on piles and their brightly lit patios. It was a mild night. Couples were strolling by the canals. As soon as they had arrived they sensed the Riviera atmosphere typical of the city that was the bolthole of the Club Fortuny.

The hotel was as luxurious as anyone could wish, built around a series of internal gardens, one of them containing a huge, kidney-shaped swimming pool. Morgenstern would quite have liked to dive straight in, but most of all she wanted to go to bed and get some sleep.

The rooms reserved for them did not have the grand

proportions of the suites in the Savoy Hotel, but they were large and welcoming, furnished with wooden screens, mats, and wicker chairs. The bathroom was the very latest thing, and had a jacuzzi too—the cherry on the cake!

With a sudden last spurt of energy the witch plunged into a deliciously soothing bath. Then she slipped into bed and fell asleep—it literally felt like falling. She slept like a log.

She woke at about eight next morning after a night of dreamless slumber, fully rested and with her head full of plans. In the Pelican she had read right through the brochure describing the city and its wonders to new arrivals. The thought of the architecture, the arts and crafts, and the botanical gardens of Mexico all thrilled Roberta. The Tlaloc festival didn't begin until tomorrow evening. It would be a devil of a shame—literally—if she couldn't find time for a little sightseeing before getting down to work on the Quadrille.

Martineau was waiting for her under a palm awning, sitting at a lavishly laid breakfast table. The witch was glad to see that he looked better at breakfast here than in London. They talked casually of this and that as they ate. The detective suggested taking a walk to the entrance of the labyrinth that apparently protected the palace, to get some idea of the challenge facing them.

Morgenstern was in favour of this idea—particularly since the main market place was in the *zocalo*, the central square of Mexico City, next to the famous labyrinth.

The two investigators put on local costume: a loincloth and a cloak for Martineau, a cotton skirt and blouse for

Morgenstern. The clothes were white with a black border; the hotel staff had explained that these colours marked them out as members of the *ciuacoatl* caste, the nobles who were only just below the Emperor in status.

Martineau had great difficulty with Aztec words; they went in one ear and out the other. Morgenstern was amusing herself by writing them down in her little notebook, where *huipilli*, blouse, and *cuetli*, skirt, stood shoulder to shoulder with the names of the Ripper's victims—names learnt in London in a grey, foggy atmosphere and at a period that now seemed to her very far away.

Tenochtitlán had been built to a grid pattern, with each traffic artery consisting of a paved road and a meticulously maintained canal. The buildings were only two storeys high, but here and there pyramids with terraces rising to the sky broke the monotony of the design. Floating gardens and flowery patios made this the greenest city Roberta had ever seen.

They reached the *zocalo* after a swift ride in a water taxi. The esplanade was busy in spite of the early hour, and Morgenstern almost forgot their mission when she set eyes on the forest of tents, shops, and craft stalls in the centre of the square. Martineau couldn't have cared less about them. He was interested only in the labyrinth, the palace, and the Quadrille.

A long wall ran down one side of the square, with the entrance to the labyrinth in the middle of it. As they approached, Morgenstern and Martineau noticed that passersby instinctively avoided going too close to the entrance. Yet there was nothing frightening about what they could see of the scene on the other side of it: a paved road, no canal, running straight for about ten metres and then turning right.

"It's not guarded," the young man pointed out, suddenly excited by the idea of making his way into the palace immediately.

Morgenstern wondered what his excitement was all about—she herself had been in enough mazes to guess the nature of the one that protected Montezuma's fortress.

"Go on, then," she suggested. "I'll wait here."

"But—suppose I get lost?"

"Other people must have tried before you. Palladio wouldn't risk having the Club Fortuny after his blood by letting one of its members accidentally disappear."

The young man marched through the entrance with his arms stretched out in front of him, as if afraid of colliding with some invisible barrier, but he got into the labyrinth without any difficulty. Roberta told him to go as far as the bend and then round it. He did so, disappeared from her sight and returned almost at once, walking in the other direction.

He looked annoyed to see the witch and the *zocalo*, turned to go back the way he had first gone, and reappeared again. Morgenstern signed to him to come back.

"It's not really a labyrinth," she explained when he rejoined her. "More like what we'd call in the trade a palindrome. It goes both ways at once."

"Brr! That's really weird! What are we going to do?"

"No idea, but personally, I find shopping a very inspiring activity. I'd suggest you come with me, but I don't want

292

to be dragging a dead weight along. Let's meet back at the hotel around midday, all right? You can tell me what you've found out and I'll show you what I've bought."

Palladio Sealines had given them each a thousand *quachtlis*, the local currency, worth several hundred cocoa pods. Roberta firmly intended to spend the lot before turning her mind to Montezuma. Exhilarated, she left the young man in front of the entrance to the labyrinth and made her way to the market in the *zocalo*, the realm of weavers and goldsmiths.

There were loincloths made of red wool (*maxtlatl*, the sorceress wrote down in her notebook); ankle-length cloaks for the nobles, *tilmatli*. Tunics made of cotton and agave fibres. Magnificent woven sombreros. Master feather-workers who made headdresses or fans for high-ranking dignitaries from the plumage of parrots, birds of paradise, and kestrels.

Metal-workers and jewellers were busy in the *zocalo* too, crafting precious metals, turquoise, mosaic, and above all jade. Jade was a material that had always fascinated the sorceress because of the difficulty of cutting it and its velvety grain. Here they patiently polished and drilled jade, and made it into pendants or small votive objects.

After much indecision, Roberta decided that her heart was set on a poncho in all the colours of the rainbow. It was really meant to keep out the wind and cold, and she wouldn't get much wear from it in Mexico in this dry, hot season. But as soon as the sorceress had tried the poncho on she knew she wasn't going to take it off in a hurry, whatever ribald remarks Martineau might make.

293

She jumped into a water taxi which took her back to the Tezcatlipoca Hotel. Martineau was in the patio studying a menu and sipping a fruit-juice cocktail. On seeing the electrifying figure of Morgenstern in her new finery, he nearly choked.

"What on earth is that frightful thing?" he asked. "Don't tell me you've gone and bought it?"

Roberta proudly draped her poncho round her. She couldn't expect the heir to Martineau Cement Industries to be an arbiter of sartorial taste. She would show the mercy befitting an Aztec princess, she decided.

The typical Mexican lunch they were served contained a great many different dishes, each more mysterious than the last. It was up to them to pick and choose and put their own meal together. The sorceress liked the notion, and began with a little steamed bread roll (*tamalli*, she noted down) covered with sweet pepper sauce. Martineau was still studying his menu with care. He didn't exactly look like a starving man.

"How did you spend the morning?" Morgenstern asked, to distract him. "Seen anything interesting?"

The detective raised his head and looked at Roberta. He felt both ridiculous in the company of this walking scarecrow and full of his mission, delicate as it was.

"I've found a good place for getting a view of the palace. Those plans of the city don't give any detail about the interior of the labyrinth, but there's a pyramid at five degrees slightly south of the *zocalo*, and you can climb to the third terrace."

"You've been up to the third terrace of this pyramid,

294

then? Good." Morgenstern turned her attention to a portion of duck in caramel and peanut sauce. The detective began nibbling a maize cake.

"From what I could see the palace is a series of buildings arranged in a U-shape, and there's a pyramid with seven terraces in the courtyard. It could be the highest in Mexico, and there's a kind of large park beyond it."

"What are your plans for this afternoon?" the witch went on. She already knew her own programme.

"I'm going to Tenochtitlán Museum. I'm told there's a model of the palace there. I'll be able to study it and—"

The sorceress rose abruptly from her chair, adjusted her poncho, and warned Martineau seriously, "Don't overdo it, Clément. The Tlaloc festival begins tomorrow evening. My sixth sense tells me that things will start happening fast tomorrow, and today's our day off, so make the most of it. Have a siesta. Go and see a game of . . ." Here she took out her notebook. "A game of *ollamaliztli*," she read, carefully pronouncing each syllable. "Their version of pelota. There's a match this afternoon on the pitch beside the *zocalo*. Perhaps you'll have a chance to admire some new athletic skill or other on the part of our friend La Voisin."

"And what are you going to do?" he asked, suddenly feeling in a good mood. The pelota idea wasn't bad, and he'd be very happy to see the clashing colours of that poncho disappear from his sight.

"I'm going to visit the Flowering Blossoms Quarter where the pottery makers, spice-sellers, and bird-sellers hang out. I fancy a little beauty treatment too, and the high-class hairdressers have their salons on a nearby *chinampas*."

"What's a *chinampas*?"

"A floating garden. I'll meet you at dinner. See you then, Martineau."

And the witch set off towards her destiny, leaving the investigator to his doubts and his burning desire to succeed. He finally folded up the menu and turned his attention a little more seriously to lunch.

If Morgenstern had passed a delicious morning, her afternoon was divine. She spent a good deal of it in the floating garden while a rather attractive man massaged her scalp with undoubted expertise. The hairdresser was even tactful enough to admire her poncho. Then Roberta strolled round the markets she had decided to explore. She had a wonderful time among the stalls of the apothecaries and spice-sellers, but the real surprise, a surprise that bowled her over when she wasn't expecting it, came in the marketplace where they sold musical instruments.

The sun was already sinking towards the horizon when the water taxi took her back to the Tezcatlipoca. She was tired but happy, and a little tune was going round and round in a corner of her mind. It wasn't Percy Faith but something else, and she couldn't place it. Finally she identified it while relaxing in her bath. She was still humming the same tune when she went to the patio for dinner.

"Under the sun of Mexico . . ."

A waiter brought her a fresh cocoa just as the detective appeared. Martineau was in a state of great excitement. He told her that the Tenochtitlán Museum did indeed have a fairly detailed model of the palace, which had shown him that the park beyond the U-shaped complex of buildings was almost a forest, and he had discovered that this was Montezuma's menagerie, where the fiercest animals in all creation roamed at liberty.

Morgenstern, her mind occupied by the song which wouldn't go away, was only half listening to him. Now and then she remarked, "A person could forget everything under the sun of Mexico," or, "Don't those tropical rhythms just drive you crazy?"

The investigator would have liked to describe the pelota match he had seen, but the witch wasn't listening. His account of it would just have to wait. He politely asked if she'd found anything nice during her exploration of the *chinampas* (a word that he pronounced with great care). Roberta seemed to emerge from her lethargic state and showed him a small potato-shaped pottery object with holes in it. Martineau took it and turned it in his fingers, unable to guess its function.

"What is it?" he asked blankly.

The witch put the object to her mouth and began blowing the opening notes of a tune. "It's an ocarina," she said, putting it back on the table. "I had one when I was a little girl. I'd almost forgotten it."

A woman with a poncho *and* an ocarina, thought the young man. This was too much!

But there must have been some magic about the pottery flute, for a highly anachronistic *mariachi* trio came over to their table and struck up a ballad. It wasn't their presence that really bothered Martineau, it was the fact that guests at the other tables might think he and Morgenstern were . . .

The sorceress whispered something to one of the guitarists,

who nodded, passed the message on to his companions and began, in strident tones, "Mexico! Mexiiicoooo!"

The other tables took up the chorus of the Luis Mariano song. You could hear them all the way to the *zocalo*.

"Under your blazing suuun," sang the restaurant in perfect unison.

Even the waiters joined in. Martineau was the only person to keep his mouth shut. He was thinking of the pelota match. He had found a seat quite close to the imperial box, which was empty until the game began. Then Montezuma arrived, acclaimed by the throng of Aztec nobles—and with a shock the detective recognized him as the bobby who had knocked him out in London when Roberta was chasing the female Ripper round the dome of St. Paul's. So Montezuma really *was* the fourth murderer. But it was an even bigger shock to recognize the man in the anthracite grey suit sitting next to the emperor. Major Gruber was sharing Montezuma's box, and the enthusiasm with which he applauded the pelota players suggested that he was not unhappy to be there.

The three *mariachis* turned to Martineau, as if to distract him from his thoughts, and sang at him:

"A Mexican adventure, 'neath the sun of Mexico, a week, a week of pleasure" (here they began furiously plucking their guitars), "and you'll never want to go!"

"Olé!" added Roberta.

Antonio Palladio was scrutinizing the rectangle of virgin forest, three kilometres long by one kilometre wide, that lay beyond the palace. A wall separated the menagerie from the safe area of the park. The wall was about ten metres high, and its jagged top bristled with bits of broken pottery arranged like the teeth of a saw. Only two structures rose above the treetops: the wooden top of a monumental aviary and the upper floor of a stepped pyramid surrounded by jungle vegetation.

"You've lost again," said the man behind him.

After hunting and sacrifice, *patolli* was one of the Emperor's favourite pastimes. But Palladio wanted to be alone with their guest. The Venetian asked Montezuma to leave them, and the Emperor left the room without demur. The other man began setting out the haricot beans on the board for the *patolli* game.

If this man is an impostor, said Palladio to himself, he's a madman too.

"A game, Count?"

Palladio brought his wheelchair over to the gaming table.

"No, let's have a little talk."

The man picked up a bean and chewed it unenthusiastically. He would rather have played another game of *patolli*.

He had gone to see the palace bird-sellers that morning. Kestrels were the only creatures that could cross the labyrinth, and the people of Tenochtitlán used them to communicate with the Emperor from the *zocalo*. In fact it was Palladio who received the messages, for Montezuma, a childishly spoilt, irascible character, was incapable of running the imperial palace on his own.

The Count had not expected to get a note claiming to

be from the Devil himself. But such, apparently, was the visitor waiting in the *zocalo* when an escort went to fetch him. Half an hour later the perfect double of Major Gruber was installed in the murderers' headquarters, armed with a change of clothing and a toothbrush.

Montezuma had spent the afternoon watching the pelota match with the new arrival. Odd as it might seem, the Emperor had taken to him. Fortunately La Voisin had not seen anything, and the newly resurrected Ripper seemed even less interested in the things of this world than her previous incarnation had been.

After the theft of the pacts from the Libreria Marciana and the disappearance of Simmons, Palladio had made inquiries about the CID, and he knew that the man in the grey suit was the brains of the outfit. The two special agents tracking down the Quadrille with such exemplary determination worked for the man known as the Major.

The Venetian had failed to discover what obscure military feat allowed Gruber to bear that title. Still, wasn't he himself, a guttersnipe from the *campi*, Trevisan's pupil Martinetto, only a self-styled Count?

This man could be either the Devil in Gruber's form or Gruber trying to pass himself off as the Devil. But it was impossible to find out which before the invocation ceremony. If he was really an impostor, there'd be plenty of time then to make him pay for his audacity.

For the time being, the Count suspected that this was the only way Archibald Fould could find to get one of his spies right into the heart of the Quadrille. Would the labyrinth have been any obstacle to the real Devil? Would the Devil travel with a toothbrush?

"A little talk," sighed the man. "I expect you got a taste for it during your time with the Jesuits. Those clerics just love to talk."

All the same, the Count decided to simplify matters by acting as if this were really the Devil. It would give him a better chance to assess the acting talents shown by the Major in his effort to put on a convincing show.

"You didn't—er—look like that on the night of the Redeemer," began the Venetian.

Against all expectation, the man roared with laughter.

"About to give me the third degree, Palladio? Trying to make sure I really am what I claim to be? I'm not inclined to remove the doubts from your mind until the invocation has taken place in due form. But I will agree," he said, counting on his fingers, "to answer three questions. So I suppose the first is, what *did* I look like on the occasion of our first meeting?"

Palladio nodded.

"I wore the habit of a Franciscan friar, an ardently enthusiastic friar, of course. I modelled myself on Savonarola. And here's a free gift: I'll tell you how I appeared to the other three members of the Quadrille. For Jack, I assumed the character of a depraved English aristocrat, a notorious rake. I looked very much like his brother." The tip of the man's pink tongue showed between his lips. "La Voisin—now let me remember. So much water under the bridge since then . . . oh yes, the classic outfit: goat's head and legs, bat's wings, smoke, all that. As for our dear friend Montezuma . . . he, perhaps, gave me more fun than any of the rest of you."

"The Emperor has never been very forthcoming about your first meeting with him."

"Really?" Reading the Count's mind, the man was aware that Palladio didn't know about it himself. "Ah, well, let me tell you—it really was a scream! Let's call this the second question, shall we?"

The man in grey rose and began pacing up and down the room. Stopping in a triangular bay, he began his story.

"I'd heard the Spaniards talk of the Aztec Empire. The modern world could no longer provide many specimens of those wonderful civilizations that honoured their gods by shedding gallons of human blood. So I introduced myself to Montezuma and informed him that Cortez, who had just conquered Mexico, was going to execute him at dawn. It was no less than the truth. And then—I made him my proposition."

"How did you appear to him?"

"In monstrous form. Vulture's head, lion's body, feet like those of the crocodiles kept in luxury in the Emperor's private game reserves. The effect was magnificent and terrifying, particularly on top of the Tlaloc pyramid." He pointed to the structure looming over the palace courtyard. "And here we have the real pyramid at last."

The man in grey sighed. Palladio couldn't smell sulphur, but that was not conclusive.

"Montezuma wanted to be incarnated as Huitzilopochtli, the God of War and a ferocious manifestation of the Sun, so that he could defeat the invader. Yet another master of the universe! Well, why not? "May your reign come, O solar power," I solemnly announced. "You shall be reborn with the morning." What a wonderful night the Emperor must have spent, thinking of the boundless empire he would build when day dawned. As for me, I made haste to go to Cortez and warn him of the danger. The conquistador was a bloodthirsty madman but no fool. He heard what I had to say, stormed the palace and took it that very night. He found Montezuma at the top of his pyramid waiting for dawn. Cortez beheaded him with his own hands." The man shrugged his shoulders. "Montezuma was a bloodthirsty madman too, but he *was* a fool. He'd have done better to ask me to incarnate him as the God of Night. Then the outcome would have been very different."

It was a plausible tale, and the man sounded convincing. All the same, if he really was the Devil, something nagged at the Count's mind, something to do with the incarnation and omnipotence of the being who had deceived him in the past.

Were the murderers really dealing with an elemental power, an entity of supernatural dimensions? The man in grey looked anything but that. In fact his suit suggested a sales rep.

"I can hear that your mind is troubled, Palladio."

"Why didn't you wait for the invocation?"

"To appear to you in a blaze of glory filling the whole horizon?" asked the man. "That's your third question." He thought for a moment or so. "Let's say I'm tired of the special effects. The exploration of the human soul is the finest journey into the dark that I have ever taken. So I've come down to your own level, Palladio, the better to appreciate you. And I also wanted to visit Mexico incognito before meeting you and the Quadrille."

A lion's roar echoed through the air outside. Ibises flew up from the tops of the tall trees in the menagerie and settled on the far side of Montezuma's park.

Palladio's mind ran through the range of possibilities available, without much success. A man posing as the Devil, the Venetian wondered, or the Devil passing for a man? Even the guessing games played by Sultan Selim in his court at Constantinople had been easier than this.

Martineau and Co.

Preparations for the Tlaloc festival had transformed Mexico, usually a laid-back city, into a hive of activity. A tall structure with seven terraces representing the Tlaloc pyramid now occupied the esplanade of the *zocalo*. Jugglers, actors, and acrobats were enlivening the centre of Tenochtitlán at sunset as the festival opened. The programme said that the Emperor was to sacrifice a slave at eight o'clock in honour of the God of War.

The sorceress had found it quite difficult to get up after her merry evening the previous day. The end of the evening wasn't perfectly clear in her mind, especially since the waiters had left a carafe of *octli*, the local spirit, on their table. She did remember exploring all the possibilities of her ocarina, and doing a poncho dance among the tables. She rather thought that Martineau had gone upstairs to bed at that point.

"How aaardent are your lovely girls!" hummed Roberta.

The sorceress dressed and went down to reception. Martineau, who had risen earlier, had left a message asking her to meet him at the Calmecac Hotel in the Mosquito quarter at noon. That was all. Roberta had no idea what he was up to now. As she had plenty of time, she went to the hotel on foot.

The Calmecac was nowhere near as luxurious as the Tezcatlipoca. At noon on the dot, the investigator still hadn't arrived. Roberta went to the reception desk and asked if someone called Martineau had left a message for her.

"Ah—would that be the young man who arrived half an hour ago?" replied the receptionist. "He was visiting a guest in Room 9. He hasn't come down yet."

"Room 9? Can you tell me who's in it?"

The receptionist's ideas of confidentiality seemed to be flexible. He consulted his register and told Roberta, "The name is Gruber."

Roberta's eyes widened. So Gruber *was* here. Had Martineau gone to see him without a word to her first?

"Could you possibly call the room, please?" she asked, hiding her fury with some difficulty.

The receptionist complied, and let the phone ring for some time before hanging up again. "There's no reply."

"And you say the young man hasn't come down yet?"

"No. That's certainly odd."

Roberta signed to him to stay at his desk, and made her way into the corridor leading to the rooms. Number 9 was on the second floor. She went upstairs four steps at a time and put her ear to the door of Number 9. Someone was groaning on the other side of it. She knocked.

The groans stopped. Then she heard a yell from Martineau.

The sorceress had not shown up when the detective came down to the patio for breakfast, which was hardly surprising after her theatrical show the night before. He had made off when she handed him a tambourine to accompany her performance on the ocarina.

He hadn't slept well. The sight of the Major in Montezuma's company seriously alarmed him. He wanted to be in the clear about it. Gruber wasn't staying at the Tezcatlipoca, and there was only one other hotel in Tenochtitlán, the Calmecac. Martineau went off to the Calmecac as soon as he had drunk his coffee.

The young man found himself outside Room 9—the Major's room, according to the receptionist. He knocked, but got no reply. He tried the handle, and the door opened, inviting him in. The detective hesitated for only a split second. Then he slipped into his boss's room and closed the door.

The blinds were lowered, leaving the room in twilight. Martineau switched on a bedside lamp and began examining the place.

It was quite a large room, comfortably furnished. A stuffed jaguar sat enthroned at the foot of the bed. The detective thought this a strange ornament, particularly given the stuffed animal's realistic look and very convincing wild animal smell.

As he explored the room, his mind was working full tilt:

either the Devil had assumed the appearance of Gruber, or Gruber *was* the Devil, or Gruber was—well, just Gruber.

He couldn't decide whose reaction, Gruber's or the Devil's, he feared most if he were caught here. But there was no sign that anyone had used the bathroom recently, and no travelling bag or suitcase in the room itself. Nor had the bed been slept in.

"This is crazy," muttered the young man, baffled.

Well, there was no more he could do here. He was about to leave when his eyes fell on a bedside table which had escaped his attention. Opening a drawer in it, he found an unsealed envelope. It contained a sheet of paper covered with fine, legible writing. The letter spoke of the Killers' Quadrille and offered legal assistance to its recipient. It was signed . . .

"Suzy Boewens!" murmured the detective, stunned by this discovery.

Fould, he remembered, had told the young lawyer to get in touch with the Devil, and she had mentioned a post office box number. Martineau turned over the envelope, heart pounding, and read the address there in black and white.

"For Satan, PO Box 666, Personal and urgent." Good heavens! So Gruber really was the Devil!

"And you're a dead man," he heard a voice say just behind him.

A violent blow low down on his back threw him against the foot of the bed, which collapsed under the impact. Martineau fell to the floor, and had enough presence of mind to roll over on his side just as his attacker came down with him. He rose, and retreated in a hurry to the blinds over the windows.

His adversary was approaching with a measured tread, in no hurry at all. The dusk showed an extraordinary figure: a young girl who couldn't be over fifteen. Naked, and despite her build extremely strong, she was approaching him with a strange, rolling gait.

Martineau instinctively slipped the letter to the Devil into a pocket in his cloak. He retreated farther, but came right up against the blind. Seeing him cornered, the girl smiled. She seemed to recognize him.

"Why, if it isn't my dear Monsieur Quinze-Juin!" she exclaimed. "So you didn't lose your head at Versailles?"

Martineau instantly realized that the creature meant his astral twin, of whose unhappy fate Morgenstern had told him. The room was full of that wild beast odour now. If he could manage to open this window . . .

And then the telephone rang. The two adversaries did not move. Both knew that when it fell silent their conflict would begin again. The detective took hold of the little cord to pull the blinds which he could feel hanging behind his back.

The phone stopped ringing. The girl jumped on Martineau. He flung himself to one side, tugging at the cord as hard as he could. The shutters opened abruptly and sunlight flooded the room. Blinded, the girl staggered. Martineau was already making for the door, but she was on him again in two bounds and brought him down on the floor.

She turned him over as if he were just a puppet, put her

309

hands round his throat and began to squeeze. The detective clawed the air. He couldn't breathe. He tried to struggle, but in vain. He must do something, anything, to make her loosen her grip.

At that moment there was a knock on the door. Taken by surprise, the girl raised her head. The investigator managed to break free and called for help at the top of his voice, although his throat hurt horribly. The door was flung open, and there stood the flamboyant figure of Morgenstern in her rainbow-coloured poncho.

Martineau thought he was dreaming as he saw the girl move away, collapse on herself, and turn into a live jaguar. Morgenstern, standing there motionless, looked at the big cat at her feet. It was weighing her up, baring its canines as it growled. Finally the savage beast of prey padded round the sorceress and disappeared without more ado along the corridor of the Calmecac Hotel.

"Sit down and don't move. Your throat's badly swollen. That viper's nails must have been poisoned."

The sorceress had taken Martineau back to the Tezcatlipoca in a water taxi. Even in the Calmecac he had been incapable of speech, and now he felt as if he were wearing a collar of burning metal and breathing through a narrow straw.

Morgenstern had opened a little box containing a number of phials and a finely adjusted set of pharmacist's scales. Brows furrowed, she was concocting her mixture.

"Three fingers of liquorice, one violet petal, three crocodile tears," she chanted, mixing the ingredients, "one ounce of powdered bone, two grasshopper eggs . . ."

Martineau didn't know if she was describing the elixir or simply performing a musical accompaniment to what she was doing. When he tried to ask he realized that he couldn't even move his jaw now. Without warning, sheer panic engulfed him.

"I said don't move! Do you or don't you want me to save your life?"

He wished he could reply.

The witch poured her decoction into a cup of warm water and stirred it, muttering. Then she put the cup to Martineau's lips. The medicine scalded his palate, his throat and his stomach, but he felt his paralysis ebbing. The swelling in his throat went down like a punctured balloon. At last he could move. He rose to his feet, felt down his body, and tried to speak.

"Thanks," he told the witch, in a voice partially restored to him.

Roberta, sitting on the edge of the bed, contemplated her handiwork with satisfaction.

"Right. So what were you doing in the boss's hotel room? In such charming company too. If he were to find out . . ."

The young man cleared his throat and announced, with conviction, "Gruber is the Devil incarnate."

The sorceress burst out laughing. It took her some time to calm down. "You're telling me, Martineau. I've been working for him for over twenty years, remember?"

He returned to the attack, trying to make his point more clearly. "No, really. Well, if you prefer, the Devil's taken on Major Gruber's appearance. Anyway, the Devil's in town." And the investigator told her what he had seen in the imperial box at the pelota game.

"Gruber's only playing his part," Roberta said reprovingly. "That's what Fould told him to do, right? If he's managed to soften up Montezuma, well, good for him."

"How about this, then?" retorted the young man, showing her the letter he had found in the bedside table drawer.

The witch examined Suzy Boewens's letter and then the envelope. Martineau never took his eyes off her, but if she was at all shaken she didn't show it. After a few seconds of silence she put letter and envelope down on the bed. "I do assure you, Major Gruber can't be the Devil."

"You're even more pigheaded than that girl who tried to kill me," Morgenstern complained. And he'd thought her just a stuffed jaguar! He'd be giving any taxidermists a very wide berth in future.

"Do you know what she was looking for?" the witch asked him.

"Same thing as me, I suppose."

"Which you have stupidly taken away with you instead of leaving it for her."

"What?"

"If that creature was sent by Palladio, you total idiot, then she too was looking for proof that Gruber really is the Devil. The Major must have left the letter behind for that very purpose, and for that purpose alone."

"What, to mislead the murderers?" said the detective, realizing his mistake. "Oh, what a fool I am!"

"Oh no, just a little too enthusiastic." The witch looked

at Martineau with a grave expression he had not seen on her face before. "We have to find a way to get into the palace tonight," she said. "And before we do it, I suggest you order a bottle of champagne."

"A bottle of champagne?"

"In an ice bucket."

"OK."

The detective did as he was asked and sent the order down to reception. The witch had something ominous about her, a definite look of the hired killer. She could have ordered him to play a tune on the ocarina and he'd have obeyed without hesitation. Room Service sent up a bottle in an ice bucket and two champagne glasses.

"Shall I open it?" asked the young man.

"Go ahead."

He opened the bottle, filled the glasses, and waited meekly for Morgenstern to make her intentions clear. She picked up her glass and sipped the champagne. So did Martineau.

"Those Vikings not bothering you anymore, dear boy?"

"I—er, no, thanks. I haven't drunk a thing but coconut milk since we arrived . . ."

The contents of the champagne bucket, about three litres of icy water, were suddenly chucked in his face. Roberta calmly put the bucket down again and folded her arms.

Martineau had jumped up. "I—you . . ." he stammered. "What do you think you're doing?"

The witch still wasn't smiling. He sensed that this was no joke.

"Witchcraft, Lesson Number One. Instant drying, as you put it. First-level stuff, nothing very difficult about it for a sorcerer."

So that was it, was it? All the same, she could have warned him.

"It's a simple spell. I won't repeat it, so listen carefully. Woof and weft, knot and seam, wet or stained, be dry and clean, as if no mishap e'er had been!"

Roberta Morgenstern, a lady in her prime, had recited the childish drying-off spell to Clément Martineau with all the gravity appropriate to such an occasion. But when he saw that the witch's face still wore that serious look, he managed not to laugh.

"It's a kind of a spell, is it?"

"A spell taught to children to see if they have any talent for witchcraft," she replied. "Hence the nursery-rhyme tone."

"That explains it. And it's supposed to clean and dry your clothes instantly. Terrific. But—er—I'm still sopping wet."

"I did it on purpose to let you have a go yourself."

Martineau prepared to cast his first spell in a loud, clear voice, but Morgenstern stopped him with an imperious wave of her hand. "Remember that conversation of ours in London when we left the Crystal Palace?"

"Yes, of course," he replied confidently. "Can I try it now?"

Young featherbrain, thought the witch.

Martineau uttered the spell in a strong voice whose range surprised himself.

So you *are* one, thought Roberta, trembling.

An untrained eye would have seen nothing. A brief flash, sudden warmth wafting through the room, a breath of hot air escaping outside. Roberta's heart pounded as a certain aroma rose to her nostrils: the smell of ozone that accompanies spells successfully cast by talented sorcerers who have a special affinity with the element of Air. Clément was feeling his body, his arms, and his hair.

"Clean and dry," he said, delighted. "Wonderful! Great! Thanks, Roberta."

The sorceress had had her suspicions of Martineau ever since Paris. Now they were confirmed, but she hesitated over her next step. Should she tell him? How would he take it?

She picked up her champagne glass again and thought the problem over, rubbing the cool glass against her cheek. This little exercise helped her to make her mind up. She put the glass down with new determination.

"There are two things I have to tell you," she began very gently. "I hope you won't hold either of them against me."

He shrugged his shoulders. He was ready to hear anything she had to say: now that he could cast spells, everything was sure to be all right.

"We're dining with your parents this evening in their house in the Quarter of the Gods."

"What?" said his parents' offspring, choking. "You mean my mother and father are here?"

"Tenochtitlán has a phone directory. I felt curious enough to look up Martineau and call the number given for the name. Your mother answered and invited us for seven o'clock."

What on earth was Morgenstern doing, fixing dinner with his parents without asking him first? Who did she think she was?

"And now that you have cast your first spell so brilliantly I really *do* have to meet your mother," said the sorceress apologetically.

"I don't know what you're talking about!" Martineau was seething.

"So you don't remember our conversation in London after all."

"When you told me you were a witch, and I asked you to teach me some spells? You said—you said . . ."

"I told you that magic spells don't count for much in themselves. It's all in the nature of whoever casts the spell, his or her ancestry, and the talent given to that person at birth. Not many people are born with it. Some are unaware that they have it at all if their particular branch of sorcery has fallen into disuse, but anyway it's rare. You are one of the rare kind, Monsieur Martineau."

The anger on the young man's face was instantly followed by an expression of stupefaction. "You—you're telling me I'm—I am . . ."

"It was a one in a million chance, but there's no doubt of it, you are a sorcerer. You have an affinity with the element of Air, as I do with Fire. In view of the quality of your first spell, I should think your talent goes back several generations. Your mother will have passed it on to you. And I have to meet her, if only so that I can draw up your family tree of sorcery, which the College will want to see when I tell them about you. Congratulations. Welcome to the club."

Roberta emptied her champagne glass in a single draught and put it down abruptly on the table.

"Well, it's nearly four and your parents are expecting us at seven. That gives us time to go back to the *zocalo* and take a closer look at the entrance to the labyrinth."

She rose and made for the door, expecting Martineau to follow. But the young sorcerer, still seated in his chair, was staring into space with his mind elsewhere. He was already imagining himself flying. And that was only for a start!

The Tlaloc festivities lasted four days: two days of games and offerings, two days of terror and penance, and the climax came with the picturesque execution of Montezuma. It was all set out in the city calendar drawn up by Palladio—not that anyone took anything but the festive part seriously.

The water taxi dropped the investigators off near the *zocalo*. Workmen were busy with the final preparations. The sacrificial stone had been set up on the top terrace of the pseudo-pyramid with the aid of a floating crane. Four braziers were already crackling in huge stone basins at the foot of the structure, casting barbaric light on the scene. A bronze idol for the act of immolation wouldn't have looked out of place in this bogus dramatic setting. Morgenstern and Martineau were rather disappointed to find the entrance to the labyrinth closed. The sorceress thought of trying various abracadabras, as she put it, to unlock the Circus Palladio's gallery of illusions. They talked to the bird-sellers, who were assembling their cages and shutting up shop before the ceremony, and were told that the gates would be closed during the festivities except for

Montezuma's own entrances and exits. And there was no other way into the palace.

Unless you flew in—and Martineau had no flying licence yet—there was no way for them to get at the Killers' Quadrille.

It was barely six o'clock. The Martineau villa was in the same part of the city, hardly a hundred metres away. The sorceress and her protégé sat down outside a café by the canal. The herons and water taxis navigating the surface of the grey water gave this arm of the domesticated lagoon a *dolce vita* atmosphere which reminded them of Venice.

"Would you like to go ahead and see your parents first? I can follow later if you'd rather?" suggested the witch. "I imagine they'll be very pleased to see you."

"Well, yes, but my mother is kind of . . . clairvoyant. If she says seven, then the cosmic forces have told her seven is the right time, and you have to do what the cosmic forces say."

They ordered tea, and the waiter put a handful of coca leaves down on the table, probably just for decoration. Roberta hadn't seen any member of the Club Fortuny actually chewing them; she had tried coca leaves herself and found them rather disgusting.

"When did you first realize I had a talent for it?" asked the young man abruptly. He had been thinking of nothing else since they left the Tezcatlipoca.

Morgenstern scrutinized her partner. How confidently he accepted being a sorcerer! He knew how to dry himself by magic, and he did it well, but so far he was unacquainted with the *Book of Dreams*, the Lesser Clavicle and the

318

Greater Clavicle, alchemy, and the six levels of spells he would have to study (let alone the intermediate stages). If he decided to embark on those studies he would have to learn dead languages, and languages unknown to the rest of mankind, and abandon any fixed ideas he might have held in the past, because everything ahead of him would be completely new.

The young man was only at the beginning of his story—did he really already see himself as elect in some way? Well, he might be. There weren't many sorcerers with an affinity for Air. That branch had gradually died out over the years, while the planet was dying under humanity's onslaught. Fire, on the other hand, Roberta's branch of sorcery, had grown in strength. So had Water.

Well, the College would teach him a little modesty, one way or another.

"I first realized in Paris, Martineau." The fact that he was walking on air had escaped the young man's notice entirely at the time, and even now he didn't seem to remember.

"You could have told me sooner. What made you notice?"

She felt like replying, "Your general incompetence in ordinary life," but that wouldn't have been fair. "Your sense of coincidence," she said at last.

"What?"

"Your instincts often precede your actions, Martineau. Anyone would have expected our inquiries to be chancy, proceeding by fits and starts, but your ideas have turned them into a set of almost harmonious events. Anyone would think we were in a work of fiction. Things don't run so smoothly in real life."

"I don't understand."

Roberta leaned over the table and explained. "I go to Paris on my own initiative to track down La Voisin. And who do I find there? Martineau. First coincidence."

"It wasn't really," he said defensively. "We were working on the same case."

"I have to get into the Libreria Marciana. Who turns up with the plans? Martineau."

The young sorcerer said nothing, but let Morgenstern go on.

"We have to find some way to get to Tenochtitlán unknown to the Ministry. Who finds the solution with his amazing mystery game? Super-Martineau!" She nodded. "I've never believed in coincidence. I hope you don't either."

The sorceress let her gaze wander over the hurry and bustle in the *zocalo*. The stone had been raised to the top of the pyramid, where workmen were busy installing it.

"The fact that Providence is on your side is explained by your affinity with Air. In the world of Air nothing ever happens by chance, it's all predetermined. From the breadth of a jet-stream to the flapping of a butterfly's wings. Unlike Fire, which no law can ever control."

Morgenstern felt her subject inspiring her. It was like those verbal and alchemical duels about the qualities of the respective elements of the Schools of Sorcery—the College organized them as competitive tournaments.

"Air gives Fire its strength," said the young man almost involuntarily.

"Let's play paper, stone, scissors, and I'll beat you hollow," she challenged.

"All right, all right, destiny wins! I'll accept having Providence on my side!" he said, laughing. "But I don't yet have any miracle solution for getting us into the palace."

"Never mind. We're dining with your parents this evening. The dice are loaded in our favour." Sure enough, the time for their dinner date was approaching. "Shall we go?" suggested Morgenstern.

Leaving a handful of *quachtlis* on the table, they rose and made for the Martineau house.

Two hours later Roberta knew what father, mother, and son had in common: the Moon. So much so that she wondered if the young man's affinity was not with the Ether itself rather than with Air.

Physically, Robert Martineau was as unlike his son as Roberta had been unlike her own mother. His generous paunch gave him a Falstaffian look. He laughed at his own jokes ahead of his audience. But he was a remarkably good and considerate host.

There didn't seem to be much communication between father and son. Not that their relations were icy; it was just that they didn't navigate at the same speed.

Robert Martineau was an inventor as well as a business-man, obsessed by his past, present, and future designs. At the moment he was working on the Verne project, the latest of the Historic Cities that Palladio had commissioned him to create.

"It will be not a city but a whole world!" he exclaimed

at one point. The rest of the time he only half-listened to the conversation, his eyes looking into space.

Morgenstern instantly recognized Clémentine Martineau as a witch. She had passed on her blue-grey eyes and the shape of her face to her son. Madame Martineau was still slender and elegant, and must have been very pretty in her youth. Mother and son were obviously close.

Like most of the people in Tenochtitlán, the Martineaus had a huge fortune. Their house was as big as the Tezcatlipoca Hotel. Strangely, however, there was no sign of any servants all evening. Martineau's mother told Roberta that she took advantage of their flying visits to Mexico to do the cooking herself—the constant round of parties in their penthouse apartment in Basle left her no time for that pleasure.

"Such a bore, all those receptions!" she confided, making a face.

The table had been laid on the roof of the house, which had a wonderful view of the city and the nearby palace. The triangular bays of the palace wing visible to them were brightly lit, and torches had been set up on the terraces of the Tlaloc pyramid. Seen from here the labyrinth looked like a flimsy set of lightweight structures.

But even standing as it did in the middle of the city, the jungle park suggested latent menace lurking in the darkness behind the palace.

"We built Montezuma's palace using the original techniques," father was explaining to son. "No mortar, all done by hand. Think of that! Martineau Cement Industries running a building site without any mortar!"

Clément let his father roar with laughter as he himself scrutinized the figures going into the palace, wondering if one of them might be Major Gruber.

As for Roberta, she was admiring her hostess's handiwork. A large platter with eight circles of different dishes on it stood in the middle of the round table. Clémentine Martineau explained that the solar stone on which the Aztec calendar was based had given her an idea—their dinner was to be eaten from the outside of the circle in to the centre.

The rim, an appetizer of shredded coconut, represented the Milky Way. The second circle was made of chillis for Xiutecutli, Lord of Fire, Saturn to his friends. The third, called the Black Mirror for Tezcatlipoca, God of Death, was an assortment of pâtés and sweet peppers in a sauce of black cuttlefish ink to pay him homage. The fourth circle, dedicated to Tlaloc, God of Rain, was empty. Clémentine Martineau didn't want divine anger spoiling her dinner party.

"But you'll discover," she told Morgenstern, "that a little later, when Montezuma pays homage to Tlaloc on top of his pyramid, it will start pouring. It's the same every year."

Singing drifted to them from the brightly lit *zocalo*. They couldn't see the show, but it must have begun.

The next two circles on the huge platter contained a spiced poultry dish with a wonderful fragrance, accompanied by golden polenta cakes. Four covered dishes, their contents still a mystery, occupied the last circle but one. An obsidian knife lay in the centre of the whole arrangement, in homage to Ollin Tonatiuh who, with his claws firmly

323

planted in the cosmos, would ensure the stability of the Martineaus' universe, at least for this evening.

"If I'd known earlier I'd have made something a little more elaborate," the cook apologized.

Horn calls rang out in the square, and the head of the family took them as the signal to sit down at table. He gallantly placed himself behind Roberta and slid the chair in for her. Dinner could at last begin.

An hour later they had finished the circle of Black Mirror dishes. Robert and Roberta took advantage of the pause provided by the empty Tlaloc circle to smoke.

"That was delicious," the witch congratulated her hostess.

"My mother is a wonderful cook," agreed the young man, taking her by the shoulders.

"And you haven't tasted her salt cod *brandade* yet!" said her husband.

"Oh, don't!" begged the cook. "The stellar conjunction was favourable, that's all, or I couldn't have got hold of the ingredients I wanted so easily."

No one pointed out that this was fantasy. Martineau's mother might be the most lunar of the three of them after all, Morgenstern told herself.

The Martineaus asked her and Clément what they were doing in Tenochtitlán, but of course it was impossible to tell them about the Quadrille. Clément left the reply to Roberta, who invented a reconnaissance mission being carried out for the Ministry of Security: Palladio, she said, had invited Archibald Fould to join a hunting party in the imperial menagerie, and it was up to Major Gruber's department to make sure that the city was safe for him.

"Mexico is the safest city in the whole Network!" Robert Martineau assured her. "It was built to the strictest seismic standards, and I should know."

Roberta brought the conversation round to the Historic Cities in general and the interest people took in them, to such an extent that they adopted the habits and costumes of the past. This was certainly an age of escapism, she said. Who didn't dream of inventing another life? She herself, Roberta Morgenstern, might have liked to be something other than an investigator for the Ministry of Security.

"So what would you like to be?" asked the mistress of the house placidly enough. She saw just where Roberta was leading her, and was beginning to wonder about the real person behind the inquiry agent. Her first suspicions had been roused when she watched Roberta, listened to her, and observed her reactions—clues that only another woman could spot. Not for nothing did the talent for sorcery pass from mother to daughter. In most cases.

"Oh, if I could be someone else I'd like to be a witch," said Roberta.

Clément had been lost in thought, but at this he came abruptly down to earth. His father, who had probably had his mind on Jules Verne and scientific realism, exclaimed, "A witch? But witches don't exist."

"This city existed in the past, before you ever delivered your cement to Palladio, my dear," Clémentine Martineau reminded him. "Go on, Roberta. And if you *were* a witch, what would you do?"

Morgenstern wondered how Clément's mother had

concealed her talent from her son and her husband so long. It seemed that they had never suspected it. Then she noticed the ring that her hostess wore on the middle finger of her left hand. At the moment the stone was turned to the inside. Its setting was very old, no doubt as old as the tree of sorcery which it must symbolize.

"Oh, what witches do in children's books. Good witches and bad witches alike."

"You'd fly on a broomstick, would you?" inquired Robert, chuckling.

"No, no. I'd leave the acrobatics to witches and sorcerers more athletic than me."

"And would you still work for the CID?" asked Clémentine, with assumed innocence. "No doubt Major Gruber would give you plenty of chances to use your talents."

"Chasing criminals who eluded the tracers? Oh yes. And I might well be clairvoyant."

"If you were, what would your clairvoyance tell you?" asked her hostess.

"It would tell me," replied Roberta soundlessly, moving her lips very slightly, "it would tell me that your son Clément is a sorcerer."

Clémentine Martineau could read lips. If the revelation was a shock to her she didn't let it show, apart from the fact that a slight flush rose to her cheekbones. She took off her ring and spun it on the table in front of her.

"Well, would your clairvoyance tell you anything interesting?" asked Robert, who hadn't noticed their guest's silent reply.

Roberta turned towards him, apparently hesitating—but it was time to bring this odd conversation to an end. "You're quite right, witches don't exist, Monsieur Martineau," she replied with the utmost conviction. "But if they did, then I really would be one."

"And you'd be the best of all, Roberta," put in the young detective, before falling silent again.

Only the covered terracotta dishes were left on the table. The festivities in the *zocalo* had taken a sinister turn. The Emperor, or the actor playing the part, was up on the top terrace praying to the sky to repel his Spanish enemies. A slave lying on the sacrificial stone was submissively waiting for his chest to be slit open with the knife.

Roberta fervently hoped that it was only a reconstruction she was watching. Palladio would never dare to shed real human blood in front of the Club Fortuny, she told herself. Yet it had become so easy to commit atrocities in a world where the dice of reality were loaded from the start.

"We don't particularly care for Montezuma and his mime shows," confessed Madame Martineau. "It's all too noisy, too garish."

The temperature had suddenly dropped and the stars, like the moon, had disappeared. Roberta searched her small rucksack, took out her poncho and put it over her shoulders.

"Oh my dear, what a beauty!" exclaimed Clémentine. "Did you buy it in the *zocalo*?"

"I thought I'd give myself a little present," said the sorceress, carefully arranging its folds.

"Speaking of presents . . ."

Madame Martineau signed to her husband, who was watching the show at a distance. Understanding her, he rose. "I'll be back in a minute," he said.

He disappeared into the house. Clément's mother was looking at her ring. Her son said nothing.

"This ring," she began with a melancholy smile, "was worn by my mother, and my mother's mother before her, and so on back to the very roots of our family tree, which are lost in the mists of time." She turned to her son. "You have inherited my talent, and now I pass this on to you," she said, slipping the ring on the middle finger of his left hand. "Don't repeat your mother's mistake—use your gifts. Study and work. And Roberta," she said, turning to the witch, "I entrust my boy to you. Please make sure that the College opens its gates to him!"

The young detective was turning the ring on his finger. Roberta thought the setting was silver-gilt, but she couldn't identify the stone. "What is it?" she asked.

"A moonstone. Transparency and limpidity. I don't know what powers it has."

"Yet you read lips, and you know what it means to be a sorceress?"

Clémentine was about to reply, but her husband came back, out of breath. He hesitated for a moment, seeing the grave faces round the table. "What's the matter? Has someone died?"

A sudden clap of thunder made them all jump. The Martineaus and Morgenstern instinctively turned to look at the *son et lumière* show. The slave had just been sacrificed.

Flashes of lightning surrounded the city of Tenochtitlán, rending the clouds.

"The heavens are about to open," Roberta pointed out.

"Yes, we'll have dessert indoors!" said the mistress of the house, setting the example by picking up her dish and leaving the roof to the coming rainstorm. "I told you so!" she said over her shoulder to the sorceress. "It's the same every year."

Tlaloc, God of Rain, mercifully waited for the guests to be safely under cover before giving vent to his fury.

Madame Martineau had made her son's favourite almond cream for dessert, and they ate it in appreciative silence. Outside, the floodgates of heaven were closing again. The rain had lasted only long enough to send the planet's billionaires scurrying for shelter.

Clément was almost sorry he hadn't stayed out in it, so that he could demonstrate his first spell to his mother—and his father. She had hidden her talent all these years. Personally, he wanted to show what he could do as soon as possible.

"Here," said Robert Martineau, "I found this in a cupboard." And he gave his son an old silver hip flask the size of a child's hand.

"The flask I got for my eighteenth birthday!" exclaimed the young man, unscrewing the top and sniffing the contents. "Still full, too!"

"Full of Grandfather's armagnac."

"Remember those Vikings," Roberta warned him. Clément closed the flask again and put it in his pocket.

"You'll stay the night, won't you?" asked Madame Martineau.

The two investigators exchanged awkward glances.

"Is there a problem?"

Morgenstern hardly liked to broach the subject, but Clément took it upon himself to announce, "We have to find some way to get into Montezuma's palace tonight."

"Tonight! But why?" asked his father. Seeing the young man in difficulties, Roberta stepped in.

"It's standard procedure. Every time Minister Fould travels we do a spot check on the security of the places where he's going to stay. It's true that outsiders might think it impossible to get through the labyrinth, but is there some way of getting round it?"

"Not round it, no, but you could get underneath it," Robert told her.

"Underneath it?" repeated his son.

"Yes, on the raft," Clémentine continued. "In case you didn't know, your father is a VIP in this city, one of the few permitted to keep a raft. We haven't used it for ages, but it should still be in working order."

"Where is this raft?" asked Roberta.

"Moored under the house. You want to try it now?" Roberta and Clément nodded in unison. "Robert, show your son and Miss Morgenstern where it is." Clémentine rose and embraced the sorceress. "My dear, I'm so pleased to have met you. We're leaving Tenochtitlán in a couple of days' time, but you really must come and see me in Basle, with or without my son." She hugged Clément. "Don't forget what I told you, and look after yourself. And don't you get lost, Robert!"

After handing out instructions to the three people

present, she turned her attention to the gods who thought they governed human existence. "And may Tlaloc and Huitzilopochtli look kindly on you!" she said, glancing up at the ceiling. "If not, Clémentine Martineau will have something to say to them!"

A roll of thunder responded, echoing round the city like a muffled growl of disapproval.

Down beneath the Martineau house, Tenochtitlán was a forest of piles planted in the lagoon.

Robert Martineau turned several controls on an electric panel. A set of light bulbs came on, casting a beam for about twenty metres ahead. They saw the raft moored to the steps where they were standing. It was a floating platform three metres wide. A double pulley system linked it by a pole to a traction cable. Robert Martineau was examining the engine that operated the cable.

"It should be in working order," he said, before jumping on to the raft. It began to sway dangerously, but the sorceress saw that, stout as he was, Robert Martineau had quite a good sense of balance.

Four torches were set at the four corners of the raft. Robert lit them, and their flames dispelled the darkness, although not enough for Clément's liking. He was inspecting the deep water below Tenochtitlán with a nasty sinking feeling.

His father climbed back on to the steps, rubbing his hands. "There you are. Once the engine's started, the raft will take you in underneath the palace. If I remember correctly, you'll find yourselves in the kitchens. You have only a couple of hundred metres to go, no more. Large red marks on the piles show you where the boundaries of the palace begin." He let the two investigators clamber on the platform and find their balance.

"Ready?" Robert Martineau started the engine, which caught at once. The cable stretched taut, and the raft began moving away from the steps at walking pace. Once they had passed the last light bulb the investigators' field of vision was restricted. They could see only three metres ahead of them now. Morgenstern, one hand clutching the pole, was trying to see through the darkness ahead of her like a lookout on watch.

The young man let several minutes pass before asking, "What are we going to do once we're in the palace?"

"I don't know, Martineau. Improvise, I expect, same as usual."

Yes, thought the young man, and what else? Were they to stop the Quadrille conjuring up the Devil? Make haste to Gruber's aid? But suppose Gruber *was* the Devil? None of it made much sense.

"It's not the Devil you have to fear," added Morgenstern, "not now you know you're a sorcerer."

They passed a series of piles stencilled with Montezuma's symbol. The little jaguar-headed character, painted in red lead, was like a warning. Abandon hope all ye who enter here, thought Roberta.

Their Aztec outfits made them look like ghosts. What a sight they must present to anyone who might be watching them! Victims floating away on the sacrificial raft. The Vikings would have fancied this kind of thing, thought the young man.

The sorceress stifled a chuckle.

"What's so funny?"

"I feel as if we're on a voyage made by our doubles before us."

Martineau did not reply. He saw nothing in the least amusing about that idea.

Without warning, the raft stopped. But they were still on the lagoon, in the middle of the forest of piles. Standing on tiptoe, Martineau shook the cable. They had stopped moving.

"We're stuck," he said.

The sorceress saw a reflection between two ripples, and a slight wave raised the raft. She followed the course of whatever was disturbing the water, and thought the torches showed her a dorsal fin like the blade of a knife caught in their light. The great fish dived and seemed to disappear.

"Phew!" breathed Roberta.

A violent gust of air whipped into their faces, suddenly blowing out the torches and plunging them in darkness.

"Morgenstern?" called the young man in a muffled voice.

She did not reply. The raft began rocking furiously, as if someone were trying to climb up on to it.

"Morgenstern!" he called again, groping blindly in the dark.

Something wrapped itself round his ankles, pulled him violently backwards, and carried him away into the depths of the lagoon.

PALINGENESIS

Suzy Boewens was getting some fresh air, hoping it would inspire her. The blue sky had relegated raincoats and umbrellas to the back of the wardrobe. It was weather for a nice walk, not for tearing your hair out over a problem of Satanic Law. She couldn't see where it ended or indeed where it began.

The lawyer had written to the Devil by way of PO Box 666, which the College ran, but she had received no reply. There were just two days to go now, and she still hadn't found a way to interpret the pacts in favour of the defence. Suzy had known better situations than this.

Perhaps she'd been wasting her time combing through the pacts so closely. She ought to stand back, take the long view, consider the documents as a whole.

Instead of tracing any cracks torn in the text by the Devil's claw to show what lay beneath, perhaps one should concentrate on the bridges between the various clauses. Suzy had thought of that already, and had drawn a quick diagram of the pacts. Perhaps she'd approached them too fast, seeing only a logical succession in the numbering of the clauses. She'd have to begin again from the beginning.

She walked to the square. It was the end of the school day, and the small green space between the apartment buildings echoed with the shouting of children. Well, the noise wouldn't do her any harm.

"Bridges," she repeated to herself, feeling more and more sure that this was a trail worth following. The Devil liked to play with words. He concealed facts even as he displayed them. His manipulations were sometimes as blatant as they were difficult to make out. Suzy had to cleanse her mind, put it into reverse. Pretend she'd never read those pacts. That she didn't know what they said.

The children, shouting merrily, were chasing each other in and out of a fibrocarbon play tube with the city crest on it. The oaks in the square stretched their bare branches skyward as if throwing alms. A dog approached and sniffed round Suzy's legs. She bent to pat its head. It retreated, growling and baring its teeth.

The young woman glanced swiftly to right and left, and then, just for a fraction of a second, turned her face into the face of a giant cat, a transformation that did not escape the dog's notice. It fled to the far side of the square with its tail between its legs, yowling.

The spells Suzy had learned during her two first years of training at the College of Sorcery were not much use for Satanic Law, but they did come in quite useful now and then.

★ ★ ★

The room was bare, and its walls were huge, irregular blocks of stone. A circular window in the ceiling let a little light fall on Martineau. He was seated on a chair with his hands and feet bound. Palladio was circling round him in his wheelchair. The only sound was the squeak of its rubber tyres on the stone floor.

The young man remembered the journey on the raft up to the moment when the torches went out. After that, nothing. He had a nasty impression that he had just been woken to order, although he couldn't be sure of it, which made him doubt whether this was really happening at all.

"Palladio," he said, recognizing the Count.

"How are you feeling, Monsieur Martineau?"

He had almost forgotten how difficult it could be to understand the ancient Venetian's artificial voice. He tried to move, but whoever had tied him up knew about knots.

"Where's Morgenstern?"

"All in good time. We'll see about Morgenstern later." Palladio brought his chair to a halt in front of his prisoner. "No doubt you know that Major Gruber's here, trying to pass himself off as the Devil. Do you think I should execute him at once or wait for his *alter ego* to show up? I'd be interested to know your opinion."

Martineau didn't have to think long before replying to the Count's implied question.

"Gruber *is* the Devil—the Devil incarnate."

Palladio brought his wheelchair closer, stuck out his cane and dug it into Martineau's abdomen. The detective felt an unpleasant electric shock go through him.

"Facts, young man, facts! On what do you base your

statement that Satan and Gruber are one and the same? Your payslip, perhaps?"

The investigator told the Count about his suspicions and the letter he had found at the Calmecac Hotel.

"Fascinating. But it doesn't get me much further. I'll ask once again: how can you be certain that Gruber is the Devil? And don't try to trick me. I don't need a lie detector to know if you're playing games."

Morgenstern had sown doubts in the young man's mind. If he replied evasively Palladio would use that cane again. And he had no reason not to give his real opinion of the Major.

"I don't *know* if he's the Devil or not, but he certainly *could* be."

Unexpectedly, Palladio smiled. "He could be?"

"He could."

"Very well," said the Count. "Thank you."

And he swung his wheelchair out of the room through an entrance that the young man couldn't see. Martineau's drowsiness, dispelled by the electric shock, returned. He struggled against it for a few minutes, and then let himself fall back into endless dark, wondering whether he might be leaving a bad dream behind.

Montezuma was no longer dressed as a London bobby. He wore a loincloth and a crown of feathers, and he was prancing around, brandishing a club and a gourd and uttering incomprehensible threats. Martineau thought he was too ridiculous to fight. He wanted an adversary up to his own weight! After all, they were dealing with a genuine sorcerer now, not just a CID investigator . . .

The Emperor shrivelled like a chrysalis in an invisible flame, and the young man finally opened his eyes.

He was lying in a clearing looking up at a pale blue sky. A couple of birds of paradise flew above him and disappeared from his field of vision, calling to each other.

"I'm dead," said the young man. "In the Garden of Eden."

"Oh, do stop talking nonsense and get up, Martineau. I've spent the whole afternoon trying to bring you round."

It was Morgenstern's voice.

"So they got you too? And we're together for all eternity?"

The sorceress knelt down beside the investigator where he lay full length in the grass. "You're alive at the moment, but that may not last forever. Look to your left."

Martineau did as she said. The decomposed carcass of a goat was tied to a stake. Its head and hooves had been spared, but the rest of the animal was savagely mauled and lacerated. Clément was on his feet at once.

"Where are we?"

"In the menagerie. You mean you didn't see anything of the palace?"

"No, I was asleep the whole time except for an interview with Palladio. And I'm still wondering if I didn't dream that bit. What happened?"

"After the raft? As far as I'm concerned it's all rather vague. I know Palladio tried to put me to sleep, but he only half succeeded. We were brought to this clearing in the middle of the day. I didn't see Gruber."

"The middle of the day? You mean it's a whole day since we left my parents?"

"Two days, Clément. The invocation will take place tomorrow evening."

"Oh, good grief!" exclaimed Martineau. "We must get out of this jungle as fast as we can."

The clearing was surrounded by tree ferns. Choosing a direction at random, the investigator resolutely walked through this ferny barrier, only to reappear immediately at the same place but walking the other way. He was dumbfounded to see the sorceress.

Taking three steps backwards, he left the clearing without taking his eyes off Morgenstern and disappeared through the ferns—and once again reappeared in the same place, but walking backwards this time.

"You can try it upside down if you like. I've been all round the clearing already. It's protected by the same charm they used on the labyrinth. But no trap is perfect. We just have to find the flaw in this one before it's completely dark."

The forest had fallen strangely silent. As a boy, Martineau had read travel books, and he knew that small animals pipe down when a large predator is approaching.

Morgenstern was right: if they didn't want to end up like that goat they had to find a solution, and fast. He began exploring one side of the clearing, not too sure what he was looking for. The sorceress was scrutinizing the treetops out of their reach. If only they could get there . . .

A stifled sound several metres behind her made Roberta turn. The investigator had disappeared.

"Aha," she murmured, and made for the spot where the young man had been standing a moment earlier. "Martineau!"

"Roberta!" she heard. "I'm here."

"Where?" she said with irritation, still walking forward.

Suddenly the ground gave way beneath her feet too. Following the route that Martineau had already taken, she found herself in a shallow trench partly hidden by the foliage. It led to a tunnel running into the floor of the clearing. Crouching down, Martineau was trying to see into the dark tunnel.

"Montezuma's forest is full of holes," he said. "This looks like a deep one."

The sorceress had sharp ears. She could clearly make out the innumerable sounds of burrowing, scratching, scuffling, and groaning. They said a lot about the melting-pot of wildlife into which Palladio had cast them. And the sky was turning dark above the trench. She examined the tunnel.

"We don't really have any choice," she said.

"Not really," agreed Martineau. "But we don't know what's in there."

"Would you rather go back to the clearing and wait for one of Montezuma's animals? You could disguise yourself as a goat. You never know, maybe whatever came for it didn't fancy goat first time round. That would explain why it didn't finish its dinner."

And without more ado the sorceress made her way into the tunnel. Martineau followed her. Reluctantly, but he followed her all the same.

Suzy had tried all imaginable links connecting the clauses of those wretched pacts. Some words, of course, were repeated. Like *name* in clauses 1 and 4, *law* in clauses 2 and 3. But that meant nothing. She had even tried writing the text of the pacts out backwards, declaiming it aloud and holding it up to a mirror, hoping that its reflection would show her some hidden meaning in the original.

In fact she had been going round in circles for hours.

Nothing suggested that she could mount a defence worthy of the name. The Devil was a fool. At least he'd soon be paying for his incredible fecklessness. Too bad for him. And too bad for the world if the Killers' Quadrille proclaimed themselves its masters.

"Oh, bother!" said Suzy, getting up to leave her study for the kitchen. She needed something to calm her nerves. Returning to the study with a cup of herbal tea, she paced up and down in front of her bookshelves. Law on the left, Sorcery on the right. Suzy's research meant she had had to mingle the two fields. *Albertus Magnus* and *The Illustrated Law Gazette* shared the same poplar-wood shelf. She picked out a book at random and dropped into the leather arm-chair her father had given her for her eighteenth birthday.

Good choice, she thought. Louis Figuier's *Alchemy and Alchemists*, published in 1860. She leafed through the book—its pages were yellowed with time—and stopped to read a passage at random: "Palingenesis: the art of bringing plants back to life from their ashes."

Palingenesis . . . she vaguely remembered it. It was a branch of alchemy somewhere between the search for the alcahest—the universal solvent—and the creation of a homunculus. She nearly closed the book again to return to work, but suddenly realized what it was she had just chanced upon: *bringing plants back to life from their ashes.*

Hadn't Palladio done just the same, in his own sinister way, when he revived the killers?

She read the rest of the passage carefully. It was about resuscitating roses. Then came the part about bringing humans back to life. "Corpses already rotting in the tomb have been seen to revive, more particularly the bodies of murder victims, for the murderer is likely to inter his victims imperfectly and in haste." She had found resuscitation and murder mentioned in the same paragraph of a book that she had chosen and opened entirely by chance . . .

Next came quite a long passage on an experiment carried out by the botanist Kircher in the presence of the Queen of Sweden, attempting to revive a plant that had been burnt to ashes. A vegetative shape appeared in crystalline form when the glass vessel containing the ashes was placed in a hot fire. The image that appeared had impressed seekers after curious facts at that time. If Mother Church had been involved it would have been hailed as miraculous.

In fact, explained the author, it was merely the effect of the crystallization of any hydrochlorate, sulphate, or ammonia carbonate that the ashes might contain. When heated, these substances condensed on the cold parts of the glass phial and produced a convincing image of a ghostly plant.

Suzy returned to the passage which had first attracted her attention. It explained spectres with delightful naïveté: "The salts of corpses, exhaled as vapour by means of fermentation, are coordinated once again on the surface of the earth, forming those phantoms which have so often terrified travellers by night, as many true records bear witness. During the nights immediately following a battle, therefore, it is surprising how often spectres may be seen hovering above their corpses."

The log burning in the stove at Suzy's feet flared up just as she reached the end of the passage. She lost herself in contemplation of the flames, letting her thoughts wander as she closed the book gently and wondered what Figuier was trying to tell her.

The killers were spectres. Was that a good enough reason to tear up the pacts and claim that they had lost their contractual force? No. Or anyway, no legal authority allowed her to say so. If the original murderers had still been alive Suzy could have used such vague concepts as intellectual property, or she could have accused the astral twins of misusing their power. But the killers, even though three of them were not the original entities, were unique. There was no way of attacking them on that point.

She had to go back to what had struck her. Figuier was talking about murder victims, using them as subjects of study. She, on the other hand, was interested in killers. In the opposite, the inverse . . . *Inversion*, she thought.

There was a humming in her ears.

"Inversion, inversion, inversion," she repeated as she rose from her chair and paced up and down her study. That was it. She had the solution. Somewhere in the contract there was a mirror effect. An inversion in the text, a mechanism which made two phrases interact and, when it was finally noticed, would allow the pacts to be invalidated, making them null and void and bringing Clause 5 about sanctions into effect.

Suzy went over to the desk where the pacts lay. Taking

a deep breath, she laid her hands flat on both sides of them, finding in that gesture the energy to begin from the beginning yet again.

They had gone about a dozen metres down the tunnel. Martineau followed Morgenstern, who was using her cat-like night vision to find their way. She told him what she could see as she moved forward.

"It's getting wider. There's a kind of little cave with dry grass on the floor. A lot of rodent carcasses. Like being back in the Marciana. Oh look, a bear. I'll just ask if it can make room for us too."

Since coming round, Martineau took everything literally. She nearly had him scared.

"Very funny!" he said, grinding his teeth.

After Morgenstern had cast the appropriate spell on a handful of dry grass, a small fire lit up the cave they had found. Something had been living there, but luckily it was gone now.

The tunnel went on in the same direction. They must be outside the magic circle of the clearing by now, but they agreed to wait for the morning before carrying on with their exploration. They weren't about to venture on into Montezuma's menagerie just when they'd found shelter for the night.

They made themselves as comfortable as they could. Morgenstern fed the fire with the vegetation in the cave, and they took stock of their assets. Martineau still had his silver hip flask. Morgenstern had only her ocarina and her poncho. Her partner had simply been obliged to get used to that garment.

"Like me to play you a tune to keep your morale up?"

The young man didn't bother to reply to this. His stomach was crying out for food. In their cavernous shelter, it made a noise like some infernal machine. Morgenstern was trying to collect her thoughts. "You're rumbling," she said.

"I know. I'm hungry. I suppose you don't have anything to eat with you?"

"You suppose right."

She went back to tending the fire while she thought about Gruber, Palladio, and the Devil. There was a question that Martineau wanted to ask, but he didn't quite dare. After seeing him bite his lips for the fifth time, however, Roberta asked, "What's the matter?"

"Did—did Palladio interrogate you? He asked me about Gruber."

"Is he or is he not the Devil? Yes, I was asked the same question."

The young man nodded.

"What did you say?" asked Roberta.

"First I said yes, then I thought about what you'd told me and said no. And finally I told him I didn't know anything about it."

"You were categorical on that point?"

"Well, yes, and I meant it. What else could I say? How about you?"

"The same," said the witch. She smiled. Her face wore the enigmatic expression that Martineau knew so well. It meant: I know something, but I'm not sure if I'll tell you.

"You know something and you'd better tell me," said the investigator.

The witch had decided to have a little fun with her junior partner. "Why do you think Palladio asked us about the boss?"

"Because he's a sensible man who wanted the opinion of two responsible people well acquainted with the Major," said Martineau.

"You think you convinced him that Gruber was the Devil?"

"What are you getting at? Yes. No. Perhaps. Palladio had only to pick one of those three answers. As for convincing him . . ."

"You know what they say about the Devil, Martineau? What's he particularly good at?"

The young man scratched his head. "Central heating?" he ventured, holding his hands above their fire.

"Deceit, pretence, turning situations upside down. What he dreams of, what he's been working at for ages, is making people think he doesn't exist."

"But why?"

"For theatrical effect, Martineau. The Devil loves surprises when they work in his favour. He wallows in his victims' discomfiture. He likes to pull a fast one. It's his reason for existence. The only thing that amuses him."

"So he does exist?"

"The Devil exists, has existed, will exist. Like fairies and dragons and witches. But those who meet him can't be sure of it. What do you think Palladio wanted to hear to assure himself that Gruber really was the Devil?"

"I don't know."

"Exactly. I don't know. Neither yes nor no. Someone

who doesn't know really has seen the Devil. You've done your job. Well done, dear boy."

"Wait a minute—are you telling me that Gruber *is* the Devil?"

Morgenstern shook her head. "You weren't listening properly. I'm telling you that by being honest you made Palladio *think* Gruber was the Devil."

"So Gruber *isn't* the Devil?" A lot of this was above his head, but Martineau wanted a definite answer on that point.

"No, he isn't."

"What makes you so sure of that?"

The sorceress hesitated before saying, "The Gustavson."

"What—you mean Hans-Friedrich? What's that hedgehog doing mixed up in this?"

"I met Major Gruber the day after we arrived, and I gave him Hans-Friedrich before going to buy my poncho."

"The day after . . . you never said a word to me about it!"

"I wasn't meaning to. Fould's plan to pass the Major off as the Devil was ingenious, but he still needed a way to carry it out. I imagine Gruber used the telepathic hedgehog to probe the killers' minds and give his character the right enigmatic, clairvoyant touch."

"What about the letter I found in his hotel room?"

"It was left there for Palladio to find. But in the end your finding it had the same effect because, thanks to that letter, you really did believe that Gruber might be the Devil."

"You've been manipulating me!"

"No, no! We've both been manipulating Palladio. And now I'm telling you the truth."

347

Martineau had the sense not to get on his high horse. Very likely their brief visit to the palace had consolidated Gruber's position there. But one detail was still bothering him.

"Why expend so much energy on making the killers believe the Major is the Devil?" he asked. "What will he do at the moment of invocation?"

"Whatever Fould has told him to do."

"Which is?"

"I've no idea."

"But the real Devil will have to show up! You think he'll congratulate the Major on his acting talent?"

"I don't know," Roberta repeated.

"There's a lot you don't know."

"Oh, you make me tired, Martineau." Morgenstern sighed. "All I know for sure is that I'd really like to be there when the Devil does put in an appearance."

"Why?"

"Oh, honestly! To get his autograph, of course!"

The sorceress evidently considered the interrogation over. She drew a square on the floor of the cave with her forefinger, and divided it into two.

"A wall separates the menagerie from the palace a few hundred metres to the east. We have to get to that wall and over it during daylight hours tomorrow."

"Then we'd better try to get some sleep." Martineau stretched out as best he could, made a few handfuls of moss into a kind of pillow, and wrapped his cotton cloak round him like a bat wrapping itself in its wings. He caressed the silver flask, now resting on his stomach.

"And don't hesitate to wake me up if I grind my teeth," he told the sorceress.

Two minutes later he was snoring.

He was making his way through an evil, black ocean.

He woke up, choking, and realized at once that something unexpected had just happened. The fire was out. They were in total darkness.

"Hear that?" asked Morgenstern, who had woken up too.

The creaking sound began again, coming from the trench leading to the tunnel. Something was moving in there, bumping against the walls.

"Don't move. I'll go and see what it is."

Crouching down, Martineau cautiously made his way back into the tunnel along which they had reached their hiding place. He was much surprised to see that day had dawned, and was casting some light into the tunnel. He felt as if he hadn't slept a wink.

The tunnel went round a bend. The young man risked putting his head round it to see what was in the trench.

A cayman three metres long was forcing itself clumsily into the tunnel and making for Martineau. On seeing him, it stopped short. Transfixed by terror, the young man didn't react at once.

The cayman opened a gaping muzzle, turning the tunnel into a pair of jaws bristling with teeth, and went for the investigator.

THE SIXTH GUEST

Martineau was following hard on Morgenstern's heels. She was forging on as fast as she could go. He kept looking back at the tunnel behind them, fear clutching his guts. The bend had slowed the reptile down, but he suspected that the monster was still following them. The darkness and the twists and turns of their path, however, prevented him from seeing for sure.

"This burrow is never going to end!" said the sorceress crossly. She had just gone round yet another corner, giving a view of a new section of tunnel running for about a dozen metres ahead of them. But there was more daylight here, suggesting that the way out was not far off. Roberta covered the distance at a run, and suddenly came up against a wall of earth. The mouth of the tunnel was above them, at the top of a shaft partly blocked by branches and roots. The outside world was nothing but a mosaic of dappled green.

"I'll give you a leg up," said the young man, crouching

down and clasping his hands. "Go on!"

Supporting herself on his hands, Roberta caught hold of the roots growing out of the walls to hoist herself up. Martineau helped as best he could. Morgenstern was no lightweight, but she had good strong arms and hauled herself doggedly up. She had almost reached the top of the shaft when the cayman's muzzle appeared. The reptile followed it up cautiously with the rest of its head, inspected the scene, and on recognizing its old friend Martineau opened its jaws wide.

Clément made a violent effort, propelling Morgenstern up into the outside world. He heard a curse followed by the sound of a fall. The cayman was making for him, rhythmically opening and closing its jaws. Clément caught hold of a root and began to climb. The damp earth offered few handholds or footholds. He climbed a metre, with difficulty, but then found he was stuck and would have to go down again. He let himself drop, thinking that the cayman wouldn't have moved very far during this first attempt. Then he froze as foul, hot breath wafted round his ankles. Clément was unable to turn round, unable to move at all.

"Come on, Martineau, what are you doing?" called Morgenstern from the surface.

He grabbed the highest root he could reach and started up the shaft once more. The cayman lunged forward. Martineau swung his legs out of the way just in time, and the cayman's jaws closed on empty air.

Clément went on climbing. Morgenstern was hauling him up into the outside world now. A glance below him showed the reptile starting up the wall of the shaft with alarming agility.

Martineau took off from his last hold, pushing hard, and heaved himself out of the shaft. Grabbing Morgenstern's shoulders, he let himself drop as far from the entrance as possible. There was a violent movement where they had been standing a second before. Then silence, scarcely broken by hissing breath—the young man knew where that came from. The jungle had fallen silent.

Cautiously, they rose to their feet. The cayman had got its muzzle out of the shaft, but the rest of its body was too wide to follow and was jammed. It was turning round and round on itself. Morgenstern and Martineau hesitated, wondering what to do next.

"It can't get out," said Clément.

"Are you sure?" asked the witch, looking at the animal in alarm. "It's terribly large."

The cayman began struggling like mad, but all it could do was shake the roots now holding its muzzle in a vise-like grip. It exchanged a long glance with Martineau, opened its jaws one last time to suggest that it was making a date for the future, and then let itself slide back into the entrails of the earth.

For a few more minutes Clément and Roberta heard the sound of its hissing breath as it crawled away. Then the silence that had fallen over the jungle was broken. Its denizens resumed their conversations, chattering and calling from the roots to the trunks of the trees, from the trunks to the uppermost branches.

"We've got a bit of a start on that monster, but let's not

hang about," said Martineau. "We'd better try to find the wall you mentioned. I'd be very glad to get to the other side of it. You said it was east of here, didn't you?"

The young man looked around him. Primeval forest surrounded them on all sides. Cypresses, palm trees, and large ferns let in only a faint light. No sky was visible at all, so they couldn't see the sun to help them decide which way to go.

"Got a compass about your person, Martineau?"

He dismissed this remark with a gesture. The forest was teeming with nasty creatures on two legs, four, twelve, or even twenty-three legs just waiting for a chance to bite them, sting them, or eat them alive. Martineau felt they were being spied on. His skin was itching as if bugs were nibbling it.

He chose a direction by guesswork, thinking it probably led away from the clearing, and made his way forward, fighting off the palms and stepping over the roots that rose in his path.

They walked on like this for at least an hour, and often had to make detours to avoid fallen tree trunks barring their way, or deep ruts opening up in front of them. The humidity made the going more difficult and added to the obstacles causing them to stumble.

"A jungle paradise, eh?" Martineau exclaimed. "And to think some people pay to see this!"

"They're in the other part of the park," Morgenstern reminded him. She was breathing with difficulty. "I expect there are well-marked beaten earth walkways there, charming wooden bridges, stalls selling coconuts for visitors to refresh themselves . . ."

"Oh, stop it! You'll drive me crazy!"

Morgenstern noticed that it seemed lighter over to their right. "It looks clearer over there," she told her companion in misfortune.

"Let's go and see."

It took them some time to cross the hundred or so metres separating them from the clearing to their right, but they reached it and stopped on its outskirts, trying to make sense of the strange machine of wood and ropes they saw there.

A pole some thirty metres high had been raised in the middle of the clearing. Three wooden platforms round it made it look like the mast of a ship, and a dozen ropes had been stretched from the top platform to the ground. As far as they could see from where they stood, the ground around the mast was covered with sawdust, straw, and assorted bones. The sky was cloudy, but the sun was breaking through just above the clearing. It must be about midday.

"You think this is a trap?" asked the young man in a whisper, although there were no other living creatures in sight.

"Not all the clearings are necessarily booby-trapped. I don't know what that thing is for, but we ought to be able to see the wall from up there. What do your ankles say?"

"Oh, my ankles are fine now they've escaped the cayman's jaws."

Leaving the cover of the trees, they set off to approach the device with the mast. The ropes were fixed to large, trellis-like wooden structures lying flat on the ground. These giant panels stopped ten metres from the mast, where the sawdust and straw area began. There were rungs for climbing the pole. Martineau hitched up his cloak so that it wouldn't get in his way and began the ascent at once.

He climbed like a pirate, head turned to the sky, leaping from rung to rung without stopping to take breath. The trainee sorcerer really was made for the air. After an impeccable ascent, he stood upright on the second of the three platforms.

Martineau was well above the vegetation now. He could see the wall ahead, more or less in the direction they had been taking, about five hundred metres off as the crow flies. The top of a black stone building emerged from the jungle just in front of them. A giant tree with a blood-red trunk stood between it and their present position.

"Can you see the wall?" Morgenstern called up from the ground.

He waved his arms to say yes, without stopping to think that this signal wouldn't convey much to the sorceress.

He could even see Montezuma's palace, the Tlaloc pyramid beyond it, and Tenochtitlán spreading out in all directions. In spite of the overcast sky, the sparkling water of the lagoon around the city was visible too.

If the young man climbed another five metres he'd reach the top platform. A little risky, but what a view he'd have!

"Where's the wall?" shouted Morgenstern, using her hands as a loudspeaker.

Martineau pointed. He saw the sorceress emerge from the circle of bones, pass the peculiar wooden panels which, seen from up here, surrounded the mast like the petals of a flower, and then make for the outskirts of the clearing. She built a small cairn of stones to mark the right direction, and then looked up again.

"Are you . . . down now?" she asked, her question partly blown away by the wind.

Martineau signed that he was going to climb on. He heard Roberta's voice.

"Careful . . . there must be a . . . up there."

"A what?"

But he couldn't hear her anymore. Never mind, he thought. He nimbly climbed the last few metres, stood erect on the platform—and immediately realized his mistake.

His feet were sinking into a nest of bones, branches, and dried mud. Three eaglets the size of adult vultures were craning their necks his way. Martineau couldn't take his eyes off their scissor-sharp beaks.

"Dear little birdies," he said. "Mummy and Daddy will be home with lunch soon. Don't mind me. I'm only passing through."

All thought of admiring the view was gone; he just wanted to get out of this fix. He retreated towards the mast as quietly as he could. The eaglets became excited and started uttering shrill squawks.

Watching from the edge of the clearing below, Morgenstern saw Martineau move back towards the edge of the platform. What was he up to now?

A roar made her look round. Martineau and the eaglets had heard it too. The cayman, emerging from the jungle, was advancing with its rolling gait towards the base of the mast. The sorceress stood as if turned to a pillar of salt on the far side of the clearing.

"Get out, Roberta!" shouted Clément from his perch.

The witch stared at the great reptile, which was now crossing the sawdust and bones on the ground. The cayman, stopping, turned its hideous head to look at the prey above, now out of its reach.

The eaglets chose this moment to launch themselves at Martineau's face. He beat the air with his arms to avoid their beaks and claws. One eaglet got hold of the moonstone ring his mother had given him and managed to pull it off his finger. He retreated yet farther to escape their attack.

A network of creepers plaited into cords lay on the platform, linked by a pulley device to the ropes going down to the ground. Martineau caught his feet in the creepers and lost his balance. Roberta screamed.

He fell through the air, ankles caught in the cords. He didn't close his eyes; he felt no fear. He had been born to fly. What could have been his worst—and last—memory became one of the most unforgettable moments of his whole life.

He fell towards the cayman, slowing down as the ropes raised the wooden panels vertically like a flower closing. It was an ingenious system. The elasticity of the creeper cords must have been calculated so that a man acting as counterweight could come down to earth safely, tie the cords to the foot of the mast, and thus keep the aviary closed. A scenario that included a cayman waiting below as a welcoming committee probably hadn't been foreseen.

Martineau arrived at ground level. He nearly caught hold of the mast, but the cayman immediately made for him, mouth open. The young man let the elastic cords pull him up again, only just escaping the reptile's jaws. He got back to the second platform with the ease of a trapeze artiste and perched on its edge.

The wooden panels had fallen almost all the way back to the ground. Furious to see Martineau escape yet again, the cayman decided to attack Morgenstern, and clambered on top of a panel to get out of the aviary.

Untangling the cord from his feet, Martineau coiled it round his wrists. Without hesitation he plunged into the void again, once more feeling that delightful sensation as the air caught him. He touched down gently on the ground. The panels were now vertical again, the aviary was closed, the reptile had fallen into the sawdust.

Jamming one leg between two wooden bars, the young man hauled the cord towards his chest, calling to the now utterly confused monster. Spotting him, the cayman stood still for a moment as it realized that they were in the same arena and at last this large two-legged goat had no chance of escape. It charged the investigator, vast jaws open wide, and blindly crossed the last few metres. Pulling the cord, Clément slipped the knot he had made round the cayman's top jaw before flinging himself aside. The cord tensed, the knot tightened between the reptile's rows of teeth and hoisted it right up in the air to the top platform. The wooden panels fell to the ground of the clearing one last time, raising an astonishing cloud of dust.

Morgenstern, who had stood watching, unable to help,

ran towards the young man.

"Are you all right? How did you do it?"

He got up and dusted himself down. Bits of old skeletons were clinging to his loincloth. The giant reptile was writhing this way and that, muzzle jammed against the pulleys thirty metres overhead. The eaglets were squawking just below its tail, which lashed the air with a whistling sound.

"Do you think they'll eat it?" Clément asked Roberta, feeling his left hand. "Oh no! My ring! I must have lost it up there."

He felt quite naked without the moonstone, and almost wanted to go back up to look for it, but Morgenstern tugged at his cloak. It was becoming a habit of hers.

"We'll look for it later if you like. Come on, time to get moving."

They had been walking for over three hours when an agonizing wail reached their ears all the way from the clearing. They stopped and listened as it died away.

"What was that?" asked Martineau.

"Donkeys bray, caymans wail. Mother Eagle must have come back to the nest."

"Tough love, eh?"

They started walking again, looking up at frequent intervals, but the branches high above them hid the sky. Nonetheless, they were approaching their destination: they had passed the red tree that Martineau had spotted.

The black stone structure suddenly loomed behind a screen of palms. It was a pyramid with its base sunk deep in the jungle. Roots had grown into the stone blocks, partly revealing the brickwork core of the building. Sculptural fragments were scattered around: stylized torsos of dancing girls, figures of men in ceremonial robes, friezes of skulls.

"Delightful," said Morgenstern. "Palladio certainly has a gift for a grand setting."

A teak tree felled by lightning lay on the ground before them.

"The pyramid is the only building in the menagerie except for that aviary," said the young man. "It was marked on the model in the museum. The notice said it was dedicated to Tezcatlipoca. Same name as our hotel, right? Don't you think that's amusing?"

Morgenstern, who had been listening to what Clémentine Martineau said about the solar stone of Mexico, knew that Tezcatlipoca was the God of Death. She did not think it at all amusing, but she refrained from saying so to the young man.

"I'm going to climb it," he announced, matching the deed to the word. "Will you wait here?"

"I'd a lot rather go for a dry Martini in the bar. Are you going to climb everything at the drop of a hat?"

"Don't be such a spoilsport. I'll only be five minutes."

Morgenstern sat down on a stone jaguar's head, sighing. Martineau was already on his way up to the fourth of the six terraces of the building. He'd certainly got the climbing bug. His element of Air was calling to him.

He reached the level of the treetops. Seen from here, the palace was reduced to its roofline, but there was a good view of the mast in the middle of the aviary. Only the remains of the cayman—its head, backbone, and feet—were still swinging in the empty air.

"Good heavens," muttered the young man, "what beast of prey can have finished off a meal like that so quickly?"

The wall was now less than a hundred metres away. He came back down to Roberta, who had taken off her shoes and was massaging the soles of her feet.

"Well?"

"That goat's been avenged."

"Good. Come on. I'm dying to get my tootsies into a bowl of warm water."

They ducked underneath the fallen teak tree and came out in a rectangular area free of vegetation. Its layout astonished them. Tiers of seats like the seating in the Aztec pelota ground surrounded it. Four towers carved in the shape of faces stood at the four corners. The faces were staring at the centre of the esplanade, where a ramp went down into the ground. A path gave access to the wall at the other side of the esplanade. Its top was still bathed in the light of the setting sun, its base was already in deep shadow.

"What are we waiting for?" said Martineau impatiently.

"This place looks like an arena."

"But the wall's within reach."

"Wait."

But the young man didn't. He jumped into the arena and started walking up and down, to show Roberta that its paving did not conceal a trap.

"Come on!" he called. "What are you afraid of?"

A low, continuous musical note began to vibrate in the air around them. The sound became a two-part, then a

361

three-part and then a four-part canon. Martineau looked round for the origin of the singing sound. At the same time he felt he was being observed.

Turning towards one of the carved towers, he recognized the features of La Voisin. The stone face was smiling, and its mouth, slightly open, was humming the same guttural note. The other three towers showed Jack, Montezuma, and Palladio, faces of red stone looking at him, surrounding him, threatening to engulf him in their plaintive song.

Suddenly the voices fell silent. A humming continued in Clément's ears, but the silence was back. Martineau waved to Morgenstern to hurry up and join him. She did not move. Like the towers, she was watching the ramp in the centre of the esplanade. The young man looked too.

Walking with nonchalant majesty, a lion was coming up from the depths of the temple. He turned his head towards the investigator and stopped, whiskers quivering.

There was nothing the young man could do. The lion crossed the few metres separating them and pounced, paws outstretched.

Martineau felt himself violently thrust aside. The shock revived his mental faculties, but too late: the lion was lying on top of Morgenstern, who had just pushed her partner out of the way. The animal was holding her down on her back, one paw on the poncho, the other scraping at the paving as if to sharpen his claws.

Baring his teeth, the lion uttered a roar that could have split stone. Morgenstern kept her eyes shut. The lion looked as if he were about to open up her chest.

Then a terrible screech rent the air. A storm of feathers swooped down on the wild beast, raised it, and carried it three metres up above the ground before dropping it on the far side of the esplanade. Martineau had not seen what had happened, but he raced towards the sorceress and helped her to her feet. A Titanic duel had begun on the other side of the arena.

The monstrous eagle was waiting for the lion to charge. The big cat's flanks were already seriously injured. When the lion did leap, a couple of wingbeats carried the eagle into the air. Fifty metres away, Martineau and Morgenstern felt the wind of its flight. The lion hit the ground and landed on his back, clawing at the air. This pitiless close combat was punctuated by roars and shrill screams.

The young man began to feel anxious about the witch. After all, he had seen the lion dig its claws into her chest—yet she seemed unharmed. She was even examining the holes torn by the lion's paw in her poncho.

"Are you all right?"

"Every day a holiday with the BodyPerfect girdle, dear boy. I'm not claiming that my girdle would stop bullets, but it's tougher than this rotten poncho."

The fight was coming to an end. The lion uttered a final roar. The eagle, perched on the big cat's belly, tore off a piece of the lion's flesh before uttering a screech of victory.

"Martineau," called Morgenstern.

The eagle spread its wings with a dry clacking sound, soared ten metres through the air and came down two paces away from the investigator, who felt no fear of it at all. It was the male, a magnificent bird, its beak splashed with blood and its inky brown feathers ruffled up by the excitement of the fight.

The bird dropped the piece of flesh at his feet, like some kind of present. Then it lowered its head and regurgitated a small metal object which rang as it fell on the stone slabs. Martineau knelt to pick it up. The bird of prey watched with its perfectly smooth, round eye.

"My ring!" he exclaimed with childish delight.

He put the moonstone ring on his finger and thanked the bird of prey by stroking its head. The eagle turned, spread its wings, and skimmed the esplanade before taking off into the sky with a strident call.

Morgenstern, who had been keeping her distance, went over to Martineau. She looked at the ring, at the young man, and then at the esplanade. The lion's carcass was evidence that a miracle had just happened. If she hadn't actually seen it, she would have thought it a hallucination.

"Anyone would think the bird enjoyed that cayman," said Martineau, trying to make a joke of it, but nonetheless rather shaken by the incident.

"Anyone might think that your career as a sorcerer had made a good start. OK, we're close to our destination now, so let's hurry. The killers won't wait long to summon their master."

The pacts as a whole were perfectly clear, the text as solidly drawn up a contract as you could wish to see, so there was no way of defending the Party of the first part on the grounds of imprecision. Although at first Suzy had thought she had found the solution, the trail suggested by the idea of inversion had turned into an impasse.

Clause 1 obliged the murderers to commit their wicked acts in the name of the Devil, while Clause 4, the *intuitus personae*, stipulated that the killers must sign the pacts in their own names. Contravening that clause would mean that Clause 5, on sanctions, could be applied.

The lawyer thought she had found the weak spot at last.

Of course, signing a pact with the Devil could be considered a crime in itself. But the act of signing involved two responsible parties, the Devil and the killer, equally accountable for their actions at the same moment, the moment of signature. It was the killer whom Suzy must show to be guilty of breaking the pact, not her client the Devil. How could she attack the former while he or she might have been acting in the name of the latter?

She had to alert Gruber. It might not be too late to get a message to the director of the CID, she calculated, working out the time difference between Basle and Tenochtitlán.

Suzy opened her address book and looked under Gruber. No, of course; she hadn't written the private number for his mobile there, she'd put it in a safe place, somewhere she was sure to find it if she needed it. She cleared everything on her desk, opened drawers, slammed them shut. No number.

You idiot, she told herself.

Could she have put it inside a book? Running her eye along the shelves she took out books at random, flinging them on her chair one after another. Where *had* she left that wretched piece of paper?

Looking at the glowing embers of her fire, she tried to

think calmly. A church clock chimed the half hour, as if to remind her that time was passing and she was getting nowhere. She rose to her feet, took her phone off the hook and rang the number Fould had given her for emergencies.

"Ministry of Security here."

"This is Suzy Boewens, Legal Department. I have to speak to Archibald Fould as soon as possible."

"Mr. Fould is in a meeting at the Ministry of War."

"Is there some way I can call him direct?"

"Try the War Ministry."

"Can you give me the number?"

"You'll find it in the telephone directory."

And the speaker rang off. Suzy almost lost her temper. Where had she put the phone book? Ten minutes later she found it in the kitchen jammed into the waffle iron.

"War, War, War," she muttered, leafing through the pages. "Here we are!"

She dialled the number and waited, tapping a bolero rhythm impatiently on her telephone pad. On the twelfth ring someone answered.

"Ministry of War here."

Suzy suddenly feared she might be talking to the same official as before, not that it would have made any difference to her problem.

"I want to speak to Mr. Fould."

"Certainly," replied the friendly voice. For a brief moment Suzy thought she was saved. "Which department is he in?" continued the voice.

Another shower of cold water had just fallen on her head.

"I mean Archibald Fould," she said crossly. "The Minister of Security! I have to talk to him, and he's with you."

"One moment, please."

Then silence. Suzy wondered whether the switchboard operator was finishing an article in a women's magazine, painting her nails, or bending her powerful mind to the problem that had just been put to her. Suzy was about to return to the attack when the same voice told her, "The line's busy. Will you hold?"

"I'll hold." She began to hope again, but then bland recorded music came over the line. The musical phrase went hypnotically round and round in circles. It was suddenly replaced by the ringing tone. No one spoke. Suzy could almost see the phone vibrating on its rest in an empty office outside the conference room where Fould was sitting at this minute. The Minister would be saying, "Can someone answer that phone?"

But the return of the music reduced Suzy's hopes to zero, before sending her back to the original switchboard operator.

"Ministry of War here."

"Look, I spoke to you just now. You have to get Archibald Fould on this line!"

Another offended silence at the other end of the line. Suzy knew she had just made a mistake; it's not a good idea to get aggressive with a civil servant when you want her to do something.

"If Mr. Fould is the Security Minister, you'd do better to call the Ministry of Security," the operator reasoned.

Suzy didn't even try to argue. She knew it was useless. She rang off, picked up the phone again, and dialled her parents' number. Miraculously, her mother the witch was in.

"How are you, Suzy darling?" she asked before Suzy had even spoken. Thanks to long experience practising her talent, which had an affinity to the Ether, plus more experience than Suzy herself yet had, the copper wire of the phone line transmitted not only her callers' voices to Birgit Boewens but also their thoughts and feelings. Suzy had found it difficult to get used to this, so she hardly ever phoned her mother, preferring to see her in person and keep her thoughts to herself.

"You have a problem," Birgit Boewens told her.

"Yes," Suzy replied in a small voice; she was concentrating on the present emergency. "I have to contact Gruber."

"This Gruber can be called only on his mobile, am I right?"

"Mother, you'd save me no end of trouble if . . ."

"Don't worry, I'll find it. But if he's using a satellite it'll take a little longer than through the wire. Keep your phone off the hook and I'll try the relays, all right?"

"Thanks, Ma."

"That's all right, dear." She paused. "So who's this Clément Martineau?"

"Oh, Ma!" Suzy said reproachfully.

Her mother did not reply to this. Was she laughing secretly, or was she already exploring the Ether to find Gruber's number? Both, probably.

Electronic crackling and magnetic siren songs came over

368

the line, indicating that Birgit Boewens was surfing the air-waves in search of Major Gruber's mobile.

Morgenstern and Martineau ran on up the pathway. The jungle formed an impenetrable screen. There was a door in the wall just ahead of them. The young man uttered a cry of triumph when he saw it, but the sorceress grabbed him by his cloak and stopped him.

A crevasse previously hidden by the irregularities of the paving opened up ahead. It was too wide for them simply to jump it.

"Oh no! Now what?" asked the investigator.

"Always obstacles in your path, never any let-up," said a female voice philosophically behind them.

Turning, Martineau recognized her at once. The jaguar woman hadn't changed since their meeting in Room 9 in the Calmecac. And now her husband was with her. Monsieur and Madame Du Parc, in their birthday suits, had cut off the investigators' way of escape.

The lion's death must have excited the young woman, for she was already half transformed into animal shape, with dense spotted fur covering her forearms. She hesitated to go down on all fours, but mewed to the man impatiently, cat-like: "Leave the boy to me."

"And I'll take the witch," added the man, dropping on all fours himself. His companion imitated him. "We'll soon see to the pair of them."

Instantly their faces turned to animal muzzles. Fur swiftly covered them, and their tails uncoiled at the same time. The two jaguars began yowling plaintively at the

369

temple and the surrounding jungle, paying comparatively little attention to the fugitives now.

"What shall we do?" whispered Martineau. He wondered whether the monstrous creatures still understood human language.

"Do you feel capable of jumping that crevasse?"

"Not the way my calf muscles are playing up just now, no. But on the model in the museum I saw moats all round the menagerie. There must be one behind this wall, right?"

"What are you getting at?"

The cries of the jaguars had produced results. A whole pack of cougars, panthers, and other wild cats was approaching thick and fast. The newcomers began a kind of round dance led by the pair of jaguars.

Martineau had taken out his silver hip flask. He unscrewed the top, tipped it over his mouth, and swallowed at least three large mouthfuls of armagnac before closing the flask again.

"Is that all you can think of?" the sorceress furiously admonished him.

Grandfather Martineau's elixir was already working: Clément was swaying on his feet. Glassy-eyed, he grabbed Morgenstern by the waist and held her close, breathing alcoholic fumes in her face. She began struggling. He held her tighter. The jaguars were approaching, tails aloft, coats bristling. In three bounds they would be on the investigators.

"Hang on tight, Roberta!" Martineau said. "Because I think the—hic!—the Vikings will be along any moment to sort me out."

Roberta understood. Of course! A moat meant water.

Dismissing her revulsion, she immediately put her arms round Martineau's waist.

The jaguars pounced on them just as an irresistible force snatched the investigator from the ground and carried them both up in the air, high above the crevasse and over the wall.

The jaguar who was making for Morgenstern realized his mistake too late. He tumbled into the crevasse, uttering a desperate yowl. His wife, who had not jumped quite so far, managed to fall on her feet. She got up at once, returning to human form. "What magic is this?" she asked, looking at the wall and the place where her human prey had been standing a moment before.

The male jaguar had abandoned his feline form too. He was lying in the middle of a network of roots five metres below her. The wood to which it was attached creaked and groaned. One false movement and the net would break and cast him into the gulf below.

"Don't move," she told him quietly. "I'll find some way to get you out of there."

She was planning to go back to the esplanade, make a rope of creepers, and go down to rescue her husband. But the many ominous growls suddenly rising behind her showed her her mistake. The other big cats! She had forgotten them. The couple had promised them blood, and blood they would have.

She concentrated on changing back, but in her fear or her confusion couldn't manage it instantly. A male cougar was the first to throw itself on her. Then the big cats went for her legs. Her cries were soon stifled by those of her second, feline family.

At the far end of the path, the faces carved on the towers had stopped smiling.

Five stone thrones were arranged on the roof of Montezuma's palace in the shape of a five-pointed star. The circle of torches surrounding the thrones gave the design the shape of a pentangle. The sun was setting beneath the horizon, and the moon, half its disc visible, was already waiting to rise and take its place in the sky until morning.

On this fourth and last day of the Tlaloc festivities the final ceremony was to be held on the *zocalo* a little way away. Cortez would soon climb the pyramid to strike the Emperor's head from his body.

Montezuma sat on one of the thrones. Knowing that the little man in grey to whom he had offered his friendship and the creature who sold him to the Spaniards were one and the same made him furiously angry. If the other three had not been there he would have cut the man's throat long ago.

While the Emperor's heart was full of hatred, La Voisin's was empty of any emotion at all. She was so divided between distrust and exultation that she was waiting for the invocation to make up her mind. This figure, who resembled a civil servant, looked very different from the Goat as he had appeared to her!

Antonio Palladio was astonishingly calm and controlled. He too had been placed on a throne, where he sat propped between its stone arms like a rag-doll or a fetish.

As for the Ripper's mind, it was as vague as the fog in which her myth had been born. Only a howl or a face contorted by pain sometimes penetrated her clouded mind. Even with the Gustavson's invaluable aid Gruber, sitting on the fifth throne, could not have said if it was her own face the Ripper saw, or if the face of one of her victims still haunted the killer.

Palladio was waiting for the last ray of sunlight to disappear below the horizon before going on the attack, so Gruber had time to reflect on the madness that had brought him here. Why had he obeyed Fould? His superior in the Ministry had sent him on a suicide mission. He would never leave this terrace alive.

The last glimmer of golden light was extinguished on the surface of the lagoon. Palladio began: "According to Clause 5 of the pacts between you and us, we are now in the right place, with a sufficient number assembled, and have the right to demand justice. Whoever you are, we insist on your performing your part of the contract."

Gruber and the Venetian exchanged a long glance. Let's hope the real Devil appears now, the Major prayed silently. Gruber wanted to save his skin at all costs.

Seconds passed, and the killers were watching him. The Major had to say something. He was about to take the plunge when his phone suddenly rang.

Palladio smiled when he saw the Major take out his mobile, put it to his ear, and turn to present his profile so that the others could see only half of his face.

"Hello?" The little man was nodding his head with the regularity of a metronome. "Yes, I understand. You're absolutely certain? Thank you, Miss Boewens. No, no, the Ministry will call you back."

Gruber switched off the mobile and looked at the

Killers' Quadrille. Taking a deep breath, he finally replied to the Count and his minions.

"Antonio Palladio, Montezuma, Miss Ripper, Catherine La Voisin, I arrest you in the name of the Ministry of Security for first-degree murder, various atrocities, sequestration of persons, and invocation of the occult powers."

He was bluffing, of course, and he was far from confident that the Quadrille would knuckle under at once, but what alternative did he have? Gruber, back in his own character, was going to play his real part as head of the CID to the end.

He was about to dial the number of the Security Ministry. But his mobile slipped from his hands and disappeared over the edge of the terrace. Palladio had just disposed of it with a casual movement of his hand.

The Venetian was wondering how to cure this impostor of his taste for impersonation. The crystal bones trick seemed to him rather too merciful. And he too was beginning to feel very angry. Not only had the Ministry of Security treated him like a fool, but the *other* entity had not yet turned up.

Was the Devil as dead as God? Or did he prefer to turn a deaf ear to the summons he had just received?

Someone applauded, just behind Palladio. The Venetian started. An intruder? He hadn't heard anyone coming. It was unthinkable!

The sixth guest moved to the centre of the pentangle as if it were familiar territory. Gruber, enthralled, was watching this apparition.

The man, who was tall and thin, was smoking a cigarette. When the killers were able to see him each of them

374

recognized a face with lean features, marked by a lassitude that made an odd contrast with the eyes, for those eyes were lively and sparkling with malice.

"Fould?" murmured the Major.

"We're grateful to Gruber for his services, but I'd prefer to take over myself now, if none of you mind."

The Major vacated his throne and left the tribunal. No one was paying him any more attention. Fould, or his exact double, sat down in the place reserved for him, crossed his legs and said, his tone suddenly brittle, "Very well, I'm listening, but cut it short. I haven't got all night, you know."

Palladio was exultant. The Quadrille had succeeded in luring the monster out of his den. The fact that he had assumed the appearance of the Minister of Security was of no significance to the Venetian. This could only be *he*.

"You have deceived us," the Count began again. "We want justice."

The Devil tapped his cigarette and let the ash fall. "I've deceived *you*? Are you sure, Palladio? Jack!" he said, addressing the Ripper, who turned an expressionless gaze on the Devil. "You asked to be left in peace. And you *were* left in peace until Palladio resuscitated you, am I right? Catherine?" La Voisin trembled. "What was it *you* wanted? Ah yes, ultimate knowledge. And I was prepared to let you have it, but the Burning Chamber got to you first. A pity." He shrugged his shoulders, looking genuinely sorry. "Montezuma, my boy, how could I help it if Cortez got wind of your divine plans? Ah, you think I could have helped a great deal! I see that from your face. Now as for you, Martinetto, I admit that I didn't play entirely fair with you—only partly fair."

"Partly!" said Palladio furiously. He made himself calm down. Anger would get him nowhere. "We have come together to demand reparation," he repeated, *moderato cantabile*. "The pacts bind you as well as us."

The Devil did not react. He seemed to be thinking. His bony fingers were tapping the stone arm of the throne. Gruber, keeping a prudent distance away, was trying to decipher the Minister's bird-of-prey profile, which looked more rapacious than ever.

None of Montezuma's rage had left his heart. It had accompanied him here all the way from Hell. The other person present was not responding to Palladio's injunction. He could disappear just as he had come. The Emperor might try plunging his ceremonial knife into his heart, for he was curious to know if this alleged *diabolo* was made of blood, guts, and muscles like the creatures he led astray for his amusement.

The Aztec unsheathed his knife, leaped down from the throne, which was too high for him, and made for the Devil. But Palladio put out an arm and ordered in a firm voice, "No!"

It was not the order itself that stopped Montezuma in his tracks, it was the way it had been delivered. Palladio felt his throat, coughed, and tried to talk without the aid of his vocalizer.

"My name is Antonio Palladio," he said in an old man's voice.

And then the Venetian looked at his hands. The age spots had disappeared. The veins were less prominent, and his nails no longer looked like claws. Palladio felt the changes taking place all over his body. The aches and pains that had built up over the centuries fell away one by one, like strips of bark flaking off a thousand-year-old tree. He was in contact with his muscles, his bones, his heart once again. He was rejuvenating.

The Devil chuckled, seeing the Count absorbed in his own metamorphosis. His eyes moved to the Poisoner.

La Voisin suddenly rose to her feet, staggered where she stood in front of her throne and took three steps aside, clutching her brow in her hands. Confused visions milled before her eyes. Ultimate Knowledge had finally been revealed to her. The fortune-teller traced her way through its innermost ramifications, through matter, the elements of matter, the elements of those elements.

"No, no," she murmured enigmatically.

Montezuma was looking from Palladio to La Voisin and back again. Was the newcomer really granting their wishes at last? A frightful tingling ran through his breast, flinging him to the ground, making him drop his knife. An army of red ants was devouring his skin . . . The torture stopped as quickly as it had begun. He rose, straight as an arrow. A blue breastplate gave his torso a heroic look. He held a sword and shield. A headdress of hummingbird feathers adorned his divine skull. He had become Huitzilopochtli, the Warrior God, the humming bird.

As for the Ripper, nothing at all was happening to her.

La Voisin had slowly taken her hands away from her temples. Palladio removed the vocalizer from his neck. He now looked like a handsome man in his sixties. White hair grew on his bald pate again. Montezuma was doing a war dance on the terrace, telling men and gods alike who was their master now.

La Voisin uttered a kind of groan. Deep circles surrounded her eyes. She knew all that a human mind is capable of knowing and saw the world as it really was, in its totality. She had only to bend down to pick up the last few crumbs of the Ultimate Knowledge that she had just devoured.

Getting to his feet, Palladio recognized the strange sensation of balance that had left him a century ago. His hair was no longer all white, but showed threads of grey. His skin grew tauter over his skull. His eyes had brightened. He looked as he did when Napoleon had known him during his Egyptian campaign.

The killers had not noticed the metamorphosis of the Devil himself. Only Gruber, standing apart from them, was watching. The visitor now had red leathery wings, and small horns on his forehead. His teeth were sharp and pointed. And he stank terribly. They must be able to smell his odour right down in the *zocalo*.

The fact that he had abandoned his masquerade as Fould reminded the Major of the reason for his own presence here among the Quadrille. The Minister had confided a very precise mission to him—"For national security, the end of Evil and the defeat of the dark." Those had been Archibald Fould's very words. This was no time to lose his nerve.

He took the little test-tube out of an inside pocket of his jacket and began turning it in his fingers, wondering just how to proceed.

"Enough fun and games, I think," announced the Devil in cavernous tones.

La Voisin, Palladio, and Montezuma turned to him.

The Devil made a sign in the direction of the Venetian, who was going round and round his throne like an automaton. Palladio bent over the wheelchair that stood behind the throne, took out a small, black wooden box, and grasped the broken glass dagger it contained. The expression on his face showed that he was trying unsuccessfully to counter the moves that the Devil was making him perform. And also that he was rediscovering a sensation he had forgotten long ago: fear.

The Devil put out a claw-like hand to La Voisin and spun her round. She went to Palladio, who turned with lightning precision and plunged the broken dagger in her heart, standing face to face with her. La Voisin spluttered, spat a little blood, and fell at her killer's feet.

Montezuma had realized what was happening, and was brandishing his sword at the very moment when an invisible force lifted him above the terrace and slung him into the void. The Emperor disappeared over the parapet without even uttering a cry.

The Ripper had not moved. The Devil took no notice, and relaxed his control of Palladio, who fell to his knees, crushed by a vast weight. The executioner had reverted to the appearance of Archibald Fould in his city suit, cold, dry, and imperious. He rose and went over to the Venetian. Palladio was trying to understand what had happened.

"The pacts—you must respect the pacts," he said, his breath coming short.

The Devil knelt down, assuming an expression of the deepest commiseration. "But I am the Prince of Deceivers," he pointed out. "I respect nothing. My signature isn't worth a rabbit's fart, and I owe no one any explanation."

He rose, preparing to leave Palladio where he was, then changed his mind and retraced his steps to deliver the final blow.

"I suppose you knew that Isabella was a member of the White Hand, utterly devoted to her duty? Oh, didn't the Ten tell you? Arnolfo Cambini, the man you killed, was not her lover but her master, in the noblest sense of the term. She was learning your own trade to dazzle you all the better. And you were indeed dazzled—or rather, I'd say, blinded."

The Venetian's shoulders shook with a silent sob that had been buried within him for centuries.

"Jealousy can sometimes be sublime," concluded the Devil, straightening up again.

Gruber was still at the edge of the terrace as the Devil walked towards him. The Major just had time to close his hand round the test-tube. The convincing likeness of Archibald Fould took a cigarette out of a packet adorned with a head of Mephistopheles. He tapped it on the back of his hand and lit it with old-fashioned sulphur matches that gave off an acrid smell.

"Tell Morgenstern I'm not dead, Gruber. She can pass the message on to the College if she likes. This is not goodbye."

The Devil waved, clicked his heels, and went down the stairs to the palace. Gruber did not move until he heard the sound of his iron heels ringing on the stone below.

"My God," he finally exclaimed, once silence had

returned. A glance at the terrace was enough to show him that he hadn't been imagining things. The corpse of La Voisin lay in a pool of blood into which the Ripper was dipping the toes of her boots with an expression of interest. Palladio was leaving the roof terrace on the other side. The Venetian had grown still younger; he now looked no more than fifteen. But the Major was thinking first and foremost of the mission entrusted to him. He made for the deserted rooftop and found the cigarette end in the gap between two paving stones in the middle of the pentangle. A Mephistophelean mask grinned between the filter tip and the centimetre of brown tobacco that the Devil had left unsmoked. Gruber picked it up with a pair of eyebrow tweezers and slipped it into the test-tube, which he carefully recorked.

"Mission accomplished," he sighed, inspecting his treasure by torchlight.

Night had fallen by the time the two investigators reached the palace. From a distance, they saw a boy of about ten run out. He was wearing a shirt three times too big for him. Morgenstern and Martineau stopped, undecided.

"Go and see what's happening up there," the sorceress told her companion. "But don't take any unnecessary risks."

The investigator plunged into the building. What was this lad doing, Roberta wondered, all on his own at this time of day in the palace courtyard? Spotting her, the child started to run away. She caught up with him easily within a few metres.

"Where do you think you're going?" she said crossly, holding him by the arm.

"Stop it! You're hurting me!" cried the boy in shrill

tones. He looked even younger than he had at first sight. The sorceress would now have put his age at seven or eight. What was more, she felt she'd already seen him somewhere. He looked like a little Italian, hair brown and curly, bronzed complexion . . .

"Palladio?"

The child's delicate features were visibly rounding out. He was a chubby five-year-old now.

Young Martinetto kicked Morgenstern's leg viciously and made for the labyrinth. The little boy was shrinking and beginning to toddle. The sorceress was just deciding to go after him when he fell, and seemed unable to get up again.

Montezuma was watching the scene from the top terrace of the pyramid dedicated to Tlaloc, where he had landed after the Devil threw him off the roof. His fury had a name now. He was Huitzilopochtli, eater of human flesh, immortal sovereign, God of War.

Down in the *zocalo* the actor playing Montezuma's part was in the hands of the actor playing Cortez. The people of Tenochtitlán who formed the audience held their breath, waiting for the fatal blow. And a good thing too; so far they hadn't seen anything.

A baby's wail brought Montezuma out of his thoughts. The woman was standing motionless at the foot of the building. The new-born child was still howling at the top of its voice. Then its cries died away. After a few moments the woman turned back to the palace, arms dangling at her sides. The baby had disappeared.

"What does this mean?" Montezuma asked the empty air.

His thirst for vengeance brought him back to himself.

He rose, turned to the menagerie, and called in a loud, firm voice, "Here am I, Huitzilopochtli!" He spread his wings like a bird. "May the night wind carry me away! May my forces be revealed!"

Suddenly he felt himself being raised to the skies. He was above the pyramid. He was flying. A great shout had just gone up from the *zocalo*. They were saluting him, applauding him, paying him tribute!

He waved his arms, uttering a fierce yell. Now he was flying above the trees of his park. He leaned over to one side, to steer himself back to the palace.

It was then that he met the eyes of the giant eagle holding him firmly in its beak by a strap of his breastplate. The bird came down to the treetops with its prize and flew to the clearing with the aviary at its centre. It dropped the Emperor in the eyrie at the top of the mast.

Montezuma had not yet gathered his wits when the squawking eaglets made for him. He tried to reach the mast, but the watchful mother bird struck him a blow with her beak that brought him back into the nest, almost knocking him out and tearing off his breastplate.

The adult eagles affectionately watched their chicks at work. The eaglets were clumsy. There was no particular advantage in making your prey suffer, but the little ones had to learn.

All the time this carnage was in progress countless beams of light swept the night sky above Tenochtitlán, and quantities of firework displays were going off on roof terraces. The Club Fortuny was celebrating Tlaloc, the death of Montezuma and renewal. *Octli* flowed freely that night in the gardens of the billionaires' city retreat.

EPILOGUE

The students arrived alone or in small groups and passed through the University gates. Roberta and Monsieur Rosemonde were sitting on the covered terrace of the Little Ladies' Café, which cheekily taunted the Great Men's Brasserie on the opposite pavement.

The café, something between a drugstore with an impressive display of jars in the window and a publisher of books on spiritualism, was the official bolthole of the teachers and students of the College of Sorcery. Below its bar were three levels of cellars, said to go on underground as far as the municipal mausoleum. It was an ideal lookout post if you wanted to see who was going into the College and who was coming out at any time of day or night. You could play table football there too.

Roberta took her gloves off and rubbed her hands vigorously together. The heater mounted above their table cast a little warmth on her shoulders, but not enough for her liking. Although she didn't naturally feel the cold much, she had found it difficult to get used to the weather in Basle again since their return from Mexico, even though winter was nearly over now.

A group of girls looking as determined as a set of suffragettes passed through the gates. Still no Martineau.

"Not many boys this year," remarked the sorceress. She folded her hands round her piping hot cup of tea, looking into it as if searching for the courage she needed to venture on her plan. She had been beating about the bush too long. The case of the Quadrille, now closed, marked a turning point in her career. Roberta had decided it was about time for a turning point in her currently non-existent love life too.

"We do have a handful of young men," said Rosemonde. "One to thirty, the usual ratio. And I had to fight hard to get them accepted."

Later, she told herself. It's still too soon. I'll let the conversation get going.

"Did Carmilla Banshee kick up a great fuss again?" she asked the Professor.

Rosemonde nodded and ordered another coffee. Banshee lectured on Practical Sorcery. She taught the students how to open doors, conjure up rays of light, and create astral twins. The laboratory was her domain. But she was a spinster, an old maid who had announced one day that sorcery was for girls and boys had no business meddling with it.

"Were you at her last Sabbath?" asked Morgenstern. "I'm told the Devil stood her up again. What a catastrophe!"

"No, I didn't go. I don't much care for society events, and I had other things to do. You can't be in two places at once."

"No, even the Devil could hardly be in Mexico and the Liedenbourg Palace at the same time . . . but I'm being catty. Not very nice of me. All the same, Professor, don't you think Carmilla is past her best? Isn't there anyone who could take over from her?"

"You could, my dear. But the Ministry of Security snapped up our best student from under our noses long ago."

Roberta blushed to the tips of her ears. Was Rosemonde reading her thoughts? Was he throwing her a lifeline? She was about to take the plunge when Eugène Bouillotte, the café proprietor, brought Monsieur Rosemonde's coffee to their table himself, proof positive of his high opinion of the eminent Professor of the History of Sorcery.

"But you're keeping me on tenterhooks," the Professor went on. "You promised to tell me the whole story. We'd just got to where young Martinetto kicked your shins."

Roberta came abruptly down to earth. Palladio, Montezuma's palace . . . she decided to sum up briefly.

"By the time I caught him he'd turned into a baby one year old, no more. I picked him up. He was very upset. The end came in only a few seconds. He turned into a new-born infant, and then his features gradually disintegrated. I held him in the palm of my hand as he was reabsorbed into himself. And then the foetus disappeared like a magic bean."

"And everything was back in its right order," added Rosemonde.

"So I joined Martineau on the roof. La Voisin was dead. The Ripper was alive, looking dazed. Montezuma had vanished. Gruber was there too."

"And no trace of the Devil except what the Major

brought back for you."

Roberta had begun her story at the end. The Devil was alive and well. In journalistic terms, it was a real scoop.

"The Major told me about that. The Gustavson confirmed it."

"Didn't you say you could find no thoughts of the Devil in the hedgehog's mind?"

"Poor Hans-Friedrich's memories are more like a mental broth than classic literary prose. Just imagine: the poor creature was reading the killers' minds and Gruber's at the same time. He didn't know where to turn."

Rosemonde stirred his coffee, creating a little black whirlpool in the cup. "So everyone shared the same vision of the Devil," he continued.

"In the form of Archibald Fould."

"Amusing, that. This story is like a vast fancy dress ball with the leading character trying on several costumes one by one. Gruber's first, then Fould's. At least he got the ranking order right."

"No, listen. The Major *aimed* to pass himself off as the Devil, but we never had any doubts of his real identity. Well, I didn't, anyway. But as for Fould, it's almost certain that— that *he* merely took on his appearance. Palladio did just the same kind of thing when he wanted to captivate his little world and hide his real face."

"But you do have doubts, my dear. Is Fould really Fould? We don't know anything about him, do we? And it's on that lack of knowledge that the Devil based his mystifications."

Whether it was reality or her imagination, it seemed to Roberta that the Professor's eyes were shining from within.

He was looking at her with a new intensity. No, she wasn't making it up.

"*Qui nescit dissimulare, nescit regnare,*" he added in slightly theatrical tones.

"Yes, dissimulation and government have always gone hand in hand," agreed Roberta.

A young man, looking anxious, was watching the groups of girls going into the College. He dared not follow them. Timidity would be one of the worst dragons that the witches might help him to vanquish. So far Roberta had failed to conquer her own.

Yet she had faced Palladio and his minions, survived encounters with a lion and a cayman, played leapfrog with Death in four impossible cities. Was she incapable of uttering sentiments as old as the world out loud?

Rosemonde was trying to decipher the sorceress's face. He seemed about to say something, changed his mind, and finally asked, "Is Martineau still attached to the CID?"

"Yes. I got permission from Vandenberghe for him to attend lectures. The CID allows leave of absence for people to learn specializations. He's already got a good training in criminology, and since the College opens only during academic vacations Clément can go on working for the CID the rest of the time."

Otto Vandenberghe lectured on magic—magic black, white, and grey—and had been appointed Rector of the College for the coming year.

"He won't get much free time."

"No need to worry about him. That young man is full of energy."

"I'm sure he is."

Roberta's blood froze in her veins: suppose Rosemonde was thinking that she and Martineau had . . . ? She must calm down. The heater was blazing down on her like a furnace. What with that and the way her hormones had been simmering for a good ten minutes . . . Rosemonde said nothing. He toyed with the sugar that had come with his coffee.

"By the way, did you know that Suzy Boewens is teaching this year?" he said casually. "She's giving practical classes in Satanic Law."

Roberta said nothing.

"And guess who was the first to sign up for her classes?"

She had to moisten her lips before she replied, in a small voice, "Martineau?"

"Your clairvoyance always astonishes me, Roberta."

Rosemonde put his hand on his former pupil's. An electric thrill ran through her, and a sudden wave of warmth rendered the heater quite unnecessary.

The timid young man had finally ventured to take the plunge: he had just crossed the threshold. Oddly enough, while Monsieur Rosemonde's slightly trembling hand was resting on hers, the ideas circulating in Morgenstern's heart, stomach, and mind were all of Martineau.

What, she wondered, what *can* he be doing?

His alarm failed to go off. The caretaker, who usually banged on his door with his broom at the same time every morning while he was sweeping round the building, had gone to see his aunt in the country. His neighbours downstairs, who had triplets, had not accustomed him to so much silence.

Clément woke with a start to discover that the sun was in the sky. Quite a long way up in the sky. It took him some time to find his watch in the general confusion that cluttered his attic room.

"Nine o'clock!"

All was not lost. He should have woken up half an hour earlier. But he'd be at the College in no time in his car.

He took a quick shower and dressed rapidly, trying to tidy his hair. Picking up his raincoat, he checked that his keys were in his pocket. He was ready.

On the threshold of his little world, he turned to look at it. The studio flat covered thirty square metres, and had a view of the rooftops. It was like a nest perched on top of the city. Come to think of it, the Air always *had* been his domain.

A rickety shelf held several books on criminology. On an old architect's drawing board Ernest Goddefroy's *Elementary Manual of Police Technique*, a paperback edition for the use of inspectors in the field, stood next to Albertus Magnus's *Somma*. The only open volume, over which he had been poring the evening before, was a law book borrowed from his local branch of the city library. It discussed the art of making a plea in court, and the author was Markus Boewens.

The young man closed his door and raced downstairs, letting his sense of intoxication carry him away. Floor after floor dropped beneath his feet like the spirals of a gigantic helix. He wasn't running. He was flying.

"What can he be up to?" said Morgenstern impatiently.

All of a sudden Martineau appeared at the wheel of his

sputtering car. He parked it, stripped off his leather helmet and driving goggles, and put them in the glove compartment. Jumping out on the pavement, he made for the University gates.

"Full of energy indeed," agreed Rosemonde, who had scarcely had time to set eyes on him.

Morgenstern sighed. And to think that a few months earlier she hadn't even known of that great oaf's existence!

"When you saw him before we left for Venice, did you realize he had talent?"

"I've never been very good at exploring the human soul," said Rosemonde apologetically. "But he turned up at just the right time. I don't even know why I asked him to meet me at the College. His determination must have convinced me, but most of all it was a matter of coincidences."

"Coincidences . . . yes, that's how I spotted him myself. How do you think he'll do?"

"Either very well or very badly. Like the rest of us."

The Professor's gaze moved elsewhere. He was thinking not of Martineau but of the witch sitting beside him. He straightened in his chair.

"You've made a great discovery there. A sorcerer who has an affinity with Air . . . we've been waiting at least three generations for one of those. You'll have to explore his family tree of sorcery—study his maternal ancestry more closely."

"You don't say!"

Without taking her up on this remark, Rosemonde continued.

"And above all you'll have to keep him alive. I mean if he goes on working for the CID . . . Furthermore, young sorcerers tend to be either introverts or hotheads. I'm inclined to put him in the second category."

Morgenstern thought of the young investigator's latest whim: he was planning to qualify as a pilot. He had signed on at a flying club in the country and taken his first lesson. He had told Roberta in detail about the fabulous sensations you got from what he called a fantastic experience. She was a witch, perhaps she'd like to learn to fly herself?

This conversation had taken place in Roberta's flat. She almost picked up a broom to hit him on the head with it, with a view to sorting out his ideas and showing him that as far as she was concerned he wasn't out of the woods yet.

And thinking of wood . . . She searched the bottom of her bag and took out the little black wooden box that had been found on Palladio's wheelchair. Putting it on the table, she slid it over to Rosemonde. He opened it. The velvet lining in which the dagger had been kept was empty. Roberta operated a mechanism which revealed the false bottom of the case and took out the fabric-wrapped package lying there. Unfolding the fabric, she showed him a collection of fragments of bone.

"The femur of St. Lazarus," said Rosemonde, recognizing them.

"There are a few bits left. Banshee can always use them for experiments."

A lock of Isabella's hair lay with the relic. The Professor folded the fabric again, returned it all to the box, and put the box itself in his brown leather briefcase.

"What will happen to the Historic Cities?" he inquired.

"They'll go on making us dream, but without any more

murders, let's hope. They are to be placed under the authority of the Mayor, and they'll certainly have to admit tracers soon. The CID has managed to commandeer the *Albatross* for its own use."

"What, Palladio's flying ship?"

"It was standing by in a floating boathouse moored off Tenochtitlán. Gruber confiscated it as material evidence. The *Albatross* is now in a hangar near the lagoon."

"Martineau must be delighted!"

"He doesn't know yet, and I'd rather not tell him."

"What about the Ripper? She was the only one to get off unscathed, wasn't she?"

"She's absolutely fine, but completely off her head. She's back in her brand new cell in the city jail."

"As for Montezuma . . ."

Roberta mimed a conjurer making a rabbit disappear and rubbing his hands with glee.

"Vanished."

Rosemonde nodded. Thoughtfully, he said, "So the Devil *is* back. We'd better set up a special commission to study that old problem again. The news has already spread like wildfire. Did you know that Albergaggi has sent the College a fraternal message? "Our united strength will be required to send Lucifer back to his evil den." That's what he wrote to me. I have it in black and white. I feel as if I were twenty years old again."

Roberta nodded. She felt the same herself.

"The Devil went undercover when the tracers were introduced. Why would he reappear after thirty years of silence?" she wondered.

"Because he was invoked, of course!"

"So you support the theory that the word creates the object?" said Roberta in surprise.

"Why not? Remember the Records Office's inquiry into Palladio? With that simple study in your hands, even if you'd never met the Count, would you have doubted his existence?"

"Reality and fiction are very different things."

"Wait a minute," the Professor interrupted, pursuing his own train of thought. "An idea has just crossed my mind—slightly mad, but suppose the pacts, the reunion of the Quadrille, were all simply intended to bring the Devil back among us?"

"You mean that he may have manufactured opportunities to be invoked in the future in case he was quite forgotten?"

"Well, isn't that what happened? He offered the pacts to the killers, didn't he? He was just covering his back. A simple question of survival."

It was a seductive theory. Almost as seductive as Rosemonde.

The Professor rose from the table. He had to go; the inaugural meeting for the new academic year would soon be beginning.

The sorceress caught hold of his sleeve and drew him towards her. They exchanged a kiss. For the fraction of a second the earth stopped turning. Rosemonde straightened up, feeling that he was emerging from a delicious dream.

He really did have to go.

He left without paying, which was not at all like him,

emerged from the café, and crossed the road walking backwards, miming the action of phoning for Roberta's benefit. He was still smiling as he went through the University gates.

"It's on me," Eugène Bouillotte told her when she asked for the bill.

The sorceress went home by the students' usual route. She found her flat looking like a temple of domestic bliss. For once it was warm and tidy, and her black-eyed Susan was flourishing.

She cooked herself a little dish from her *Alchemical Cookbook* for lunch, scallop risotto with mandragora, a great success. The mandrake root her friend Strudel had given her was nice and fresh. Then she had a siesta in the company of Beelzebub, who was purring and unusually calm. Her cat had never been so affectionate before. After that she spent the afternoon with her feet up on the radiator, knitting mittens in colours to coordinate with the poncho from Tenochtitlán. She had mended the places where the lion's claws tore it.

The sorceress looked at the city rooftops, gilded by the setting sun. The mynah bird was asleep on his perch, the Gustavson was asleep in a little box lined with wool, Beelzebub was sleeping on her lap. Her heart felt warm.

At last, she thought. At last.

The radio was on. There was a news flash, and then, without prior warning, an army of violins invaded her flat. Roberta emerged brusquely from the dreamy mood induced by the gathering dusk.

"You are listening to 'Reza,' played by Percy Faith and his Orchestra."

She lay back in her armchair and gave herself up to the enchantment. Her vision blurred. The scene in her flat was replaced by a screen showing a jungle in smooth shades of green. Languorous violins were echoing everywhere. Palm trees swayed in time to the music before Roberta's eyes. The piano appeared behind a drift of ferns. The music grew louder. The sorceress approached the scene. The green of the jungle grew more intense, exploded, and parted like the two halves of a magnificent theatrical curtain.

The sorceress was carried away by Percy Faith as never before.

A stairway with pink steps wound its way up to the sky, with a trumpeter on each step. Roberta climbed the spiral staircase, leaping lightly from step to step, feeling the tempo of the music take her over. Three explosions of baby-chick yellow marked the beginning of the next flight of fancy. Drifting cotton-wool clouds lazily accompanied the spiralling movement of the staircase. A hundred violinists in white tuxedos cast dizzying flights of sound into infinity.

Martineau appeared at the controls of his striped biplane. He waved a hand to Roberta and flew off into the distance, his white scarf drifting after him.

Finally she reached the top of the staircase. The dusk had turned the sky into a Burning Chamber. The notes mingled in an absolute, perfect shade of pink.

Monsieur Rosemonde was waiting for her in a leopard-patterned suit, holding two dry Martinis. The sorceress threw her mules away into the void, sketched two calypso steps, and merged with her dream.